My ^Dead Friend Terry

Jeff Hawksworth

http://www.jeffhawksworth.com

My Dead Friend Terry
Jeff Hawksworth

Paperback Edition First Published in Great Britain
in 2015 by aSys Publishing

eBook Edition First Published in Great Britain
in 2015 by aSys Publishing

Cover illustrations taken or adapted for this book by
Teresa O'Neill Photography

Disclaimer

This is a work of fiction. Names, characters, businesses, places,
events and incidents are either the products of the author's
imagination or used in a fictitious manner. Any resemblance to
actual persons, living or dead, or actual events
is purely coincidental.

ISBN: 978-1-910757-33-8
aSys Publishing
http://www.asys-publishing.co.uk

To Pam

Acknowledgments

Penning a book is a lengthy project, full of surprises and an educational weight of research. There are plenty of contours too, when passages can be an uphill struggle, mixed with thrilling gallops through those that raced away from me, faster than I could write.

But the journey needs companions at times too. The support and encouragement provided by family and friends cannot be overstated and I thank them all, unequivocally.

More specifically, I would like to thank Rob Whitehead, once again, for his advice on Police procedures. Steve Lockwood, Eugen Winter, Emma Wilson and Linda Skingsley did wonderful work proof reading, before Nicola Makin of aSys Publishing turned a manuscript into a book. Not forgetting Teresa O'Neill who did a magical job on the cover.

Above all and as always, I owe particular thanks to you, because you're reading this.

Chapter 1

I use the *Skype* messaging service quite a lot, not least of all because it's free, but there is also great value in being able to activate the camera and actually see the person you are speaking to, wherever they are, be that in Hong Kong or Los Angeles. Those two examples were prompted by the fact that I have clients in both of those cities.

I also have a client in Shanghai, but the connection with him is never robust enough to use the cameras so we converse 'blind' so to speak. Sometimes the system keeps 'falling over' even then and we resort to the written word, using the *Skype* IM, or 'instant messaging' facility. In each case the exchange is immediate.

More importantly still, my two kids could communicate with me when they were away on their gap years, but that was when they were talking to me.

Even so, I was startled to get an IM message from Terry Caplan, since it had been almost a year since we'd last spoken,—just two hours before he died.

Well, committed suicide, actually.

He chose one of the softer exits, by means of alcohol and sleeping tablets, which would probably be the one I would choose if I ever felt so inclined. Not that I would be, which explains why I felt so angered by what seemed a cowardly departure by my best friend.

Six months before his exit from this life, he was widowed, when Amy succumbed to cancer after a hideously long battle.

Then, two months after he died, I lost my wife as well; to a solicitor from Nottingham. It must have been a whirlwind affair since he had only been staying at the local hotel for a two day convention when he met my wife, Dee, at the leisure centre she attended. Both departures came as a shock, though in hindsight I realised I had my marital loss coming.

I once employed a business consultant, which is to say I agreed to meet with him, after winning the consultation in a raffle at the local Chamber of Commerce ladies night. That was ironic in itself, given the warnings he gave me, after a somewhat gruelling day spent answering his questions.

He considered everything, from my work diary to leisure time and concluded that I was a pathologically 'Task Based' personality as opposed to the 'Time Manager' sort, which he considered to be preferable. He explained that by dint of delegation, control and a professional allocation of time spent in meetings, preferably with higher net worth clients who would provide me with higher fees or commission and slicker administration, I would be left with far more free personal time. That, he explained, would enhance my lifestyle and enrich my family life.

Well he was right on the last count, given that my wife walked out on me shortly after, but I'm still glad I hadn't had to pay for his views.

In the meantime I ignored his advice. Many clients have become friends, thanks, perhaps, to the time and patience I afforded them, whilst by contrast, I was providing little of either for my wife and two daughters. That epiphany came with the benefit of hindsight; something I *have* had time for, since Dee left.

That said, I wasn't a villain; I didn't play away or lose everything at the poker tables, though I came to accept that I am 'task based', which I take to mean that I wouldn't stop work until the outstanding workload had been tucked up. That often entailed working through to the small hours which simply meant that I would sleep all the more soundly. As a result, I passed off a five bed roomed house, two BMW's and a respectable investment portfolio as an adequate observance of my familial obligations; still do, to some extent. I still have them, of course, apart from one of the BMWs.

* * *

I should explain that my name is Ian Barber. I am fifty four years old and an Independent Financial Adviser, operating from my home in Markfield, Leicester, with a large bank of clients, of all types; from multi-millionaires to those struggling on minimum wages. I value every one of them and whilst the consultant was right in identifying the relative differences in my rewards, I often gained more satisfaction from securing a mortgage for young families who had all but given up on owning their own home. Their lack of experience often called for more time and lengthier explanations, but it never bothered me. That said; I'm not naive. If a millionaire expressed a wish to use my services he'd get first shot at the appointments diary.

On Tuesdays, Thursdays and sometimes Fridays, depending on my schedule and workload, the long suffering Libby worked for me as an administrator. She always seemed to cope, no matter how heavy her workload; with a calm, unruffled resolve that the clients found reassuring. Unlike the hysterics or panics she sometimes witnessed on my part; in the privacy of my office of course and never in front of clients.

Curiously, I know that Terry would have still been there for me, during my turmoil. After all, our friendship went back a ways, to the days of short trousers, marbles and conker seasons.

Odd then, that our marriages had been so different.

Mine began in the mini skirt era when a straightforward desire for carnal knowledge and a sloppy, if you'll pardon the expression, approach to contraception, resulted in marriage vows. It wasn't quite that banal, for by the time Dee conceived we had developed a real affection for each other. Even so, the partnership was founded on harsh times, when neither sets of parents were willing to throw funds our way and I've never forgotten what it is to be poor. I had a real fear of going back to that. Still do.

Terry was the complete opposite.

He began dating Amy when they were both attending the Sefton Grammar School, along with yours truly. Their love remained constant ever since, in spite, of parental disapproval; the only thing we did end up having in common. Amy, by her own admission, was a relaxed Methodist but Terry was Jewish, albeit with a growing indifference to the mantras sought by his faith.

They both decided on teaching as a career but because of Terry's choice of subject; woodwork, they attended different colleges. He to Shoreditch, in London and Amy to Portsmouth, where she studied for a teaching certificate in Geography. Both sets of parents were delighted by the distancing and therefore doubly startled when the couple were married, two months after graduation.

I never doubted that they would and was best man for the ceremony; held at the registry office in Birmingham. The guests numbered around a dozen or so; none of whom were aged over twenty three and with funds as short as the skirts at that time, we held an impromptu reception at a non-descript pub in Handsworth, where we enjoyed a 'Chicken in the Basket', washed down with a few pints of *'Brew Eleven'*.

Their honeymoon was spent in a tent beside Lake Bala in North Wales, until a force eight gale and torrential rain stopped play. Bits of torn canvas were swept out onto the lake and never seen again, but the lovebirds seemed unaffected by it. After spending what was left of the night in a barn, they hitched-hiked back to Birmingham and simply got on with life.

I should add that I had completed a BSC course in Business Studies at Warwick University before inseminating Dee, though in a rather lack lustre fashion, (the course, not the 'other') and scraped a 2.2.

I often wonder how my life would have panned out if I'd gone ahead and joined the Royal Navy when I was eighteen. In fact I was accepted for a short-service commission that would have only required a three year commitment. Fortunately, common sense prevailed; or rather Terry did, when he pointed out my continual aversion for rules or authority. He insisted that I would need an entry level of at least Captain, so that I could dole out more than I was given.

But in any event, we all began married life with no parental support, no money and no firm views on the future. After all, the US and Vietnam were still beating the shit out of each other and the Cold War was in full swing.

Yet, Terry and Amy seemed to thrive, while Dee and I panicked and argued.

Even when Terry lost his job, after the authorities decided to keep kids away from sharp tools, he drifted across to nursing where he rose to the rank of Staff Nurse. No doubt that was how he knew which drugs to use and where to get them, when he did what he did.

He'd been offered an opportunity to teach another subject but always said that his move into nursing was the best thing he'd ever done, apart from marrying Amy, that is. At some point, the authorities had co-opted him on to some sort *Civil Defence* committee that planned for large scale disasters. Everything from nuclear fallout to flu epidemics apparently. He didn't say much more about it, other than it was another government quango that did little more than pay well.

I remember once, he gave me a ten point list of things to do in the event of a nuclear attack. It bordered on the ridiculous, urging defenders to bottle water, prop mattresses against the kitchen table and get underneath it; all that sort of thing. I can't remember all of it but someone had added a number eleven, which gave one final instruction; 'to place one's head between their knees and kiss their ass goodbye'.

Later, I was to discover just how disingenuous he'd been, but by then it was too late.

Chapter 2

Of course, I ignored the *Skype* message. It was a scam, had to be. Someone looking to hook up with me, or rather my computer and all the saved passwords I had in there. I'm a bit of a Luddite when it comes to computers, but I'm not that stupid. That said, after Terry died, I tried to delete the box that contained his ID and picture but couldn't, which is how the sender's identity appeared to be known.

The following morning another message appeared.

Hey, Ian, are you there?

I didn't give it a second thought as I hit the delete button. This time I selected the option to stop any further messages from this sender, whoever he or she was. Probably ensconced in Albania, or somewhere similar.

Two days later another appeared,

Hey Ian, wake up man. It's your mate, Terry.

I had been irritated by the others, but now I was downright angry. To try and perpetrate a scam was one thing, but claiming to be someone so close to me and so very dead, was either stupid or callous. I realised that I must have made an error when blocking calls from this nasty little sod and tried again, paying particular attention to each key I pressed.

It took three more days for the next one to arrive, but this one shocked me,

Ian, please answer. It's me, honest and I need to have a word. Taz.

Taz was the nick name we agreed on when we were kids; just three letters to chalk on tree trunks in the local wood, when we were British soldiers ambushing Japs, or troopers tracking Red Indians. At least they were called that then and I'm not sure how daring we'd have felt if chasing 'Native Americans'. My name needed no abbreviation and in time, both three-letter names appeared throughout the place.

In spite of that, no-one else knew who Taz was and more importantly, the last time we used it was when we were twelve years old.

I stared at the screen, trying to make sense of it, yet yielding to the pleasure of recalling those special times, when such things as secret names seemed so profoundly important.

Well it bloody well felt like it again. Stupid, I know, but he'd been my best friend for nearly fifty years. He was dead too.

I decided to do four things, ranging from prudent to daft and I even listed them in my diary, perhaps as a record. It was a Friday and I'd allocated the day to admin anyway. The list read;

1. Back up

2. Check Anti Virus Software is up to date

3. Try IM message

4. Run Anti Virus system check.

I left the computer making another back up of my data, even though I had made one the night before; at least it gave me the opportunity to go and make a coffee and think about it.

Half an hour later I sat at my desk staring at the computer screen while the Anti-Virus software updated itself; it didn't take long since the automatic daily update had been done that morning, when I switched on.

In less than an hour the next message appeared.

Ian, please mate.

I still hesitated. There was no one to discuss it with and while logically it had to be a scam, the tiniest part of me wished it were true. I had no wife and few friends outside of my client bank.

My two daughters no longer spoke to me and I missed my best friend terribly.

Finally, I numbed out and began to type without much conscious thought;

Who are you?

The reply came back within five minutes.

I've been telling you. It's me, Terry!

I responded to the anger that suddenly overwhelmed me, at such a callous response.

Where are you?

Can't tell you.

Well it can only be one of two places.

Why?

You're dead.

Ha ha

I can't see what's funny about that.

It is,—from where I'm sitting.

So switch your camera on.

Not possible, sorry. Not from where I am at the moment.

I thought I would play along, for the moment.

But you won't tell me where that is.

Can't.

What, Official Secrets Act?

Sort of.

Bollocks.

Still as succinct as ever.

You may recall that I was the executor to your estate. Thanks for the inheritance by the way.

He had bequeathed most of his estate to their only daughter, Caroline, now living in France, teaching English, but I received thirty thousand pounds, which for the want of anything else, was placed with 'ERNIE'; more popularly known as the National Savings Premium Bonds. They doled out one or two twenty five pound prize warrants to me, most months.

Terry, or whoever was pretending to be him replied,

You're welcome.

I tried a modest test, knowing though, that wills were a matter of public record.

How much did you leave me?

You're testing me lol!

I didn't answer and just waited. After a few minutes;

30K. What did you do with it?

I thought ghosts would be all seeing and told him so.

You probably know.

No- but interested.

This was surreal, but I continued to play along.

Premium Bonds.

How very tame, especially for you.

Whatever.

Sorry about Dee by the way. Really sorry.

I wasn't expecting that and at a certain level it was as though the real Terry was asking the question; with the sincerity and concern only he would have. Once again, the emptiness her departure had left, overwhelmed me. I rubbed at the tears from both eyes with the heels of my hands and would later ascribe my next question to an emotional state. In that moment, I felt he would know the answer.

Is she happy?

As soon as I hit the enter button I felt stupid and the response was unsurprising.

Don't know mate. Had no contact with her.

Yeah, I guess. I was thinking Ouija Boards.

You're still off track. Believe me.

I don't know what else to say.

How about, Hey terry, good to hear from you—how are you?

I would need to know I was messaging with Terry first.

This time it was Terry who played silent, until I felt the need to move on.

OK, I'll play along, Hi terry, how are you.

I'm well, better than you could imagine.

Ain't that the truth.

Here's the thing Ian, for the sake of progress , will you take things at face value,—just for now?

Why?

I have some information for you. V. Important.

Go on.

I have an inside track on something you could use.

It was enough to bring me back to my senses. This had to be one of my clients, taking the pee. It was a little sick but they would have a lot of sport in the coming weeks, all at my expense. In spite of that, a sense of relief washed over me. Quite a number of clients had met Terry and recently we had talked about him without any sense of melancholy on my part, so mention of his name wouldn't be a surprise. But that thought brought back the wave of confusion and a little fear, for none could have known the name 'Taz'. I typed;

Go on.

Bridle Homes—trading at 23p. Buy today. Sell Monday before 10am. Timing critical.

Again, I played along.

How many?

100,000. Any more will make a market.

He meant that the purchase or sale of more than that number would in itself affect the share price. I typed;

Sounds a tall order; at every level.

Trust me.

Yeah, right.

You don't?

Well, see, it's like this—you're dead and telling me to spend £2,300.

I understand your concern.

Thanks.

Look at it this way—you will be risking less than 10% of the 30K I left you.

When you died you mean?

There's stuff I can't tell you at the moment.

Terry, is it hot where you are at the moment?

Ha ha.

I couldn't think of anything else to write and whilst I knew it couldn't *be* him I didn't feel able to sign off with 'sod off'. Another message appeared.

Just do it mate. I've chalked 'TAZ' on this one, just for you. Will make contact again early next week.

I'll think about it.

By the end of trading, today, it will be too late.

I'll think about it.

Oh, and be sure to buy a Telegraph and an Observer on Sunday.

Why?

Tipsters.

That clinched it.

It was a Friday and much of the copy would have been written for the Sunday papers, including the tipster's columns in financial sections. The tips were highly confidential and closely guarded until Sundays, to prevent improper trading, but at times, people had found ways of finding the information in time to buy shares on Friday. It was illegal and there was no way I was getting involved.

I did buy the Observer and Telegraph though.

* * *

Since Dee left I tended to slob out on Sundays, by getting up late, eating brunch and reading *The Times*, so it demanded little more to buy a *Telegraph* and *Observer*, particularly since I was only concerned with one article in each.

The *Observer's* tipster was someone who wrote under the name of *Poulter* and the company, *Bridle Homes* was featured, just as Terry, or whoever he was, promised. In fact it was rated as the tip of the week and read,

After five years of using their innovative approach to pre-fabricated building, which has brought the cost of their houses down by 30%, **Bridle Homes** *seem to have gained credibility at last.*

Market acceptance has been reflected in record sales and more importantly, profits, which are rumoured to have doubled. I understand that some of them have been used to acquire a significant land bank. One source suggests that they now have enough for a further 10 years of developments. Results are to be released tomorrow at 10 am.

At 23p this share looks cheap. **Strong Buy.**

The *Telegraphs'* tipster was pretty well identical and whilst I had stayed by my decision not to buy, I was keen to see what happened the next day, not least of all because I'd been instructed to sell them *before* ten-o-clock.

Fifteen minutes into trading and the share price had risen to thirty pence. By ten-o-clock, as the meeting began the shares were trading at thirty four pence.

It started well and in line with market expectations, as the chairman announced that profits were up by ninety four per cent, but as a sporadic applause broke out, he held up his hand and called for silence. The expression on his face achieved that much, in short order.

He went on to explain that they had become aware of certain shortcomings with parts of the pre-fabrication process and the board had decided to set six million aside to deal with remedial and litigious contingencies.

There were gasps from the audience and a rising swell of voices, until the chairman raised his hand, and voice, as he asked for a chance to explain. It took a little while for things to settle down but finally, he continued. Discussions with the manufacturers were ongoing, though it was too early to determine cause and effect.

Or in other words, blame had yet to find a resting place and would be a matter of bitter dispute. Inevitably, it would end up with litigation, from all directions.

Meanwhile, one thing did become clear during the angry question and answer period that followed. Someone had done a great job of keeping the homeowner's complaints under wraps.

The market doesn't forgive cover ups and this one was as bad as they come. Not in the same league as Nick Leeson, the rogue trader who brought *Barings* Bank down, but the result might easily be the same.

By ten thirty the price had fallen back to six pence and trading in the shares was suspended, pending enquiries.

* * *

I expected a *Skype* message the same morning and by Tuesday evening I was beginning to wonder if I'd imagined it. Of course, I hadn't, but I still felt compelled to boot up the *Skype* application where our text messages remained. I'd considered all sorts of things, since that messaging, with a mix of emotions. Most important was the question of legality. Whoever 'Terry' really was, the information could have only been obtained by way of a 'leak', or worse, commercial espionage. I realised that I hadn't actually been given any information, simply a tip to buy and sell, but that still smacked of *'insider trading'* which certainly was illegal. That said, I had spent most of my working life investing and advising others to, so the frisson of making such a return, in such a short space of time was compelling. Not that I would have succumbed, of course!

Finally, on Wednesday morning my computer beeped to announce the arrival of a message. I was in the middle of preparing a pension presentation to the workforce of a small engineering company in Leicester and had to save and close the file before opening *Skype*. It was him, whoever he was.

Hi Ian, you there?

I was prepared for this.

Yes.

Great. Did good didn't we?

I wasn't prepared to tell him I hadn't done anything just yet. Instead;

It was certainly startling. No-one else knew about it.

Some did. I was one of them.

How did you come by all that info?

Very easily.

Good for you, but how many laws did you break getting it?

None.

Not possible,- in my opinion.

It is, trust me.

So how many laws did someone else break?

No-one did.

So tell me how you, or they did it.

Can't.

Yes you can, or this session is over.

You sound angry.

No, just relieved I didn't get involved. When the regulators come knocking on your door, wherever that is, I'll have nothing to fear.

You're joking, are you saying you didn't buy any.

Damn right.

You silly, stupid sod!

I couldn't help grinning at that one.

Oops, you sound angry now.

I waited for a few minutes and then made a cup of coffee. After fifteen minutes I shut *Skype* down, knowing I had done the right thing.

* * *

The next message began with petulance.

I want my money back.

Fine, it'll be in cash only and I insist on giving it to you personally.

Can't.

Fancy that.

You're playing games with me.

Hey teapot to kettle, do you read, over!

Yeah, I know. I don't really want the money back, but jeez Ian, why don't you trust me.

I know I was being repetitive, but with due cause.

Because you are a dead person.

We've been through all this before.

We've been through a lot before Terry, when I could see and hear you. I still don't know why I'm calling you Terry.

The next message startled me. As much as seeing him sign off as Taz and for much of the same reason. It was something else we had never shared with anyone.

Remember Carol and Megan?

I was stunned and while I tried to think of a response, he signed off with;

Think about it chum, it really is me, (me and you). Call you tomorrow.

I stared at the screen as memories came back, of that summer evening, so long ago, when we were two fearful thirteen year olds. I whispered, "Shit."

In spite of the surprise, I couldn't help smiling.

We were fearful, not the girls. In fact we were terrified, at both the prospect of our first sexual encounter with the opposite sex and of being caught in the act.

There was a very good reason why it should have been such a secret then, though with the passage of time, its significance fell away with the realisation of how relatively innocent it was. Yet in spite of the diminishing gravity of our deeds, they remained secret, so far as I was aware.

It was still a milestone though and I could picture the living room of that house in Mackley Road as if it were yesterday.

They were the first, no, second pair of female breasts I had handled; with a thirteen year gap in between.

At the time, Terry would have been in all sorts of trouble for persuading his cousin, Carol and her friend Megan to provide us with the sexual encounter. Carol was a chunky sort of girl even at that age, but amiable and compliant enough to oblige me.

I remember that Megan was the prettier of the two girls, but Terry said that there were strict laws against doing that sort of thing with cousins, which would end up with us both being sent to *Borstal*. He seemed pretty informed on the matter and since he had organised the event I was happy enough to go along with the arrangements.

Carol's parents, Terry's Uncle and Aunt, were out for the evening and with jangling nerves we knocked on the front door of their small terraced house with a mix of anxiety and anticipation.

The girls seemed very calm about the whole affair and directed us into the living room. I can't remember what Terry was told to do, but Carol instructed me to sit on her lap as she unbuttoned her blouse and removed her bra. I do remember being startled, by the way she could do so without taking her blouse off and how large and white her breasts were. It was time to be a man.

I puckered my lips and squashed them against hers as I grabbed a breast. It fell a long way shy of a caress, for I knew nothing about female arousal then, obviously. I'm not sure that she did, but after an extended mauling I remember trying to head 'south'. Carol called out a warning to Megan and we were both told, in no uncertain terms, that excursions below the waist were out of the question.

Even so, it was a grand adventure, tinged for some time by the fear of her parents finding out.

I felt certain about one thing though; it was still our secret.

* * *

After a night's sleep I didn't care who knew about Carol or Megan, or why it should be a secret. Clearly, Terry hadn't thought so either, when he told someone about the affair. I was ready for the message when it came through.

Hi Ian.

WHO ARE YOU!

Stop shouting.

BOLLOCKS. ANSWER THE QUESTION!

(Sigh), Ian. Please, believe me.

ANSWER THE QUESTION

No exclamation mark. See, you're calming down already.

When did Terry tell you about the girls.

This Terry has told no-one, ever. After all, it was my cousin I allowed you to fondle.

In spite of such determination earlier, I felt my resolve slipping. I certainly didn't feel in control of the situation and realised that for the time being I could only play along, until he or she slipped up.

Do you want another tip?

Where are you? And how are you getting this info?

Can't tell you, but I <u>can</u> tell you that I'm safe as houses and the info is too.

I couldn't think of a reply that would be anything short of tacit collaboration. After a minute or so his next message appeared.

Jaygen Engineering Plc. Should be able to buy them for less than ninety pence. Will rise within two days. Price should settle back slightly, within a week and not go much further for a while so either sell on good news or see as a longer term hold.

It didn't take two days but in the meantime I had checked it out and discovered that they specialised in alloy fabrications, more usually for the marine industry. Like all marine enterprises they had experienced feasts and famines but had managed their affairs reasonably well. Borrowing was well within the norms and the brokers forecasts were for a modest increase in the share price, indicating stability, at least. There were no rumours or media tipsters showing interest.

By nine the next morning their shares had risen from eighty eight pence to one pound forty. I checked their website and discovered that at eight thirty, they'd announced the award of a fourteen million pound government contract which formed part of the construction of two new naval destroyers. It was their first government contract and the popular view is that if a contractor keeps their nose clean, more follow.

* * *

I expect you didn't buy any.

I'd been waiting for the message and replied promptly.

Correct.

What can I do to convince you?

Not sure, but we can start with these.

The previous evening I racked my brains for stuff only he and I would know and wrote down a few questions. Inevitably, I suppose, the secrets most often shared by two lads are often of a sexual nature, but my first was tame enough.

When did I get my first bicycle?

The reply came straight back.

> *Just before I did. We were ten years old but mine was a brand new 'Blue Flash' though, and you sulked. Your dad made yours from bits and pieces he collected. It was a big old heavy black thing—like a butcher's lad's delivery bike. You lost control of it on the first day and crashed into the back of the Co-op baker's wagon.*

He was right, on all counts. I could still sulk about his bike today. It was time to get back to sex. There was one secret I hadn't shared with him; I'm not sure why, but it meant so much to me and the experience was so profound, I hadn't shared it with anyone, so an informed reply would suggest that I was dealing with another intelligence source. Though God only knew who. I keyed;

When did I lose my virginity and who with?

Once again, the reply was immediate.

> *I know who you __didn't__ lose it with. Deirdrie Fox, behind the pavilion in the rec'. You persuaded her to shed her draws but when push came to shove, if you'll pardon the expression, she started to yell blue murder. I was keeping guard at the corner of the building, but watched everything, with a keen interest. You were on top and going through the motions and I thought you were actually doing 'it' but you never managed to 'make the connection'. Meanwhile she was belting you over the head with the heel of her shoe and gave you a couple of nasty cuts. We were fourteen I think.*

He'd startled me, again. I've never told anyone about that ignominious episode and he'd sworn never to as well. I moved on. Having only ever been to hospital once in my childhood I asked;

When did I go into hospital and why?

> *I think you were six or seven, very young anyway. Your foreskin 'locked on' and you were top and tailed, just like me! I don't*

remember mine of course; I was only eight days old at my brit milah. We compared them, do you remember?

I did.

I also decided that further questioning was not going to achieve anything. Different strategies were called for, but in the meantime I wrote;

What now?

Convinced?

No.

Well, for the moment I have another tip for you and remember, I'm asking you to use my money, not yours.

It's not your money anymore, not since you died.

Whatever.

I waited, but he'd tweaked my curiosity and after a minute or two I wrote;

Well?

Currentsea Plc. Trading at 4.2p. Go for it.

* * *

I'd never heard of them and began by looking up their website. They were self-proclaimed 'Leading edge developers' of sustainable energy but a quick check of their RNS's, (Regulated News Service, as required under stock market rules) established that they were far more trailing edge.

I checked them out on *Google* and discovered pages of bad news. They had tried most things and failed spectacularly, so much so that I wondered how they'd managed to get away with three rights issues. They must have had unreasonably forgiving shareholders, coupled with the markets' current fad with sustainable energy, but there were signs that even their patience had run out.

One tale of woe involved the wind farm they constructed on the foreshore of the east coast, south of Gibraltar Point.

It seems they found a soul mate in Tovey Construction Ltd, the faltering ground works company, owned by two Irish brothers who made more money from dodgy insurance claims than they did from doing their job.

I discovered a couple of examples, from later newspaper articles that chronicled the insurer's prosecutions for fraudulent claims. One involved having two lorries stolen from a site in Kent. That part was true, but the thirty thousand pounds worth of equipment that they had claimed lay in the trucks was pure fiction.

Similarly, when they were working in the Scottish Highlands, they discovered bogs that could swallow up entire diggers, with scant chance of recovery. A discreet swap with cousins in Ireland meant that the two which sank without trace were eleven years older than the ones they claimed for and worth little more than scrap value.

Bankruptcy was inevitable, at some point, if only as a matter of veiled justice, but the story of the *Currentsea* debacle was hailed as their primary nemesis, in the bankruptcy hearing. In fact, it was family.

The award of that contract to the brothers coincided with the arrival of another Irish cousin, who wanted a job as a digger driver. He was just in time to excavate the base footings for one hundred wind turbine masts.

Maybe it was the pronounced cast in one eye, or more probably the five pints of *Guinness* the digger driver had for lunch each day, but the surveyor discovered a slope to the floor of every hole.

The cousin was told to carry out the remedial work, but it had been a dry summer and the clay spoil had hardened into rock-like lumps, making the delicate task of levelling extremely difficult, so he used topsoil instead.

In time, months after the wind farm had been completed, the topsoil compacted and each mast began to lean towards the sunken side.

It didn't take long for the whole farm to look like a drunken mess and the local authority declared the site to be unsafe; banning unauthorised visitors and closing an adjacent road.

Which was how I discovered all this information. The closures had become such a public issue, that the web was full of newspaper articles, though mostly from the east coast locals.

Rather than face the cost of a complete re-build, *Currentsea Plc* sold the site for a fraction of the cost.

I looked back further and found a history littered with, as one impassioned investor yelled from the floor at an AGM, "fuck ups!"

Back at their website I discovered that things at the top were just as I'd feared. Apart from the finance director, who I suspect was a failed accountant; the entire board of directors were scientists. It is a common enough mis-match in concerns like that, or in other words, ideas *sans* acumen.

Until eighteen months ago, at that same AGM.

One of the newspaper articles I read on *Google* reported the stormy confrontations during the meeting with obvious glee, where a vote of no confidence very nearly succeeded. Had it done so, the board would have been dismissed and trading in the shares would have been suspended, until new arrangements had been made.

In fact, a little more research showed that while most of financial press were having a field day, pressure from the institutional investors ensured that a new Managing Director was appointed and within six weeks, the appointment of Howard Long was announced.

I decided to check him out.

The internet is a cornucopia of information about such people. In fact *Google* provided two whole pages of items, from press reports to blogs. *LinkedIn* and *Companies House* filled in most of the gaps though I wasn't surprised to discover that he hadn't gone on to *Facebook*. People like him tended to avoid that sort of social media.

Yet the picture of him on *LinkedIn* was surprising. Instead of the lean, mean, corporate machine I'd expected, he looked quite homely; jolly even. In spite of being two years older than me, at fifty six, he had a shock of dark wavy hair, thick rimmed spectacles and a round face that bore a beaming smile. Given a white beard and wig, he could have made a good Father Christmas, which left me wondering what he was like in the world of commerce.

It was a pedigree of mixed successes, with a couple of failures and a number of appointments that entailed disposals of failing companies, for as much as he could, either by asset stripping, or finding buyers for the company as a going concern. He sounded more like a liquidator than a captain of industry. So far as I could tell, it was a patchy record too, with longish gaps between some of the appointments.

In spite of all that, his first RNS on behalf of *Currentsea Plc* was extremely upbeat, suggesting that great news was at hand and the company's future assured. Whether it was their Welsh wind farm, the solar panel sales arm or the hydro-generation experiments, he didn't say.

Since then there had been little news of note. Even the last AGM was a lacklustre affair compared the earlier one, probably because there were no more disasters to report, or pleas for more money.

On balance, it still looked negative, so probably out of perversity I bought a hundred thousand at two pence.

After all, it wasn't my money.

* * *

Four days later, they made their announcement and within twenty four hours, the front page of most dailies.

They had patents pending on a revolutionary design of tidal turbine, one that seemed to tick all the boxes and which was proving to be spectacularly efficient. The test site was in the Severn estuary, a little north of the two motorway bridges linking Wales with England, near the east bank and due south of Lydney. The authorities deemed it to be well away from the bulk carrier sea lanes into Swansea and Cardiff, yet still in a position to benefit from the regular tidal ranges of up to fifteen metres; second only to the Bay of Fundy in Canada, with its tidal range of over sixteen metres.

Elsewhere, in the estuary, one of the more traditional designs, employed by a competitor, was a strengthened variant of the fan blades used in land-based wind farms, while another more recent design, which was proving to be more efficient, was a shrouded turbine; a sort of short duct containing a turbine blade that looked similar to the arrangement seen on top of a hovercraft.

Both were subject to great stresses and the single-blade design was still causing engineers headaches with cross-sectional distortion and buckling. Even when functioning well, they were difficult to manage and had a considerable ecological impact, while the ones *Currentsea* had developed were more of a helix design, with no apparent risk to fish stocks or migrations. Even a few conger eels had tried to take up residence in the tubes, without apparent harm, or success. Furthermore, maintenance was a fraction of the cost because the loadings were reduced. In effect, it relied on the cumulative effect of a current over forty feet of helix instead of the one-off hit by a propeller blade. Most importantly, the efficiency of the *Currentsea* design and the power produced by it was startling. They had a winner.

Even the 'green' lobby expressed cautious support for it and within hours, Howard Long was giving television interviews.

After two days of hype, their shares were trading at eighteen pence.

Terry contacted me that morning;

Well?

Ok, I'll admit that I was grinning as I typed;

That's my line.

Mine this morning. Did you buy?

Yes.

What price?

2p

Nice one.

Thank you, whoever you are.

Now don't start that again!

Will they carry on going up?

Should do. I'll keep you posted.

How do I contact you if I need to?

Click on my Skype icon of course. If I'm not here leave a message and I'll get back to you.

Though I didn't realise it at the time, that was the moment I began to accept that Terry was real. Why else would I have asked a dead man for his contact details?

I was half hoping for the next message, which read;

Now, try this one.

Chapter 3

MV *Erebus* was a Panamanian registered general cargo vessel of four thousand tons and typical of the many that sailed European waters. She was carrying timber from the Baltic port of Riga to Britain and would be returning with a cargo of scrap metal

The voyage had not started well for Captain Jansons, with three of his crew confined to Police cells in Riga after a drunken brawl. However suspicious the circumstances, he was forced to sign on three men the ship's owners had sent. Any thoughts he had about exercising his right of refusal, as captain of the vessel, vanished the moment he saw them and their kit. In addition to kitbags, the two large chests they stowed below bore stout padlocks and were treated with caution. An offer of help from one of the other crew members was tersely declined.

They were different to the usual 'temps' he'd had foisted on him for earlier voyages. For one thing, they soon demonstrated seamanship, of a high order, but these three were not merchant seaman and with that he knew better than to ask questions. Not that they would have provided answers anyway. He should have expected something like this, when loading had been delayed for a week. Obviously, timing was an issue.

Previously, 'guests' had dressed like sailors, but behaved like *litllle lielie viri,* (little big men), unwilling to get their hands dirty and concerned only with the hidden cameras and sensors they operated when the ship entered and left port. Only the strategic ones though, like Portsmouth, where the British Navy was kind enough to line their warships up, as though for inspection, while ships like his sailed past on their way to '*Portsmouth International Port*'.

So their choice of this voyage posed another question. The two ports they were heading for had no military or strategic value.

Latvia was a democracy and had joined the EU in May the previous year, but legacies remained from their time as part of the Russian republic. Almost thirty per cent of the population were ethnic Russians and the 'Bear' still slumbered next door. His ship was owned by Russians just as they had owned Latvia, until nineteen ninety one. Then, he knew better than to question anything and routinely carried personnel who were there for espionage, plain and simple. Voyages would be timed to coincide with NATO manoeuvres and sonar buoys were dropped in strategic places.

It had been a long time since he had hosted such people though and a little more subtlety was called for, now that everyone was so chummy. Discreet it may have been, but it was still business as usual.

Both he and his family knew that to refuse would be almost as calamitous now as it was when the KGB had watchers on most corners. At least now, he could and would use his mother tongue during the voyage. Eighty per cent of Latvians could now speak their own language and over half were using it as their primary language. It was only a gesture, he knew, but at least it was something.

Sad times; Jansons was getting old and felt like it. Clearly, *Aukstais kars,* the Cold War, had not finished. In fact, it suddenly seemed to be warming up; or getting colder, he couldn't decide which was correct.

They set sail in weather that was as grey and depressed as his spirits, bound for the first port of call; Portslade, in Sussex.

* * *

As an IFA, (Independent Financial Adviser), I was licensed to advise on certain things only, such as life assurance, income and health protection, taxation, inheritance planning, trust laws and 'Collective Investments'. The latter included unit trusts, investment trusts, bonds and such like, where fund managers carried out stock selection and fund management. I was forbidden from recommending specific stocks and shares.

Of course, I did.

It was a sharing thing, from which I earned nothing more than a client's gratitude, and perhaps a bottle of malt now and then. But shares can go down as easily as they go up so I only passed intelligence on to clients I knew well enough to be certain they wouldn't complain to the regulators if money was lost. I also made certain they had the wherewithal to sustain losses. They were few in number and to some extent, friends.

Sharing. There's a word that conjures up all sorts of thoughts; of charity, compassion, information, hardships, good days, bad days, a life and so much more. I don't believe in self pity, in circumstances or situations I can't change; it's simply a form of self-indulgence, but I missed Dee most when I got in at night and when I got ready for bed.

All I had were the usual 'let down' rituals for the end of each working day, followed by a microwave dinner.

I don't drink a lot, although some might think otherwise. All I will admit to is that I'm in denial.

At the end of fifteen hour days I had a few stiff drinks during the hour or so it took to log the answer phone messages and call the most demanding clients back. I prefer the term used by a doctor I used to know, who was an out and out alcoholic;—vodka on his cornflakes sort of thing. He called it self-medication.

Finally, I would turn the television off and climb the stairs. It was the stairs I dreaded most, and the silence; a deafening reminder of my failure to keep a partner. Every evening, the same thing happened. By the time I reached the top of the stairs, my self-pity had been re-classified as self-indulgence, and despatched to my mental quarantine area; but I hated that journey.

By morning, I rose refreshed and ready to start work again. Whilst I was reasonably well off, the prospect of making money, either for me or my clients, never failed to excite.

In fact, in addition to my house, which was worth three quarters of a million, I owned two buy to let properties, a quarter share in a small industrial complex, a pension scheme worth half a million and a rising investment portfolio that stood at over two hundred thousand when Dee left.

No doubt Dee would come after her half at some point and many had urged me to start hiding funds, but I was determined to play things with a straight bat. Not that I expected her new partner to; he was a lawyer, after all.

That morning I had good reason to reflect on my lot and more importantly, those much less fortunate than me. I valued all my clients but that didn't always mean that I always understood their lot in life.

I had a meeting at ten, with the Pelhams; an elderly couple who lived in Great Glen. Their solicitor had suggested they call me after seeing the state of their affairs, whilst preparing wills for them. It was my third visit and we were going to put a number of invest-ments in place, which would provide them with tax free income and the comfort of knowing that in the event of one of them dying, the survivor would be well cared for.

Thomas Pelham was already a stroke victim, with the usual impediments; a lopsided gait, gathered in arm and frozen lips that hindered speech, though in spite of those, I detected a cultured background when he did attempt to speak; or was allowed to.

Emily Pelham was from a very different background. She was a large woman, who must have been fearsome in her day, but by the time we met, she was more concerned about what others might think of her crippled husband and his laborious attempts to join in conversations. In fact, he was banished to the kitchen for my first meeting and only allowed into the second one under sufferance though even then she continually shushed him into silence.

The first meeting with new clients involved a lengthy session of fact finding, which could often take several hours, so to my later shame, I welcomed the expediency of talking to her alone.

The second meeting was a matter of discussing possible solu-tions and recommendations but the third was a more profound affair; of implementation. Detailed illustrations were to be con-sidered, agreed and contracts signed. For that reason, I specifically asked that they both be present.

The status quo remained in place for that meeting, with Thomas being silenced continually by his wife; until the telephone rang. She hurried out of the room, with a promise to be back momentarily, but it was a call from her daughter in Sussex, in a state of some distress and Mrs Pelham ran back into the room in one of her own, to explain that she would be a little longer than anticipated.

The poor man had been reduced to silence by then, leaving both of us with our own thoughts. I struggled to find something to say and gazed around the room for inspiration. It was pretty sparse, with furnishings that were worn and faded. Even the television was the sort with buttons rather than a remote and somehow, it didn't seem appropriate to talk about television programmes. So the silence continued, broken only by the murmurings coming from the hall; until I noticed a framed photograph of him in military uniform, which finally gave me an opening. I pointed to it and asked, "Which unit were you with?"

Any impatience I might have had with his laboured response fell away, as he told me, with discomforting modesty, that he'd been a Major in an armoured division. I can't remember which one he said, but I will never forget learning that he'd been in the first wave to hit the Normandy beaches. His tank was destroyed within the first ten minutes, after which he climbed into another and continued to command the attack. I asked about the medal ribbon in the picture and he was almost embarrassed to tell me that it was the Military Cross.

It was a meeting I would never forget and a salutary lesson.

* * *

But time moved on, with the routines and schedules of everyday life.

It had been six months since I succumbed to 'Terry's' temptations and bought the *Currentsea Plc* shares, since when, they had risen to forty nine pence; an increase of almost three thousand per cent, which represented a gain of forty seven thousand pounds.

Their turbine was attracting worldwide interest and all augured well. Two new test sites; a second in the same estuary and one in the Menai Straits were at advanced planning stages, with the Banks suddenly keen to lend them money. In fact, the company had never been so heavily geared, but the market capitalisation justified it, easily.

But it hadn't stopped there. Terry continued to feed me with tips, albeit at irregular intervals and without such spectacular results. All were good though and the small group I was sharing the information with had taken to telephoning me daily. I was taken to lunch frequently and my liquor cabinet was full to overflowing. When one bottle came with a note of gratitude from someone I didn't know, I realised that the tips were being passed on, in a ripple effect. This was helpful when a share was rising, since the added demand would strengthen the price further, but the opposite would hold true if a share began to fall and the call went out to sell. I decided that if Terry told me to sell I would be sure to do so before passing the advice on.

I ran a check on my share portfolio, as I did most days and confirmed what I already knew. In just three months, it had risen by almost eighty thousand pounds. I extrapolated that to an annual growth rate of one hundred and sixty per cent, if things continued as they had.

It was then that I began to become a product of my good fortune. Firstly, I persuaded myself to let communications with 'Terry' to continue a little longer and see what developed. Secondly, growth rates like that get talked about. I decided to avoid attracting attention by limiting the amount of information I shared.

I had long since passed my *Capital Gains Tax* allowance and was facing a hefty bill so all other share deals were being done via my pension scheme which was a SIPP, (self-invested personal pension). Under pension scheme rules all capital gains from allowable investments were free from taxation. That said, all deals had to be run past the SIPP provider, whose job it was to ensure that only eligible transactions were effected.

* * *

There was no preamble to Terry's next message, which was a real sphincter clincher.

Ian, go get yourself a three month put option on Currentsea. At the lowest price you can.

After a few moments of freewheeling panic, I focused and typed;

Why?

Just trust me mate.

Trust you? I've got fifty grand's worth and you're suggesting that they're going to fall out of bed.

Yeah, I was coming to that. Buy the option and then sell your shares on the drip over the following few days.

You're scaring me.

No need, not if you do as I say. Remember, trust me. Haven't let you down yet, have I?

This is like blind man's bluff. You've got me staggering around without a clue about what's going on.

Just get on with it, we can talk later. Ciao.

That brought me to my senses. I tried to ask more questions but he didn't respond. Hell's Bells, I thought, what had I gotten myself into.

I should explain. A '*Put Option*' is a way of playing a stock without actually buying any shares. In fact, it's an option to sell rather than buy shares. In return for a premium, an investor can purchase the right to sell a share at a pre-determined price. It works like this; say that shares in *ABC Plc* were trading at one pound and an investor thought they were in for hard times. He could buy a *put option* which is set at a price of fifty pence, for a modest cost. The option would have an exercise period; usually three, six or twelve months and the option price would reflect the odds of the share price behaving in that way. If the share doesn't fall and the option is not exercised, the premium is lost, but if, say, the share fell to forty pence, the investor would exercise the option and buy shares on the market to meet the contract, thus making ten pence a share.

Investors can do the same thing for the other direction; by buying a *Call Option* to buy shares. In that case everything is reversed. If *ABC Plc* were trading at fifty pence and rose to a pound, a person who had bought an option at, say, seventy five pence, could exercise it and buy shares for twenty five pence less than they were trading at.

Fund managers often use options to protect their position from large movements, if they are already holding the stock and in that sense the principle is one of insurance. So why wasn't Terry telling me to do that with my own shares, rather than sell them? There could only be one answer; the fall, if it happened, would be precipitous enough stop trading, in which case any actual shares held could be worthless. In effect, he was telling me to cash in my gains and hope for a double whammy, provided they were still trading when the price dropped below my option price.

That sort of investment in options is only a small step up from gambling and not for the man in the street; in fact, not for anyone who has an attitude to risk of less than twelve on a scale of ten.

So, in telling me to buy a *Put Option* at the lowest price possible, Terry was indicating that bad news was just around the corner; very bad, by the sound of it.

Share dealing was an allowable investment under SIPPS and so were derivatives such as '*Options*', though most providers didn't like seeing them in a pensions wrapper and needed persuading. Mine certainly would.

I struggled to find an option, probably because the market thought a demand for them in this stock was unlikely, but eventually I purchased one with an exercise price of thirty five pence, for next to nothing.

After that I began to sell my shares off in parcels of twenty thousand. I reckoned it would take a few days which left me on the horns of a dilemma. If things went tits up before my clients could sell I could expect censure. In the end, I compromised, by passing the news on three days later, when I had sold eighty thousand. I'd made so much money I was tempted to hang on to the last twenty thousand; after all, they didn't owe me anything and the fall might not be as bad as Terry indicated. I realised that would be stupid though, for the intelligence was obviously reliable enough for him to propose the put option; a nugget I did not pass on.

Not surprisingly, they all questioned my advice. After all, there seemed no end to the good news and no hint of adversity. All I could say was that the tip came from the same source that told us to buy in the first place.

Sure enough, the sell off by my band of followers and their networks caused the price to ease back, from fifty one to forty nine pence. Thankfully, the chat lines and trading commentaries put it down to profit taking, which was certainly true, in part. I had sold one hundred thousand shares for a total of forty eight thousand seven hundred pounds after paying only two thousand for them.

I tried to make contact with Terry by clicking on his icon, as instructed, but there was no response.

Two days later the shares had recovered and moved on by another two pence, something I pointed out when *he* finally made contact. His response was unequivocal.

Don't even dream of going back in Ian.

Why are you so certain?

Questions being raised internally,—about the turbines.

What questions?

Don't know, but info is reliable.

When will we know?

Soon. Did you buy the put option.

Yes.

Good, probably best to exercise your option before price falls below twenty five pence.

I was stunned, again. Not only was he forecasting a crash, he was telling me how bad it was going to be. His next message appeared before I had chance to respond.

Nothing for you at the moment and must dash. Just called to make sure you'd sold them. Will be in touch soon.

He didn't make contact for three weeks and by then, it was all over.

Chapter 4

They'd made good time from Portslade on the Sussex coast, but as always, timing for the last leg into Sharpness was critical, if they wanted enough water beneath the keel to get into the lock. The channel north of Portishead, in the Bristol Channel, careered from one side of the river to the other and the pilot needed all his skills to manage the currents that hammered up behind them. The captain always took the opportunity to admire the grace and beauty of the two bridges that crossed the river, in defiance of the treacherous brown currents and fierce Atlantic gales that swept past them. New *Cardinal* buoys marked the zone designated for the hydro power experiments but otherwise, little had changed.

In fact, Sharpness Docks were the most limited in the Bristol Channel/Severn Estuary, in that they could only offer berths to ships of less than one hundred and forty metres length, sixteen and a half metres beam and a six and a half metre draft. All that equated to a dead weight tonnage limit of around ten thousand tons. The outer lock was rarely used as such, apart from when the largest of ships went through or when traffic was heavy enough to need the outer lock as a basin. For that reason, the outer gates were usually left open.

By contrast, further downstream, Bristol (Portbury) could handle vessels of three hundred metres, with a beam of forty two metres, a draft of fourteen and a half metres and a dead weight tonnage of thirty thousand tons.

Jansons's relief as she nosed into the lock was keener than usual, for reasons he couldn't pin point, save for his instincts, which were on high alert. He'd expected the three new crew members to jump ship at Portslade and on reflection, it would have been welcome, but they were still on board, expertly heaving the lines down to the dock workers, who would help to warp her in. At least now, they were safely within the protection of a harbour that had no military value whatsoever.

Piles of timber on the western edge of the dock signalled their destination, just as the mountains of scrap metal on the eastern side signalled their point of departure, scheduled for four days time.

Three hours later, the Customs and Immigration had finished inspecting the ships' manifesto and crew's documents. Unloading could begin. He'd been bringing cargoes to this port for so many years there were few concerns, particularly these days and formalities were sealed with a glass of vodka. A practice that was wholly improper of course, though customary; with such a well known skipper.

Just after the unloading began, one of the new men, Dominiks, entered the bridge and said that he and his friends were prepared to man the night watches while they were in port; all of them. It sounded much more like an order than an offer, but what the hell. None of the other crew would object, with beer, women and Bristol's night life so close to hand. Jansons felt very much like joining them.

* * *

Sundays were always quiet; uncomfortably so these days, with little more than the *Sunday Times* and mediocre television to pass the time. In fact, I had taken to doing my weekly shop at the superstore on Sundays, as a way of filling in time.

I was still on tenterhooks, waiting for news about *Currentsea* and hoped for a call from Terry. In spite of his assurance, I continued to hit his icon on *Skype*, without success. It was worrisome and frustrating, but as I sat in the silence of my kitchen, nursing a mug of coffee, that concern triggered another; one that I should have acknowledged weeks before.

I missed him, terribly. We could have kept each other company on Sunday mornings.

Both my parents were dead, but I realised that Terry would still have been able to go to his parents for Sunday lunch, if he was alive. Both were in their eighties and still living in Loughborough; in the semi-detached house they bought when Terry's dad, Jack was demobbed after the war.

I should have thought of it earlier. It was time to pay them a visit.

They always joked that it was a poetic match rather than one made in heaven, which was as good a way as any to pass off their names. Jack and Jill.

It was the twentieth of March and a beautiful spring morning, so the drive over had been delightful. The hedges were showing a hint of green and the roadside verges had started to fill with wild daffodils. I stopped off at a convenience store en route for a couple of gifts and as soon as I reached their street, my spirits lifted.

Parking was always a nightmare on Sundays, when everyone was home and people were visiting, but I didn't give it a second thought. The small estate had been built in the late nineteen forties, when cars were luxuries and therefore rare. The width of streets reflected that and had now become single track highways, with passing places at driveways and road junctions. I counted myself lucky in finding a space to park within four hundred yards of their door and set off with a bunch of daffodils for Jill and a bottle of decent Aussie red for Jack.

On the way over I wondered how to play things. Did I act as though Terry was alive and kicking, since they should already be party to that much, surely? Or should I wait for them to tell me?

Her welcome was spontaneous, but the lines in her face, the sadness in her eyes and the desperate need reflected in her voice told me everything. I was doing for them what I thought Terry could do for me, on a lonely Sunday morning. She smiled and held out her arms as she spoke, "Oh Ian, I'm so glad you've come to see us."

I died a death; several in fact.

As we hugged, I realised how dreadfully I had treated them; visiting once or twice maybe, since Terry had died and they had been like an aunt and uncle to me.

I also realised that Terry was still dead.

I didn't dare think about what I'd gotten myself into.

She hung on for a little longer and quickly swept the tears away as we parted, "Oh how silly of me, come on in, Jack's in the back."

He was already out of his chair and marching towards me with his hand outstretched as I led the way into their living room. "Ian, it's great to see you. A sight for sore eyes, I can tell you!" He glanced at the wine and added, "My, and so is that;—something to celebrate with."

My eyebrows popped up, "Oh, what celebration is that?"

Jack winked, "When you're my age, any day with a 'Y' in it is cause for celebration lad."

It was an act, of course, and Jack's hand trembled enough to spill some as he poured the wine. Jill had been a strikingly handsome woman, with a great shock of black hair, but she had shrunken somehow and her hair had become steely grey. Jack's hair had all but disappeared, though he'd shown signs of thinning for years. But like Jill, he'd *diminished,* sitting in his chair like a little gnome.

We chatted and reminisced for an hour, mostly about Terry and me as kids but never of more recent times, as though fearful of the proximity to his death. When they invited me to stay for lunch I excused myself by pleading prior arrangements elsewhere. There was no smell of cooking and I suspected that the fare would be like their lives, frugally scant.

I drove home in a state of unspeakable sadness and the silence of my own home maintained it. At six-o-clock I had a very stiff whisky, followed by another. At six thirty, I opened a bottle of red wine and shoved a frozen meal into the oven.

At eight-o-clock, I managed to remove the foil container from the oven, with its blackened, smoking contents and dropped them into the sink. The alcohol had done away with my appetite, but at least and against the odds, I was going to sleep that night.

The following morning I rose with a mild headache and much clearer state of mind.

I had made a ton of money under very suspicious circumstances and so had others. It was time to draw a halt to things.

And hope we hadn't broken any laws.

Or if we had, unwittingly, hope that no-one found out.

It was a Monday and apart from a couple of portfolio reviews that morning, I had little else to do. Normally, I would have settled down to some client admin, or begun the preliminary work on my company accounts for the current trading year, which ended on the same day as the tax year.

But, I was enjoying a sense of release. Finances were more than shipshape and looking less threatened now that I had made my decision to stop acting on Terry's tips; wherever he was, or indeed, *whoever* he was. Simple greed had been my only motivation and now it was over. The *put option* was probably the most damning thing in my portfolio, in that it indicated prior knowledge of a fall, but I reasoned that if it wasn't exercised, the transaction would probably go unnoticed.

It was a beautiful day too and like *Mole,* in *Wind and the Willows,* I decided it was time to head over to the riverbank. Well, the canal side actually, or at least nearby; to the *Dog and Hedgehog,* in a small village called Dadlington; a pleasant twenty minute drive away. There, I could expect one of the finest Fish and Chips in the Midlands. Their menu was broad and excellent anyway, but by making their batter with tonic water, they elevated a simple basic to something special.

Since it was Monday lunchtime, the Inn was only a third full, though I knew that from Thursdays to Sundays, the place would be heaving and reservations were necessary.

Bill met me at the door with his usual smiling welcome and handshake. After a short chat, he showed me to a table in the corner of the lower dining room. A couple of minutes later, a middle aged lady dropped a lunch menu and wine list on the table in front of me. I had been miles away and hadn't seen her approach, but I quickly looked up, smiled and said hello. I'm pretty sure my greeting wasn't noticed because she had already turned away, murmuring over her shoulder that she would be back for my order. Since I knew exactly what I wanted, I called to her and said as much. She stopped, dropped her head slightly and paused, before turning back, as though my haste was an inconvenience.

Undaunted, I tried another smile when she returned with a pen and pad to hand and hoped for a more positive response after giving her my order. There was none; either to my obvious efforts to be pleasant or to my order. Not a glimmer. There'd hadn't been a smile, hello, how are you, or thank you. She might have been young enough for PMT, but only just.

She offered me a choice of sauces when she brought the food but, again, there wasn't a trace of a smile. A couple of minutes later, a bowl containing the tartare sauce was placed on the table; close enough for me to reach, but far enough away to remove the need for further communication. At least, the fish and chips were delicious, as was the glass of *Chardonnay* I'd chosen to accompany it. Both the batter and the *Chardonnay* could have been described the same way; light and crispy. In fact, I ordered another; wine that is.

I had finished my meal by the next time I saw her and as she made to remove my plate I said I hadn't had the second glass of wine. Before I could tell her not to bother; that I would settle for a coffee, she let my plate drop back onto the table and stalked away without a word.

It was enough; I had tried to be pleasant and she had been all but rude. Valiant stoicism was turning into rage.

I never believe in shouting in places like that, in fact I believe that a softly spoken threat is far more effective than a yelling match. So when she returned with the wine I no longer wanted I signalled at it and said quietly, "I told you that I had finished my meal, and you charged off before I could request a coffee instead." She made to grab the glass and I placed my hand over it before continuing, "Wait, let me finish, or I'll continue this conversation with Bill and I promise you, you wouldn't want that." I took a breath, "You have been surly and unhelpful to the point of rudeness. Is this how you normally treat customers? Because I have to tell you that this customer expects an apology."

She looked at me then; I think for the first time and then stared at one of the pictures on the back wall as her eyes filled. She tried to stop them, but tears began to flow and she tried to search her pockets for a tissue while continuing to face away from the steps up to the bar, from where Bill was beginning to show interest in what was happening.

I have never been able to cope with a lady crying, particularly when I have caused it and my anger disappeared as I handed her an unused paper serviette from the table. I murmured, "I'm so sorry, I didn't mean to upset you like that."

After a quick facial wipe down, she pocketed the serviette and glanced back at the bar before looking at me, "No, it's me and I'm sorry. Had some bad news at home, but I shouldn't have brought it to work." She signalled towards the wine, "Please, have that on the house."

I tried to provide her with a gentler smile as I thanked her, but I was concerned. To begin with, I told myself, I should have realised something was wrong, for the owners would never tolerate that sort of service as a norm, but instead of leaving her be, I'd gone and threatened her.

I felt compelled to speak with her again and began by ordering a coffee. When she brought it, I spoke in a much gentler tone, "What's your name?"

She pointed to the small badge that was pinned to her left breast, or rather, the cream blouse that covered it, as she said, "Stephanie."

I gave a little grimace, "Yes, I saw the badge, but they always make those badges too small and I couldn't read it without peering too closely. It must be discomforting for ladies to experience that."

She gave me a small smile, "Some see it as an opportunity."

I was heartened by her response and pressed on with what I'd rehearsed, "I'm sorry for what I said Stephanie. Could we start over do you think?

I was rewarded with a bigger smile, "Yes, let's." She paused before adding, "Shall I get the menu and wine list?"

This time I chuckled, "No thanks, a smile is all I have space left for." I became serious, "I'm also sorry to hear you've had bad news, truly. It's a pity you couldn't have taken the day off."

She shrugged, "I'm on my own and only a casual, so time off isn't an option."

There were other diners waiting for service so I knew that time was short. I pulled out a pen and one of my business cards as I spoke, "Look, I don't want to pry, but I have some specialist skills. If your bad news was of a financial nature, I might be able to help." I pressed on as she made to speak, "There'd be no charge, just a sympathetic ear and sound advice." I held up the card with the number I'd written on the reverse, "Please, take this. My private number is on the back."

With a nod and smile, she took it and moved away, to attend to another table.

When the bill arrived, I noted that the second glass of wine had been left off, but I guessed that in the circumstances, she would have paid for that herself, so my tip was more than enough to cover it.

* * *

Even though it was towards the end of March, a bitterly cold south westerly swept up the estuary, bringing with it a persistent drizzle of rain. The crew were all in Bristol, save for the three strangers and Captain Jansons, who knew when it was time to stay in his cabin. He also knew that none of the crew would be back before six thirty in the morning, ready for their departure which was scheduled for high water at ten-o-clock.

Had he been on the bridge, he'd have known that there was no-one on watch. He'd have also noticed that the light at the head of the gangway had gone out, though there was enough ambient light for him to have caught a glimpse of three figures moving down on to the dock. One was carrying something dark and bulky on his shoulder, another seemed to be carrying a small outboard and the third was making hard work of carrying a holdall, suggesting that it was the heaviest load of the three.

It was one-o-clock and desolately quiet. The captain raised his vodka glass and mumbled a Russian toast, "To your health!" Then added sombrely, "And mine actually."

The three men kept to the shadows whenever possible, as they made their way along the side of the outer lock. At three hundred and twenty feet long and fifty seven feet wide, the scale of the lock seemed much larger when empty, where the inky black water in the bottom was too low to reflect light; giving it a sense of menace. But it was of no concern to these men, as they slipped past the outer gates and descended the steps on the seaward side of the lock in absolute silence. The tide had been on the ebb for an hour and they could smell the stench of exposed mud, which served to caution them against the treacherously slick lower steps.

The first man allowed the mat black roll to slip from his shoulders as he reached the water. Moments later he located a cylindrical tank and eased the valve open; just enough to inflate the dinghy without being heard by anyone on the dock.

As soon as the transom popped up into the upright position he moved to one side, so that the second man could clamp the outboard on. By the time he had completed that task, the dinghy was fully inflated and they all slipped on board; the last man pushing them away from the steps. The ebbing current raced past the end of the approach to the lock, causing an eddy that swept them back into the lock gates and two of the men hurried to locate and employ a pair of extendable paddles. They strained against the current for several minutes, past the long, timbered jetties that bridled the approach to the dock, before their raft was snatched out, into the mainstream, with a contrast of forces that startled all three of them. None had spoken a word and their departure had been without a sound. The whole ensemble was matt black, ensuring that they hadn't been seen either.

The man at the helm flicked a switch before turning the throttle and an electric motor purred into life. He knew that they would need to conserve the cadmium batteries, but the timing of this mission had taken that into account. It things went to plan they would only need the motor for positioning. The tides would do the rest.

Having entered the channel, they were swept downstream by the twelve knot current. The man with the holdall, who now sat in the bow, had already removed a hand held GPS and was waiting for it to acquire enough satellites to give them a fix and a course down the navigable channel, which had already been programmed in. Despite the rain, they could see the lights of the distant cardinal buoys within minutes, so the bowman had only to concern himself with the channels. The dinghy only had a draught of six inches, but they couldn't afford to run aground on one of the many mud banks being exposed by the falling tide. Jumping overboard to push off would have been unpleasant at best and probably dangerous.

After covering the five miles in less than half an hour, the helmsman brought them around to face upstream and steered slightly to starboard, so that they moved across the current in a 'ferryman's glide'. In no time, the man in the bow lashed a line to the *Cardinal* buoy at the northern end of the navigational hazard.

One of the two interconnected *Portakabins* on the bank, housed the monitoring equipment, evidenced from the dim light that shone from within. They already knew that the other cabin provided accommodation for the two men on site and it was in darkness. Soon, they would need to be watched carefully. A third unit looked much more industrial; used as a store and of no concern.

All three began to empty the holdall. Four light nylon tubes; open at both ends and black, like everything else; looking like narrow, but long windsocks, were lashed to the sides of the dinghy, allowing the current to straighten them out. Then, using only the glow from the GPS, they began to arm the small plastic charges, which were similar in appearance to golf balls, though half the size. By two-o-clock they had divided them equally between four sacks and were ready to begin.

The mooring was loosened and line paid out as the dinghy was allowed to drift further downstream; until the man at the stern signalled that it was time to tie off again. Sixty feet away, they could just make out two large pods mounted on upright posts, each being driven by two of the four underwater turbines. The soft hum indicated that things were still operational. At that point, another man donned a mask and small diving re-breather before slipping over the side, with a heaving line around his chest. The current had begun to slow as low tide approached and time was short. A current was necessary for their mission and slack water was only an hour away.

When one of the nylon tubes was tugged by the diver, one man paid out the line that still connected it to the dinghy, while the other figure stood and began to pay out the diver's heaving line that would be used to haul him back. The man in the dinghy knew that his charge was working by touch alone and was ready for any sign of trouble.

Below, Dominiks fought his way from side to side, trying to make contact with one of the huge tube casings, while constantly being buffeted by eddies. The darkness was total and the lack of bearings became complete. Surfacing would do little to help, since visibility up there would be limited and in any event, lacked any indication of where the underwater targets lay. Time was slipping by and the air in the miniature tanks was extremely limited, notwithstanding the bitter cold that was beginning to affect him badly.

It was those eddies which had pushed him to towards the bank and past the casings.

On board, anxieties were rising too. Both were feeling the cold almost as badly, for whilst they were all wearing dry suits the rain and bitter wind were taking effect.

Suddenly, the end of the heaving line was at hand and it was time to bring Dominiks back on board and re-position. Their margins had all but disappeared. Straining against the weight, they began to haul on the heaving rope, causing the diver to arc through the current as he was dragged back. Within a minute or so two things signalled the target location. A faint murmur of machinery, or it might even have been vibration that reached him, moments before he was slammed against the side of the casing, ejecting the mouthpiece from his jaws. Retrieving it is one of the most basic skills in diving, but training didn't include exhaustion combined with spinning. The effect of current and a tight rope caused his body to spin like a propeller; constantly bringing him back to collide with the casing and causing a sickening disorientation. His ears began to sing as his lungs burned, until finally, instinct took over and he kicked for the surface.

When the man hauling on the rope caught a glimpse of surface froth; caused by something on the surface and in line with the rope, he stopped pulling and considered the options. Should he haul like mad and perhaps retrieve a casualty or wait. Training came in to play. If Dominiks was dead, he could wait a little longer, but on the other hand, if it was a temporary situation, he should allow time for it to be sorted out.

Moments later, he was rewarded with a double tug on the line and began to pay it out again.

Below, Dominiks soon found the turbine entrance and drew the nylon tube towards him. It was then a simple matter to fix the large plastic clips that had been sewn onto the downstream collar of the delivery tube, to the protective grill and from then on, even simpler to locate the three other entrances, which lay alongside, in line. It was simply a matter of being pulled back to the dinghy for another tube and following the line that still attached the first tube to the dinghy. Within twenty minutes, including short breaks to help with exhaustion, the job was done.

They helped him back on board, though by then, he was in a state of collapse. Like so many missions, things never turned out as expected and chaos took precedence. He shifted his head so that they could hear him, "Do it."

One gave slack on the mooring line while the other cautiously hauled on one of the tube lines. As soon as the top of the tube appeared it was tied off and the bowline was secured before both men set about retrieving the three other tubes. Then, they quickly poured the balls into the tubes, before easing each collar back beneath the surface. From then on, the slackening current had just enough effect to sweep the charges into the turbines.

The 'droplet' charges had been designed to take out strategic machinery, such as the pumps and valves in gas and oil pipelines. They were such a simple concept and because they were bio-degradable, save for the detonation device, evidence of their use would be virtually irretrievable. The detonation device was half the size of a SIM card, and without any indentifying features, so that any that weren't destroyed would be extremely difficult to identify, notwithstanding the impossibly slight chance of even finding one in the Severn estuary.

They might have heard something, a series of faint noises which sounded like the purr of a cat, but it was impossible to be certain in that wind, so the first definite sign of success was the sound of alarms coming from one of the *portakabins*. Lights came on in the accommodation unit followed by the main ones in the monitoring area.

Sharp snatches on the nylon delivery tubes snapped the plastic hooks that tethered them to the entrance grills and all four were retrieved. Then, they waited, certain that they couldn't be seen in those conditions and equally certain that no-one would be venturing out on to the water at that time. The only real risk was if someone onshore had a powerful lamp and in that case they would slip the mooring and quietly motor out into midstream. Otherwise, their plan was to wait for an hour and ride the incoming tide, back to Sharpness Dock. Five minutes later; someone opened the cabin door and poked their head out, to peer in their direction, before retreating back inside.

They were safe.

An hour later, they cast off and moved into midstream, where the incoming tide delivered them back to Sharpness within half an hour. It was four thirty; an hour shy of sunrise and two hours before the dock workers would be arriving for work. By that time, they would be aboard *Erebus* and asleep.

* * *

'Noddy' Pope wasn't the brightest bulb in town, but then few would be prepared to spend six nights a week as a security guard for minimum wage. Forty eight hours a week, without a sniff of overtime pay. The scuffed shoes, creased uniform and dishevelled appearance served to confirm that he lived alone, just as his seventeen stones reflected a taste for junk food.

The ships were expected to take care of their own security so he was left to wander around the dock itself. On nights as lousy as this one, he would make his way along one side of the dock before making a swift circuit of the lock and retracing his steps; to the warmth of his cabin, at the main gate.

The rain had stopped at last, but he sought temporary shelter from the wind behind a crane stanchion, beside the bows of a freighter and was thinking about the next warm Cornish pasty when just fifty yards away, a dark, glistening figure appeared from the direction of the river. Noddy, who had been standing in a shadow was startled by the appearance and took a few moments to collect his wits. By then the figure was within thirty feet and obviously wearing some sort of diving gear. It had been used too. That much was evident from the water dripping from the figure, which started in surprise as Noddy illuminated it with his torch and called out, "'Ere boy, what you up to?" Had he stayed in the shadow and taken a few more moments to consider his options, he would have seen another two figures appear, in which case, he would have remained hidden and survived.

The other two had seen how exhausted Dominiks was and had sent him on while they followed with the gear, but adrenalin and training overrode everything.

Smiling, he continued to walk towards the guard and waved over his shoulder, "I been for a night dive. Vairy cold."

By then only eight feet separated them and Noddy held up a hand as he began to instruct the man to stay where he was. Dominiks winced and cried out as he lifted his foot and bent, to remove the imaginary stone from the sole of his bootee. His return to the upright position brought with it a battering ram of a right fist, which plunged into the fat man's stomach, lifting him off his feet and delivering him to the ground with a thud. Severely winded; he couldn't utter a word as two other men appeared, silently and from nowhere, it seemed. The assailant simply pointed, before they gathered the heaving form up and ran along the dockside, before laying it on its back, at the edge of the lock.

Still too winded to speak, Noddy felt one of them take hold of his feet while the other two grabbed his armpits and eased him nearer the edge. It was all happening so quickly and things blurred further as a shadow fell across his face. Two hands clasped the sides of his head in a vice-like grip.

In a single fluent movement, Dominiks lifted the head and smashed it down, onto the concrete edge of the lock, while another undid the guard's fly and pulled out the penis. Still without a word from any of them, the man holding Noddy's feet hefted them up until gravity took over.

By the time Noddy hit the water the three killers were already yards away, about their business. Two returned for the gear while Dominiks checked the area for witnesses, though as expected, there were none.

Even if Noddy had been conscious, he wouldn't have lasted long in the frigid water, but the blow to his head ensured that he would never know the agony of drowning.

* * *

The portly figure, still in his dressing gown, stood at the window of an apartment in Henley, not seeing the view over the Thames, while listening intently to the telephone. Eventually, he thanked the caller and broke the connection.

He'd been waiting for the call and remained where he was while he assimilated the intelligence, along with the instructions that accompanied it. They both served to remind him how kind the fates had been; which was when and why, he gazed out and appreciated the view outside. Dawn was bringing form back to the cruisers moored along the opposite bank. There was no movement on the river at that hour and little expected at that time of year.

Many of the cruisers opposite were sheeted up for the winter, just like his own fifty three foot cruiser, moored beneath him. Twin Volvo engines provided enough power for a top speed of twenty eight knots and a high freeboard ensured excellent sea keeping qualities, not that he had ever used it on the sea; at least not yet, but he was comforted by those capabilities.

Whilst few could ever tire of the view, fewer still could afford it, though the call had re-enforced his tenure, by several more million pounds. There was still a great deal to do, but there was nothing he hadn't done before; it was simply a matter of subtlety and direction.

* * *

They dragged Noddy's body out of the lock at seven thirty three, according to the police record. Death was pronounced at the scene but as they prepared to remove the corpse, a paramedic drew attention to the wound on the back of the head. Calls were made and more Police arrived, including the SOCO; Scenes of Crime Officer, who reasoned that since no other crime had been reported, they were struggling for a criminal motive. Ergo, he suspected accidental death and became certain of it when someone pointed out that the fly was open. Somehow, Noddy's penis had retreated back inside the trousers but remained outside of his underpants. It had obviously been out in the air at some point, prompting the SOCO to theorise, "He was having a piss in there and slipped, let's have a look at the edge of the lock."

Minutes later he was called over to a patch of moisture that discoloured the wet concrete. Closer inspection revealed hairs embedded in the chipped surface and a spray of what looked certain to be blood fanned down the vertical face of the lock. Samples were gathered and the consensus was; job done. Simply a matter of checking for witnesses, confirming a blood and hair match, writing it up and filing it with the post mortem.

* * *

Since Dominiks was supposedly on watch between two and eight, he was called to the bridge where a Police Constable waited with the Captain, who didn't bother to make introductions. Instead, he merely gestured for the officer to begin his questioning.

But when the first question was asked, Dominiks shrugged his shoulders and looked to the Captain, who translated into Russian, deliberately, instead of Latvian.

That much was lost on the Englishman but Dominiks responded immediately, with a denial of any knowledge, as expected and a translation was passed on. After noting the response, along with their names, which had to be spelt for him, the constable thanked them for their time and bade them farewell. The smoke from the stack and presence of a pilot indicated an imminent departure, so he added a 'Bon Voyage' and left.

Another death and God only knew what else. Jansons hoped he would never know, but he was sick of it; of them.

Now though, the pilot was waiting, but before dismissing Dominiks the captain murmured in an aside, "Your English is less fluent than I recall."

Dominiks merely shrugged, before replying in perfect English, "I did not want to be misunderstood."

It might have been ill-judged, but Jansons needed to have the last word, "You haven't been. Go to your station."

One of the three men remained on deck for the journey downstream, until they reached the experimental turbine site. It was mid-morning yet there was no evidence of a crisis. A cluster of vehicles were parked around the *Portakabins* but no-one was in sight.

There was ample evidence of one inside though, where there was every sign of rising panic. All feed had ceased in the early hours and so far no-one had any answers. All the sensors; temperature, vibration, output and pressure were dead, as though someone had made off with the turbines. Nothing more could be done from shore and the surveying team; with their boats and cameras, weren't expected until after lunch.

When they did finally arrive, late that afternoon, it was too late to venture out on the water and arrangements were made for them to begin the next morning.

In the meantime, some news might have been leaked and the first sign of a reaction was a fall of five pence on the shares, after several hundred thousand were dumped. Worse, all of the deals were 'Ordinary' trades. Normally there would be a mix of 'Ordinaries' with 'Automated trade executions' and each would be shown with either an 'A' or 'O' against it. The 'Automated' deals demonstrated that the buyer had pre-planned the purchase at that particular price and the transaction would be triggered automatically if the share reached that figure. The opposite holds true for selling too, but over thirty 'Ordinary' deals suggested that many were unplanned transactions; immediate and 'at best', or in other words, at whatever price they could get for them. By the close, they had fallen by eight pence on the day.

I was startled and concerned, once again, but in spite of everything, intrigued. It looked as though the fall would continue the next day and I knew I would be monitoring it, closely.

The next morning *Currentsea* shares only fell by a further three pence within twenty minutes of the market opening and stayed there. The chat lines were still full of confidence, along with scorn for the *lightweights* who had jumped ship instead of recognising the longer term value. Those sentiments seemed to hold good for the rest of the day and by the end of trading, the shares had rallied by two pence, to close at forty three pence; thanks to those who saw the earlier fall as an opportunity to buy or worse, to increase their holding.

* * *

That morning, on the Severn, the surveying team couldn't credit what they were seeing on the monitors.

Each turbine was the same. Little remained of the innards, save for the axles and the stanchions that secured them to the casing.

Although it was a different concept, the tolerances in the engineering were just as fine. Balancing turbine blades is crucially important; to avoid vibration, but by the same token, when part of the whole is removed, or blown apart, the integrity of the entire assembly goes west, or in that case, south west, down the River Severn. The first few charges would have ensured that the innards had beaten themselves to death; a little like the main rotor blade of a helicopter striking the ground.

The damage was therefore total and catastrophic.

An emergency board meeting was called for four-o-clock that afternoon, in which it was agreed that they should wait until the full report was received from the surveyors. The next day was *Good Friday* and the markets were closed until Tuesday. At least that would buy time, enough to span a long weekend; so often a useful means of softening blows. Since they already knew the essentials, a statement was prepared for release on Tuesday the twenty ninth of March; one which declared the extent of damage, as they were legally obliged to do, but which went on to point out that the cause had yet to be established. It also drew attention to the hugely successful results they had already demonstrated and that technical difficulties had always been anticipated with such a leading edge design,—and they would be resolved.

There was a flaw to that logic. Not only was it 'leading edge' and therefore speculative; it had been the only working model in existence. The funds for more were coming from the banks. Worse still, the *Environmental Agency* had been called in and was already expressing concerns about the clean-up costs, including the retrieval of the casings.

During the conference call with the chief surveyor, one director raised the question of sabotage. The surveyor was unequivocal, "Can't see that. To wipe all four out, so comprehensively, you need people with military capabilities and you're not that grade of target." There was a short pause before, "Are you?"

Howard Long cut in, "I rather doubt it. We are working on something new, but we're still minnows in the power industry."

The surveyor replied, "Fair enough, I thought as much." Otherwise he would have added that if it had been a military attack, there would be traces of incriminating evidence. In the event, when the casings were finally lifted out of the water, five months later, all definitive traces had been sluiced away.

* * *

Steph telephoned me on Saturday morning, on the private line, "It's me, Stephanie Newell."

I was struggling to recognise either the voice or name and the pause was eloquent enough for her to add, "We met at The *Dog and Hedgehog,* I served you."

I was delighted, "Oh, yes, of course, I'm awfully sorry; I'm terrible with names, great with numbers." I allowed a moment before adding, "I'm pleased you remembered this one; number I mean. How are you?"

"Much better thank you. I 'phoned to say I was sorry for my behaviour. It's just, well, my dad died two weeks ago. Yours wasn't the only complaint and the bosses were getting..," She paused, searching for the right word before, "*Anxious*, too."

I softened my voice and spoke with absolute sincerity, "Don't be Stephanie, the bond between father and daughter is a strong one. Losing a father brings a special grief."

"Steph"

"Pardon?"

"Steph, everyone calls me Steph."

I smiled, "All your friends that is."

There was a hint of a chuckle before she said, "Yes, I suppose. What do your friends call you."

I said the first thing that came into my head, "Bogbrain."

This time she laughed outright and we began to chat, though not for long. Just enough to establish that she'd spent half a day checking me out, which gave me confidence enough to ask her out.

She said yes, so I spent the rest of the day behaving like a youth facing his first date. I was excited, nervous and ridiculously pleased with myself. I didn't bother with the exact maths, but it must have been over thirty years since I'd asked a girl out.

Sunday was just the same. I worried about what I should say and more importantly, what I shouldn't. The venue needing some thought too. Whilst I had no intention of suggesting that we 'go Dutch' with the food bill, she could be emancipated enough to insist. That wrote off any thoughts of a posh restaurant, since she'd already told me that she was reliant on the casual wages from *The Dog and Hedgehog*. There may have been some welfare benefits, but she would still be strapped for spare cash.

With that conclusion, I found it easier to decide on dress code. Smart casual would do it. But then, I wondered if I should telephone and confirm that much. I think it was then that I laughed at myself. I knew so little about this lady, nothing I did might be right. What would be; would be.

* * *

The *Currentsea Plc* RNS was released at eight thirty on Tuesday morning, to coincide with the start of trading and by nine thirty, they were sinking fast. At eleven that morning, I checked again, just before leaving the house and saw that they had stabilised at thirty four pence, against my option at thirty five pence. If I had exercised the option, I'd have made one penny per share, but they looked certain to keep on falling. Even the chat lines were struggling to find anything positive to post.

* * *

I didn't exercise my option. In fact, I took Steph out for lunch instead, which served to keep me from temptation. It worked too.

I'd been pleasantly surprised to learn that she lived in Coalville; just ten minutes from my house and therefore only half an hour away from Leicester, where I planned to take her for lunch.

I drew up outside a block of four maisonettes, on what had once been a council estate, since when most of the tenants had bought their homes, which now boasted the *de rigeur* emblems of ownership; double glazing and a new front door. I would learn that hers was privately owned too, but by a landlord.

It was immediately clear that I did well to be on time, for Steph must have been waiting for me; bolting out of the door before I had chance to switch the engine off.

I smiled, waved and watched.

She wore a bright red ski jacket over a light mauve jumper with a large roll neck and made of wool that looked soft enough to cuddle. A flattering pair of jeans and beige lace-up shoes completed the ensemble.

Firstly, I had to establish whether she liked Indian food or not. I received a definite 'yes' to that one, which was good news, since for all my worrying the day before, I hadn't thought of an alternative.

I'd chosen a Sikh restaurant on the Narborough Road, which was a simple cafe that served home cooked vegetarian dishes to die for.

The drive in had been laced with polite, if slightly stilted conversation, though part of the reason for that was the traffic. Leicester is the only city I've driven in where the red traffic light triggers wild acceleration and seems to mean, 'Keep going, another three can get through yet'. By the same token, therefore, green means, 'Go, but with caution.'

I was perfectly happy conversing with clients and often addressed groups of a hundred or more, but I was not good with small talk. In fact, Dee used to say I was an embarrassment to be with at social occasions and I began to think that this was going to be another example.

Not so. From the beginning, she showed genuine delight at my choice of venue and allowed me to talk her through the menu, cutting in now and then with a quip or sign of preference. There was no alcohol on sale, but the mango milkshakes were stunning.

Within fifteen minutes, I felt we'd known each other for months. She had checked out my website and a couple of newspaper articles I had written for the local 'money page' but had lucked out on finding anything of a more personal nature. Then, thankfully, Bill had directed her toward two couples who were clients of mine and dined at the *Dog and hedgehog* regularly. Both spoke well of me.

Steph was clearly intelligent and up to date with World news. There was a genuine air to her as well, apart from the blonde hair and even that had been expertly coloured and bob-cut.

We over-ordered, massively, but the food was excellent and for once I didn't begrudge the smells that would be left in the car by the doggy bags she asked for.

At one point, well into the meal, she referred to her behaviour at the *Dog and Hedgehog*. "I'm so sorry about the other day Ian."

I put up a hand, "Please don't feel the need to apologise."

She shook her head, "No, I need to explain things a bit. You see, it wasn't just him dying, it was the *way* he did. The cancer just consumed him, literally ate him away and it took so long. He was fifteen stones when it began and six when it ended" Her eyes filled, "And I loved him to bits too."

I reached forward and took her hand, "I'm really sorry and you're right, I did need to know that." I watched as she gave herself enough of a mental shakedown to re-establish an equilibrium and she smiled.

Inevitably, the conversation got around to marriage partners, if only to establish that neither of us was misbehaving.

She led, with the tale of a husband who'd been a manic depressive for most of their life together, but the combination of redundancy and eviction from the home they were buying pushed him over the edge, to suicide.

I commiserated once again, but she shrugged her shoulders, "We didn't have any children and I haven't found anyone else since, so that was probably why Dad and I became so close. Mum died when I was a kid and he didn't find anyone else either."

I was tempted to mention Terry, as a suicide candidate I had known, but didn't know where I would end up with the tale. I could have frightened her off in our first date with that one.

Whenever the opportunity arose, I looked at her; really looked, taking in the ready smile, brown eyes, bow-shaped lips and, thankfully, modest use of make-up. When she rose to go to the toilet I stared after her as she walked away, noting that her bottom was wonderfully mobile and whilst it might have ample by a model's standards, I found it unutterably sexy.

I'd already fallen in lust and couldn't help wondering what the future might hold.

I told her about Dee, her new *amour* and two daughters who'd decided that since I'd been incapable of keeping their mother, I should lose them too.

Steph didn't say she was sorry. Instead, she asked, "How do you know when a solicitor's been run over on a pedestrian crossing?"

Startled, I said "Don't know."

"No skid marks."

We laughed and toasted that one, before ordering more mango milkshakes.

It was three-o-clock before we knew it and time to go home.

When we drew up outside the house, Steph asked me if I wanted to go in for a coffee, but I knew that there were things to check before the market closed at four thirty, simply in case of anything unexpected. "I'm sorry, but I have a few things to attend to that won't wait." I hastened to add though, "Steph, I've *really* enjoyed today."

She smiled, "Me too."

I hesitated to look her in the eye, in case there were signs I wouldn't want to see, when I asked, "Do you think we might do this again?"

She snorted, "Did you think for one moment I was getting out of this car before you'd asked me that?"

We laughed and with fluid ease we leaned towards each other and kissed. No rubber lipping, or tongue, just a lovely, gentle kiss and a wonderful beginning. I said, "I'll call."

She poked me in the ribs, "You'd better, or you'll be wearing the next meal you order at the *Dog and Hedgehog.*"

* * *

I'd been saved from temptation in more ways than one. The time was four fifteen when I got back to the office and checked on *Currentsea Plc;* to discover that trading in the shares had been suspended at two thirty, after the price had collapsed to twenty two pence. I checked the commentaries and discovered that the permits for the other two sites had been withdrawn, pending a full report of the disaster. One fund manager wrote that with only a few, modest income streams, the company would probably have been technically insolvent before the calamity, but surviving on the back of the new project. With that gone, insolvency was no longer a technicality.

He was right.

As soon as trading was suspended I couldn't have dealt anyway. As an unexercised option under such remarkable trading conditions, it was probably more noticeable than if I *had* exercised it, but at least this way, I had a chance of defending myself.

If I had exercised my option at twenty six pence, as originally planned, I'd have made another nine thousand pounds. As it was, I had lost the premium of a few hundred.

It felt great, well, not *great* exactly, but very comfortable. Having bullied him into allowing the deal, my SIPP provider was going to have a fit, but I'd explain that I'd had a day full of appointments and couldn't check things until late afternoon. Who, I would ask, could possibly have expected a collapse on that scale, in just a few hours.

The answer machine was full of messages from the band of people who I'd passed the tips on to, all asking me to call back and I did so, that evening. They all wanted to know how I came by such quality intelligence and finished the calls none the wiser. One stupid man hadn't sold, believing my tip to be either ill-considered or premature. I made a mental note never to include him again and hoped he didn't take it into his head to lodge a complaint.

All I had to do then was wait for the next *Skype* message.

Chapter 5

*H*ey Ian.
     Five minutes later, *Come on dude, talk to Taz.*
  I continued to ignore him

Ian, are you there?

He knew I would be, of course. It was only eight in the morning; a Wednesday and the sixth of April. The beginning of a new tax year, which signalled a flurry of ISA's and the closing off of my year end accounts. Others take months to prepare their accounts but I've always been a bit anal about mine, preferring to get the job over and done with.

Ian, are you ignoring me.

I had prepared for this;

Plan to.

You didn't exercise the option.

No.

Guessed you wouldn't.

Really?

Yeah, it was a step too far for you.

I bridled at that,

"I'm perfectly capable of dealing in derivatives, but not on the back of suspect material."

Nothing suspect about it, they crashed didn't they?

I'm referring to the source, not the material.

Me you mean?

I went to see your mum and dad. Both are well but still mourning the death of their son.

It took a few minutes before the reply to that one appeared.

Shit, wish you hadn't done that mate. What was said?

Oh, you mean did I tell them about my recent messaging with their son?

Yeah.

They send their love.

Christ, Ian, that wasn't a good thing to do.

I suppose the exhumation won't be either.

There was a lengthier pause before the next one.

Tell me what's happened.

I have done, though I'm certain you haven't been dug up yet.

No, I need the details. Who's been involved and when. Christ Ian, this cannot be allowed to happen.

Why, afraid they'll take your PC off you when the lid comes off?

I'm not laughing Ian. Please, fill me in.

That was too good to let slip by. I typed,

Poor choice of words, that.

Stop being a SHIT.

OK, I'll tell you, but not now.

When?

When we meet. I'll tell you face to face.

Can't do that.

Then my lips are sealed.

We will meet up Ian, I promise, as soon as appropriate.

Not good enough.

If I tell you something, do you swear to keep it secret?

It was my turn to pause and think a while. I was curious, intrigued even and eventually, decided to play along, but with a caveat.

Fair enough, I promise to keep it a secret, provided I am not compromised in any way.

That's not much of a promise.

It's the best you're going to get. Anyway, a friend wouldn't want to put me in a difficult position. Your choice.

He obviously accepted my terms.

Look mate, there were things I didn't tell you about. Couldn't. Please, you have to trust me, for both our sakes. The crisis committee I was on had a hidden agenda, stuff I am still involved in, but while this is going on I also have access to information that I can share with you. A sort of added benefit, if you like. I've already disclosed more than I should have, but whatever you've done poses a real threat to the work I'm doing.

I was startled and couldn't think of a response that didn't smack of *James Bond*. Yet somehow, there was something dreadfully credible about it. He, or whoever was on the other end knew so much about me, stuff that only Terry had known and I realised that I had already accepted his credentials; at least to the extent of following his instructions and making a great deal of money out of it too. I needed more time to think and in the meantime, decided to stop playing games. I typed;

I didn't tell your folks anything and so far as I'm aware, you're not going to be disinterred.

There was a pause, before;

Sheesh partner, you had me going there.

Now you know how it feels.

I wish I could have done it differently. Just wanted to do good by you.

That was a barb that caught, enough for me to try and lighten things.

Hope the fright doesn't give you a heart attack. Wouldn't do to die twice.

Ha ha.

What now?

I'll be in touch shortly. Have some important info. Have to sign off now though; being called away.

I sat back to try and make sense of it all. In effect, he'd told me that his death was faked and he was involved in some sort of secret work.

On reflection, there were times when he'd been less than open about that committee, which I thought was understandable, given some of the threats they would have considered; not least of all terrorism and the nasty things those folk could come up with. Dirty bombs and biological weapons sprang to mind immediately.

Overall, I decided that whilst it had been a series of new revelations; at least they were now tinged with some credibility.

I made a mug of industrial strength coffee and returned to my desk, to reflect on the intelligence he had been passing on to me. Even that word, intelligence, held a new significance now.

Much of it could have been routine stuff, if the sources had been well placed or high enough, including many government agencies, whose tentacles stretched everywhere.

There would also have been agencies close enough to the Severn Estuary trials, with access to drawings, manufacturing processes, and data, if they so chose. Their own experts, probably naval, might have become aware of shortcomings and might even have shared them with *Currentsea,* who would hardly have made them public, not when their survival depended on the success of the project

But where did that leave me, a shrimp in the scheme of things.

If I were to continue with what might be an unholy alliance, would I be hung out to dry if anything went wrong? After all, who trusts a government? Should I seek a guarantee of immunity?

I set about writing a list, beginning with 'Immunity'.

However bizarre things seemed, the information *had* been authentic; the results, spectacular.

And I was going around in circles.

Yet, he had been terrified when I mentioned disinterment. I remembered then, that Terry had specifically asked to be cremated in his suicide note, in which he'd also explained that he couldn't continue without Amy and apologised to his parents.

Since that note lacked any legal force and his will didn't mention funeral arrangements, Jack and Jill would have none of it. They were traditionalists and probably needed a grave to tend, in remembrance.

That must have given him a fright too.

Now that Terry had admitted to there being a secret part to his work, I didn't doubt that his death could have been faked. He'd posted the suicide note to the Police, who called at the house when they received it, two days later and discovered the body. In the note to them, he'd explained that he didn't want a relative or friend to find him. Amen to that, though I couldn't recall who identified the body. I felt certain it wasn't Jack or Jill and it certainly wasn't me. Cause of death was a given though.

I added another note to my list.

* * *

'Be in touch shortly' turned out to be five days later. By then I had extended the list and taken Steph out to the cinema, where we saw the picture *Miss Cogeniality 2*. We both agreed that it wasn't a feature we'd have chosen normally, but it appeared to be the least violent one showing. In any event, it was a fun sort of film, which we followed with a pizza in the Italian restaurant opposite.

It was a Sunday when the next message came through. For the want of anything better to do, I was working on a report. Steph was working that day too and I didn't feel inclined to eat at the *Dog and Hedgehog*. It wouldn't have felt comfortable having her serve me, not now.

At least I could work without all the usual interruptions of a working day. Well, save one. The computer beep told me I had a *Skype* message.

Hey Ian?

I typed back, immediately, *Hey.*

Any more thoughts about our chat the other day?

A few.

Go on.

I pulled the list out of my diary and set it down on the desk, beside the keyboard, before typing;

I see all sorts of issues, which might prompt enquiries at some point. Not least of all, 'insider trading'. Do I need some sort of immunity?

You have it.

That was a bit definite and prompt.

So I do need it then?

Doubtful, but I put it in place at the outset. Didn't tell you though, you seemed nervous enough as it was.

Can I have that in writing?

You just have.

I was tempted to write, 'from a dead man', but thought better of it. Instead, I referred to the list,

Who identified your 'body'?

Don't know.

I made a mental note to check that one myself and moved on;

Do you, (and your new friends), come by the information legally?

All authorised.

That's not necessarily the same thing.

Same difference, trust me.

Then I don't suppose you'll tell me how each bit of info is obtained?

Correct.

That didn't really surprise me, not if he had an 'M' for a boss, so I ploughed on.

Are the regulators involved?

Indirectly, yes.

So they know about me.

No and they won't.

That didn't give me any comfort, so I went back to the beginning;

So if they do find out, am I on my own?

Terry did too,

Please refer to immunity.

How long will this go on for?

Don't know, but will tell you when I do know.

Do you want a share of the profits?

No. Defo, no.

My last question was written with tongue in cheek;

If you're so well connected, what about tax?

Ha, ha. No change there, I'm afraid. I'm not God!

That's it, for the time being.

OK, then it's my turn. Stop sharing the tips, unless I sanction it.

He had managed to throw me off balance yet again. His instruction was too specific and therefore well informed for me to try and deny it, but I had to ask;

How did you know?

It was easy. You received the tips before the market knew anything and your buys were always followed by a cluster of others.

Oops.

Whatever, but no more in future, please. Others will notice too and ask questions.

I had no choice and anyway, I realised how stupid I'd been by sharing the information with so many. I typed,

OK, sorry.

No need mate. In fact having told you that, I'm going to suggest that you share this one anyway.

Go on.

Do you have any clients in PREVEX EUROPEAN?

Yes!

That was an understatement. I had a shed load of clients in there. The PREVEX stable had a score of funds, from the 'Gilt and Fixed interest' to 'Japanese Small Companies'. All were unit trusts covering the whole range of risk ratings, from low to high and with varying performance levels. A few were in the bottom twenty five per cent of the ratings, otherwise known as 'fourth quartile'. But their flagship fund was the 'Prevex European'. As the name suggested, the fund manager invested in European companies and other investments in that sector. It had outperformed ninety eight per cent of its market peers and looked set to continue. I tried to figure out how many clients I had sold the fund to and took a mental stab at a hundred and fifty before typing;

100, give or take. Why?

Get them out.

Just like that?

I'm beginning to sound like a parrot, but trust me.

Why? I realised my error and quickly added, *get them out I mean.*

Rule breach. I'll tell you more when I can.

The workload he was suggesting was way more than a simple rule breach warranted, even a serious one. A hefty fine, slapped hand

and a bit of bad press wouldn't destroy a fund and even the dismissal of the fund manager wouldn't negate the underlying assets, which should ensure that any exodus from the fund wouldn't necessarily cause a crash.

But it was the workload that really affected my reaction.

That seems a bit too radical. Do you realise how much work that will entail and what if things aren't as bad as you suggest? My clients will want my blood.

His reply suggested that he knew more than I expected, again.

I'm guessing that you have a bunch more than a hundred clients. Believe me, you need to do this.

I was becoming irritated, by the prospect of so much work and by being corralled into a corner. The mercenary in me came out.

So, without giving me a valid reason, you want me to embark on a giant task that will cost me a bundle in time. Why can't I leave things to play out naturally? I couldn't be held responsible, IF anything untoward happened.

That's a bit cynical!

I thought of something else then;

Anyway, can't be done. My compliance people would have a dickey fit if they saw me moving people from a top-performing fund to another without a very good reason. People used to do it for the commission. It's called 'churning' and it's highly illegal. Can't be done, sorry.

It was an extremely valid reason for not doing anything and a wave of relief swept over me. He wasn't giving in though.

OK, there have been some investment anomalies. Extraordinary ones, which will come out at the next AGM. You can protect yourself by asking for the latest details of their portfolio. It won't mean much, yet, but it will do when the sticky stuff hits the fan. Enough to justify your action, I promise.

I don't understand why I need to do this. I can't just tell half the clients, it's all or nothing and I don't have the time. I added, *Why me?!*

The answer was succinct.

Credibility.

I immediately railed against that one;

I have enough thank you.

Jeez Ian, I'm trying to make sure that you are bomb proof. This sort of pro-active work will buy you enough cred to justify any number of other investments, past and future.

Are you saying that I'm vulnerable?

Look mate, no matter how careful we are these messages are a matter of record and all the tips have been kosher and legal,—including this one. So you ask are you vulnerable? Yes you are, if you fail to act, now that you hold this information.

Looking back, I realise how deftly he'd handled that one, but at the time I was too concerned by the logistics and my blood pressure was rising.

But you haven't given me enough intelligence to draw ANY conclusions.

The AGM is on the 6ᵗʰ May. You won't have a leg to stand on then—if you haven't done anything.

Answer the last note,—please!

Ian, you have to accept that I have access to information before it becomes public, just like the Currentsea affair. I would never give you anything less than 24 carat, you know that. By the way, do you have any money in there?

No.

OK, so there's no self-interest served there then. Just good advice, plain and simple.

There was a petulant note to my next note;

I'll have to think about.

And Terry realised it, by signing off with;

Well don't sulk for too long. I'll be in touch.

I stared at the screen and murmured, "Shit". Then I continued, progressively raising my voice to a shout, "Shit, shit, shit, shit, shit!"

I thought back to his tips and realised how far out on a limb I'd gone, for they were often based on very privileged information, well before it became public. As he'd reminded me, 'just like *Current-sea*', which in the meantime, had foundered. An administrator had been appointed and was seeking a buyer, though he was reported as saying, in an unguarded moment, that there wasn't much to sell. He was right of course. Some office furniture, a couple of cars, a few small solar cell sites and the intellectual rights for a failed tidal turbine design.

Howard Long had been retained for the time being, having offered his services on an expenses only basis. Clearly, he was winding yet another company up and presumably, he was job hunting too.

Chapter 6

A good nights' sleep always helps.

I knew as soon as I woke, that I had no real choice, at least morally. My clients trusted me and so long as I trusted the source of the information I had no choice.

Libby arrived at nine and as usual made two coffees. On the odd occasion I declined, she seemed not to hear and I still received one; of industrial strength as usual. On that morning I followed her into the kitchen to break the news, "Libby, we have a problem."

As impassive as ever, she poked around in the cupboard for the sweeteners and said, "So did Houston." Sweeteners found, she glanced at me and sighed, "How come when things are going well you use 'I' but when bad stuff happens, it's always 'we'?"

I acknowledged that one with a shrug, "Perhaps, it's a problem shared and all that."

She turned her back to the warming kettle and faced me, "Does that mean I should feel honoured?"

I grimaced, "Perhaps not. How does a couple of extra days this week sound?"

She didn't hesitate, "Like tooth extraction."

The database informed me that I had a hundred and sixty six clients in the *Prevex European* fund and I knew that many saw it as their sole exposure to that particular sector. Most will have already had enough exposure to others, such as UK, America, and the Antipodeans, while the more adventurous would also be invested in the Middle East, China, and other less certain markets. Which meant that I would have to offer an alternative European fund and since *Prevex* didn't have one, new providers needed to be found. There was a large choice, of course, but new contracts would mean new commissions and the regulators were always on the lookout for that type of exploitation.

I began by contacting *Prevex,* who promised to email me an up to date investment schedule by lunchtime that day. I then printed off a schedule of alternative funds and made my selections, noting as I did, the reasons for each choice. I then spent over two hours preparing a report that recommended the transfer, based on my research, with enough detail to appear credible. I then went on to recommend alternatives with my reasons for doing so. Finally, as a salve for my conscience rather than anything else, I declared that I would forego half of the commission.

Each letter had a pre-printed response, which would only require a signature at that stage, *if* they chose to proceed. After that, I would sort out the details and have them sign a bundle of paperwork. By five the following afternoon, Libby and I had the lot ready for posting. As she left, with two carrier bags full of envelopes, she asked, "Do you want me in on Thursday and Friday?"

We had completed the task a day earlier than I'd hoped and I hadn't planned on asking her to work any extra days, but I realised how intuitive she was being. The letters would be falling on doormats in two days time, so Thursday and Friday looked set to be full of telephone calls from anxious or indignant clients.

That evening I scanned the *Prevex European* portfolio and while I recognised a number of companies, I'd never heard of many, partly because they were based all over Europe, from Scandinavia down to Spain and from the UK across to Germany and Latvia. I certainly didn't find anything to support Terry's allegations.

* * *

Thursday, Friday *and* Saturday were absolutely dreadful. Most clients were willing to trust my judgement, thanking me for my attention and commission sacrifice. But even the most straightforward call was extended by pleasantries and other topics.

A significant number were less convinced and their calls were the longest and most difficult. Eventually, the majority agreed to the transfer, albeit with varying degrees of confidence.

Perhaps fifteen per cent discussed matters with me but chose to keep their funds where they were and a few, usually the ones with the smallest portfolios and therefore, conversely, the most to lose in relative terms, showed varying degrees of belligerence. Some actually accused me of 'churning'; doing it solely for commission.

By Saturday afternoon I switched the telephone on to answer phone and drove over to the *Dog and Hedgehog* for a pint. It was past three o'clock when I arrived and lunchtime serving was coming to an end, which suited me perfectly. I just needed a friendly face and sympathetic ear.

Steph was about to go home and readily volunteered for the role.

By the time I had finished she had snuggled up to me and suggested, "Tell you what; I'm not working tomorrow night. How about I do a meal for us?"

It was a perfect idea and then I realised how therapeutic it would be for me to spend the day preparing the meal instead. I asked, "Are you working tomorrow lunchtime?"

She nodded, "Yes, but that won't matter".

I returned her snuggle and said, "Sure, but how about I do the meal. It'll give me something to do during the day, tomorrow."

She grinned, "I accept. If you're promising to spend a whole day on it I'll look forward to something special".

My grin bordered on the idiotic, "Count on it!"

* * *

Adam West inspected himself in the mirror once again and found his second attempt at shaving wanting.

His face was as smooth as he could ever manage, but achieving the same degree of hairless perfection with his genitals had always been a challenge, or at least since it had begun to matter.

Now, with another assignation with Bernhardt in prospect, there could be no blemishes. They wouldn't be tolerated, he knew, just as any other imperfections would affect their time together.

He would spend the whole afternoon preparing his body, beginning with what he called an 'inner cleansing', followed by a long soak in a fragrant bath and shaves. He used a favourite body lotion, savouring the sensuality of the treatment and lingering where he favoured, while dreaming of the oils Bernhardt would use, with such devastating effect.

The heating in his three floor terraced house in Putney was set at a tropical temperature but he'd spent so long naked that it was necessary to don the super soft dressing gown before heading back to the bedroom.

Then came the difficult part, beginning with foundation cream and progressing through the huge range of colours and hues he had to choose from. Each component required co-ordination, just as he waited until the choices had been made before choosing the eyelashes. The eyebrows were always a given; feminine but not flirty.

The air around him became laden with *Givenchy Fleur D'interdit;* one of Bernhardt's favourites, along with the pearl necklace, that had been a birthday gift last month.

Tonight, he would wear the medium length wig; the one with such wonderful waves.

So far so good, but all those decisions were so exhausting. It was time for a cup of tea, as usual.

There followed the ordeal of combing the wardrobe rails for just the right dress, while moaning softly to himself that he had simply nothing to wear. Each dress was lifted off the rail and held up beneath his chin, in front of the full length mirror, before being discarded onto the bed. But eventually, when patience, fatigue and time made their demands, he made his selection; often with a comment like, "Well this old rag will just have to do."

The ritual of putting the padded bra, panties, stockings and suspenders on then followed, though they had already been selected, just after lunch, after he had finished doing his nails.

Lastly, a pair of patent leather shoes, with medium heels completed the ensemble. The choice of coat was the least demanding, since he only owned one, on the principle that he wouldn't spend long in it anyway. He giggled at that thought, conceding that he wasn't planning to stay in anything for long.

His pulse spiked and an unwelcome flush bloomed across his cheeks when a car horn announced the arrival of his taxi, but Adam paused in front of the hall mirror, on his way out, for one last, inspiring assessment.

Outside, the taxi driver turned to watch as the *trannie* wobbled down the path. It was a caricature that could have graced the pages of *Punch*. He shrugged; shuffled back into his seat and thought, 'Not for me to judge'. Then, to himself; aloud, "But, it takes all sorts."

* * *

I was quite excited at the prospect of doing something special. When I concentrated on the subject of food, which wasn't often, not when cooking for one, I could produce some decent meals.

On that occasion, partly because I welcomed the diversion but mostly because it was for Steph, I poured through the recipe books over breakfast and came up with a menu I hoped would impress.

The first course was my own invention, born of necessity, during our holidays in France. Dee loved raw oysters and I hated them, so one day, after shucking them, I set mine to one side and dropped a teaspoon of white wine in and another of crème fraiche with a topping of grated *Gruyere* cheese before grilling them until browned. I couldn't believe the difference; in fact it marked a new found love of oysters, *al la Ian*.

Morrisons at Coalville had a wonderful fish counter, so supply wouldn't be a problem.

The second course comprised crispy chunks of fried hake on a pesto salad. A bottle of *Pouilly Fume* would accompany both, admirably.

The main course was set to be crispy confit of duck with sauté potatoes, braised celery and baby carrots. A decent *Merlot* would do well with that and the next course. Since my French experiences had influenced most of the menu I decided to do as the French do by having the cheese before sweet, which would be *Crepes Suzette* in an orange liqueur. I would get a half bottle of desert wine to go with those, though after pre-dinner drinks and a bottle of wine each, I doubted that either of us would be able to tackle it.

We agreed to embark on this odyssey at seven-o-clock, though by six thirty I had the second and main courses cooked and in the hostess trolley. The oysters were ready to go under the grill and the pesto salad was adding a fresh and welcome fragrance to the fridge.

The pre-dinner nibbles were croutons laden with a tomato and parmesan paste, topped with a sliver of anchovy, though I added a bowl of peanuts in case she didn't like my first choice.

After that lot, I had just enough time to shower and change.

Steph arrived at seven prompt and stepped across the threshold to take the front of my shirt in one hand and draw me close enough for one of her deliciously lascivious kisses. We lingered for a while before she broke away and presented me with two small boxes wrapped in crimson paper. She pointed to one, "That, you may open now. The other one can only be unwrapped when I say so and that may not even be tonight. Agreed?"

I gave her a small nod, "Oui mon colonel."

She nodded, "Good, I see we're already coming to more than one understanding."

Once the door was closed, she slipped out of her ski jacket to reveal a light beige jumper and brown check skirt that flared away from those wonderful hips. The blue shoes were kicked off into the corner and jacket dropped on to the newel post at the bottom of the stairs, before she gestured with open arms, "So, Monsieur Blanc, show me the way."

The anchovies, along with the gin and tonics were a great start. I was reminded which box I could open and did so, to reveal a bottle of *Calvin Klein* cologne. Before I could say anything Steph said, "Don't thank me, I did it out of self interest. The stuff you're using at the moment smells like an old tom cat."

Somehow, I managed to look surprised, grateful and affronted at the same time and sought an adequate response, "Well thank you for that, not that I know what an old tom cat smells like."

Her jaw dropped theatrically, "You do, believe me."

This time, I went for the moral high ground, "I'd be at a loss to find anything to improve on you."

She snorted, "That is exactly the sort of smarty pants answer I should have expected of you. I suggest we kiss and make up without delay."

The crispy hake wasn't; crispy that is, but otherwise everything went according to plan. Not just the food, but the comfort of being with someone special as well. I'm certain that the ease and joy of the evening was mutual, in fact in light of what happened, I'm certain of it.

We nibbled at the cheese, but in truth we were both full and Steph suggested taking a break.

I agreed and asked, "Do you want to stay here or shall we head into the lounge?"

She avoided looking at me; gazing down at her plate when she said quietly, "When I arrived, you called me Colonel. Does that still apply?"

I grinned and gave her a Gallic shrug, "Mais oui."

When she looked up at me, I saw the mischief in those deep brown eyes as she whispered, "Then I order you to advance on all fronts."

I didn't speak, but stood and offered her my hand. She grasped it and rose from the table, before we ventured silently upstairs, both deafened by racing hearts.

She entered the bedroom first, but closed the door behind me and leant back against it. I closed the gap between us and kissed her gently, before she whispered, "Explore me first."

Her lips seemed fuller, swollen almost, as we kissed and she gave me a small sigh of encouragement as I cupped her bottom with both hands and leant against her. My hands followed their own volition in tracing their way up her sides, to lightly cup and graze each breast, finding and teasing both engorged nipples.

A minute or two passed before she moved her hips forward to press against mine, signalling another need and I let one hand slip down to her waist, gathering the material of her skirt up towards her hip. The cloth tightened from being drawn up on only one side and I crouched slightly, until I was able to reach beneath the hem. She shifted and parted her legs slightly as I slipped my hand between them and moved upward. Almost immediately, I felt the wonderful warm softness of bare skin and couldn't help myself. I broke away from the kiss and gasped, "Oh God, stockings!"

It was more of a gurgle than chuckle before she whispered, "I decided we were both old enough to remember those."

I'd reached her panties by then, gently stroking and she murmured, "Now, undress me and take me to bed."

* * *

It would have been nice to say that what followed was romantically perfect; it certainly was in a visceral way, but certain odds were stacked against it, or rather me. Notwithstanding the discovery of stockings, followed by the sight of her in them, topped as they were by a creamy pair of satin panties; all easily capable of bringing a premature end to things, we were both out of practice. It had been a long time since either of us had made love.

I decided to opt for extended foreplay, while keeping her hands away from my explosive parts but she would have none of it and pulled me over into the vee of her thighs before clasping my erection and guiding it to her entrance. She gave a sharp upward thrust and I was inside. My whole being slipped through a sensual vortex, into the part of me that had entered her moist warmth; no other sense mattered. But then she clasped my bottom to draw me further, into a complete and beautiful penetration.

I reacted like an inexperienced youth and surrendered to the inevitable, almost immediately.

I lay there, spent, with my head resting on her shoulder and trying to figure out what to say. Soon, I felt myself begin to soften and made to roll away, but she held me in place and murmured, "No, stay there." In spite of the obvious anxiety I felt wonderfully relaxed in the physical sense and could easily have dozed off, as she began to stroke my back.

In time, we kissed gently before I raised my head and whispered, "I'm so sorry, that wasn't what I'd intended."

She slapped one buttock and chuckled, "Don't be. I'm flattered. It's nice to know I can still have that effect on a man.

I mumbled, "That isn't what I meant."

She conceded that much, with a small shrug and, "I know, but there'll be plenty of time for me to put *you* through the hoops."

That notion made me giggle and in no time we were both laughing, before slipping back into a comfortable silence, that allowed me an opportunity to realise how important Steph was becoming to me.

Eventually, I rolled off her and when we 'spooned' I draped an arm over her and she clasped my hand.

We must have dozed for half an hour or so, before I was woken by the chill of her absence. I heard a tap running in the en suite and moments later she stepped back into the bedroom, gloriously naked still, but with her arms wrapped around her torso, "Have you got anything I could slip on?" I pointed at my dressing gown; hung on the back of the door but she shook her head, "No, you'll need that. What have you got in the wardrobe?"

We both explored until she selected a woollen lumberjack style shirt that extended to just below her waist, "This'll do fine. Now, how about those Crepes; sex always gives me an appetite." She considered that statement for a moment and added, "For food that is."

This time, she insisted on doing the cooking and I sat at the kitchen table gazing at her. Her legs were beautiful. Not stick insect by any means but then I have never found skinny girls attractive. For most of the time she had her back to me and occasionally, for example when she bent to retrieve something from the fridge, I would be rewarded with a tantalising glimpse of her indescribably sexy buttocks. Eventually, she asked, "Are you ogling me?"

I didn't hesitate, "Damn right I am."

Instead of sitting opposite each other we ate desert snuggling side by side and I wondered at how quickly our relationship had changed into something so much more intimate. I said as much and she obviously agreed, for she held a spoon laden with crème fraiche and liqueur up and gave me an impish grin, "You can do all manner of things with this stuff too you know."

I leant over to kiss her while scooping some off my plate and easing my hand down the front of her shirt. She gasped slightly at the coolness of the cream but then sighed as her nipple responded to my gentle manipulation. Suddenly, she broke away and pulled my hand back into view, "Enough, already, it's time to open your other present." She hesitated before adding, "First though, switch the central heating back on and turn it up."

She lay on the bed, on her front, waiting for me to retrieve her second gift; a bottle of aloe vera massage oil, from the bowl of hot water. I loved massages so I had a good idea of what to do, though I also knew that this one had an additional agenda.

I poured the warm fluid onto the small of her back to form a reservoir from which I made broad, slow sweeps up to and around her shoulders, taking time to ease under her hairline and work on her neck. Sometimes I would knead her back with straightened fingers or trail my nails down both biceps to provide some textural variety, though always without rush. Little was said until I moved down the bed and poured a trail of oil across her bottom, some of which trickled out of sight into her cleft.

I didn't pursue it but she gave a murmur of appreciation as I continued with a slow and deep massage of those globes. I went on, with the same variety of techniques, along her thighs, calves and feet. One leg at a time with sweeps up from the knees until I reached the top, where I would move over a cheek while allowing the side of one hand to err closely with or sometimes brush against her vee, as though by accident.

She eased her legs apart and shifted slightly, to signal her readiness but this time I was in control. The teasing continued until, finally, I broke away and moved to her left ankle. Slowly, very slowly, and using both hands, I advanced along her leg but this time, in a smooth sweep upward I extended one hand and penetrated her with my thumb, cupping her mon veris with the palm of my hand.

Now my actions were much less subtle, though I struggled to stay in place, as Steph's movements became more frantic, until, at last, her climax overwhelmed her. I slowed as she came down but suddenly felt her grasp my wrist as she rolled over.

There was no subtlety about what followed, but within minutes, we had both enjoyed a second climax.

* * *

I was up early the next morning and on my second coffee when Steph joined me in the kitchen, looking dishevelled but refreshed and this time, she was in my dressing gown. I decided to take the credit for both states, though I on the other hand, was exhausted. With a gesture towards the table I said, "There's coffee, toast, eggs and jam. Take your pick."

She settled for toast and jam, and just a little small talk, thankfully, but while sweeping a smear of strawberry jam off her upper lip with a finger, she appeared to notice something, "You look the worse for wear, if you don't mind my saying."

I hadn't planned on saying anything, but decided there was nothing else *to* say, though I tried to make it sound observational rather than whingeing, "You snore."

She didn't apologise. Instead she asked, "Why didn't you wake me?"

"Didn't know how you'd react."

She raised her eyebrows, turned her mouth down and rolled her head onto one side, before nodding, "That's true; I'd probably have blacked both your eyes."

I gave a single nod, "Thought so. In that case, next time we sleep together I'm taking a broom handle to bed with me so I can prod you from a safe distance."

"Ha, better make sure you've got running shoes on as well. Anyway, who says there'll be a next time?"

I smiled at her but said nothing.

She took a sip of coffee and set the cup down before looking at me. There was no brevity when she next spoke, "Ian, last night was the loveliest experience I've had in years, maybe ever. Thank you."

I reached forward and placed my hand on her arm, "Don't thank me; just say you want this to continue."

The telephone started ringing at eight and by eight forty five, when Stephanie retreated to the bedroom for a shower, there were already nine messages for me.

* * *

The following two and a half weeks were chaotic. In fact, they would have been worse, had it not been for Libby's stoic calm. She remained unflappable, throughout, in spite of having to work a full five days each week, something she so hated having to do.

When I found something to panic, or have a rage about, she would calmly take the file from me. It would be given back later in the day, with the problem attended to.

There were piles of client files everywhere and for once I encouraged people to come to my house for the completion of the paperwork.

Many did and a significant number were happy to effect the transfers by post, but I still had sixty visits to schedule in the time Terry had allotted. I didn't give much thought to any further *Skyping* with him, but near the end of week two the screen beeped;

Hey Ian.

I was in no mood for chatting, *What?*

Busy huh?

No time for stupid questions, sorry.

I'm sorry, I really am.

I didn't bother to respond and tried to concentrate on the current client file, but eventually, another message appeared; one I couldn't ignore, or believe.

Ian, you already told me that you didn't have anything in Prevex European, but you need to invest 2K now.

I stared at the screen and tried to make sense of that one. After committing a couple of hundred hours to getting my clients out of there he was telling me to go in. I was lost for words, save one;

Explain.

It's OK, I've transferred the money into your account so there'll be no pain.

Explain.

It's OK, just a means of getting you into the AGM.

Explain.

Well, you're going to need to be there so you can ask some salient questions.

Explain.

Well, unless you are press, you have to be an investor to get into the AGM and that is where and how their naughty ways will be drawn into the spotlight. Don't worry, I'll brief you on what to ask.

Hey, whoa there, you didn't say anything about making me into a public watchdog, or Doberman, more like. In fact you made it feel as though the bad news was already known and just waiting to be made public.

No mate, sorry. The info is kosher, I promise, but you need to kick the hornet's nest.

No I don't. WON'T.

You have to, for your own sake.

What!

You are the only person I know who can expose the rule breaches.

I was angry, very, very angry.

What fucking rule breaches. You never told me what they were and now you're saying that no-one else does either!

It's complicated.

Bloody right! So you're saying that if I don't do what you're asking the problem won't be found and I've spent nearly three weeks frantically working myself into the ground for NOTHING!

No.

YES! YES YES YES. Because even if I do it and then fail, life at Prevex will carry on as normal, but over 150 of my clients will be after my blood, let alone the regulators.

No, the truth should get out anyway, in time.

In the meantime, I'll have a lot of explaining to do to my clients.

Please Ian, buy the units and wait until I get the questions to you. It'll make sense then, I promise.

I need to think.

OK, but buy the units.

It was then that realisation struck. I typed;

I've been led by the nose haven't I? You've used me.

No, no, no. This is me, Terry, and all that I've, no, we've done has been primarily for you. The day after the AGM, you'll be an absolute hero, I promise.

I need to think. Bye.

I didn't bother to see if he replied, I just needed to get up and pace around; to try and string some logical thoughts together. Even if Terry was on the level, why keep this bit until now? Was it because an alternative means of exposure had failed, or had this been the only plan all along?

I'd been to AGM's of course and speaking in public didn't bother me, but this could be very messy and public. The national press wouldn't be there, but the financials and specialist weeklies would be represented.

For want of anything better to do, I logged on to my bank and found the two thousand pounds he'd transferred. I ran to get Terry's file out of the archive cabinet and checked his details against the source shown for the transfer. They matched; it was the *Hinckley & Rugby* bonus account I'd recommended to him, years earlier, though I hadn't realised he'd opened it. More importantly, I had signally failed to find it when I wound up his affairs, as executor to his estate.

I made a cup of tea and sat at the kitchen table to cool down, which helped, in that it restored a measure of equilibrium. I sensed, however unwillingly, that I would have no choice in the matter. I was committed, because of my actions, if nothing else. At least, if I failed, my clients *might* believe I'd transferred them in good faith. I would have to wait and see what the briefing notes contained.

In the meantime I had nothing to lose by spending his money. I began to complete a *Prevex* application form.

Needless to say, I didn't sleep well that night and rose at around six, the next morning. At that hour I preferred to throw on a dressing gown and go downstairs for a coffee because the central heating didn't come on until six thirty. Before then a shower, or rather drying off and dressing after one, was too much of an ordeal.

A large brown envelope lay on the doormat, void of any marking, but from the weight of it, there was plenty inside. I didn't doubt who it was from, but the time and manner of delivery seemed a little secretive. The thought struck me that it might have been Terry himself, but I soon dismissed that idea. He, or they, would have used a courier. In any event, I waited until I had a coffee to hand before emptying it out onto the kitchen table.

Everything was typed. No hand written notes or even Terry's signature, though the pack didn't just contain scripted questions. I was spellbound. There were too many names and dates and too much detail for it to be wrong. I read it twice before accepting that someone had gained access to an astonishing amount of privileged information and then furnished me with a detailed briefing of the fund manager's malpractice.

I allowed my imagination to cast forward, to the grateful acknowledgements I would receive, if I carried it off and in so doing, realised that my anxieties had evaporated. My worries were over.

I was wrong. They were about to begin.

Chapter 7

I hate driving in London; not because of the traffic, which has never bothered me; the quality of driving is, by way of necessity, pretty good, but the costs of parking and the *Congestion Charge* are outrageous. Therefore, on the morning of the AGM, I stuck to my usual practice of parking at Finchley Central station and completing the journey on the tube.

In hindsight, I realised that my initial disinclination to attend the AGM had been replaced with a frisson of anticipation. The amount of intelligence, with confirmation of what had been made public and what had been hidden, was so complete, I felt empowered and not just for my part, for I knew that their investors were entitled to know the truth too.

The *Regency Ambassador Hotel* on the Bayswater Road in London was aptly named, with a light stone facade and the beautiful proportions that exemplified classical Georgian architecture. Even the faux Corinthian columns astride the entrance looked appropriate.

I was early for the meeting; intent on finding a strategically placed seat. Well forward, yet far enough into the body of the audience to be part of it. I knew that being heard wouldn't be a problem as soon as I saw the sound desk at the back of the room; manned by a technician who was still carrying out sound checks with a girl on the stage. They would be certain to have roving mics for question time.

The room was large enough to seat a couple of hundred, I guessed and thanks to its age, was lofty enough to be comfortable.

Unlike modern hotels with their low lights and ceilings, which felt so claustrophobic. Moreover, that number of people could turn a modern room into an oven. A long table had been set up on stage, with the usual array of microphones, water jugs and glasses. Clearly, the public relations team wanted to re-enforce the audience's focus by erecting a large screen behind the stage, with the words *PREVEX EUROPEAN* projected onto it from a hidden source. A multi-hued blue background moved, as though it had a life of its own, which given time; something I'd allowed plenty of; had a soporific effect. Not good if you're up on stage, trying to keep the audience's attention. I wondered if any of the PR people had sat where I was.

To remedy the problem I pulled out Terry's brief and scanned it for the umpteenth time, even though I knew it off by heart. But I'd suffered enough 'blank spots' in my time and took comfort from having the data to hand. There would be no room for error either, so I intended to refer to the notes for some of the specifics.

The glossy booklet they had presented me with at reception was standard corporate 'fare' in that it was an easily digestible homily of self congratulations, with a commentary from the fund manager, a chap called West, an abbreviated statement of accounts and promises of a wonderful future. I had no doubt that the stage performance would be similar.

It was.

The group chairman boasted; the sales manager sold and the fund manager gave a dry resume of what they had done, their investment philosophy and where they were heading.

My pulse spiked a little when the chairman rose to take questions and though I was already holding my hand up, someone seated twenty feet away beat me to it. I barely heard the question but focused on the guy who was in charge of the mic and waiting in the aisle to retrieve it. I continued staring until the chairman began his response and Mr 'Roving Mic' looked around for his next customer. I managed to catch his eye and smiled while signalling discreetly with my half-raised hand. I was rewarded with a half nod and felt my heart beat spike again.

The chairman smiled and asked me to identify myself.

I smiled too when I replied, "I am Ian Barber, an IFA from Leicester.

Another smile. "Good morning and thank you for coming such a long way. May we have your question please?"

I focused for a moment before beginning with, "Is it true that fifteen per cent of the fund is invested in the Scandinavian company named *Premier Exact?*"

The smile stayed in place, but the tone of his voice indicated a willingness to indulge me, "I cannot confirm or deny an investment in that company, since I don't have the degree of detail here this morning, though if it is in our published portfolio then it must be so."

He remembered something then, "But, I can assure you that you've been misinformed about the *level* of investment in that or any other company. As I'm sure you know, the regulations don't permit more than ten per cent of the fund to be invested in any one company."

I pressed on, "And then there is a further six per cent of the fund invested in *Johannsen Kugghjul International,* also based in Sweden."

The smile still stayed in place, "As I said, if it is in our published portfolio then it must be so."

I gave him a smile and nod that might have been taken as gratitude before continuing, "Then no doubt the same would be true of the eight per cent invested in *Horizont International AG?*" I quickly added, "Who are based in Frankfurt.

He chuckled lightly that time, "Same response I'm afraid. Is there a specific issue you wish to address?"

I nodded much more vigorously, "Then, I guess you wouldn't know that *Premier Exact* and *Kugghjul international* are both wholly owned subsidiaries of *Horizont International AG*, effectively raising your exposure to one organisation to a staggering twenty nine per cent of the fund."

At last, the smile had gone, "I don't know where you sourced this information, but I can assure you that it is incorrect,—mischievous even."

By then, any background murmuring had gone. The audience was silent and attentive.

I continued, "In that case, in the interests of everyone here, would you allow the fund manager," I glanced at my notes, "Mr West, to answer the questions himself?"

At a signal from the chairman, the fund manager sat up to attention and ruffled through a sheaf of papers; quite audible in the pregnant silence that had followed. Finally, he leaned forward and grasped the microphone in front of him, while remaining seated. He coughed and glanced down at his notes again, before speaking, "I stand by my chairman's response, though out of interest, please advise us all how you came by this insidious information."

I stuck to Terry's brief, which had prepared me for this question, "My source is impeccable sir and I cannot bear to see this information so blandly denied."

The chairman sprang to his feet, "Your response sounds like a threat."

I glanced around me as I spoke, "And so it should;—if all that I've said is correct."

His response bristled with indignation, even though the tone of his voice was calm and measured, "I can certainly assure you that your facts are incorrect, though I am sorry that we cannot discuss specific investment choices here, this morning. With the greatest respect, this meeting should not be used as a platform for erroneous and scurrilous scandalising. Please submit your concerns in writing and I will personally respond to them in good time." He thanked me, with all the sincerity of a sewer rat, before addressing the audience, "And now, ladies and gentlemen, we must move on."

The microphone man had moved into my row to retrieve the mic, but I fended him off with a straight arm and raised my voice, "Then, if I *am* wrong, and I'm not, I call on you to allow for an external audit or would you prefer me to pass on all of my intelligence to the regulators, who will carry out an audit of their own."

There was nothing left of Mr nice guy now, "I believe we've heard enough of this mischief, now . . . " With a sharp nod towards the sound desk he added, "May we have the next question please."

I continued to speak for long enough to realise that my mic had been switched off and sat down to review things. I looked down at my notes and realised I was shaking, yet I knew that I'd done as well as I could have hoped, in the circumstances. Question time continued for another thirty minutes and a couple of people referred to my input, but they were dealt with fairly deftly.

As expected, none of the daily papers featured the AGM the next day, but the following day was Sunday and several included it in their 'money' sections. The storylines were all similar; along the lines, '*Unexpected dissent at AGM of Prevex's flagship fund, with allegations of rule breaches. All dismissed by Chairman as spurious and unfounded'*.

The *Prevex* denials had been re-enforced by a press release from their public relations team and as a result, the tone of the articles suggested that the reporters had little regard for my allegations either. I bought five different papers and thankfully, found that only one mentioned me by name, and then, only in passing.

So much for that I thought. A waste of time, but at least I was off the radar.

It was then that the full implications began to dawn on me and how far out on the limb I was sitting. I began to feel rather stupid; *very* stupid in fact and gullible. I'd gone down there with a detailed brief, scripted questions and not a shred of hard evidence. Worse still, I was going to have to explain as much to my clients, because I had a feeling that Monday was going to be a pretty shitty day.

I did the only thing possible and began preparing a commentary of my own; one that was as scant of detail as I'd thought the *Prevex* response had been. Deep down, I felt certain the brief had been accurate, but it wouldn't count for much without proof.

I tried to *Skype* Terry several times, without luck.

Steph came round that evening and tried to lift my spirits, but eventually even she conceded that things looked challenging. I'd told her most of the story, though in place of 'dead Terry' I invented an old friend in the city.

We made love, though it was more an act of comfort than anything else. Nevertheless, it was welcome. Even her gentle snoring helped me to realise that I had someone in my life that trusted me.

I was right though; Monday was shitty, in fact the whole week was. The nicest clients said that they just wanted to have a chat about it and it was clear that they had no intention of acting prematurely. The ones in the middle ground were a little more hostile and voiced more concern. All I could do was promise everyone that my position was unchanged and that time would tell. As I spoke the words, my fingers and toes seemed to cross of their own accord.

Just two advised me that they wanted to initiate a complaints procedure. I assured them that even their verbal warning would instigate the process, but I would also need something in writing. My heart sank, not only because they could represent the first of many, but any complaint was an expensive and time consuming affair, with an uncertain outcome. At best, my compliance officer and ultimately the regulators would rule that I had acted correctly. That would be an end of the matter, but if their ruling went against me, they could impose a fine and award damages. Even if they found for me, both the compliance people and regulators would charge me almost a thousand pounds.

A few blessed souls didn't contact me, but not many.

Finally, after countless attempts to contact him, Terry contacted me on Thursday. By that time, I wanted to be a refuse collector.

Hey Ian.

Where the fuck have you been?!

Sorry

Not good enough. You never respond when I try and reach you and this time it really, really mattered.

No, really, I am sorry, but I cannot leave this programme running. I've just logged on and seen that you've been trying to reach me.

No good. Can't go on like this.

I understand. Let me think about it.

So, now I'm in a really bad place thanks to following your advice about Prevex.

Not bad advice. That's why I'm calling.

Go on.

Everything as we thought. Regulators going in tomorrow.

I stared at the screen in disbelief. Eventually I typed;

When do they go public?

Don't know. Tomorrow or Monday I would guess.

Before I could respond he added;

Well, that's all for now, but will be in touch on Monday, defo.

* * *

I slumped back in my chair and tried to take stock.

I didn't cry, but it had been such a terrible week that my eyes did leak as I took huge gulps of air. I was a drowning man who'd just found his straw.

I telephoned Steph at work, something neither she nor her bosses encouraged, but she gave a whoop of delight when I told her the news. She was working that night but offered to come round when she finished. I was tempted, at several levels, but she didn't finish until after midnight and it wouldn't have been fair. Instead, I arranged to pick her up from work after the Sunday lunches and find somewhere nice to go."

I dashed out and bought all the daily newspapers I could find on Friday morning, yet couldn't find a single mention of *Prevex*. I reasoned that if the regulators were aware of the problem on Thursday, word should have leaked out, but it turned out that the regulators didn't know about it.

By lunchtime, I would learn that on Thursday, the Chairman of *Prevex* had merely invited them to attend their offices on Friday morning.

Normally, when I'm at home at lunchtime, I fill a sandwich and watch *Bargain Hunt*. After that, I watch the news for long enough to catch the headlines, before getting back to work.

It was the second headline, right after news of heavy exchanges of fire on the border between Israel and Lebanon.

The presenter said, "This morning the city was rocked by yet another scandal when *Prevex* called in the regulators, following an internal investigation."

They had little more to add at that time, since the regulators had only just started work, but clearly, the Chairman had decided to carry out his own checks, in spite of his public denials of malpractice.

By teatime, the public learned that after irregularities had been found, Adam West, the fund manager, had been suspended and the *Prevex European Fund* had been frozen; pending a full investigation by the regulators.

It was Friday the thirteenth and one of the happiest days of my career.

Ironically, I only received a dozen or so calls from clients, thanking me.

* * *

On Saturday it was front page news, with most of the correspondents citing the scandal as justification for their continued vilification of the financial services industry.

I was used to that. It was either the politicians, us, the police or the NHS. We all took it in turns to be targets. At least this time, the scorn was appropriate.

I was still fearful of press exposure though, not least of all because they would want to know how I came by such a wealth of intelligence, when the auditors and regulators had failed to uncover the anomalies. One consolation was how quickly the chairman of *Prevex* had gone public, together with an assurance that every investor would be compensated, in full. All of which would help to defuse the situation and the press would soon lose interest, for only bad news sold papers.

I was wrong, of course.

* * *

As a result of all that had happened, I hadn't seen much of Steph in the previous month; perhaps once or twice a week and even then it wasn't particularly 'quality' time, which is not to say that I wasn't grateful for her company. It was just that half of me was elsewhere. She seemed to understand that, while realising that I wouldn't have wanted a mother hen, fussing around with dusters and making meals. Sometimes, a companionable coffee did the trick.

It was time to make up for things. We began to see each other three or four times a week and if anything called for an impromptu outing I would almost always accept, even at the expense of my work. For the first time I could remember, it didn't matter. I had no hesitation in postponing an evening call in favour of one spent with her.

Often we would go out for a meal and whenever something reasonable was on, we would include a visit to the theatre or cinema. I had eaten at her place on a number of occasions too, though initially, she was either apologetic or defensive about her modest maisonette; no matter how much I played it down, saying that her company was my only concern.

Yet as we grew more comfortable with each other I took pains to say how beautifully clean her place was compared to mine and it was furnished in a slightly quirky style. Feathers she'd picked up while walking in Bradgate Park were arranged around the hall mirror and she could identify all of the original owners. I also learned that the wild flowers she had, in frames and vases scattered throughout the place had been picked, dried and pressed by her. Nothing matched, yet there was a warmth and abstract continuity to it all. Her bookshelf held an eclectic mix of fiction, some of which I had read while others I borrowed and mostly enjoyed, save for the overtly romantic ones.

Once, a *Mickey Mouse* soft toy had been pinned face first against the back of her front door, so that only his ears gave his identity away. When I asked her about it she explained, with a wry grin, "That was the last financial adviser who tried to sell me something."

I feigned fear, "I'll keep that in mind."

* * *

Libby seemed to know whenever Steph had stayed over and was still in the house. Without a word, she would make a third coffee and leave it by mine. The two women became friends quickly, to the extent of chatting away for ages. Eventually, I would have to interrupt, with some comment about paying for work not gossip. They would stop then, but neither looked particularly put out or bothered.

Two months flashed by, during which time news of my advice had passed by word of mouth and as a result my client bank had grown nicely. Moreover, the new additions to my flock were high net worth individuals. People who wouldn't even grant me an interview were now willing to transfer their entire portfolios over to me, which meant that I would receive the 'trail', or renewal commission as well payment for the new business they transacted. Yet in spite of that, I continued to make space for Steph.

The *Prevex* affair had been a defining one for me too, in that I was prepared to believe anything Terry had to offer.

Down in the city, the regulators were having a field day. Rumours of a record, multi-million pound fine signalled more bad news for *Prevex,* who had already put eighty million in to shore up their *European* fund and had allocated over two hundred million to cover the compensation bill.

The fund manager, Adam West, had been charged with conspiracy to defraud investors and eight counts of dishonestly concealing salient facts. He was out of custody, on bail, while investigations were continuing.

* * *

Terry had *Skyped* me a few times, with information of sorts, but nothing on the scale of his earlier tips. I made a few thousand but chose to do so alone, even in the face of a constant stream of calls from the previous beneficiaries.

The next biggie appeared on the twentieth of July.

Hey Ian.

Hey back at you.

We exchanged a few pleasantries, something I'd felt better able to do, now that I believed in him, but eventually I asked;

How are things in finance?

All good and all the better for what I have for you today.

Great, I'm all ears, or rather eyes.

LOL. OK , so have a look at BEARING STRAIGHTS. Been a bit of a dodo, but looks set to fly. Goods news on their R & D.

New product then?

Very much so.

What about timescale?

A week or so. Don't leave it any longer.

OK, I'll check it out, thanks.

No probs, ciao.

* * *

I did the research. They didn't have any recent press coverage, broker ratings or RNS's of any significance, other than to confirm their commitment to research and development of specialist components for the oil industry. They had yet to show anything in the way of profits though; on the contrary, they had shown consistent losses since their listing on the market. So much so that they had sought further funding on two occasions by way of 'rights issues'; the process of extracting more money from existing shareholders by issuing more shares, which in turn, diluted the value of the original shares.

Terry was adrift with his timing, in that it took three weeks for the good news to break. In the meantime though, he had bad news for me.

A week after his *Bearing Straights* tip I received his next *Skype* message.

Morning Ian.

Hi. How are you?

Standing by.

What for?

Your next tantrum.

I wasn't that concerned. People didn't use words like tantrum if things were serious. I typed;

OK, Give.

Seems there's a freelance reporter named Agatha Symons, who's been doing an in depth thingy on Prevex.

My breathing slowed,

And?

Well, it seems likely that she'll contact you.

She can do what she likes, but I don't have to see her.

That's the problem.

What is?

She WILL do what she likes if you don't see her.

What does that mean?

Come on Ian, you know what reporters are like. If they are denied the facts they'll make stuff up, even if it's by way of hints and innuendo.

She can do whatever she likes.

Don't be naive.

I'm not being anything and that includes co-operative.

So how will you explain all that we've been up to, when the shit hits the fan.

Explain.

Easy. Right now, her focus is on Prevex and what went on behind the scenes. OK, your part in exposing the problem too. She's going to want a bit of info regarding your sources, but you can be coy about that and still remain convincing. Just don't tell her anything that will point her in this direction. That way she'll only be interested in the main story. In the end, you were a small part of it.

This sucks.

Well one thing is for sure, you have to deal with it.

I need to think.

OK.

* * *

On the twenty fifth of July, a Monday, I took Steph down to Padstow, in Cornwall, to share some of my childhood memories. The hotel overlooked the harbour and was described as being quaintly authentic. We discovered that 'authentic' meant that the floor had a slope of five degrees. The walls, where they met the ceiling, were covered in the fur left by wintertime moisture and the bed could have belonged to *Blackbeard,* with springs that were so creaky, everyone in the bar downstairs could hear any attempt at lovemaking.

In spite of all that, the weather was wonderful, cream teas delicious and the evening meals, a joyous trek through a fabulous range of seafood. With that calorie intake, we deemed it wise to embark on lots of walks along the cliffs, with sneaky nude dips in bays, whenever we could.

She had to be back for Friday lunches, but in those four days I discovered two things. Firstly, making love on the beach, without the benefit of a mat is not what it's cracked up to be. In fact, it became distinctly unpleasant in places and I'm not referring to the geographical sort.

Secondly, I realised that I had fallen in love.

Chapter 8

On the tenth of August, *Bearing Straights* issued an RNS, stating that they had perfected and applied for patents, for a radically different design of bearing, most notably for the oil industry. The design comprised a mix of metal alloys and composite materials which were bound together in a manner capable of withstanding the temperature ranges found on rigs. It was also very much lighter than the designs currently in use, which would result in much lower operating costs and easier on-site maintenance.

More importantly, they confirmed that two major oil companies had been involved with the development and had indicated a willingness to sign option contracts for the supply and fitting of the bearings. The share price quadrupled within a fortnight.

It was no more than I'd come to expect.

* * *

Needless to say, I was feeling fairly positive about things, so when I received a call from Agatha Symons on the twelfth asking for an interview, I agreed, instantly.

I felt less certain as the day wore on and decided to *Skype* Terry. Surprisingly he answered, immediately.

Hey Ian, how are things?

Not bad. Just hope I've done the right thing.

Tell me.

I've agreed to meet with that reporter woman.

Good! You need to. Just be polite and coy. Play a little shy too.

OK, I'll prep myself. Surprised to find you on line.

Oh, just sorting stuff. By the way, have I ever told you to invest in an outfit called BIO MANAGEMENT SYSTEMS?

No.

Good. I was going to say get the hell out. They are set to collapse.

Oops.

Too right. Now I've got to try and remember who I did tell. Bugger.

Haha. Good luck.

Yeah, thanks. Bye.

* * *

She was diminutive. Dressed in jeans and a filmy, floral top that did nothing to conceal her white bra. Her auburn hair had been cut beautifully, forming a perfect frame to a pale face. All this I noted as she walked towards me from her car. She wore a bright smile and great big round glasses; in fact, she'd have made a perfect Aunt Sally for Wurzel Gummidge.

She'd called me from two streets away, for final directions, so I had gone to the front door, to wait. As she approached, her smile brightened further as she extended her right hand, "Hi, I'm Aggie Symons."

I confirmed who I was and invited her in, noticing as she stepped across the threshold that she was wearing a battered pair of moccasins. She had a cross between a handbag and holdall across one shoulder, that looked quite heavy, but she declined my offer of help.

I knew where she was based, from previous correspondence and asked, "Have you come up from Guildford today?" It was still only ten in the morning.

She sighed audibly, "Yes, all the way through those bloody road works at Luton. To be honest, we could have done this over the telephone, but I have someone else to see in Coventry this afternoon and that *will* need a face to face interview."

I shared her view of the Luton mess, "Then I would guess you'd like a coffee. Or tea?"

"Ah yes, coffee please. Definitely NOT decaf, if you've got it."

I smiled, "Won't have the stuff in the house and the regular sort comes in industrial concentrations."

She chuckled this time, "OK, on that basis and provided we can get onto first name terms, this trip has just improved, exponentially."

Coventry seemed a bit close to me and I asked, "So, is the Coventry visit to do with the same feature?" I was relieved to see her head shake, "Oh no. I can't tell you much, but it's a scandal that's local to Coventry. It should make the nationals though, so keep your eyes peeled."

She was charming and disarming; enough for me to relax. We chatted for a while in general terms and then set up in the kitchen, across the kitchen table, where she placed a pocket tape recorder and large note pad.

After switching the machine on she gave me excellent news, and apologised for it.

"Now, Ian, I've come up here because I need a little background as a fill-in to my main story. I say that now, because I wouldn't want to suggest that you are going to be anything more than that. Fact is, there is so much more to the *Prevex* scandal than anyone realises; more than enough for a feature."

It was easy to remain pleasant throughout, though I was coy about my sources, adding that they only formed part of a much larger whole. I claimed a reliance on hard work, detailed research, reading between the lines and sensing when things are not as they should be. Most often, it was a matter of methodology, which I needed to keep to myself.

The interview was over in less than an hour and she seemed satisfied with the material I'd provided, except for one small transgression on my part, when I reacted to an inflated ego and provided a tip, of sorts. She returned to it as she packed her bag, "Are you sure you can't give me anything more on your sources."

I feigned sorrow, "I'm really sorry Aggie, but I've spent years making connections and I could lose them with one hint in your article."

As I waved her off I wondered if it had been enough. She was certainly telling the truth when she said I was only a small part of things. In fact, the main article had already been written and accepted, ready for inclusion in Saturdays' *Guardian*.

It was, too, though the piece featuring me was exactly as she'd warned; just a fill-in, literally; halfway down the page in a small box of its own. She described me, my home and hospitality favourably but added that I was secretive about my sources and methods.

Her piece concluded with, '*However secretive, Mr Barber's sources have been remarkably well informed thus far. On that note, let me share a snippet he did give me. His advice to anyone invested in the company BIO MANAGEMENT SYSTEMS is to get out of there, as quickly as possible. Make of that what you will.*'

Terry *Skyped* me that morning.

Hello Ian. You there?

I was feeling pretty upbeat,

Yep. Have you read the Guardian?

Yeah, seems OK. As good as we could have hoped for really. Why pass on the tip though?

I could have told the truth and said that after having my ego massaged for an hour, I felt the need to boast. Instead I typed;

Didn't feel like a tip. Didn't concern me either, as I recall.

Ah well, should be OK. Well done you for doing the interview anyway.

Thanks. You were right. No harm done.

* * *

Adam West sat in his lounge, watching a soap without paying particular attention; he couldn't have even named it, if asked.

He regularly crossed and uncrossed his legs, relishing the brush of nylons and tug of suspenders. Subtle physical reminders that he'd spent most of the day preparing himself for the night's encounter, though this time he wore an angora sweater over a chamois leather miniskirt. When he paraded in front of his mirror, the stocking tops were clearly visible and a flick of the wrist completed the imagery, with a glimpse of sheer black panties. It was dated and a little tart-like, but entirely safe, within the confines of his own house. More usually, he would visit Bernhardt in his hotel, whenever he was in the UK on business, but this time, his lover was visiting him and the encounter would be unequivocally sexual, he knew. Just as he knew that this trip had been especially for him. Two days earlier, Adam had wept and pleaded down the telephone line, for some comfort.

There was no one else he could turn to; no one else able to understand what he'd already gone through and all that lay ahead. The horror was scheduled to begin on Monday, at the *Old Bailey*.

Bernhardt would understand and soothe the anxieties away, with his calm, logical reasoning and wonderful touch, just as he always did. Adam had done so much for his lover and would do so again, without hesitation.

He had been ready by seven thirty and installed on the sofa in the lounge, but there was nothing on television that could hold his attention. Minutes dragged by slowly, while he tried to avoid thinking about the debris of his working life, in favour of those concerning the comforts his evening had in store. Eventually eight approached. There were just five minutes to go, exactly, for he knew how much Bernhardt hated tardiness. Punctuality had always been observed and demanded.

Sure enough, the bell rang on the hour, precisely and Adam hurried to the front door, pausing for just a moment at the hall mirror to fuss with his wig; a blonde one this time and check that everything else remained in place.

Bernhardt stood on the step, dressed in a denim shirt and black trousers. He smiled and handed over a bottle of chardonnay after they had exchanged kisses. Adam ushered his lover in and directed him into the lounge, where two glasses had been placed ready, on the mahogany coffee table.

As the 'dominant' half of their relationship, Bernhardt was left to open the wine while Adam hurried into the kitchen for a plate of canapés. When he returned, Bernhardt's glass was already half empty and he explained, "I'm sorry my dear, I started without you. Please, we must toast to a return of happy times." Adam placed the canapés on the table and took the offered glass. The crystal chimed as they toasted each other and Bernhardt watched Adam empty half of his glass in one gulp.

It took just ten minutes for the *Rohypnol* to declare its presence in Adam's bloodstream. He began to feel overly intoxicated and to begin with, they both laughed about it, but minutes later conscious thought fell away.

Bernhardt said something about a glass of water and left the room. In the kitchen, he unlocked the door and almost immediately, a large man with close cropped hair stepped into the room. "He's ready for you." The visitor nodded and removed a small rucksack from his shoulder for Bernhardt to take. Still without a word, the man followed Bernhardt into the lounge, who said, as they entered, "Adam, my dear, I've brought Dominiks along to meet you."

Adam may or may not have noticed the rubber-gloved hands that eased the coffee table to one side, though he probably felt a spur of anxiety when the man's bulk loomed overhead. At some level, the anxiety would have persisted as he was hauled up from the sofa and thrown over the man's shoulder, but hopefully his senses were dulled enough for him not to see Bernhardt's blank expression as they trooped upstairs.

The stranger lay him down gently on the first landing before taking the rope Bernhardt had removed from the sack. One end was tied securely to the newel post of the banister rail before the loop at the other end was loosened enough to slip over Adam's neck. By this time, however sedated, the primeval sense of survival kicked in and he began to make mewling sounds.

As the large man lifted Adam's loose form, he spoke for the first time, to Bernhardt, "He whines, like a little girl."

In one fluid movement he hefted Adam over the rail and into space. They had only allowed for a modest fall yet the banister made a cracking sound as the rope snatched and knots at both ends tightened.

Neither man paid any attention to the figure struggling for life, as they moved through the hall and into the lounge, to remove any trace of their presence. By the time they moved on to the kitchen, Adam's bowels had voided, though still, neither showed any reaction.

* * *

His failure to appear at court and the concerns expressed by his counsel, prompted the police to visit the house, where they found a curious sight. What some might have thought obscene in life looked pitiful in death. A bloated purple face; partly obscured by a blond wig that had been shaken awry. Two bony male legs; housed in stained stockings and topped by improperly filled panties within a pelmet of an impossibly short skirt.

Suicide; it was no surprise, to anybody.

That same morning I had a call from the regulators, who wanted to carry out a compliance visit just two days hence, on Wednesday. Unless there was a very compelling reason, such as death, you didn't put these people off, but either option was as palatable.

Steph came round that evening and listened to me whingeing, until at last, I ran out of steam and as they say, normal service was resumed. Neither of us heard the news headlines.

So it was Tuesday morning before I heard the news of Adam West's death reported on the breakfast radio. Apparently, his body had been found by the police after his failure to appear at the Old Bailey. I popped down the newsagents and discovered that all of the papers featured the story, though most carried a straightforward headline. One of the more salacious tabloids differed, with a banner headline that read 'TRANNY FUND MANAGER FOUND HANGING'. I opted for one of the others and read the article in the car. It was a bare bones affair really, as sad as it was shocking, though the police statement advised that there were no suspicious circumstances.

* * *

I spent most of the day checking on my administration and gathering the basics together, such as up to date company accounts, the complaints register, new business register and enough attendance certificates to establish that I was maintaining my 'Continuing Professional Development' or CPD. All those were the basic 'knowns', which they always asked for, but after the routine rituals, the compliance inspectors would embark on my client files. Because I had no idea which ones they would choose there was little I could do to prepare for it.

The following day, they arrived at nine thirty on the dot. Both were young and looked fresh out of college. He looked like a tailor's dummy, in his pin striped blue suit, crisp white shirt and a tie that might have signalled attendance at a public school.

She wore a very dark brown two piece over a cream blouse and had her hair drawn back into a ponytail. There was no jewellery in sight, no make-up and an expression that was equally austere; all the information I needed, to see that she would be the one to watch out for. Civil service on steroids.

I took them into the dining room after asking Libby to make coffees, but while waiting for the drinks to arrive, my attempts at small talk felt as welcome as a fart in a *Michelin* restaurant so that finally, I gestured towards the pile of basic documents at the end of the table and left them to it. On the way out, I stepped aside to let Libby by, rolled my eyes upward and relieved her of one coffee.

Thirty minutes later the boy, sorry, man, came out to the kitchen where I was struggling with a *Sudoku* puzzle and asked me to rejoin them. I'd already given them names of my own and followed 'Junior' into the dining room where '*Boudica*' sat with my new business register, compiling a list. In no time, I was despatched to retrieve twenty client files.

I popped back in at one, to see if they needed anything; a risqué joke perhaps. That thought didn't dare make it as far as my vocal chords, but I noted that lunch comprised of neatly trimmed sandwiches, fat free yoghurts and bottles of mineral water. God, they were a cliché.

They certainly worked to schedule though, for at four o'clock they invited me back in to be given a list of minor procedural infractions, including ridiculously trivial omissions from reports, that were already too long for the poor clients to wade through. They indicated what remedial steps were required, before I wrote to each client, to secure their signed acknowledgement of my shortcomings. Once that lot was done, I would have to send copies of everything to them. Bless.

Thankfully, there were only five files to work on. It could have been worse.

She leant forward, with both elbows on the table and I yearned for a serving spoon. If one had been to hand, I'm pretty certain I'd have done what my mother used to do and rap both joints sharply, with, "No elbows on the table!"

These visits always followed the same routine and this was their last act. Her face was as expressive as a tortoise's as she asked, "Now, Mr Barber, do you have any questions?"

I'd been waiting for this, "Yes, as a matter of fact I do. My last compliance visit was only eight months ago and like all the ones before it, there was little to find. So why so soon for this one?"

"We do not have a set schedule for these visits Mr Barber. Selection is most often random."

Her reply insulted my intelligence and I reasoned that she'd done all she could to me, on this visit at any rate. I held her gaze, "Bullshit."

She stared back, perhaps wondering how to fit me in for another visit next week, but eventually, she shrugged, "Well, I can tell you that this visit was triggered by recent press coverage, which implied that you were heavily involved in Stock Market dealings. As you know, your licence does not permit such dealings, at least on the part of others and we were sent to ensure that none of your clients had been involved."

It wasn't worth arguing. Besides, I had actually been involving clients by sharing the tips with them. Thankfully, nothing was on paper. It would have been poetic to send them home with a bottle of scotch each though. A matter of ill-gotten gains all round.

I sat watching them pack their things away and managed to smile politely as I saw them off the premises.

I knew I'd need cheering up that night and had arranged to take Steph to the cinema. We seemed to do that a lot, but the truth was that apart from eating or drinking, there was little else to do mid-week in Leicester. There was an Elvis Costello concert that night, but all the tickets had been sold long before. The choice of movies was pretty limited too and we ended up watching *The Forty Year Old Virgin*. It wasn't as bad as I thought it was going to be.

Instead of stopping off for a drink we opted for laced hot chocolates and uninhibited sex.

While she made the chocolates I nipped into the office to see if there were any messages and sensed something out of kilter straight away. I know it sounds like OCD, but at the end of each day I cleared the desk and placed the mouse out at the corner of the blotter. It just made the place look tidier and therefore easier to come back to each morning. As such, it was a really simple ritual, just like ensuring that the computer screen had been switched off, after shutting the processor down.

The processor was off but the screen remained on and the mouse was sitting in the centre of the blotter.

I called Steph, who wandered in carrying two mugs. I was looking around for other clues as I said, "I think someone's been in here." I explained why I thought so and she thought I was being silly, "After the day you've had, it's small wonder you forgot to switch the screen off."

I shook my head, "But I would never have left the mouse there, slap in the centre of the desk. For me, it offends the eye."

Steph knew that Libby had a key, "Coo, get you! So maybe Libby came back for something."

"Nope, she'd have left a message, I'm certain. Come on, let's check the house."

We searched every nook and cranny. I even dropped the steps and clambered into the loft. Close inspection of the downstairs windows and particularly the door locks also failed to suggest anyone had broken in. Finally, I conceded that it must have been me and waited for Steph to nuke the chocolate drinks in the microwave before turning the lights out behind us en route for bed. By the next morning I'd have forgotten about it, if Steph hadn't insisted on using a twelve inch ruler to set my breakfast cutlery out with a geometrical precision. She could be quite mischievous at times.

Chapter 9

Based just south of Cambridge, *Bio Management Systems* were becoming accepted as a leading supplier of specialist equipment and mediums to the biological research facilities in the UK, including the groundbreaking pioneers of genetic engineering. They had over a hundred mediums to choose from, with plans to branch out into an even broader spectrum. Yet they had been on the edge of bankruptcy just two years earlier, when they were saved by a huge injection of capital.

The three man team from *The Health and Safety Executive* had spent two days there, though their visit had been arranged three weeks earlier and seemed no more than a matter of course.

As managing director, Alistair Phillips had been their primary contact and by lunchtime on day two, he sought closure to the matter by having his secretary organise a small buffet lunch in the boardroom for him and the inspection team, led by a chap called Colin Jackson.

The visit seemed to have thrown up a host of questions but they had all been dealt with by Phillips and his team, to the extent that the chief inspector *seemed* impressed; relaxed, certainly. But who could say for sure with HSE officials.

Nevertheless, when they returned to his office he felt at ease, certain that they would be out of there that afternoon.

Jackson *was* relaxed, for the moment. They hadn't expected to find anything, but had to make sure before the next stage. He wasn't a man to waste words; in fact his delivery suggested a military background. That much was evident after lunch, when the inspector and one of his team were seated with Phillips, in his office.

The first sentence was the verbal equivalent of a kick in the groin. He had smiled slightly when he said, "Now, Mr Phillips, we would like to inspect your premises at." He referred to his file even though he knew the address by heart, "Twenty Four, Anglian Way, Ely.

Phillips's pulse spiked. No-one knew about that place, apart from two of the directors and the people who worked there. The tiny industrial unit had been a very secret and discreet operation and had even been registered as a private company. Funding had been from the outside and therefore never featured in the parent company's accounts. In fact, the place shouldn't have featured anywhere.

Yet he had prepared for this contingency anyway. He'd done so, the day they took the lease on.

He shrugged, "Of course, I'd be delighted to show you the premises, but we've only been using them for secure biological storage. Maybe the fact that we don't have any processing down there has resulted in a reduction of our usual standards, because only last week we discovered an unexpected contaminant in some of the stock. We believe we have isolated it but naturally we have quarantined the site and only authorised personnel are allowed on the premises. I'm assured that the problem will be resolved within a week, so if we could defer your inspection until then, we can ensure that our main stocks are safe and secure.

It would be ample time to clear and sanitise the place.

Jackson had been well briefed. "We are well versed in carrying out secure biological inspections Mr Phillips, particularly in contaminated areas. We have the personnel, equipment and protections to complete the survey, or would you prefer us to affect a quarantine order of our own?"

Phillips's tone of voice sharpened, "What do you mean by that?"

"Well, we could return in a weeks' time, but our people would continue to quarantine the site in the meantime."

There was the slightest inflection on 'continue', which was worrisome, but Phillips pretended he hadn't noticed, "That really isn't necessary Mr Jackson, I trust that by now we have established our credentials as a secure operation."

Jackson conceded that much, "On this site, certainly, though in light of what you've just told me, I'm sure you will understand our need for diligence, in respect of all your establishments."

Phillips forced a chuckle, in spite of his growing anxiety and the heat that was blooming across his face, "You sound as though you're going to surround the place in the meantime."

The inspector's face was unreadable, "Our people are already in place Mr Phillips, ready to establish our own quarantine. Nothing will leave that place until we have carried out our inspection. Moreover, when we do gain access to the premises, any evidence of destruction will be subjected to the most intensive forensic study and it goes without saying, that you, in particular, will be held responsible."

Phillips snarled back, "I have no intention of succumbing to those threats."

"Are you therefore refusing to co-operate."

"Damn right I am. This inspection is at an end, now!"

"In that case.." Jackson handed over a document, "I must exercise our right to carry out a full search of both premises and if anything improper is found we shall secure this establishment too." He pressed a single button on his mobile and waited for a few moments for the screen to signal the connection, before issuing the instruction, "Go." He glanced up at Phillips, who looked stunned and decided to take another turn on the screw, "I must advise you that these premises will undergo a more thorough examination, by the team we already have here. At the moment though, our other team is exercising the same right, to enter and search your Ely premises."

Just then, Phillips's telephone rang and he snatched the receiver up, more as a momentary diversion than anything else. He listened for several minutes; his only responses deliberately monosyllabic, but when he replaced the receiver he turned to the inspector with a very different expression. The relief was evident.

"So you're set to assault our premises? Well I suggest you go and get a warrant first. In the meantime, I want you and your minions off the premises."

As if on cue, two uniformed guards, who Jackson hadn't seen before, burst into the room. The uniforms didn't disguise the fact that they were thugs, waiting for an opportunity to 'use reasonable force'.

Just then, Jackson's mobile rang and he glanced at the caller ID before answering. He listened, mostly, while the voice on the other end said, "Boss, an army of guards have appeared out of nowhere, in a couple of minibuses,—along with two dirty great dogs. They've surrounded the place. We'll need an army of our own to gain access."

Jackson glanced at Phillips who was clearly enjoying the moment. There was little more they could do, until they had warrants. He spoke into the telephone, "OK Carl, form your own perimeter, use the cameras and call me if so much as a teacup comes out of there. On no account, get into a brawl with their lot." With that, he snatched up his briefcase and left the room without a word.

Later, on his way back to London he reviewed the meeting and considered his options. Their intelligence was that there was no radical threat, yet, but they'd certainly been outmanoeuvred. Checking the main premises out had been straightforward and to any observer, a matter of routine, though as expected, nothing untoward was found. But it was a necessary process of elimination that could be carried out without triggering alarm.

Their knowledge of the other premises had genuinely startled Phillips though. All the signals were there, indicating shock and alarm; until that call came through. Whoever was on the other end knew everything, which meant that someone had been listening to their conversation, someone with enough authority to order a major response. It only proved that they had something to hide; the very reason that two of the team down there were from *Porton Down,* the UK's own facility for the research of chemical and biological defence.

* * *

Otto Rilke was a skinny, gaunt looking individual whose clothes hung on him, as though they'd been slung onto the back of a chair, which was partly due to the fact that his height, at six foot three, was at odds with his frame, but mostly because he lacked any dress sense. Not that his appearance mattered to him.

Numbers did, in fact he lived for them. They were his creed and sustenance. He had difficulty in remembering names, but his memory for numbers bordered on the paranormal, which explained why he had chosen accountancy as a career.

Lack of social skills ensured that his employment, at the accountancy firm of Boeker, Schmidt, Koch & Co KG in Frankfurt had been a solitary affair, but his skills were valued, particularly with the more challenging accounts, where financial malfeasance had been buried by experts.

He looked set to be there indefinitely until the Russian, Sergey Osokin had made contact, three years earlier. The man had been charming and persuasive, during the months it took to tempt him into private practice, which in itself, should have suited Otto's predilection for working alone, but the financial security enjoyed from working in a large practice had been a compelling factor. Osokin had explained a need for European expertise in managing the accounts for a number of companies spread around the EEC, which was logical, given the global misgivings about Russian practices, but even with a package that seemed too good to pass off, Otto continued to decline.

The Russian, or rather the principal he was working for, offered to cover the costs of setting up in private practice, while permitting Rilke to operate from his home. From the outset, he would enjoy the certainty of enough fees for the venture to be more than viable. The monthly retainer alone exceeded his existing salary and all of it confirmed, contractually.

Osokin had been patient and understanding, but eventually, he pointed out that Otto's skills would always find employment anyway, so that if all else failed, there was little risk, in career terms and everything to gain. Finally, when they offered him a minimum contract period of ten years, he gave in.

So it was; that in December two thousand and two, Otto entered into private practice, from the bedroom he'd converted into an office. Only then was he introduced to Osokin's boss, who was just as charming.

Before he bought his own place, Otto had lived with his parents, in Wurzburg; an hour's drive to work. But he had chosen to live a further half an hour away, in Rothenburg, so the ninety minute commute would not be missed. It seemed too good to be true.

That was over two and a half years ago. He glanced out of the office window, at the car park that was full to overflowing. Beyond, lay the walls of the old city, a medieval survivor that was crammed with tourists. The window was open, but the hint of a breeze did little to exchange the stifling air inside. August was his least favourite month.

On his desk, lay the closing accounts of the English company, *Currentsea Plc*. He'd been asked by the new owner to check their accounts for hidden gems, but he'd had no luck so far. The only thing they had been able to hide, for a long time, was a consistent record of mishaps and ineptitude.

He allowed his thoughts to drift to the review of his situation, something he kept returning to, of late. He was being ridiculously well paid, for a remarkably light workload, while living in a beautiful place.

He was also very, very frightened.

* * *

It was a small unit, tucked away in the rearmost corner of the industrial estate. At only two thousand square feet, it would normally have been part of a terrace, but instead, it sat in its own enclosure of chain link fencing, with fields on two sides, and the estate's perimeter road along the other two. A huge biscuit company sat on one side with a self-storage warehouse on the other.

The building looked different to those around it too, as though it had happened by accident, which was entirely true. The farmer who sold the land to the developers had built the machine shed before there had been mention of planning permission and because of the value of the equipment stored in there, the construction was much more secure than a barn might have been. In the event, it was positioned conveniently out of the way and good enough to leave in place.

There were no signs on the building, save for a board on the gate, bearing the name 'SMB Ltd'.

Not very imaginative they thought, given that the real owner's initials were the same letters, reversed. The inspection team were in four cars and remained highly visible initially. High grade tele-photo lenses captured shots of each of the six employees as they left work, but as the evening wore on a call came through for half of them to stand down. Thanks to there being a road on two sides, the whole perimeter could be monitored from two cars.

At eleven thirty, the guards and dogs clambered into the mini buses and drove away, after securing the gate with a heavy chain and padlock. The watchers took more photographs but stayed where they were. They couldn't effect entry without a warrant and besides, there were only four of them. The rest of the team would be along in the morning, bright eyed and bushy tailed. In the meantime, the holders of the short straws hunkered down in the cold, to continue watching the premises, and the minutes, as they dragged by.

At two o'clock, the walls of the building seemed to bow out as the incendiary devices that had been installed throughout the place months earlier, responded to a telephone call from Cambridge.

Somehow, the roof and walls withstood the blast, but the inferno had been arranged by professionals and the heat soon con-sumed everything but the girder work, which softened enough to twist and turn into strange forms, as though in agony. That much would be seen at dawn, when a single fire crew were left to con-tinue dampening the site down. All of them were wearing breath-ing apparatus and none were allowed within the twenty five metre perimeter, defined by the government people who had been wait-ing for them.

Meanwhile, the area had been evacuated and Jackson's team were continually taking samples of the smoke and surrounding ground. It hadn't been necessary though. The heat had been so intense and the destruction so complete that nothing survived, active or inanimate. By teatime, Jackson declared the site to be safe, and void of any evidence.

Meanwhile, the local police had been given photographs of the staff, taken as they were leaving work the previous evening. After obtaining a list of names and addresses from the Inland Revenue, officers were despatched to bring them in.

Neighbours recognised and identified the individuals but none answered their doors. Warrants were soon obtained and entries were forced, only to discover that each employee had abandoned their home. Food lay on tables, newspapers had been left on sofas and clothing remained in wardrobes. The only things that were conspicuous by their absence were cash and passports.

The authorities would carry out checks but Jackson suspected that aliases had been used and therefore the scientific expertise of the individuals would remain a matter of speculation. They were probably foreign nationals anyway, which would make tracing near impossible. They would sweat Phillips, but both knew that there wasn't a single document that connected the two concerns. In fact, it appeared that two of the missing employees had been registered as directors, by the only registered owner, a trust formed in Northern Cyprus.

They had one certainty in the bank though. Iran wouldn't be receiving their order.

Because of the bank holiday, it was three days before Jackson and a larger team returned to *Bio Management Systems Plc*, with a vengeance and this time with warrants. They effectively disabled the company by removing the computers and stock records. Every inch of the property was searched, but they were too late to discover anything of real value. The only apparatus they found that might have been used to manufacture biological weapons, could just as easily been used for other purposes.

Eventually, they did establish the link with *SMB Ltd* and whilst the attempt at secrecy was telling, the destruction at the Ely premises had been so complete that nothing of value had been found there either. By then though, it was old news and the link failed to become public.

But a price was paid. The stock market reacted badly to the news of a major *Health and Safety Executive* investigation and the agency's refusal to divulge any information served only to make matters worse. In the meantime, the company had effectively ceased trading. The share price fell out of bed.

The chairman, Alistair Phillips and two directors resigned.

* * *

I was sitting in the lounge with a glass of wine and trolling through the television channels when the door bell rang. It was Saturday the second of September and a little after nine, the time when Steph would be rushed off her feet. I struggled to mine and threw the remote down in disgust before making my way to the front door.

I opened it to reveal an extremely large man, with a shorn head and dressed in a black leather jacket over denim jeans. He was also wearing a smile and holding an open hand up as he asked, "Mr Barber?"

After my confirmation, I noted two things, in less than a second. Firstly, the Eastern European accent and secondly, the hand closing; into an enormous fist which smashed into my face like a battering ram. The explosion of pain disappeared as quickly as it began, but that was thanks to my loss of consciousness.

When I came to, I was seated on the lounge floor and propped up against the front of the sofa. Both slippers had disappeared and the collar of my shirt was nearer my shoulder blades than the nape of my neck, making it difficult to breathe. Later, when I found both slippers in the hall, where they had been dragged of my feet, I would figure out that he had taken me by the scruff of my neck and dragged me into the lounge. For the moment though, I grasped the front of my shirt to ease the airway, realising as I did so, that I couldn't breathe through my nose. I remembered the punch; some of the agony had remained in place to ensure that, but when I touched my shirt it was sodden. I looked down to discover that my front was covered in blood. I glanced across the floor and saw a trail of the stuff, which served to confirm that my nose had been broken.

When I heard movement in the kitchen, I felt real terror, on a level I'd never known before. There was nothing in there for a thief, but lots of knives for a killer. He reappeared as that thought came to mind, so a tea towel was a welcome surprise. From where I was sitting, he really was huge.

He walked across to me, crouched down and handed over the tea towel. But instead of moving away, he stayed where he was, crouched down in front of me, waiting as I sought to control the flow of blood. Eventually though, he began to speak. I remember thinking how relaxed he seemed as he said, "Now, I ask you some questions and maybe you answer them. Maybe not, but then I will hurt you some more, yes?"

I had a little difficulty following that, but knew it was wise to nod, which I did.

He did too, "So, you ever heard of company called *Currentsea?*"

I made a noise that sounded like, "Deh" and nodded again.

He asked the same question of *Prevex, Bearing Straights,* and *Bio Management*, though in hindsight I realised that he was simply laying down the basics. His next question took things to a different level.

"Where you get information?"

I managed, "A Fuwend."

His slap seemed casual, but it rolled the eyes in my head and split my ear. He explained, "Don't make me ask same question again, or I hit you again." He was obviously getting stiff and repositioned himself, onto his knees before saying, "Where you get information?"

I suddenly realised that this ape had only been playing with me thus far and the range of pain he could inflict could be endless. An inner voice called out, 'He could kill you'. My conscious half added that he might do that anyway.

Those thoughts flashed through in seconds, but when I saw him shift slightly I called out, "Terry. Terry Caplan!"

"Ahh." It sounded as though it was the answer he'd wanted, or maybe expected. "So, you tell Terry I want to meet him. I just want to talk. He safe. But . . . " He placed a huge hand over mine, the one I was holding the tea towel with and rocked it from side to side, enough to cause an explosion of pain I'd never, ever have thought possible. He waited for a while, as I rocked from side to side, keening in agony, but eventually he arrested my movements by taking a shoulder. He leant in closely, so that I might hear him through the pain and spoke into my ear, "If he not contact me, I come back and hurt you again, only more, much more."

My eyes were closed, but I sensed his move away from me and then heard him leave the room. Moments later he came back and said, "I have left number for Terry to contact me on your desk." I still didn't dare to open my eyes, even after I heard the front door open and slam shut.

I stayed that way for what seemed an age, but in reality was more like fifteen minutes, before struggling to my feet and staggering into the kitchen. As I approached the sink my eyesight clouded over with speckles and I began to feel faint, particularly when I dropped the blood-soaked tea towel on the drainer. Somehow I held it together for long enough to remove the washing up bowl from the sink and throw it to the floor. Once I'd managed to turn the cold water tap on, the dripping blood was swept out of sight while handfuls of cold water spread around my face ensured consciousness and provided a little comfort.

Incredibly, the bleeding began to ease, though I knew it would need fixing, sooner rather than later. I went upstairs to change my shirt and get a large towel, which I wrapped around my head, while leaving a gap to see through. A glance in the mirror was enough to tell me that it looked like a burka on a mumps victim, but I was fond of the leather trim in my car and knew that blood would be difficult to get out.

I made it into Leicester Royal Infirmary's A & E at ten to eleven, along with a few dozen similarly splattered drunks. The knife wounds seemed to be given preference and the only person who asked me what had happened was the triage nurse who saw me early on, but that was only because the form in front of her told her to. I blamed a gang of drunks in the city who obviously wanted to pick on an older guy. Having established that I wasn't a priority case I was sent out to wait with the others. Eventually, I was given an X ray and much later saw a doctor, who told me that since there was no mis-alignment he wouldn't need to do anything, other than prescribe painkillers and a decongestant. Beyond that, he told me to use ice. After putting three stitches in my ear, long before the local anaesthetic had taken affect, he sent me home.

I poured my first scotch at four in the morning and poured the second very shortly after, before sitting at the kitchen table to take stock.

My first question; put to myself, was why hadn't I called the police the moment that monster had left? The answer was clear. He was untouchable; I just knew. If I called the police, they would file a report, put out his description and hope for the best. Twenty four hour protection was out of the question, yet it was the only thing that could give me comfort.

Scotch didn't usually clarify my thoughts; quite the contrary in fact, but maybe it's deadening effect on the pain did, for once.

Another scotch brought some harsh realities into focus.

The first epiphany did away with any guilt I'd been feeling about bubbling Terry. The attack and threats were outside of anything I'd experienced before and there was only one person who could get me out of the mess; the same so and so who got me into it.

This lot was because of his tips;—ergo he had to help me deal with some of the consequences. With that, I realised that I was still the only one looking set to get hurt though. If Terry didn't say or do the right things 'apeman' had already assured me of that.

* * *

The improper mix of alcohol and painkillers served to make me drowsy and I tottered upstairs and fell into bed, still dressed. The relief didn't last long though. Within an hour the pain took precedence again, yet my bed still felt safer than anywhere else. It was warm and comfortable enough for me to try and take my mind to other places; daydreaming if you will, which worked to some extent and intermittently.

At eleven that morning further chemical relief was vital, though *sans* alcohol that time. The area around my nose ached like a diseased tooth but the face that stared back at me from the bathroom mirror actually looked worse than it felt. It was as though someone had stuck a pig's trotter onto my face, along with two slices of black pudding, with slits I was trying to peer through. Thankfully, my ear was encased in a dressing, so I was spared from seeing that.

I returned to bed and sought refuge in my patchy dreams.

At six o'clock in the evening, I finally took my shirt off and forced myself to have a shower, in an attempt to remove the dried blood that covered my torso. After drying off, approximately, I felt able to don my dressing gown and go downstairs, checking the front door on the way, for signs of entry.

There was a spray of blood on one wall and a patch on the carpet, from which I followed a trail of bloodspots into my lounge. At first glance, things didn't seem so bad. A table lamp had been knocked off one of the occasional tables and the coffee table still lay askew, but then I stared at the blood. It seemed to be everywhere; on the carpet, sofa, wall and fireplace. I considered having a go at cleaning up, but a wave of pain counselled otherwise. Instead I stuck to the original plan and micro-waved a mug of *cuppa soup,* before heading back upstairs. On the way past the kitchen table I glanced at the bottle of scotch and remembered the nurse telling me not to mix alcohol with the painkillers. I recall thinking two things as I picked it up. Firstly, 'Fuck it' and secondly, 'I could use the soup mug when it was empty rather than try carrying a glass'.

As expected I had another mixed night, so I was startled to see that it was nine thirty when I woke, after hearing movement downstairs. My racing heart began to settle when I peered at the bedside clock. It had to be Libby and this was a first. I struggled into some casual clothes and eased down the stairs slowly enough to avoid jolts.

Libby met me in the hall; stared for a moment, with eyebrows heading north and said, "Oh dear." After a moment, she added, "I've put a strong salt solution on the bloodstains in the lounge and hall. It should work but I'd call in professional cleaners, just in case" She passed me a mug of coffee and saw my expression, "OK, I'll call them." Then she realised what she'd forgotten to mention, given that the bloodstains may have evidenced a fatality, "I did look in on you and you were snoring; well snuffling, so I knew you were OK." She didn't ask any questions for she knew I would tell her all I wanted to, when I was ready.

Well, she did have one question, "I take it you'd like me to cancel your appointments."

I smiled, nodded and went through to the office, where I tried to *Skype* Terry, without luck.

The answer phone showed that there were eight messages. The absence of beeping told me that Libby had listened to them without erasing any, which was our normal practice. So did the *post it* label she had stuck to the receiver, with the note, 'nice name'.

Seven were from Steph.

"Hi love, call me when you can."

"Hey, Bogbrain, where are you?

"Bogbrain, answer please."

"Ian, FFS, answer!"

"OK Bogbrain, if you're dead, can I have your car?"

"Ian, not funny any more. Call me!"

The last message was left at eight thirty that morning, "Please Ian, you're scaring me."

I thanked the stars she hadn't taken it into her head to come round to the house yesterday and she answered on the second ring when I called back; intent on withholding most of the details, though I had to explain enough to prepare her for the sight that would greet her. She would certainly want to come over, I knew, and that made me realise how much I needed her to, as well.

After the usual pleasantries she said, "I wondered what was happening. Had I done something to upset you or had you gotten tired of me, but it sounds as though you've got the flu."

I could hardly stick to the story I'd provided at the hospital, not with all the bloodstains, so I told her some truths, at least. I said that a thug had thumped me on the doorstep and dragged me into the lounge. After that, I ventured into fiction, saying that he had searched the place without finding anything of interest, which hadn't surprised me since I never kept cash in the house and all the jewellery had left, with Dee.

She wanted to come straight over and took some dissuading, until we agreed on six o'clock, when Libby would have gone home and I could look forward to a cuddle.

By lunchtime time and by contrast, I felt able to tell Libby pretty well everything. The pain was still there and then some, but it was no longer interfering with cogent thought. We sat at the kitchen table over mugs of soup while I explained how all those tips came about. I'd never mentioned Terry's *Skype* messages before and wondered whether I should, but then she worked in this house and needed to know the measure of risk. I ended the meeting by offering her paid leave until things sorted themselves out, but she would have none of it.

Her first suggestion was sound, "You never set the alarm. The first thing you should do is have the system checked and then, start using it." I'll admit, I hadn't bothered to set it for ages and didn't even know whether it worked

I put our discussion on hold and telephoned Jimmy Vaughan, the alarm fitter, who also happened to be a client. He began by suggesting the following week, but when I explained what had happened he promised to be there within the hour.

When I returned to the kitchen Libby was waiting, with a pad and pen in front of her, "So, if you're not prepared to involve the police, we need to work out where 'apeman' comes from, or who sent him. Perhaps then, you *will* involve the law and we can sleep at night."

I shook my head, "I've explained why Libby, we just need to have Terry call him."

She shook hers, "You've been trying to get him all morning and besides, how do you know he'll play ball, *or* even if he does,

I can't see how *Skype* messaging is going to satisfy this man. I reckon he wants to arrange a meeting and Terry wouldn't do that, even for you."

I tried to reason that one through, "Yes, but Terry has hinted at being involved with the Secret Service and that is where our salvation lies."

"You told me that he seemed to know about Terry. You said he wasn't surprised when you said the name."

I cast back to that moment again and remembered the tone of the 'Ahh'. I also realised that the agenda had changed then. 'Apeman' had stopped asking questions and moved on to giving me instructions.

I said, "True, but what does that tell us."

"That we're out of our depth. It sounds like the cold war."

My swollen eyelids helped to hide my anxiety, while I continued to use reasoning, to reach safer ground, "I think we're jumping the gun a bit there. Somehow, playing the stockmarket at the level I did, wouldn't concern the parish council, much less Her Majesty's Government."

Libby thought for a while before admitting, "I can't think of an answer to that one. But it does have something to do with those tips. Don't you think?"

She was right, it *had* to. I pulled my own portfolio file and we listed every company Terry had mentioned. I waved a hand over it, "I reckon the answer is in there somewhere, but what and where?"

She picked up the list, "Well we won't know until we make a start."

I gave her the thumbs up, "OK, we'll split the list into two. You use the office computer and I'll use the laptop in here."

She began to scribble notes down as I thought of ideas, "Check out *Companies House* for director's details, the financials, subsidiaries and anything else you think looks interesting. Print it all off and have a look at the websites for these companies. Oh, and *Google* them too."

Shortly after, Jimmy Vaughan arrived and I told him the basics. He was obviously appalled by the damage, particularly to the carpet, explaining that the sight of blood always affected him badly. After a quick inspection, he declared the alarm system to be defunct. "Blimey, Ian, when did you last use this? Wait a minute." He was standing by the control box and plugged two probes into its innards before looking at me askance, "Fifteen months ago! Why did you bother getting me to fit it in the first place?"

I tried to look forlorn, but it didn't show through the swollen tissue, "Erm, sorry Jimmy."

"Don't apologise to me, just thank your lucky stars you haven't been turned over. At least it wouldn't have affected what happened to you, working or not."

Now that personal attack was to be included, or rather protection from it, he drew up a fresh schedule, which included panic attack buttons in my bedroom and by the doors, three closed circuit television cameras outside, which relayed images to a monitor in the kitchen and an up to date control box. He presented me with the quotation which made me wince, mentally at any rate, but at least he promised to complete everything the next day. Jimmy added, "I shouldn't think your visitor will come back, or if he does, we'll be able to ID him."

I said, "I think he could be back."

"Hell's bells Ian, what makes you think that!"

I shrugged, "Sixth sense."

"In that case, maybe you need to be hooked up to a monitoring station."

I asked how much that would cost and vetoed the idea immediately.

Jimmy dug into his briefcase and extracted a sign, "Well, we can still put this on the wall outside." It said,

24 HOUR CENTRAL MONITORING

"See," he said cheerfully, "I can lie like a Persian rug; should've been a financial adviser."

He never missed an opportunity to take that dig.

The carpet cleaner arrived at four and by ten past, had completed his testing and declared the stains to be permanent. The idiot suggested dying the whole thing a rusty brown.

* * *

At six, I think the look on Steph's face startled me as much as mine did for her. She remained on the doorstep with her mouth open, until she cried, "Oh my God, what a mess."

I grinned, "That's not much of a chat up line."

She didn't find that attempt at humour funny, but she did step in and hug me.

It came from nowhere, I hadn't even thought it possible, but suddenly, I began to cry. She held on to me, stroking my back and making gentle shushing sounds. Then it was over, as quickly as it had started. I apologised but she would have none of it and then she saw the bloodstains, on the carpet and wall. She groaned, "Oh, Ian!"

I huffed, "You should see the one in the lounge, where he dumped me."

I followed her through and watched as she covered her mouth with a hand. I thought that was enough and guided her into the kitchen, where a bottle of *Merlot* waited.

Glasses were filled and we both sat at the table. Neither of us had made a move towards the lounge, understandably, though I made a mental note to sort out a new carpet very soon. That prompted another line of thought; I wondered if it was included under the 'accidental damage' section of the home insurance. Or 'burst pipes' perhaps.

Naturally, Steph wanted to know everything, and after repeating what I'd already told her, I went on to describe my experiences in the A & E.

By the time I finished Steph had emptied and refilled her glass, before looking at me. Her voice contained a mix of hurt and anxiety, "Ian, you're holding something back. People don't get smashed in the face on the doorstep, just on the off chance they've got stuff worth nicking."

I shook my head but before I could speak she held up a hand, "Please, don't lie to me."

I managed to sound exasperated, "Steph, for heaven's sake."

She stared at me, "You're in some sort of trouble aren't you?"

I tried to sound upbeat, "Oh no, nothing like that. I haven't broken any laws, I just,—don't know."

"So it's some sort of nutter."

"Perhaps, I don't know."

Her reasoning continued en route to nowhere, "Look, if he *is* a nutter, he could come back at anytime and have you considered this; he could do it to someone else; might've done already. Ian, you *have* to call the police!"

"It's too late for that Steph and besides they'll only make a report and file it."

"You're not listening; he's probably out there now doing the same thing to someone else."

"I don't think he will."

"Don't be so sure. Christ, Ian, he could kill someone. Do you want that on your conscience?"

I shook my head, "No, this is someone with a grudge."

She paused then, to assimilate the new information. "So there *is* something you're not telling me."

I sighed, "Just a deduction at the moment, not based on anything particular, but he said some things that were connected with my work."

"OK, keep going. Now you've started you may as well tell me the rest."

"There isn't anything; or least anything I can think of at the moment, but I think it would be best for you to stay away, for the time being."

"You think I'm just going to run away and leave you?"

"I just think it would be best if you kept your distance for the time being; just till I sort it out."

She looked stunned and lost for words, but then I saw her eyes filling up. My shoulders sagged, "I love you Steph and I don't want you to get hurt."

"I'm not going." It was spoken with a flat finality.

My response sounded as though I was speaking to a disobedient child, "You most certainly are."

Children don't generally respond with, "Fuck off." But Steph did.

I began to reason with her, but she seemed not to be listening. Later, she admitted that her thoughts were directed at a strategy rather than me. Some thought process clicked into place and she interrupted me, "OK, I'll go, if you make me, but there is one thing you *can't* stop me doing."

She leaned forward, to emphasise the point, "You chuck me out of here and I'm going straight to the police. I'll tell them everything and then some, probably. Like how you think it's connected with your business."

"Please Steph, don't do that."

"Your choice; are you going to throw me out or what?" Tears began to roll down her face then, as the thought of rejection caught a nerve.

Tears, I never could handle seeing a woman cry. I remembered that our relationship had been founded on her tears and I hadn't been in love with her then.

I told her everything.

A little way into things, she reached forward and took both my hands in hers and we stayed that way until I'd finished.

We didn't make love that night; I'm not sure that I would have been capable anyway, with the sustained mix of alcohol and pain killers, but we held on to each other; both now in need of comfort.

I woke in the night with a need to visit the toilet and returned to warmth that felt secure. Paradoxically, I think it was the comfort I derived that made me realise how exposed I was; *we* were. I still didn't know who or what I was facing, but if they had any clout, or worse, were official, my credit and debit cards could be cancelled in a trice. With so many ANPR cameras in place my car could also be clocked within five miles and what about my passport? I couldn't do anything about all those things, but I could accumulate plenty of cash.

I decided that I would withdraw cash from all of my Building Society and bank accounts. Not enough at once, to arouse suspicion; perhaps a couple of thousand at a time and if necessary, I could move ten thousand into Steph's account by electronic transfer. We could say that I'd given her enough for a car, which would explain why she withdrew it immediately.

It was a plan at least and something more than being a rabbit trapped in headlights, even though it represented a waking nightmare, of being on the run from a potential killer.

Chapter 10

The following morning I was up in time to greet Libby, who reminded me that she didn't care for full time work, adding, "But in the circumstances . . ." Shortly after, she greeted Steph with a bright, "Good morning" and an offer of a coffee. The ordinariness of it was surreal.

Half an hour later, with the post opened, Libby convened another meeting at the kitchen table and dropped a bombshell, "You know how 'apeman' seemed satisfied with your answer; when you said Terry?"

I said, "Yes."

"Well I was thinking last night, if he wanted to meet up with Terry so badly, why didn't he just ask for an address and telephone number."

That was easy, "Because I don't have one. He knew I would be . . ." my voice fell to a whisper as the truth dawned on me and I finished the sentence, "*Skyping* him."

Libby nodded, "Funny how he knew that already."

Then another memory began to clamour for attention, "The mouse. Someone had moved the mouse and left the monitor on, the night of the compliance visit. To begin with I was certain someone had been in there, but in the end, I put it down to the stress of the day.

I told her about that time, when both Steph and I had laughed it off. The thought of someone being in the house that evening chilled me, along with another possibility. I asked Libby, "How much information do you think they took."

She thought for a moment before, "Well, if I was them, I wouldn't waste time going through your files here. It'd make much more sense to do a global back up and leg it to somewhere quiet and private."

That presented another set of threats. There was a staggering amount of client information on the computer, many of whom were high net worth individuals. Also, while the compliance people hadn't found any evidence of share dealings in the client files, there were plenty of emails that would do that for me.

I tried to *Skype* Terry again.

* * *

We opened files for each company and by Wednesday lunchtime they all had a significant thickness of print outs. When not at work, Steph helped by collating the information into sections that included records of company registrations, ownership, trading back ground, directors, accounts, stock market activity and anything else that seemed worthy of printing out. We reviewed the stuff regularly, but without particular focus. There was still so much information to gather; it would have been like looking for a jigsaw piece when you knew that dozens were not present anyway.

But there was a more pressing concern. It had been three and a half days since 'apeman's' visit and I still hadn't been in touch with Terry. I hadn't been given a time limit, but in a sense, that made things worse. In the absence of any contact with Terry, another visit would be inevitable and could be anytime soon.

In the end I decided on a pre-emptive act and telephoned 'apeman', myself.

It was a mobile number, with a caller ID display, because he obviously knew who it was when he said, "What *you* want."

I couldn't keep the tremor out of my voice as memories of the previous Saturday flooded back, "I, well look, I've been trying to get hold of Terry, non-stop, since last weekend, but without any luck so far."

His reply was succinct, at least, "Keep trying." Then the connection was cut.

I sat back in the chair with a sigh of relief. I'd managed to buy some time, though heaven only knew how much.

After lunch I opened the *Currentsea* file and saw that the company had been sold for one penny, along with an obligation to salvage everything from the River Severn. The purchaser was a newly-registered company whose ownership lay beneath a blanket of nominees, heading up a trust company in Northern Cyprus.

Only three people attended the final creditors meeting; the administrator, his assistant and Howard Long, for by then, it had already become a distant, if uncomfortable memory. The banks, creditors and investors would receive nothing.

Libby was doing a hell of a job.

There was a print out of an article from the *Bristol Post,* with a picture showing a floating crane, lifting one of the turbine tubes out of the Severn. It looked OK, but I figured that the damage must have occurred inside. Four bulk carriers, the sort that needed police escorts, were lined up on the bank.

I knew from the earliest reports that the alloy used for the tube construction had been hideously expensive and I'd assumed that the buyer would have bought the company for the salvage, so why go to the expense of hiring a floating crane and carting them away intact. Surely, a team of divers with cutting torches would have been a cheaper option. I made a note in the margin. 'Going to be used again—where?'

I tried to read the name on the nearest truck, but the print out wasn't clear enough, so I went back into *Google,* where the image was much crisper and after expanding it, I could read the name easily. Another search located the haulier; a specialist outfit based in Oxford.

Then, I telephoned them and spoke to the transport manager, who was most helpful, after I'd explained that I'd been an investor who'd lost everything, apart from an interest in what had happened since, "Yeah, I remember that one. It's unusual to have four of those rigs on one job. In fact, we had to sub-contract one in. Because of the scale of things and the distance involved, I went in the escort van myself. It had to be done overnight."

I asked, "Where did you take them?"

"Felixstowe,—they were loaded straight on to a ship there."

"Where were they going?"

I sensed a shrug when he replied, "Don't know. Funny that, but no-one else seemed to know either. Mind, the ship was Russian and no-one seemed to speak a word of English."

I thanked him for his time and made another note, 'Gone to Russia?'

Then I added one more, but this time put a circle around it, 'Apeman is eastern European'.

That gave me pause for the thought; a long one, until Libby wandered through to add more sheets to the files.

I asked, "Libby, why are we doing this."

She sat down opposite me, "What do you mean?"

"Well, what if we do find something, what can we do with it?"

She thought for a moment before, "Good point. We've not discussed that."

I huffed, "Well one thing's for sure, 'apeman' isn't going to like it and that will put you in danger."

"Not if we get protection from the authorities first, which answers your first question, I suppose."

"How?"

"Easy, we need to find enough to make them interested. We already know that 'apeman' has an interest in those companies, and that he wants to speak with Terry, so it must have something to do with what those companies have been up to. From what you told me, they've done enough to make you a lot of money."

I agreed, "Yes, but usually by failing." That triggered a thought and I grabbed the *Bearing Straights* file, "This is the exception. It's the only one of Terry's tips that has 'flown' and stayed up there." The share price had slipped back considerably, but I was still showing a eighty per cent gain. The recent RNS's suggested that their claims for a bright future had been a little premature, due to funding difficulties. Libby had also found some newspaper articles on

Google that referred to an acrimonious split in the boardroom. A couple even suggested that writs were imminent, but one of the latest reported that the chairman had resigned, with a sum of money they had yet to disclose. The market showed little sign of comfort from the news. Perhaps, the writer thought, because they had yet to find a replacement.

Even so, it still didn't fit the mould.

Libby had the last word, in answer to original my question, "Anyway, what else *can* you do, other than simply wait for the return of 'apeman'?

* * *

Our first break came on Thursday morning, from the least expected source. Because of the nature of the beast, in that it was now, effectively, a closed fund, I hadn't expected any information of value out of *Prevex,* until the regulators had completed their investigations and published a report, but Libby located the site of *Bolagsverket,* the Swedish Companies Registration Office, with an English language option. From then on, it was pretty straightforward. She entered the names of the two Swedish companies I'd used at the *Prevex* AGM; *Premier Exact* and *Johsnnsen Kuggjhul International.*

I was startled to see that both had ceased trading on the fifteenth of May. Nine days after that AGM and only two days after the fund had been frozen. There were lots of documents available and we ordered most of them, which were emailed to us within minutes of entering my credit card details. A minute later Libby was printing the reports off.

It took some time to wade through things, not least of all because the format was different to that of *Companies House;* the one I normally used. Even so, there was a commonality about the content, which included dates of formation, director's details, the financial calendar and a summarised version of their latest accounts. The director's names were very typically Swedish, tricky to spell and even more challenging to pronounce, though it didn't surprise me to find that three names appeared on both company files.

Eventually, we established that both companies had three other things in common. Both had folded and were under the control of a bankruptcy manager, who had already completed the winding up process, giving the reason for each *Konkurs*, or bankruptcy as failure to secure payment for their goods. He expressed concern at the size of the debts and actually named the debtor. Just the one name that is, to account for the collapse of both companies. A Turkish company, *Karadeniz Ticaret*. I made a note to check them out and continued reading.

Having only one debtor suggested that in trading terms, they had all their eggs in one basket, another commercial folly.

There was no mention of the parent company, *Horizont International AG,* which I assumed was still trading in Frankfurt. It was obviously an 'arm's length' association, with no sign of the cavalry when needed.

The bankruptcy manager went on to suggest that the directors should be censured for not abiding by the most basic of principles for international trading, where payment should be secured at the point of shipping, or guarantees put into place, at the very least.

He also pointed out that the year-end accounts for both companies were eight months overdue and the subject of concern at the *Skatterverket,* Sweden's tax agency. The company auditors, were deemed partly at fault for those omissions.

There was a long list of creditors; mainly suppliers and the tax agency; all of whom would have already learned that they would receive nothing.

In spite of so many allegations, I couldn't find any evidence of action against the directors. In fact, that seemed to be an end of the matter. The total loss in share value certainly would have accounted for a chunk of the eighty million pounds *Prevex* had already had to inject into the fund.

There was an increasing number of calls from troubled clients, not out of concern for me, but rather my lack of support for them. I'd taken some of the calls and knew I would have to start back to work soon, or see transfers to other advisers take place.

I tried to *Skype* Terry once again, before we broke for lunch.

We retired to the lounge, me with sandwiches, crisps, a yoghurt and a Satsuma, while Libby had a *Tupperware* tub filled with salad.

The television stayed off while we reviewed what we had found out so far; or at least thought we had.

In essence, a fraudulent fund manager, with personal issues, who was heavily invested in two dodgy companies and very possibly, a third. I hastened to add I had nothing against transsexuals, rather that it made someone in his position vulnerable. External influence would certainly explain why he'd invested in the way he did.

Libby was scribbling down bullet points on her pad, in between grabbing mouthfuls of lettuce. She added, 'corrupted by lover' to the list then scrubbed out the 'by' in an attempt to avoid any graphically sexual reference. Still unhappy, she scrubbed the lot out and wrote, 'sexual preferences—blackmail?'

The list went on.

'Said, dodgy companies had ceased to exist in the very week they were likely to come into the spotlight.'

'Dodgy companies only traded with one customer who didn't pay them; same one for both'.

By the time we'd finished lunch, each had a try at being devil's advocate, but there was no doubt in our minds. The connections were there and they all pointed to a conspiracy.

We sat in silence for while, until Libby voiced another thought, "Speaking of connections, Terry must fit into this somewhere you know. Is he a goody or baddie?"

I didn't feel able to answer that question anymore. Every part of me wanted to believe he was on the right side, but Libby was right, he was implicated, one way or the other. She agreed to go into the kitchen and use my laptop to search for more, while I dealt with some essential post in the office, but she did close with a bit of advice, "I think it's time you treated everyone with caution."

At four o'clock, I started when I heard the beep and stared at the screen in disbelief for a moment, then scrabbled to open the *Skype* programme before his call timed out.

Hey Ian, what's up?

Well, a busted nose and two black eyes for a start off.

Ouch. What happened?

A bloody great hulk beat the shit out of me last Saturday, all because he wants a meeting with you.

Why?

Must be about your tips.

Explain

He mentioned Currentsea. Oh, nearly forgot, I'm pretty sure he is eastern European

Won't meet.

Must. Fucking must!

Why?

He promised that he wouldn't do YOU any harm, but if you don't agree to meet, he's going to come back and do a lot more damage to me.

Clever.

Glad you think so. Do you want his number.

Yes.

I gave it to him before asking,

So you will?

Can't say. If he makes contact with you, tell him I have to get a meeting sanctioned before I could agree. May take a while.

I'll telephone him then, I don't want him on the doorstep again.

As you wish.

I hadn't expected to mention anything else but I found myself typing without conscious thought;

I'm out of my depth Terry.

Don't worry mate, he's probably just a ticked off investor.

Don't think so. I've been doing some research too. I spent a few minutes typing in a summary of our Prevex findings and waited for some time before his next message appeared.

Ian, wait five. I'll get back to you.

Five minutes or days?

Mins.

He broke the connection, leaving me to wonder how much had been achieved and more importantly, how 'apeman' was going to react.

* * *

A few minutes later, he re-established contact with;

You are right. Everything connected. Been authorised to tell you that evidence of weapon grade components found in both Swedish companies. Sapo are investigating.

Who are Sapo?

Swedish Secret Service.

Shit.

No worries. I'll sort things out.

Please, and quickly.

Will do, standby.

* * *

I reflected on his 'wait five' and 'standby', both military terms and for the umpteenth time, wondered what hell I'd gotten mixed up with. One thing was for certain, Libby was right when she told me to question everything and trust no one and that included Terry Caplan.

It was time to retrace some of my steps, beginning with a visit to Jill and Jack. After printing off a copy of the *Skype* conversation, I left Libby to lock up and drove towards Loughborough.

On the way there, I saw the sign for *Beacon Hill* and turned off my route, on the spur of the moment. The drive had given me chance for some solitary thought and I knew I needed more time. The top car park was fairly empty and I strolled up to the top of the rise, where I found a small outcrop to sit on. There was a fresh northerly wind that hastened its way over the peak and I was soon glad that I'd slipped an anorak on, but the peace and view settled me. I gave a passing thought to 'apeman' and my exposure out there on my own but after checking the car park for new arrivals, I reasoned that he had no call to beat me up again, yet.

With the exception of *Bearing Straights Plc,* all the companies had failed, yet someone must have profited by them as well; it would hardly be done out of spite. Like derivatives on the Stock Market, money can be made from failures, but they rely on the share continuing to trade. *Put Option* holders lose money like everyone else if the company founders.

I realised that I had to take a lateral view of things, to try and see how anyone could have taken advantage of the calamities. It would need a broad mind, for each collapse had been triggered differently.

Eventually, my thoughts drifted to the Swedish concerns and a chill settled on my stomach as I realised an awful truth. I may have been their nemesis. I felt certain that my questions at the AGM hadn't been anticipated, but they sparked off the series of events that might have exposed them, or would have done if they had remained in business.

So, illicit arms manufacturing, with the stuff being shipped to Turkey. That had to mean the Middle East. But who was behind it all? The third company, *Horizont* something, in Frankfurt, was the only live lead I could think of, but how to tackle them? Knock, knock, excuse me, but would you be kind enough to tell me all about your arms dealing please?

Perhaps not.

Still, I was in a bad place and trapped. I knew enough to get hurt but not enough to get myself out of it.

Half an hour later, I made my way back to the car with some sort of a plan.

I stayed in the car park and after getting the number from Libby, called *Prevex*. Eventually, I got as far as the chairman's PA, who made it clear that any enquiries had to pass by her. She suggested that I sent an email detailing the nature of my business, which she would refer to Mr Hudson and then get back to me. The flat tone she used signalled that she already knew what the reply would be.

I refused her offer, "I have some very important information that I will only share with the chairman in a face to face meeting."

Clearly, she was speaking to a difficult child, "I'm afraid that won't be possible Mr Barber,.."

I cut in, "Tell him I have information about the conspiracy that brought the *European* fund down; for his ears only. Just tell him that, now. I'll hang on."

With a mix of concern, or more probably intrigue, and exasperation, she told me to hold. I did, for a few minutes, until she came back on the line with the boss's appointment diary to hand, "Are you available anytime Mr Barber?"

"Yes, anytime at all."

I was startled by her suggestion, "Then perhaps eleven am on Saturday morning?"

He obviously took it seriously; enough to see me within forty eight hours and on a Saturday. One more step.

I started the car and headed for Jill and Jack's house. They were as lovely as ever and like the last time, I resolved to visit more often. This time I took a large iced cake and a few bottles of posh ginger beer, knowing that they both loved it. As usual, we spoke about the old days and the mischief Terry and I used to get up to. I allowed Jack all the time he wanted for the stories I'd heard many times before; it seemed a tiny thing to do.

Sometimes, I would find an opportunity to interject with a question of my own, but most of the information I sought lay in fractured, emotive territory. In the end, rather than tip toe around the subject, I decided to take things head-on.

I sighed, "I miss him, not as much as you do, but I do miss him."

The room was silent for a few moments, until Jack spoke, "Yes lad, no parent should have to bury their child."

I started, "I'm sorry Jack, I didn't mean to.."

He smiled sadly, "Don't be, we can talk about it easier these days, can't we love?" Jill smiled at him, though she didn't look as certain. Jack went on, "You can't hide that sort of thing away. It *needs* to be talked about, especially with others who loved him."

Jill seemed lost in her own thoughts as she spoke, "I wished Amy had come over." She meant to the Jewish faith, "It would have made things better, especially in the beginning. She was good for him too, I realise that now. She loved him."

It was an opening; I said, "There were plenty of those who did Jill. Funny though, there were fewer people at the funeral than I'd hoped to see."

Jack answered, "Ah well, you have to remember that a lot of the family were living in Israel; still do and Jill was an only child so there weren't that many from her side either."

I needed to keep this going, "Forgive me asking Jack, but as his best friend, I'd expected to be called on to identify him. I know that you two were advised not to."

"No, well, we were both in a bit of a state and the police said that they thought we'd be better off remembering him how he was. As it happened, Benyamin was over visiting, from Israel. Did you know him?"

I shook my head.

"I am surprised. He came over fairly often; he and Terry were cousins. They got on ever so well. Terry went over there a couple of times too; usually for a week or so at a time, 'cause Amy never wanted to go there. They'd known each other for years; him and Benyamin."

Jill cut in, "It was just after the six day war, when he first came over."

Jack looked pleased with the reminder, "That's right, he was in the Israeli army and was wounded. They let him have an extended leave to come over here while he recuperated. Anyway, as I said, he was over here when it happened and he identified Terry."

There was the slightest hint of a pause before 'Terry' and I real-ised that he couldn't bring himself to say the word 'the body'."

He finished with, "Funny you never met him."

Not only that, I thought, but until then, I'd never even heard of him.

It was after seven when I got home and Libby had left a message on the desk before she went home, having already arranged to take the next day off.

Found some more info on the web. Will share on Monday.

Stay safe,

Libby.

* * *

I had one last job to do.

"What you want?"

I began to hurry, "Terry, I got hold of Terry today. I gave him your message, but he said, I mean wrote, that he has get permission to do that. He promised to let me know."

He just grunted, "Tell him be quick. You are running out of time mister."

I had accumulated over thirty thousand pounds cash, in only five days and wondered if it would be enough to buy him off, if he came calling.

Doubtful.

Chapter 11

I arrived at the *Prevex* premises in good time and was taken up to the top floor where the same PA I'd spoken to on Thursday, directed me to sit down on a leather chesterfield that sat behind a low table, laden with prospectuses for each of their funds. I'd read them all before and settled down for the wait, noting the absence of an offer of coffee, a courtesy that would normally have been extended to anyone waiting to see the top man.

I let it go, with a mental shrug and took in my surroundings. The walls were papered, with a muted green regency stripe that had been intended to contrast with the plush, dark green carpet. The paintings on the wall were originals; mostly impressionist and definitely not off the shelf. The lighting was subdued and indirect, without a light bulb in sight, but the dominant effect was the silence. I guessed that nothing less than a gunshot would be heard from the chairman's office and couldn't help but wonder at the PA's isolation. She might just have well been in a retreat. Even the telephone rang with a soft warble, when twenty minutes later she was told to usher me in.

His office reminded me of a gentleman's clubroom. Lots of leather, floor to ceiling bookshelves and a huge mahogany desk. The place smelled of polish.

Two men had been seated at a meeting table, on one side of the room, next to a large window that overlooked a park and both rose as I entered the room. It was the chairman and a man I didn't recognise. As Hudson shook my hand he introduced his colleague, this is Charles Davies, acting manager of our *European* fund."

Or what's left of it I thought. My first reaction was to refuse to share any information with anyone other than the chairman, but I quickly realised that anything I said would be passed on to this individual as a matter of course. I shook his hand and was shown to a seat facing them, on the opposite side of the table.

If Hudson had been startled by my appearance, he hid it well, for while my nose had become less swollen, both eyes were still black, making me look like *The Lone Ranger* on a bad day.

I sensed that there would be no small talk, so I didn't thank him for seeing me, or for a coffee, but I did say, "I didn't expect you to be working on Saturdays."

His voice had a resigned air, "Mr Barber, we have people working seven days a week at the moment."

I'm sure he was tempted to add, "Thanks to you,"

He came straight to the point, "You have some intelligence for us Mr Barber, which promises to be as informative as your last disclosure."

Oops. I nodded, "Yes sir, I do." I laid my briefcase on the beautifully polished surface and removed my notes, "But first, I need to ask for the basis of this meeting to involve an exchange of information."

Hudson's response was clear, crisp and unequivocal, "I can't agree to that."

I put my notes back into the briefcase, "Then I'm not prepared to share this information with you."

I was closing the hasps when he asked, "Exactly what information would you want?"

"I would like to see a list of the investors, probably significant ones, who withdrew from the fund during the week between the AGM and when you called the regulators in."

"That is confidential information Mr Barber."

I waved a hand at the briefcase, "So is mine and believe me, yours is less valuable."

"And what are you planning to do with this information, if we did give it to you."

I looked hard at him, "Save my life."

That did take them by surprise. I pointed at my face, "This was only the first course of what promises to be a banquet."

They glanced at each other and an unreadable exchange seemed to take place. He turned back to face me, "Then perhaps we could listen to what you have to say first and then we'll make a decision."

I knew then, that the decision had already been made, subject to the worth of my intelligence. I began, "I'm sure you know that *Premier Exact* and *Johannsen Kuggjhul International* have been wound up. In fact, they went to the wall during the week of your discoveries."

He nodded. I continued, "Did you know that there was only one debtor; the same one, for both companies?"

He nodded again. I continued, again, "And that the debtor is a Turkish company, named . . ." I read from the notes, "*Karadeniz Ticaret,* based in Northern Cyprus?" The chairman didn't look perturbed, but Davies began to take notes.

I added, probably gratuitously, "Where we know a great deal of money is being laundered at the moment. My last piece of information should close the loop for you, or at least enough to count. Both Swedish companies were producing components for arms. That, I believe is privileged information, along with the fact that they are now being investigated by the Swedish Secret Service."

Their posture changed, so subtly I wouldn't have noticed it, had I not been watching closely and needed to see it so badly.

Prevex had always adopted an ethical approach to all its investment funds and anything to do with arms would have come close to the top of their no no's. The damage such a revelation could do to the group as a whole was incalculable.

It was Hudson's turn, "And what do you propose to do with this information, assuming that it can be substantiated?" The manager stopped writing notes and both of them looked at me for an answer. I addressed Hudson alone though, "Nothing sir, I promise you, provided you feel able to share a little information too."

Hudson's thoughts were almost audible. The information would become public before long, inevitably, but there would be great strategic value if they were to disclose it, as part of their remedial housekeeping. He said, "I assume that you will be as reluctant to divulge your source as you were at the AGM."

"I'm sorry, but that has to remain secret." I sought for more, something that would clinch things for me and I chose wisely, "One more thing, I promise to share anything else I discover, with you and no one else."

He took an audible breath before coming to a decision and giving a nod to Davies. He turned back to me, "Very well, Mr Davies will show you our redemption records for that week, but we cannot allow you to remove any documents from the premises and that includes copies, obviously. Also, we will require you to sign a 'non-disclosure' agreement."

I expected nothing less and said so.

Davies took me down to a cubicle of an office, compared to the one we had left and within five minutes a clerk entered with a folded sheaf of print-outs. In that time, Davies had also ordered coffees. I was startled by the volume of transactions. Clearly a number of people had been unnerved by the allegations I'd made at the AGM, but my search was still easy. Most of the transactions had been for less than twenty thousand and I was looking for much meatier ones.

Only forty or so exceeded six figures and half of those were institutional investors, such as pension schemes. I scanned the list three times, but only one entry stood out. He'd taken his two million out of the fund on the Monday after the AGM.

His name was Pavel Ankudinov.

* * *

Howard Long was charmed by the peace of his Dacha, but only in short doses. He could never leave his beautiful apartment on the Thames or the vibrancy and culture of London, for long. Moscow was two hours away and apart from the ballet, was left wanting in his view.

It might have looked like a Finnish log cabin had one corner of the building not been formed into three parts of a circle. There was so much space around them he did question why the new dachas were built in small estates and couldn't get a sensible reply. Someone said something about difficulties with utilities, which made no sense at all. He pulled himself up with a mental reminder that gift horses shouldn't be looked in the mouth.

Even the man and wife employed to look after the place had been paid for, though their insistence on growing root crops in his garden did irritate him and even now, in the new Russia, they dressed and behaved like peasants. On the one occasion he'd invited them in to eat with him, he'd been appalled by their manners and eventually, allowed them to seek temporary oblivion through a vodka bottle.

September was still relatively temperate, but he had yet to experience the place in winter; it would be interesting.

He stood in the kitchen, nursing a coffee while waiting for his visitor to arrive. A first, for Pavel usually chose to meet at his office in Moscow.

* * *

I waited up for Steph; to tell her the news. Saturdays were always the latest shifts, so I also wanted to make sure she was back safely. Since my revelations, she'd pretty well moved in permanently and already, thanks to a number of feminine influences, the house began to feel like a home again. She had also relieved me from a pet hate, by ironing my shirts, but more importantly, it was a matter of mutual support.

Sunday felt curiously void. I didn't feel up to more research, not without Libby and after 'slobbing' around all morning, reading the papers, we drove over to *Fosse Park* shopping centre for a junk food lunch and a pair of trainers for Steph. After that, we went back to 'slobbing'. By five, I felt depressed and ashamed of myself, for wasting an entire day. The sack cloth and ashes routine went on for an hour until Steph interrupted my whining, "Ian! You've left it a bit late for this, the day's over. Now go and find a jigsaw or something."

But then the cricket highlights came on. Flintoff had taken five wickets, sending the Aussies down in flames. By the time it was over I'd forgotten all about my earlier concerns.

On Monday, Libby began by making coffees, as usual, before we sat at the kitchen table to share information. I began by describing my visit to Jill and Jack, the previous Thursday and we agreed that it had thrown up more questions than answers.

I also described my meeting at *Prevex* by referring to the minutes I had written up and placed in the file.

"Great." She said, when I'd finished, "I'll add them to the *Word* file I've created. This 'Pavel' chap sounds important."

"Let's hope so." I signalled with a wave of the hand that I had nothing more to add, so she began, "Right, scary stuff first. I have only been checking the first two pages on *Google* search, so after you left on Thursday I decided to repeat the exercise but go on for a few more pages." She placed a copy of a newspaper article in front of me, which bore the headline, '*INVESTIGATIONS CONTINUE INTO ARSON ATTACK ON BIO COMPANY*'. I checked the top of the page to find that it had been an article in the *Ely News*, on Saturday the twenty seventh of August. "Hmm, parochial stuff."

Libby nodded, "That's why we missed it. If any of the nationals had featured it we'd have found it sooner. It was the reference to 'Bio' that tweaked my interest. Read on."

We would never have found it if someone hadn't leaked the information, perhaps in an attempt at exposing the *Bio Management Systems* connection, but it failed, for none of the nationals had picked it up and the *Ely News* only mentioned it in passing.

We wouldn't know until much later, that the links between the two companies wouldn't be officially established, by a team from *The Health and Safety Executive*, for another week.

The article described *SMB Ltd, as* a subsidiary of the Cambridge company, *Bio Management Systems Plc*, a scientific instrument and materials supplier, but the main theme questioned the apparent lack of motive and the scale of the damage. The Fire Chief was quoted as saying that it was the most devastating work of arson he'd seen, in over twenty years of service. He went on, "This was more than mere arson. Sophisticated incendiary devices were used throughout the building, resulting in total destruction."

I said, "It's close enough to be a fit with our research. Let's include it."

Libby made a note, slipped it into a file and continued, "I had another look at the Swedish Companies House reports again. In particular the accounting side of things, since their last return was so overdue. The last ones on record had been signed off by an Otto Rilke, which wasn't much help, but the previous year's accounts had been signed off by him too and that time, the practice name had been included. Boeker, Schmidt Koch and Co KG, of Frankfurt."

There were a number of other less significant details she had added to the files, but I decided to check out the accountancy firm. To begin with, I wondered how a German accountancy practice could be authorised to sign off a Swedish company's accounts, but a smidgeon of research established that they were; under the EU 'Mutual Recognition Directive.'

I found their website and telephoned the number listed. It was answered on the first ring but my schoolboy German wasn't up to the job. To her credit, she tried just as hard with her schoolgirl English, but eventually she put me through to a man who greeted me with a crisp, "Guten Morgen."

I set forth, again, "Entschuldigen sie bitte, aber mein Deutsch ist nicht gut."

His English sounded better than mine, "That is quite alright, I can speak English."

I introduced myself and asked if it would be possible to speak with Otto Rilke.

"I'm sorry Mr Barber, but Herr Rilke no longer works here. I have been told that he has gone into private practice."

I sounded startled, "Oh, in Frankfurt?"

"No, I believe he is operating from his home, in Rothenburg. May I ask the nature of your enquiry?"

I had prepared myself for that question, "Well, I invested in two Swedish companies which have both gone into liquidation and

I'm having difficulty in contacting their parent company, *Horizont International AG,* which is based in Frankfurt."

"I'm sorry Mr Barber, but we no longer hold that account. Perhaps it would be best for you to speak with Herr Rilke."

I didn't push my luck and ask him for Rilke's number, he'd been helpful enough. If it had been a UK accountancy, they would be more likely to say he'd left the planet than to tell me he'd set up his own practice and then tell me where.

I thanked him and broke the connection. So, not only had Otto left there, but he'd taken at least three clients with him too.

International directory of enquiries furnished me with his number and my call started off well, in that he could speak English very well too. But it ended there. I began to explain that I had been an investor in the two Swedish companies and that was as far as I got. He cut me off mid-sentence with, "Where are you from?"

I said, "England."

He snapped back, "No, who do you represent?"

"No one, just me, I was an investor."

"Then that is unfortunate, but how can I help?"

"I was just trying to glean some more information. The circumstances seemed so strange."

"Then you must speak to whoever is taking care of their affairs. I am no longer involved and cannot help with any enquiries. Good day."

The line went dead. I replaced the receiver slowly as I considered things. The tension in his voice, after I mentioned the Swedish names, was evident, but could that have been because he was a creditor too and smarting? I dismissed that one very quickly. If they were eight months late with their accounts, it was likely that little or no work had been done on them. Also, if they had crashed before he'd done any work, he'd have only felt relief. At least he wasn't one of the creditors. Finally; the only certain conclusion I came to was that he didn't want to answer any questions about them.

I expected the Russian rat; who'd jumped the good ship *Prevex* before anyone else knew it was sinking, would be off the radar, so I was startled when my *Google* search came up trumps. He had been featured in the business section of the *Telegraph,* in two thousand and two. The report had sought to describe what was going on in the new Russia, where Putin was waging war on the *Oligarchs* of the perestroika period under Yeltsin. His KGB background was deemed significant as the report highlighted a campaign of attrition, which included oppression, corruption and a series of trumped up charges that ended up in staged show trials which in turn, ended with closing statements and sentencing, from Judges who were obviously reading from scripts.

It was acknowledged that the original *Oligarchs* had done a pretty sound job of raping a country and its people, but Putin was using the opportunity to get rid of the old and put in new. Often, they were former KGB, just like him.

One of the new 'grace and favour' *Oligarchs* was Pavel Ankudinov, who had acquired a diverse conglomerate after the previous owner had fled to the west, from where he agreed to sell the outfit for a tiny fraction of its worth. The purchase had been funded by Russian banks who knew better than to say 'no'.

The article went on to name more, but the principal stories remained similar.

It was enough.

I had little enough evidence on paper, but enough smoking guns to blot the room out.

Except for *Bearing Straights Plc,* every one of Terry's tips were either involved in or suffered as a result of criminal actions. If I accepted that the Northern Cyprus connection included Russians, then the failing companies had all involved Russians too, particularly that Pavel chap and not forgetting 'apeman'.

I could hardly go down to Police HQ at Enderby with this lot though. For a start off, I had little or no hard evidence and apart from my beating, which I had omitted to report, none of the crimes had been committed on their patch.

On the other hand, time was running out, and I had enough now to be certain of one thing. 'Apeman' posed a very real threat.

I didn't think about it, I just did it, but when the MI6 screen came up I couldn't find a number, anywhere. They provided their address; Secret Intelligence Service, 85 Albert Embankment, London and perhaps predictably, their web address was sis.gov.uk. A couple of the pages referred to the work they did, past and present, but it was pretty bland. The remainder were different takes on the one theme; careers and recruitment. Eventually, I found a 'contact us' page which suggested telephoning either the MI5, police, or the 'Anti-Terrorist hot line, if I had information relating to imminent threats to the UK, life or property.

I was then given a postal address, PO Box 1300, if I had a general enquiry.

Finally, I was directed to their 'contact form' with a mix of options that could be ticked and a text box; the latter being limited to fifteen hundred words.

Bugger that I thought, someone could sit on that for weeks, yet no matter how much I searched, there wasn't a telephone number.

I wracked my brains for someone who might know, until Paul Gregson came to mind. His parents were clients and keenly proud of Paul's success in the Met. I'd met him a couple of times, but thought it prudent to make contact via his parents, particularly since they would have his number. In addition, their involvement would be a tacit sanction for my question, or at least I hoped he'd see it that way.

They were more than happy to provide his number and asked me to pass on their love, but when I did try, he was obviously on day shift, since he didn't answer my answer phone message until after six, though he had obviously spoken to his parents in the meantime. After a slothful Sunday, we'd realised the need for some food shopping and were in *Sainsbury's* when the call came through on my mobile. He sounded very cheerful, "Ian, what can I do for you?"

It was down to business, straight away. I asked him to hold for a moment and ran out of the shop. This was not going to be anything I'd want to share with the other shoppers, "Hi Paul, thanks for calling. I'm not sure what you'll make of this and I'll understand if you can't help, because it sounds strange, but *if* I wanted to contact MI6, would you be able to give me a telephone number?" I hurried on, I wouldn't mention your name, I swear, and I promise you I have a genuine need to contact them. I just need their number."

He sounded much more guarded this time, "Why?"

"Paul; it's best I don't tell you. Please, it's nothing you would want or need to know."

"Let me be the judge of that."

I began to feel trapped, knowing that Paul wasn't going to let go of this now. After taking a deep and very audible breath, I struggled on, "I don't even know Paul, I can't explain, but I need to contact them with what I do know and then, maybe, they'll make something of it. Please Paul, I'm desperate and I know the police couldn't help me, so please don't involve your lot."

There was a long pause before he spoke, "Not good enough Ian, I'm not going to rattle their cage based on what you've given me."

"Oh Christ." I murmured to myself, where to start. It needed to be concise, yet with enough detail to convince him. I began, "Quite by accident, I have come across a number of companies that are being used by Russians to ship arms to the Middle East." A sudden and horrifying thought came to mind, "When I say arms, I think that could include biological weapons."

He seemed to chuckle, "That sounds a little derring-do for an IFA, if you don't mind saying so."

I replied with feeling, "Tell me about it!"

It was clear from the tone of his voice that I hadn't convinced him, "Ian, I'm sure you believe what you're telling me but if I passed that on, verbatim, all the way up there, I'd be back on the street directing old ladies and tourists in no time."

"Ok, try this, please. Pass that message on and tell them to check out *SMB Ltd,* in Ely, and two Swedish companies; *Premier Exact* and *Johannsen Kugghjul International.* I spelled the last one for him and added, "They will need to speak to the Swedish Secret Service about the last two. Then give them my numbers please. Do you want me to repeat any of that?"

He spoke slowly this time, as though lost in thought, "No need, it's recorded." I waited, unsure of what else to say and finally, he reached a decision, "OK, I am going to speak with my boss about this then we'll see where to go from there. From the sound of things I suppose I ought to say take care."

It was a start, at any rate, "Thanks, Paul, thanks a lot."

I put my mobile away and headed back inside the store, thinking about a little unit in Ely, that someone had felt fit to destroy. SMB were linked with *Bio Managements Systems Plc,* who could well have cultured nasty things as well as good. That would give them something else in common with the two Swedish arms manufacturers, besides being one of Terry's tips.

The following morning, I couldn't settle to any real work and left Libby to catch up with some administration.

I did check my share portfolio and saw that *Bearing Straights Plc,* were having a bad time of things. Their largest lender had refused to renew their facility and there was renewed talk of a 'rights issue' to fund the remaining development costs; something the market didn't seem to like. In addition, they had yet to find a replacement for the chairman who had departed so acrimoniously, a month earlier.

Acting chairman Howard Long, was reported as saying that the fickle attitude of their leading lender had threatened the launch of a truly excellent and innovative product.

The share price had fallen out of bed again. My four hundred per cent gain had shrivelled to fifteen per cent and I got out.

But something in the report had struck a chord. I re-read it and discovered what it was almost immediately.

Howard Long.

"Who's he?" Libby asked when I repeated his name to her, "His name popped up before, months ago. I checked him out and discovered that his track record suggests that he was better at selling companies off than running them. He was also a director of *Currentsea.*"

"Ooooo, that is a coincidence."

"Yeah." I said, "Isn't it just."

Chapter 12

At first, I thought they were Jehovah's Witnesses.

It was late morning when the bell rang and I opened the door to find two men on the step. The older one wore a dark raincoat, another dead giveaway. He must have had a shock of curls once, since enough were still evident in the sandy coloured pelmet that surrounded a shiny bald dome.

The younger man wore a dark blue jacket over a woven brown shirt and dark trousers that might have been *Chinos*. He looked fresh from college.

The elder spoke, "Good morning Mr Barber; Hargreaves;- MI6." He flashed an ID card in front of me, "May we come in please?"

I showed them into the dining room and offered coffees, which they accepted, so I rushed through into the office, to pass on the order; trying to signal the gravity of things to Libby, with a frantic rocking of my eyes and head.

When I returned, he got straight down to business. "We were in the area so they asked us to pop in and have a word."

My emotions were a mix of relief and trepidation when I asked, "So this is about my message."

He graced me with a tight smile, "Quite so. We always take these things seriously, though I doubt we'd have visited you at the mention of Martians at the bottom of the garden."

I always say silly things when I'm nervous, "Oh no, I save them for elections. Candidates are willing to discuss anything then."

There was an awkward pause, as though he was at a loss for words and I felt myself blushing.

He began to speak but Libby entered with a tray of drinks. I didn't know where she'd found them, but a plate of chocolate digestives appeared too. I wondered whether I should introduce Libby to them, not knowing the protocols for dealing with secret agents, but on balance, I decided that secrecy should be paramount, at least until they'd gone.

As soon as the door was closed he continued, "Your information was intriguing and the office checked every detail." He pulled out a slim leather case that contained a notebook which he referred to, "Ah, yes, we spoke to our Swedish counterparts who advise that their fears were unfounded. All they found, in fact, were components for agricultural equipment, which was all the companies had ever sought export licences for."

I didn't know what to say, so I waited for him to continue.

"As for *SMB Ltd*. We have spoken to the HSE people who have just completed a most thorough investigation, particularly in view of that arson affair and they have failed to find anything untoward. I trust that in due course, the business will be up and running again."

I blurted out, "What about the *Prevex European* Fund? That crashed because of their investments in those Swedish companies."

"Ah yes, your enlightening expose at the AGM."

That startled me; I hadn't mentioned it.

He remained inscrutable, "Our people ran a check on you too, as a matter of due diligence, but the timing of the Swedish company's collapse was inevitable, since their somewhat limited credibility had been propped up by the fund manager's ill-judged support. His demise merely triggered theirs. Sapo's investigation was no more than a formality; based on erroneous information provided by the receiver, or whatever he is called over there."

I offered the title, "Bankruptcy officer."

"Just so."

This was going awry. I racked my brains for more, "But what about them only having one debtor, the same one,—in Turkey?"

He shrugged, "They were both manufacturing agricultural components, for the same market. It's a specialised area and therefore, not surprising that they were supplying the same customer. In fact, I don't doubt that it was the buyer who found them rather than the other way round; simply a matter of finding manufacturers capable of producing the products. The logistics of having them in the same country makes sense too, with shared designs, resources, shipping and so on. After all, Sweden is noted for engineering excellence."

The meeting with the *Prevex* chairman sprang to mind, "So how about Pavel Ankudinov? He had two million in The European fund and bailed out, three or four days before the scandal became known."

"His nationality is nothing more than a coincidence Mr Barber. An enormous amount of Russian money is invested in the UK these days and I'm sure he wasn't the only investor to have been unnerved by your disclosures."

I struggled on, "Then there's *Currentsea Plc.*" I explained about the failed Severn trials and how the scrap had been bought by an unknown buyer and shipped out on a Russian ship."

He didn't falter for a moment, "Ah, the Russians again. That would have been nothing more than a coincidence Mr Barber and a welcome one for the ship owners, I imagine. Supplies are being brought over from Russia all the time these days and return cargoes are always sought, which is not to say that the ship was bound for Russia. It could have been any of the North Sea or Baltic ports. The stuff might easily be in Holland now; or halfway up the Rhine."

He had spoken reasonably throughout, which made everything he said sound so plausible. In a tone that might have been used to ask what I wanted for lunch, he asked, "May I ask how you came by your information. Was it all your own research and if so, how much of it was supposition."

"Educated guesses you mean."

He blinked slowly; a silent 'just so'.

I only had one thing left, "No, guesswork, but here's a thing." I explained about Terry, his suicide and *Skype* messages.

They exchanged glances when I finished, like a lion training a cub and signalling, 'watch this', before a kill, "Our people thought as much, though they weren't aware of the conduit. I'm afraid you have been the victim of a particularly well-informed hoax. I'd have said 'unfortunate' victim, but I would guess that you've made a significant enough sum out of it.

Nevertheless, someone has hacked into your dead friend's computer and used his *Skype* account to play games with you. Remember, the *Skype* account is subscription free, so it could easily have remained open.

The information you received would be available to someone with enough time and resources to research those companies in depth. Whoever it was clearly had an agenda of their own and they used you to implement it."

I waved my hand at my black eyes, "Played games with me? Do you think this was just someone having fun? An Eastern European thug paid me a visit, wanting to speak to Terry."

"Ah, that simply serves to re-enforce my points. I don't believe for a moment, that you should suspect the Russians, *per se*. There are large numbers of Eastern Europeans in the UK these days, and their number will include individuals willing to do that sort of work. But your assailant might just as easily been any one of a host of nationalities. That apart, his employer is the one you should consider. He, she, or they, want to know where you've been getting your intelligence from. I would urge you to report the matter to the police."

They were making me feel as though I was reporting a UFO. I asked, "What makes you think I haven't?"

His responses had been seamless, throughout, just like the next one, "Because you wouldn't have asked that question if you had and because you are committed to your conspiracy theories. I'm sorry Mr Barber, but that is all they are, unfounded theories."

He reminded me of a Doctor, confident and well-informed, with a pleasant bedside manner. Like a compliant patient I lay back accepted it, for the time being.

* * *

It was lunchtime when they left and I joined Libby in the kitchen. She listened to me without interruption as I tried to recall all that had been said and at the end she asked, "Do you believe it?"

"I don't know!" But even as I said the words, something came to me and I said, "Yes I do, I mean, no!

I should have picked up on it at the time, but by then, they had me doubting everything we've discovered. When I mentioned 'apeman', he passed it off as someone who wanted to know where I'd been getting my tips from. I skipped a track then, by not remembering that 'apeman', or an accomplice, had been into my computer and *already* knew about Terry. That suggests forethought, prior knowledge and planning, rather than a need to know someone's name and address and besides . . . " I looked at Libby as another belated revelation came to mind, "Terry had already as good as told me he was working for a government agency."

Libby thought for a few moments before, "So, you think they did a whitewash job on you."

I still wasn't certain, but I was tired of it all, which was reflected in my voice "I don't know Libby, we can keep checking while I give it some thought."

"What about 'apeman'?"

"Oh Christ, yeah, I was forgetting him. I suppose all I can do is to tell him everything, including this morning's visit and promise to keep on at Terry to meet up."

* * *

'The midday train from Leicester to St Pancras was comfortably empty, allowing the two officers to review matters.

The younger asked, "Will this morning have helped Sir?"

Hargreaves had already considered the question, "Perhaps, but only temporarily, though I must credit him with knowing more than I'd expected. Unfortunately, I fear the Russians will continue to be heavy-handed."

"Is there anything we can do?"

"No, not with the resources we've been given for this operation."

The younger also noted, "It's not as if it's our affair."

Hargreaves nodded his agreement, "Just so."

The train slid through Northamptonshire like a bionic eel, as the refreshment trolley arrived. The coffees were non-descript, but the egg and cress sandwich was particularly fresh and flavoursome. The young officer knew how his senior hated to speak while eating and therefore waited until it was prudent to ask his next question, "Do you think the principals might offer some protection?"

"Oh dear me, no. They will lose interest as soon as the asset loses its value, which I'm afraid to say is imminent." He allowed a mile or two to fly by before reaching a decision, "In any event, I'm afraid our friends in Tel Aviv will have to manage without our help in the matter. I believe it's time to pension 'Terry' off."

What will happen to Barber?"

"From the Israeli's?" He shook his head, "Nothing, he cannot know anything about their operation and isn't likely to, after all we've been their ring-fence, so they won't even see him as a loose end. Besides, they've achieved most of their aims. On the other hand, we can only hope that the Russians don't hold too much of a grudge."

"Nothing we can do then sir."

"We've already done all that we can, by telling him to involve the police."

* * *

A little before five, I left Libby to close down and lock up. Steph had gone into Leicester, shopping and we'd arranged to meet up and see what was on in the cinema complex at High Cross that evening. There was plenty of traffic at that time of day, though I would be travelling in the opposite direction to the main flow, which would give me a chance to review the meeting.

There was a short queue to get on to the A50 and when I became number two from the traffic island I checked to my right. As expected, there was nothing much heading into the City and I made ready to move off, but just as I was about to go, a red Citroen raced around the island. Since there were no signals, I braked sharply, in case it continued around in front of me. Instead, it left beforehand, to head down the road I'd arrived on; still at some speed and I glanced at the driver to shake my head.

'Apeman' glanced at me in that same moment and when I saw the shock in his expression I realised he'd been heading to my house. I glanced in the mirror and caught a glimpse of his bulk as he wrenched on the wheel and completed most of a 'U' turn, ending up across the road, intent on forcing his way into my queue. A horn sounded from behind as I took off like a scalded cat, thankful that I was in the BMW five series and he was a Citroen, but I was also scared shitless.

We were on a dual carriageway, so losing him in traffic was out of the question, at least until we were closer to the city, but the route was also speed camera fest so that much would be restricted too. That thought went out of the window as I watched through my rear view mirror and saw him flick out into the outside lane to barrel past the cars that separated us. By then I was doing sixty and his approach was making me look like a cyclist. A speed camera flashed behind me and moments later, behind him. I think that was the moment I realised he was out to do me harm; serious harm.

I was lucky with the next camera, on the drop down into Groby, when a *UPS* truck passed it at the same time as me. He was driving within the forty mile an hour speed limit; while I was doing double that and I felt some small satisfaction at seeing the flash of light triggered by the Citroen.

When I look back, there is little I remember about that eight mile journey, apart from the stomach wrenching fear, but I do recall how much safer it seemed when we were in heavy traffic. So much so, that by the time we reached the northern bypass I changed plans and continued on the two way road, towards the city centre. The bypass would have been busy, but fast and I didn't like to think about the opportunities that would open up for him.

Horns blared, fists appeared from windows and the cameras kept popping, but I discovered a small advantage by knowing Leicester protocols when negotiating traffic lights. I jumped as many red lights as I could, sometimes dangerously, but by the time we reached the inner ring road I was three cars ahead.

The gains I'd made in heavy traffic told me that I needed crowds and police. There was only one place I could think of; *The Shires Shopping Centre.* If I'd been James Bond, I would probably have dumped the car in the street and run inside, but instead I took the ramp up to the overhead car park. I was still two cars ahead, but halfway up I realised I'd made a terrible mistake. At the top of the ramps the approach split into three lanes, for three barriers and ticket machines. One was about to be vacated and I raced for it, at the same time as the lady waiting in the next queue decided to switch lanes. The car rocked slightly as the corner of her car grazed the side of mine, but I ignored the blaring of her horn as I pressed the button for a ticket. The wait seemed an age, in which I heard a car door opening and her shrill voice, "Hey, you!"

Finally, the ticket appeared and I wrenched it out of the slot, ready to scream at the barrier, which eventually rose to let me through. By then she was at my window, demanding attention. I smiled weakly and said I was sorry, before taking off; the tyres screaming on the painted surface. She was standing in my lane scribbling on a piece of paper; my registration number, probably, but at least she was blocking one lane and her car another. I gasped; there might just be a chance.

I raced around the site but there were no spaces that were close to the *Shires* entrance, so I tore around the last corner, intent on moving up to a higher level and was faced with a solid queue of cars, moving from left to right towards the exit ramp.

Moments later, I heard the scream of his tyres as his car came into view. How the hell had he managed that?

There was the tiniest space between the two cars in front of me and I lurched forward, inserting enough of my car into the space to ensure that the car behind couldn't advance, at least not without causing damage. The driver blasted his horn and when the car in front moved on and I drove in, he leaned out and yelled, "Fucking Beamers; think you own the road."

The other drivers saw what had happened and the Citroen's approach, at a suicidal speed, so they did what most commuters do and closed to within an inch or so of each other. I caught a glimpse of the Citroen's nose; lurching as though it was a crazed dog on a chain, but the line was having none of it; not that I was racing away, but I realised that if he was held there for much longer I might get a chance to hide the car. I thought of pressing a fire alarm, before deciding that a wait for the Fire Brigade to arrive wouldn't do me any good. But thinking of an emergency service did give me an idea; one that I would never have contemplated seven months earlier, out of fear of the consequences. But after all I'd been through; it didn't merit a second thought. I dialled 999 on my mobile and as soon as the operator answered, I yelled, "Shires car park! Someone's just been shot!"

We were passing the entrance to the shopping centre when my blood turned to ice, again. He was out of his car, perhaps eighty yards away and striding towards me. I leapt out of the car and found the CCTV camera, apparently pointing in my direction and I waved at it furiously, but he kept on, seemingly oblivious to his surroundings. He snatched something out of his belt and dropped that hand to the side of his leg, out of public sight, but not before I'd had chance to see the knife.

I couldn't run, I was nowhere near fit enough, so I began to sign. I'd learned to sign as part of my *Duke of Edinburgh Award* and whilst I'd forgotten a lot of it, I knew enough to make it look convincing. In those forty seconds, I also signalled over my shoulder a couple of times, hoping that he would be camera shy.

Then, incredibly, my pulse seemed to slow as I turned to face him, with my arms outstretched, ready to try and fend off his attack.

Two things saved my life that night. Finally, he glanced up to where I was pointing, just as the camera swivelled in his direction and then the first sirens heralded the arrival of police.

He didn't falter, not one step, as he smoothly switched direction through the nearest door and into the shopping centre. After just one flight of the escalators, he'd be lost in the crowds.

* * *

I was allowed to park my car before they took me down to the *Shire's* offices and I stayed in the car while I made a call to Steph, which she answered instantly; her bright voice, void of any anxiety, which caused my stomach contents to roil at the thought of what I had to say.

"Hiya, Bogbrain, where are you?"

"Steph, I want you to go home, now! Better still, have you got a friend you could spend the night with?"

Her bubble of joy had disappeared, "Why? What's wrong? Has something happened?"

"Sort of, I can't go into detail now, please, just do as I ask."

"You're scaring me."

Somehow, I had to convey the urgency without passing on my rising panic, "Don't be; just do as I ask. I'll be in touch with you later, I promise."

"No, tell me now and tell me where you are."

I was beginning to sound angry rather than frightened, "I can't! There are too many people around. Please love, just do as I say. I'll be in touch—promise, I have to go." As an afterthought, I added, "Love you," before ending the call.

As they escorted me down to the office, I reasoned that 'apeman' couldn't have known about my plans for the evening, or he wouldn't have been heading for my house when he saw me, but I couldn't bear the risk of leaving Steph to go back to the house.

They gave me a bollocking and a notice of possible prosecution, though I didn't know that a witness had reported seeing a man appearing to make for me. I claimed not to know him and thought that perhaps I'd done something to upset him on the drive in, which would explain why he pursued me. They logged it as road rage and let me go.

* * *

I can't even remember the name of the hotel I checked into that night. It was large, comfortable and anonymous; sited in a business park near the motorway junctions by Fosse Park. All I sought was a temporary refuge; somewhere to take stock of the situation.

No matter how many ways I tried to explain things away, there could be no doubt that 'apeman' was going to kill me. It bordered on the surreal, just as my next conclusion did.

I needed protection.

The authorities; even the MI6 were not going to provide that, which confirmed that I was alone and frightened and helpless. I didn't telephone Steph that night, or answer the dozens of calls from her. I knew I should have, but what could I tell her?

At one point, a little part of me thought 'fuck it', let 'apeman' find me and get it over with, but it was only a passing thought.

I needed someone good enough to protect me from a Russian assassin, preferably as able as those that surrounded politicians, for whom nothing short of the SAS will do.

And then I thought of Smudge. When we were kids, he was part of our gang, yet he wasn't. Somehow, he failed to make much of an impression, with a quiet, thoughtful manner that should have made him a target for the bullies, but he was never picked on. On reflection, it was as though he'd been able to stay under their radar and they couldn't be bothered.

It was well over twenty years later when he contacted me for financial advice. A full army pension gave him all the income he needed and I did suggest a couple of modest investments, but it was when the 'Right to Buy' programme was in full swing; allowing council house owners to buy their homes at hugely discounted prices. The longer they'd been tenants, the bigger the discount. He was less than certain when I suggested buying the council house he was in, because he'd only been in there for a year, so the discount would have been tiny and he was less than certain about taking the responsibility of a mortgage on.

I did a little research and discovered that service in the armed forces counted as a tenancy period, which put him in place for the maximum discount possible. As a result, after some bullying from me, he bought a house worth fifty three thousand, for seventeen thousand and was delighted.

As part of the advisory process I am required to complete a 'fact find', which covers pretty well everything from birth to the present day and beyond, if you count future planning. In his case, I remember being startled, when he told me in that soft neutral voice of his, that he'd been in the SAS.

I remembered that his first name was Neil, from our last meetings rather than childhood, probably because I had to keep stopping myself from calling him by the name we had always used; 'Smudge'. But I simply couldn't remember his second name, so the directory enquiries was useless. In any event, it was two in the morning and whilst I couldn't sleep, others would. The call would have to wait until morning.

Another call came through from Steph and I let it ring out before texting her, 'All OK. Will contact soonest. XX'

I called Libby at a minute after nine, knowing that she'd be in the kitchen making coffee and therefore not surprised at the time it took for her to answer.

"Libby, it's Ian."

"Hello, where are you?"

As with Steph, I'd decided to keep that information to myself, "Best I don't say at the moment."

"Anything wrong?" She sounded as calm as ever.

"Too much to try and explain in a phone call. I'll tell you later, but for now, would you look up a surname and number for me please? It's a 'right to buy' mortgage case I did a while ago, for Neil something. He's ex-army; around fifty two years old and the purchase price of the house was seventeen thousand, give or take."

She asked, "How long ago."

"I'm not sure; five, maybe six years ago."

"OK, I'll have a look and call you back."

I didn't know where I'd be or what I'd be doing and I certainly didn't want another encounter with the police, if they caught me using the phone whilst driving, "No, best text it to me. Oh, one other thing, would you telephone Steph for me and reassure her please. Tell her I'm OK."

An hour later, I received the first fright of the day, when a call came through to my mobile from a withheld number. I sat on the bed, watching the screen until it rang out and waited. A few seconds later a beep told me that there was an answer phone message which reassured me. I couldn't imagine 'apeman' wanting to have his voice on record, but when I called it up, the message was still unwelcome. It was the police, wanting me to make contact in connection with the previous day's incident; either by calling the number given or calling in at the Mansfield House police station, which was in the city centre. The caller didn't give any reason for the call, which was probably a bad sign.

Moments later another ping signalled the arrival of a text message, from Libby.

You have a lot of Neils. Think this is the right one. Neil Foley 01455 784326.

I kicked myself; Foley, of course.

We exchanged greetings, but I was too wired to waste time, "Neil, I need help. If you can't I'll understand, but maybe you'll know someone who can."

He sounded as though we were discussing the weather, "Sorry to hear that. Go ahead and try me."

I'd been rehearsing for this, "Because of some confidential stuff I've been given, someone's tried to kill me. The police are no use and even MI6 don't want to know. The thug who . . ."

He cut me short, "No more. Where are you now?" I told him and in the absence of a reply, began to speak again, but a sharp "Wait," shut me up. I heard papers rustling and a minute or two later he said, "End this call." The line went dead before I had chance to do it and I sat and stared at the phone, nonplussed. Two minutes later, the room telephone rang and he gave me my instructions.

* * *

I left the hotel and took the route he'd given me, which was certainly not the one I'd have chosen. Instead of slipping around the outer ring road he had me drive in towards the city and head north through Braunstone, before getting onto the A47, where I headed back outwards to *The Red Cow*, a modern pub come eatery that sat beside a *Premier Inn*. His instructions had been specific, so I bought a half of lager and sat down, waiting for him to arrive. Fifteen minutes later a text message came through; a welcome diversion in what was becoming a tedious wait.

The tedium soon disappeared though. It read;

You were followed. Go park at St Marys Road car park, Hinckley, then walk into town and up Castle street to the top. Act casual, window shop. Turn left at top by pelican. Will be along there. NB. Behave normally.

It took three attempts, with trembling fat fingers, to set the sat nav and every shred of will power not to scan the vicinity for anyone waiting in a car. Once out onto the A47, I was able to use my mirrors, but in the whole ten and a half miles, I didn't see any single car following me. I found the car park in Hinckley easily, and inserted enough money into the 'pay and display' machine for two hours. I recalled the route to Castle Street and the main shopping area from previous visits and made my way in that direction. It was a reasonably steep hill, restricted to pedestrians only, with many small individual traders, so my interest in them wouldn't have aroused concern, but my attempt at a casual walk felt more like the gait of the *Tin Man* in *The Wizard of OZ*.

The pedestrian only section petered out and Castle Street became a two way highway that came down the hill and veered to the left from where I was standing, next to a *pelican* crossing. It had to be where he meant. I began walking along there, but there was no sign of him. The first car was parked seventy yards away and clearly empty, but beyond that stood a truck, blocking whatever lay behind from view. Uncertain by then, I turned back towards the *pelican* crossing to reconsider my options, just as a black VW golf GTi hurtled around the corner and snatched up alongside. I looked in and recognised him immediately, along with the urgency of his signals for me to get in.

I think it was the force of his take off that closed my door; it certainly accounted for the g force that pressed me into the seat and I had barely done my seat belt up when we approached the traffic lights, two hundred yards further on. They were full on red; even Leicester rules couldn't apply. They did though. Neil deftly wove his way across the junction, through the stream of conflicting traffic. Horns blared and the driver of the car waiting at the red light on the opposite side was making masturbatory gestures with his right hand as we passed him.

I took the opportunity to note that he hadn't changed; same pleasant round face and brown hair, with a smallish frame that looked lean but not particularly muscular. In fact, so ordinary-looking he'd be safe in any identity parade.

Little was said on the journey but for the first three miles or so, I noticed the attention he paid to his mirror. I did ask if I had still been followed on my walk through town and he shrugged, "Probably, but if you were, he had a long jog back to his car before getting back on the job."

Another thought occurred to me, "Won't he have your car number?"

"Won't hurt, the plates are temps."

Eventually, we pulled into a van hire lot near Sapcote and parked around the back amidst a range of vans and trucks. He switched the engine off and swivelled towards me, "OK, talk to me."

I began with Terry's first *Skype* message and for the most part, stuck to a chronological path. He didn't interrupt once. I finished with my flight to the hotel and call to him, which is when he made his first observation, "MI6 do not send two case officers out to put a civilian's mind at rest. You, my friend are mixed up in some serious shit."

I huffed, "I think so too!" But in that moment, I realised that he'd been the first authoritative individual to confirm I was. It was both reassuring and frightening.

He said, "We need to get those files from your house, but first, I need to organise something." He gestured towards the office, "Go in there and hire a car. They're expecting you. Do you have any cash on you?"

I nodded, "A couple of hundred or so."

"That'll do; give it to them."

I asked, "What about my car?"

He held out a hand, "Give me the keys, I'll have someone take it back to your house."

After giving him my address, I remembered the 'pay and display', "I've only paid for two hours."

"Shouldn't be a problem, but a parking ticket is the last of your worries. When you get the car, go lose yourself for a couple of hours and meet me at your house at five."

A thought suddenly occurred to me, "Libby, my assistant, doesn't leave until five."

"OK, make it five thirty".

I waved him off and checked for two hundred in cash before walking into the office. A tall thickset man was waiting and as I began to speak, he pushed a set of car keys across the counter without a word. I handed over the fold of bank notes which he took without counting and said, "It's the Vauxhall Astra, out front."

Slightly nonplussed, I asked, "Isn't there some paperwork we need to do?" It was as though I hadn't spoken. He simply repeated, "Astra, out front."

Puzzled and slightly intimidated, I picked the keys up and thanked him, before going back out of the door and around the building. It was a four year old, rather tired looking, silver Astra, but I was certainly not prepared to go back in there and ask for anything better. This was obviously something that had been pre-arranged and, I realised, discreet.

The M69 was close by and the *Leicester Forest East* motorway services beckoned, until I thought of 'apeman' and the possibility of him doing the same thing. Instead, I headed south and hid in a *McDonalds* at Walsgrave, near Coventry, where I thought the food was hideous, but the coffee, surprisingly good. They had complimentary newspapers there too and I read the lot, but even so, two hours drag by when you're preoccupied by an attempt on your life.

The car had been owned by a smoker and I reckoned he had died in there too, but it drove well and had a surprising turn of speed. When I approached the scrap *Mondeo*, parked outside my house I saw two men sitting in the front seats and almost fled. At the last moment, I recognised Neil who was seated in the passenger seat, signalling for me to join them. With a hoop of exhaled air, I parked behind them and noticed that my BMW had already been parked on the drive.

I slid into the rear seat and almost gagged at the sickly, sweet smell of body odour. Suddenly, the Astra's bouquet didn't seem so bad after all. Neil introduced me, "This is Techy, or at least that's what you will know him as." Then he gave me my instructions, "OK, so go in there with Techy, get the files, pack a few clothes then come straight back out and don't say a word. Leave Techy to get on with his job. I'll wait here."

And keep watch, I thought.

Techy looked at Neil, "You want me to wipe the hard drive?"

Neil shook his head, "No point, they've already copied it. Have a peak though."

The thought of having my computer wiped sent a shudder up my spine, but I said nothing and got out of the car when Techy did. As he stepped around the back to open the boot, I guessed his weight to be nineteen or twenty stones. The normally capacious jogging bottoms were under stress and folds of skin draped over the tops of his grey trainers. It was clear that he survived on junk food too; there was enough of it stuck to the front of his T shirt.

He pulled an aluminium case out of the boot; the sort posh photographers use and signalled for me to lead the way, which I did, in absolute silence. One thing I was discovering about being frightened was that you did as you were told.

* * *

He took over an hour, but there was nothing tardy about his departure from the house. He waddled down the drive, placed the case carefully into the boot and threw himself into the driver's seat. Neil asked, "Anything?"

Techy started the engine as he spoke, "Not now."

Neil turned to me, "Follow us, in the Astra."

I hurried back to the car behind; now enveloped in oily blue smoke from the Mondeo, which given the parlous state of its engine, startled me by tearing off at a rate of knots. We joined the A50 and drove down to the junction with the M1, but on the approach to the island, Techy bounced up over the kerb and parked on the grass verge. I followed suit and by the time I had joined them both front windows had been opened. The traffic noise was dreadful.

Techy had waited for me to arrive before addressing Neil, "The place is covered, top to bottom. There's even some sort of data transmitter in the computer, though I'm not sure why they bothered with that because they've hacked into it anyway. You told me to be discreet, so I didn't try to identify it, but someone is monitoring everything, remotely. I don't know what you're up to or what you've done, but I want no part of it. That kit is twenty second century stuff."

I began to speak but he interrupted, "I said I don't want anything to do with it,—which means that I don't want to discuss it."

While waiting for Neil to say something, I thought I ought to check and see how much I had left in my wallet. The guy would need paying.

I was wrong. He caught the movement and held up a hand, "Keep your money,—use it to find a cave somewhere. Anyway, I left everything where it was."

Neil spoke so quietly I barely heard him, "So, military."

Techy nodded, "Has to be."

"Thanks mate, I owe you." They shook hands and we got out of the car, into another cloud of blue smoke, as Techy took off.

I was just about to move off when a call from a withheld number came through on my mobile. I waited until the caller left an answer phone message and as expected, it was from the police, asking me to contact them. I asked Neil, "What do I do about them?"

"Don't know yet, let's see."

* * *

On the London Road, in Leicester, Dominiks sat in his hotel room, listening to the metronome-like beat of the bed head, striking the wall of the room next door. As if to confirm the activity, the girl was panting loudly, with the sincerity he was used to seeing on cheap pornographic DVDs. He knew that many rooms were rented by the hour, which suited him perfectly, for the owner never asked questions; or answered any either.

He'd been serviced by a couple of girls in the last few weeks, but on reflection, he thought the DVDs were better value.

The hotel was well placed too; with the railway station nearby and a motorway system within minutes. He could be anywhere he needed to be within a couple of hours, which was not to say he was comfortable, particularly after the last telephone call, from his current employer; the one he had been sub-contracted out to by the *Spetsnaz;* more usually known in the west as *Special Purpose Forces.*

They'd spoken in his native tongue, or rather he had listened, to a long tirade that ended with, "I was told you were the best, yet you couldn't deal with a simple civilian situation. Thanks to your clumsiness, the overall situation is getting out of control. Deal with it, or I'll have you replaced with someone who can."

Stung, Dominiks sat quietly, wishing that he could have used the connection to reach through and snap the caller's neck, for those insults. But he was a professional, just like his accomplice, who had been responsible for the electronic surveillance and was now waiting in a room upstairs, for instructions. It *had* been shambolic, but he had been cautioned against carrying a gun in the car on a casual basis, because of the English attitude to arms, where a simple spot check could compromise everything. Which was why he had only bothered with a knife; intending to deal with the target at his house. His mistake, he'd realised, lay in doggedly pursuing the target into that car park, when he should have waited for another opportunity.

This time, there would be no stupid drivers, cameras or witnesses. The naive little mischief maker and his elderly ex-army friend would be dealt with in more discreet surroundings.

Chapter 13

After collecting his car from where he'd left it, in Kirkby Mallory, we ate at an extremely unremarkable eatery in the middle of nowhere. The only saving grace was that they kept a nice *Bass* bitter. By unspoken agreement, we spoke only about old times, kids we knew and what they were doing now; all the usual stuff. Anything, except for the mess I was in. By nine o'clock, I was beginning to feel flaky and Neil said, "Come on, let's call it a day."

I did as directed and parked at the back of a pub, a few hundred yards away from Neil's house, before completing the journey in his car. It was one of the original council houses, soundly constructed, with an ample front garden and huge back one. I noticed that both were lawned and the only concessions to colour were a couple of small beds with hardy annuals in them.

Inside, the furnishings were functional, bordering on Spartan. A few cheap prints had been hung on the walls and there were a couple of regimental photographs, but the place was spotless.

He showed me up to my room and left me to settle in while he went downstairs, to make teas. When I got there, my files were on the table and Neil looked set to start, but not before he let me off the hook, "Go to bed Ian. You probably didn't sleep much last night and you need rest."

I couldn't argue with that. As I crawled into bed, I suddenly realised, that for the first time since 'apeman's' first visit, I felt safe.

* * *

I rose at eight the next morning and slipped a sweater on, before padding downstairs in my borrowed sleep shorts. Neil must have heard me coming downstairs and was in the kitchen making teas. The files were neatly stacked, but the A4 pad beside them looked full of notes and I felt sure that he hadn't slept much.

There was a photograph on the top of his television that I hadn't noticed the night before; of him, in dress uniform, holding a young and very pretty girl in his arms. I guessed her age to be around two and she clearly took after the fair haired woman standing beside them. All three were smiling for the camera. When he entered the room I asked, "Your family?"

He answered as if an aside, "History," which served to cancel out any further enquiries on the matter.

After setting the mugs down on the table he gestured for me to sit opposite him.

"Four hundred a day plus expenses; that's bargain basement, but I owe you."

It wasn't far removed from my earnings, which didn't include dealing with assassins, or at least it hadn't, so I agreed, reasoning that the money I had earned from Terry's tips would cover the fees. Ironic, really, though I did think to ask, "How long do you think I'll need your services for?"

"As long as it takes for them to either kill you, or us to persuade them not to. Once we've discovered who *they* are of course. In the meantime, how much cash can you lay your hands on?"

I explained, "I've been working on that. There's thirty thousand in my bag upstairs, but because of the limits Building Societies have on cash withdrawals, I've been withdrawing cheques as well and paying them into my current account. Cleared funds should stand at around sixty or seventy thousand."

Neil acted as though it was nothing less than expected, "OK, we'll get the money out today. I can place it safely, if you trust me?"

"Of course!" I didn't add that there seemed little choice in the matter anyway.

His next question sounded as though it might have been triggered by my mention of his family photograph, "You mentioned a woman, Steph. She anyone special?"

"Very! A fairly recent relationship, but," I cast for the right words, "Important to me."

"Then tell her to stay away from the house, same goes for the woman you employ, but if you call her while she's at your house, be careful what you say, they'll be listening to every word."

I knew that was the wisest thing to do, yet at the same time tried to gauge the chaos it was going to cause, "That means the business will shut down, effectively. I'll have to instruct my locum, Pete Marston." I explained that current legislation required all advisers to have an appointed IFA, to take over the practice in a caretaking capacity, when the owner was incapacitated. The choice of locum was often forged out of friendship and mutual regard, but it was a dreadful responsibility to dump on someone, and never taken lightly.

Neil put things into perspective, "Well, whether you were dead or alive, the call would still need to be made. Oh, speaking of which, give me your mobile."

I passed it over and he flicked the back cover off and removed the battery, "You are not to use this again, unless I tell you to, understood? Use a call box for those three calls and I'll sort something else out in the meantime."

I looked glum. Losing that device felt like losing a limb.

He continued, "I've been thinking about the calls you've been getting from the police. It can't be bad news for you; they don't invite people in to charge them with an offence, so something else must have come up. We could do with the intelligence and the next twenty four hours may be the last we spend in the open, so you should call in there today, when you go to the bank. You'll be on your own, but I'll be watching your back throughout.

Oh, there's one more thing, from now on," there was a trace of a smile, "Call me Smudge."

I used Smudge's mobile to telephone the Police and was soon put through to the CID, but the officer dealing with my case was out and the one I spoke to was reluctant to go into detail, so we made an appointment for me to see the right man at noon.

We used Smudge's car for the trip into Leicester, which included a detour into Braunstone where I used a telephone box to make three difficult calls.

Libby answered with her usual, calm voice, "Barber Financial Services, good morning."

"Libby, it's Ian, I've gone away for a few days, to try and think things through and I think it would be better for you to take that time off as well; paid, of course."

I could sense the shrug in her reply, "No need. I'd rather stay on the top of things; the work will only pile up if we're both not here."

"Well, thanks Libby, but I think it would be best if we both had time off, the clients won't miss us for a few days."

"It would still be better if one of us is here. Don't worry, I'll sneak some time off when you're here."

She could be quietly resolute at times; I'd seen it with some of the less reasonable clients, but I still had two more difficult calls to make and was not prepared to reason with her, "Will you do as you're told, just once. Now shut down and go home please, immediately. I'll call you later."

I had never been so short with her and the response mirrored her reaction, "Fair enough." She put receiver down without another word.

I'd made that call first, believing it to be the easiest, which didn't auger well.

"Hey Steph, it's Ian."

"What the hell do you think you're playing at, you little shit!"

"Pardon?"

"You heard me, you've been an absolute shit."

I struggled for mitigation, "Didn't Libby get in touch."

This time she almost screamed down the line, "So you think it's alright to piss off into nowhere and just have your secretary give me a courtesy call!"

"But love.."

"You're a shit."

This was going nowhere. I'd planned on giving her a sanitised version of things, which excluded 'apeman', but in desperation I blurted, "He tried to kill me."

After a stunned pause, she asked, "Who did?"

"The same man who broke my nose. He chased me into Leicester and came at me with a knife."

I heard her gasp, "What happened?" Then, a note of panic, "He didn't get at you?"

"No, too many cameras and witnesses, thank God."

"Where are you now?" I could sense her readying herself for a dash out of the door and knew then, that the only way I could keep her safe was to tell all. She would only keep her distance if I could justify it.

"Steph, I need you to listen to me carefully. First, I'm safe and I have employed someone to keep me that way. He's someone I trust, but 'apeman' is still out there, so I need you to do as I ask, for both our sakes. The house is bugged and I've sent Libby home for a few days; you must stay away from there too."

She almost wailed, "Oh God, Ian, what the hell is happening? What are you going to do?"

"Well, for a start off, I'll do my best to telephone you as often as I can, but for the moment, we have to play things by ear."

There was little more to add and soon, I had no choice than to end the call. We both wanted to spend longer talking to each other, in the way that lovers should, but circumstances dictated otherwise.

My last call was to Pete Marston, my locum; in its own way, just as difficult as the other two. His initial concern on learning about a family crisis was less evident when I explained that his services would be required and all sympathy disappeared when I was unable to answer his questions as to the nature and timescale of the emergency. He already held a set of keys to the house, for access to my client files and I gave him the code for the alarm system, but by then, the conversation had become formal and awkward. Smudge and I reasoned that he would need to access my house and no doubt use the computer and telephone, but provided he remained

totally ignorant of what was happening, he could never give anything away to the listeners.

I was absolutely drained by the time I got back into the car.

Our next stop was the bank, where an assistant manager invited
me into a cubicle of an office to enquire why I should need to
withdraw such a large cash sum. I explained that it was towards the
purchase of some land, for investment purposes and he questioned
the need for cash, when electronic transfers were so much safer and
reliable. I pointed out that such transfers constituted a record too,
which, as the 'cash' element of the deal, would have been uncomfortable for the farmer selling me the land. Eventually, the cash was
handed over; by the bank to me and me to Smudge. We parted
company then, while I walked around to my appointment at Mansfield House Police Station.

I had to dodge a couple of constables setting off on their bicycles as I crossed the car park, before climbing the steps into the station lobby, which seemed quite contemporary. It might easily have
been a doctor's waiting room, were it not for so many uniforms
and an absence of magazines. The constable behind the counter
took my name and details before telling me to go and sit down,
but I spent a few minutes studying the notice board before settling
down next to a youth who looked very uncomfortable. I judged
him to be something of an authority and asked, "Do they keep you
waiting long?"

He sneered at my naivety, "Depends what you done. Last time
I was 'ere, it was three bleedin' months." The sneer remained in
place but he snickered at his own wit. It took me a moment or two
to catch on, in the silence that followed and I realised that further
conversation would be both enlightening and depressing. I opted
for silence.

Ten minutes later, a plains clothes officer, who introduced himself as DC Leeson, escorted me to an interview room and offered
a choice of tea or coffee. I opted for the latter and settled down for
a long wait, like everyone did on the reality television shows; so I
was startled when the door was kicked open, just five minutes later,
by an older CID officer, balancing two loaded cups, while gripping

a file under one arm and trying to ensure that the plastic bag protruding from one of his jacket pockets, stayed there. His concentration on the task in hand was total, until the cups had been set down safely on the table and then he greeted me with a smile and proffered hand, "DS Owen; thanks for coming in Mr Barber."

DS Owen's figure spoke of an unhealthy diet and his slightly shabby dress code might have signalled a bachelor existence. Both were totally at odds with the young officer who had shown me in, but there was an easy assurance about this chap, that gave me comfort. He didn't waste time either, "I'm afraid we owe you an apology." He sat down, placed the file on the table and appeared to ease his genitals into a comfortable position, before continuing, "Your emergency call from *The Shires* was treated as," he searched for the word, "Mischievous, but one of the their security personnel ran back through the CCTV tapes and noticed something we had all missed earlier on. In fairness, I have to say that there were a lot of people milling around at the time and the act of disposal was so slick and casual that it could easily have been missed, had it not been for that eagle-eyed chap later on. The camera had caught the suspicious movement, by a very large man as he passed the car park payment machine on his way into the shopping centre. Anyway, they sent someone up to check." He pulled the plastic bag out of his pocket and placed it on the table, "And they came back with this."

It looked unutterably lethal.

I couldn't recognise it, given the distance involved and my panicked state at the time, but I had no doubt that it was 'apeman's' knife, or rather dagger; of the sort I would expect commandos to use. It was obviously designed for covert use, since the blade had been treated in such a way as to give it a dark, non reflective surface.

Owen was watching me closely as he continued, "In light of this, we recovered all of the CCTV tapes, which showed him making his way through the centre until he slipped out onto Church Gate. We lost him after then, but we also had our people work on the car park CCTV footage and they came up with these." He pulled two large stills from the file and placed them in front of me. The first was a wider angle shot that showed me signing frantically at the camera and at the edge of the picture, just yards away from me; was 'apeman'. Someone had drawn a circle around the hand he held at his side, in red ink. The second image was poorer in quality, because of the enlargement but still clear enough to identify the weapon, protruding from behind his leg.

He was still watching me closely as I stared, transfixed, by the second image which re-enforced the menace of the actual thing, now sealed in a plastic bag. It felt like an age, but must have only been a minute or so, until finally, he said, "So Mr Barber, I have a whole bunch of different questions for you today."

I looked up and began to focus on what Smudge had told me, when we discussed this contingency, "Listen, it will be a case of all or nothing. If you involve the police, whoever signed 'apeman' up for the job will recall him and another will be sent; someone we won't be able to recognise. Secondly, the police won't be able to offer you twenty four hour protection and even if they did, I wouldn't give much for your chances, because I wouldn't be able to stay in the frame. So don't involve them; it'll be a lose, lose situation. Make no mistake, everything we've seen so far, apart from that shabby piece of work at the car park, tells us that we're up against professionals."

Owen dragged an interview pad across from near the wall, next to the recording machine, which I noted, wasn't operating. After writing down the date, time, my full name, address and date of birth, he put his pen down and folded his arms on the table, "Let's begin with motive shall we? Why does someone want to kill you?" He corrected himself, "Why does this man want to kill you?"

My lying began with, "I have no idea."

He smiled, "Try again."

"I tell you, I have no idea. Don't you think I'd have told the police at the time, if I did? Remember, they seemed pretty intent on charging me for wasting police time." I then thought to add, "And that was the softer option. They were pretty ticked off about me reporting it as a shooting."

He switched direction by pointing at each of my eyes in turn, "So that was just a coincidence?"

I was well on the mend, but the vestiges of a broken nose were still evident, "Certainly, unless a bunch of drunken yobs in the City Centre were part of it, which I doubt."

"Ah yes; the unprovoked attack." He withdrew a notebook from a pocket, eventually found the right page and read from his notes, "On the third of September. Why didn't you report that to the police?"

I was surprised by that one. They had obviously been making enquiries about me and had secured that much information from the Royal Infirmary's A & E. I gave the same reason I'd given the doctor, "Why bother? Forgive me, but how many drunken brawls do you have to deal with each week and how many end up in court? It would have been a waste of time; yours and mine."

"So you had a fight with them?"

"Pardon?"

"Well, you called it a drunken brawl, rather than an assault."

My thought processes kicked up a gear; this was beginning to sound more like an interrogation than a statement request, "I was generalising, merely to make a point and I'm not in the habit of picking fights with anyone, let alone a bunch of drunks."

"Where did this attack occur?"

"Just off Humberstone Gate, I was making my way back to the car park."

"Which car park?"

"Lee Circle car park."

He was noting down everything I said by then, "So, after the attack, presumably, you retrieved your car and drove to the infirmary?"

I nodded.

"What time would that have been?"

"God knows, somewhere between ten thirty and eleven."

"Not a good time for anyone to attend casualty."

I huffed, "You can say that again. The place was full of drunken brawlers." I suddenly realised how far off-piste we seemed to be, "What's all this got to do with the attempted knife attack?"

Owen's expression was unreadable when he said, "Humour me." It felt more like an order than a request. "If I showed you a street map, could you point out the exact location of the attack?"

"Not a chance, I was simply strolling along, in my own little world, when they jumped me."

The questions went on for another forty five minutes. I had to confirm details of the collision I'd had at the barrier and to some extent the chase that led up to it, but most of my answers merely added to the existing fiction; until finally, he seemed to be satisfied, though I waited in silence for the few minutes taken to make more notes.

Then he pocketed his pen and smiled at me, "Thank you for coming in Mr Barber, that'll be all for now."

I smiled back and had pushed my chair away from the table and made to rise, when he continued, "I need time to digest this pack of lies and then I'll be in touch again. Meanwhile, we'll check our CCTV footage for the night of your attack near Humberstone Gate. We have a hundred per cent cover for that part of the City Centre."

He allowed a pause, while I continued to sit, two feet away from the table, and then continued, "See, drunks are one thing, but attempted murder is quite another and something we take very seriously. Now I don't know what you are trying to hide, but I am certain you're still at risk, which means that you'll very likely be calling for us again. Let's hope we get there in time again, but don't bank on it; you probably won't see him coming next time."

A moment later, his expression and manner shamed me, "But if any copper gets hurt trying to stop that happening; I'm coming after you. In the meantime, get out of my sight."

* * *

I did as Smudge instructed and caught the 158 from St Margaret's bus station and bought a ticket for Nuneaton, a town that lay twenty miles to the south and halfway to Coventry. The Police Station was only a minute or two from the bus station and the bus was already loading when I got there, so I was still trembling when I sat down. Lads like the one I waited with at the station, would no doubt laugh the experience off, but I was in shock. To have someone in authority call me a bare-faced liar was appalling; worse, he was right.

It was early afternoon and the bus was almost empty, with few getting on at later stops either, so the driver reduced speed to stay within his timetable. Once, he pulled into a stop and waited there for a few minutes, as a queue of cars raced by; some using their horns to express their frustration. I stared out of the window and allowed my mind to skip from one incident to another, like a pinball machine in turmoil.

I got off at Earl Shilton library, just over halfway to Nuneaton and waited at the lay by for about ten minutes before Smudge raced up to me. He gave me a thumbs-up sign and I responded with something between a smile and grimace. As we pulled away, he said, "So, they let you out."

I gave out a great sigh, "For the time being, but he called me a liar; said they couldn't be sure to get there in time if it happened again, thanks to my refusal to tell all."

Smudge seemed reassured by the news and added some of his own, "Well, at least you weren't followed this time."

At the house, he retrieved a new rucksack from the car boot and once inside, unpacked two pre-paid telephones, an *iPad*, a four pack of lager and three pizzas. He passed me one of the telephones and the rucksack, "Here, pack your gear in there, it's easier to carry than a case and less obvious." He glanced at the pizzas, "It's my turn to cook dinner tonight."

The *iPad* had been loaded with most of the *apps* I used, including *Skype*, which I managed to access, after arranging for a new password. I'd long forgotten the old one, because it had been pre-loaded in my computer. Smudge watched as I called the main screen up, which showed that no one had tried to get in touch with me. I'd already explained that Terry never responded immediately and that it could be days before he made contact but Smudge told me to try. I said, "OK, here goes," and began to type.

Hey Terry.

I stared in shock as the reply came back, within a minute;

Good evening.

A tad formal I thought; until another message came through;

Please state your business.

I whispered, "It's not him." Smudge tapped my shoulder, "Ask."

Who are you?

The next message did little for me;

Please state your business.

My breathing became shallow as I typed;

Where is Terry

Please state your business

I wish to communicate with my friend Terry Caplan

Not possible.

Why not?

Please state your business with Mr Caplan.

Please put Terry online.

Not possible.

Why not?

Mr Caplan is no longer able to use this facility..

I stared at the screen, trying to figure out what this would mean for me and what might have happened to Terry. I typed;

Is Terry OK?

Unable to advise, sorry. Mr Caplan is no longer with this unit.

Somehow, the word 'sorry' imbued the news with some humanity, but that bubble burst as the next message appeared.

This line of communication is no longer valid and is being closed down now. Goodbye.

I tried for another ten minutes to get a response; with messages that became more and more frantic. In the end, I even used some pretty foul language; perhaps hoping for a note of censure in return, but there was nothing.

Finally, still staring at the screen, I slouched back in my chair with, "Fuck." I looked up at Smudge, "What do you think that means?"

He sat down opposite me and said, "Motive, strategy and operational details I don't know, yet, but the effect is clear. You've just been dumped."

"Where does that leave me?"

His reply was typically succinct, "On your own." Then, as an afterthought, "'Cept for me.

That night, over dinner, he asked me to relate everything about the police interview. I told him all that I could remember and when I described the knife, with the strange letters etched onto the blade, he had me sketch it on a piece of paper. After studying it for a moment he said, "It looks like a 'Shaitan'."

I looked askance, so he added, "They're issued to the *Sptetsnaz*, Russia's special forces.

* * *

They had watched the targets leave that morning; two fifty year olds, who by chance or design, had gotten themselves involved in a game that would end that night.

A casual visit to the front door, followed by one to the back door, as if the occupants might not have heard, established that there was no dog or evidence of an alarm. Modern double-glazed units had been fitted, including the back door and the multiple locking mechanisms left the removal of glass as an only option, but for some reason the front door had not been changed. It was still the traditional council house variety and apart from being painted, it remained as plain and ordinary as it had been, the day the house was built. Even the lock might have been the original, with what appeared to be a simple *Yale* latch and that would take seconds to compromise.

Normally, they would have maintained some sort of surveillance in the run up to an operation like this, but the use of a car in such a small street wasn't an option and all the surrounding houses were occupied. At home, they would have just ejected the occupants of a convenient apartment and set up an observation team, but this was not Russia. Even so, they were unconcerned; ops like this one didn't come much easier.

Escape was equally assured. They were expected at the embassy, where they would be given back the identities they had used to get into the UK, which afforded them diplomatic status and an immediate exit out of the country.

Chapter 14

There'd been dates and liaisons, some of which had extended to the bedroom, but Steph had stopped looking for love long ago; real love that is, the sort that envelopes a person in an emotional cloak and now that she was a captive of one, fate was dealing her a hand she couldn't cope with.

For the first time since starting at *The Dog and Hedgehog*, she'd cried off with a sickie; one that felt more authentic than a broken limb. Limbs healed, but hearts didn't.

Worse still, with her father gone, there was no one she could turn to, no shoulder to cry on and she did weep, often.

She'd been sworn to a secrecy that might mean life or death, and while the threat existed, she felt powerless. For want of anything better to do, she flicked through her address book and when Father Ewan's name cropped up she was tempted, knowing that his vows would ensure discretion, but it had been so long since her last attendance at church, she felt unable to go there now. Besides, he'd probably have moved on after so long. With that page still open, she clasped her hands, wept and prayed aloud, "Please God, take care of him." Her sobs overrode any further attempts at speech.

In time, they eased and without conscious intent, she continued to flick through the pages, until the name of her only possible ally appeared.

Trevor, her husband answered the telephone and soon, Libby came on the line. Her wonderfully calm voice was balm-like, "Hello Steph." She heard the sobs and said gently, "Take your time."

Steph tried so hard to curb her tears, knowing the comfort that lay on the other end of the line and in time, she managed to find words, "I'm so sorry Libby, I'm OK, really."

Though she managed to conceal it, Libby became afraid, "Have you heard any news?"

Steph realised how things might have seemed and said quickly, "No. No news." The tears began again, "But I'm so worried.

"We both are kiddo, but I have a feeling he's found a friend; someone who can take care of him."

"Who?"

Reluctant to give too much information away on the telephone, Libby settled for, "A friend, from way back, with some experience in dealing with this sort of thing."

"Is that all you know."

"No love, it isn't, but I think Ian believes his house has been bugged and who knows where that has stretched to."

They'd chewed things over for twenty minutes, before Steph returned to the sentence she used often, "Oh Libby, I'm so frightened."

Libby was too, though she hadn't shown it, but Steph's rambling needed to be given focus, "It's obviously got something to do with this 'Terry' person he's been exchanging messages with on *Skype* and these companies he's been buying shares in, but how does the MI6 fit into it all?"

"Do you think MI6 are responsible for the break-in and bugging?"

Libby sighed, "I really don't know, but why don't we meet for a coffee in town, tomorrow? Maybe we can talk more freely then." They arranged to meet at the clock tower at eleven and maybe stretch coffee into lunch.

* * *

The lock was as easy as expected and lubricated enough to move back without a sound. The intruder slipped inside and eased the door shut, before waiting in the darkness for five minutes; time enough to ensure that no one had been disturbed. Silently, he slipped through the ground floor looking for movement detectors and to make sure that no one was sleeping downstairs.

Upstairs, Smudge had quickly silenced the alarm that sat on his bedside table. It couldn't be heard beyond his bedroom anyway, but he now knew there was someone inside the house. Three tiny contacts on the front door; two fitted to the hinge side and one inside the *Yale* lock could detect movement of more than two millimetres and had done so.

In ghost-like silence he slipped out of bed and straightened the quilt on his side. He was tempted to pat the figure that lay beside him, but instead, grasped the cosh that lay beside the alarm. The curtains had been left six inches apart, allowing enough ambient light in to enable both him and the intruder to see what they were doing. The sap in his hand felt comfortable. It was clad in dull black leather, which housed a spring loaded handle and at the business end, a core of lead shot. A rap across the biceps would disarm anyone and probably break a bone doing it.

The intruder was much lighter than Dominiks and therefore better suited to this type of job. Always sure to use the outermost part of each step, he waited for a couple of minutes after every other one. They had thought to simply storm the place and get it over with, but after the last attempt at liquidation, Dominiks wasn't prepared to take chances. This had to be a text book covert op. Nevertheless, once he'd begun, things would need to happen quickly.

The first door on the landing was just ajar and the absence of any noise troubled him. No snoring, rustling or even heavy breathing. Even so, the room would need to be checked out; he couldn't afford to leave an uncleared area behind him. Slowly, as he eased the door open, his view into the room broadened and the stale smell of sleep told him that there was someone in there, after all.

Smudge watched the door open, a millimetre at a time and readied himself for action. He was guessing it would be another knife attack and once the killer was committed to the form in bed, he would make his move.

Two 'phutts' accompanied by two dulled flashes changed things. The figure in the bed leapt as the bullets tore into it and Smudge sensed the man moving out of the room. The use of a silenced gun had achieved two things. Firstly, Smudge knew that it was game on; there were no longer any doubts. Secondly, another twenty kilos of force would be delivered with the sap; mere disablement was no longer an option.

The assassin now focused on the door at the other end of the landing. The sound of a dripping tap had already told him that the half open door in between was to the bathroom. He began to move quickly; with one down, there was little reason to waste time with stealth, a sentiment not shared by the shadow that had followed him out of the first bedroom.

* * *

It sounded as though someone had fallen out of bed. I saw a glow shine underneath the door and switched my bedside light on. Smudge spoke through the door, in an urgent tone, "Put that out!"

I did and struggled out of bed, to the door, where I thought to ask, "Can I open the door?"

"Yes."

Even today, I would swear that he was looking at me and even in the torch light; I saw the life fade from his eyes. Smudge had rolled him onto his back and was patting down his pockets. The only thing he found was a spare ammunition clip, which he checked for rounds before expertly switching it with the one in the gun. After slipping the spare into his pocket, Smudge looked at me, "He won't be alone, stay here and stay away from the doors and windows. Oh and no lights. In fact, get back into bed."

I was nodding, but still staring at the corpse at my feet.

"Oh, for fuck's sake." Smudge grabbed my arm, hard enough to cause pain, "He ain't gonna hurt you, but he was planning to." I saw the gun being waved in front of my face and came to my senses. Without a word, I scuttled back into bed.

He went back to his room and allowed his vision to normalise before using a thermal imaging weapon sight to scope the rear of the house. He continued to do so until a passing cat served to confirm the device was working. As expected, nothing else had shown up.

Once out of the back door he made his way across enough back gardens to give him the margin he sought. A couple of dogs barked, briefly, but they were indoors and of no concern. Soon, he crept out to the front of his chosen house. It had an ornamental cherry in the centre of the front garden that served as cover, while he scanned the street.

The car was exactly where he'd expected it to be. Thirty yards or so beyond his house and facing in the opposite direction, ready to make a break for the main road that crossed the end of the street.

Smudge had no doubt that the man in the car was a professional, with every sense on high alert and time was running out. Very soon, he would know that something had gone wrong and therefore, a covert approach would take too long.

It was very early, he guessed at around two; chucking out time for professional drunks.

To begin with, he could barely be seen, leaning as heavily as he was into the hedge, but when he pushed himself away, brushing an imaginary spillage from his trousers with exaggerated care before struggling with a recalcitrant zip, it was clear, he was a drunk.

Each yard counted, as he wove his way down the pavement; ricocheting from parked cars into hedges or walls. The approach began at a hundred yards, by estimate and at twenty he would begin firing. Long odds, with a hand gun and through car windows, but he would be closing all the time, while the target was keeping his head down.

Seventy, fifty five, fifty. The figure in the car hadn't moved an inch, but at fifty yards, the engine started with a roar as the clutch was let out at the rush. The take-off was accompanied by a squeal of tyres and any attempt to shoot at that range would have simply wasted bullets. One thing was for certain, they were up against professionals.

* * *

I lay in bed, staring at the vague form outside my door. Part of me wanted to get up and check the man's pulse myself; just as another wanted to close the door on the scene, but both options faltered, with the fear that he might just come round and then I wouldn't have a clue what to do.

No amount of films can prepare someone for the real thing. Strangely, in that first period, I didn't give a thought about the man's actual intentions; they seemed too abstract in the face of his own violent death; a mere eight feet away from me.

Time dragged on though, enough for darker thoughts to creep in, accompanied by a growing nausea. I thought about bullets and the horror of their impact; the lonely, frightening end, in a strange bed and then, my mind's eye saw this house, silenced by the deaths of its occupants. Two bodies left in their beds to decay. How long would it have taken to find our bodies?

In hindsight, I believe I came close to giving up then, as the fear of my imagination began to outweigh the fear of the act itself. To go and find 'apeman', for a quick, clean end began to look better than the debilitating fear of the inevitable. Time passed.

My heart spiked when I heard movement, but the landing light came on and Smudge said, "It's OK, it's me." I listened to cupboards and drawers being opened and closed, while I stayed where I was. Finally, he came into my room and made a quick assessment, "Get dressed, now and pack your gear. Don't think, just do as I say."

I did. He hadn't raised his voice, yet there was such an air of authority; of dominance, I clambered out of bed immediately and began to get dressed. Meanwhile Smudge went out on to the landing and began to ferry things downstairs.

I waited at the door, holding my rucksack in front, but fearful of treading on the body, until Smudge appeared and snatched the sack out of my hands. He thrust a pair of surgical gloves into my hands, "Put these on and wait there."

He was back on the landing by the time I'd donned them and I glanced down to find that the intruder was still lying face up. I noticed his brown hair, dark clothing and two slivers of reflected light from between partly closed eyelids. Smudge began to unravel a dark blue nylon pack, the size of his hand, which grew into a full size bivvy bag; the sort climbers use for survival. He shook it, enough for the air to open the collar and knelt down to begin feeding the man in, feet first, "Give me a hand."

I stared at him as though he'd lost his mind.

He stood and grasped the front of my jumper, "Ian, wake up, I don't know how long we've got." My failure to respond instantly caused him to pull me closer, "Do you want me to kick some sense into you? I'll beat the shit out of you if I have to."

I nodded then and satisfied, he released his grip to point at the body, "You're going to have to lift that while I draw the bag along." I did as directed; lifting the man's hips by his trouser belt and his torso by the armpits. In no time, Smudge had enclosed the corpse and drawn the cord at the end tight, leaving a collar of around four inches through which brown hair protruded, like an obscene parody of birth. I made to help with the lift, but Smudge shook his head and hefted the whole thing over his shoulder. Grabbing my cash and keys, I followed him downstairs and out of the front door, collecting my rucksack on the way. As we approached the car he signalled for me to put my sack on the back seat while he flicked the rear hatch and dumped his burden in the luggage space. I noticed that the interior light didn't come on, but there was enough ambient light to see that Smudge's rucksack was already on the other side of the back seat.

He'd gone back to the house and obviously expected me to as well. Inside, I was told to go upstairs to turn the lights out and when I returned to the kitchen a box of provisions sat on the work surface. Smudge was on his knees, reaching under the sink and I assumed he was turning the water off, but then I heard a loud click and he reappeared with a box. I couldn't help noticing the economy of effort as he placed it on the counter and began to withdraw and load two handguns, ammunition clips and some other bits and pieces I didn't recognise. All disappeared into the army tunic he was wearing, save for one of the guns, which he passed to me, "You ever used one of these?"

My jaw dropped, "Christ, no."

"It's a semi automatic; that's the safety. He pointed to a lever beside the trigger, "You must press that as you pull the trigger, or nothing will happen." He flicked the ammunition clip free and checked that the chamber was clear before thrusting it at me, "Try it."

I took it, though he might just as easily have handed me an angry cobra. He snapped, "Get a move on."

Once satisfied that I would actually be able to fire the thing, he re-loaded the clip and passed it back to me, "If anything crops up, you point and shoot, just like the movies. You've got thirteen rounds there, if you run out, you're fucked."

As we left the house, he asked, "Have you got the Astra keys?"

I struggled with the box of provisions as I patted around my pockets, until I found them and held them up, to show him. He said, "And your house keys?" I'd already felt them in one of my pockets and whispered, "Yes," in a voice that still seemed unnaturally loud compared to his.

By the time we reached the pub I knew exactly what was expected of me and soon I was following him north out of Hinckley. Incredibly, it was still only three in the morning. Less than an hour had passed since the break-in.

There was no traffic to speak of and at Market Bosworth, Smudge turned off onto even quieter lanes. As we drove through Thornton, he slowed to allow me to pass, just before the left hand turn for the descent to the reservoir. I drove across the dam and stopped at the far end, with my engine running and lights off. If any car approached I was to switch them on with main beam, to blind the other driver. As I pulled into the side of the road I saw Smudge's lights go out at the midway point across the dam.

He got out of the car and scanned the area for fishermen, but it was still too early. A distant owl hooted, as if to re-enforce the solitude of night, when he hauled the body out of the car and rested it on the parapet. The rope he had tied around the waist back at the house made the job easier and moments later he hefted a concrete block onto the body. The rope that was tied around that had a carabiner attached to the loose end, which he used to clip onto to the ex-assassin, before rolling the lot off the edge. Moments later, there was a loud splash, but by then Smudge was already closing the hatch of his car.

Four minutes later, he was parking it in my garage, after I had turned the alarm off. I re-set it as soon as I heard the door close and within ten minutes, we were heading south on the M69.

Smudge took over the driving and little was said on the one and a half hour journey. He seemed to be lost in thought and I couldn't think of anything intelligent to say. In truth, I had surrendered myself to his care, entirely and waited for him to tell me what to do.

We skirted beneath Birmingham before heading south on the M5, until we reached the Strensham Services, where we both bought large *Costa* coffees. Smudge accompanied his with a 'full English' breakfast while I settled for a bacon roll I barely tasted. Eventually, he pushed the empty plate to one side and replaced it with his coffee mug, before asking, "I want you to think, did you mention my name to anyone else?"

I looked offended, "No, of course not!"

"Then we need to find out how they managed to track us down so quickly. If it happened once it'll keep happening."

I was keenly aware of the weight in my pocket, which seemed to be pulling my jacket out of shape, in a graphic betrayal. It prompted me to ask, "What happened to his gun?"

Smudge said off-handedly, "It went in with him." He must have read my thoughts, which were asking why we'd thrown a weapon away, "It was a *Makarov PB* nine millimetre; they come with a silencer attached, which makes them a specialist weapon. They'll find the body before long and when they do, I want the authorities to be looking further afield than our houses. A lot further in fact. That is a classic *Spetsnaz* weapon, so they won't know the why, or who, but they will know the where from."

I asked, "Where are we heading for now?"

"A cottage; somewhere quiet and well off the radar, but first, we go somewhere quiet and go through all of your stuff."

We took the M50 from there; bound, I was told, for Hereford, where we would collect some more supplies.

Silence ensued until we reached Ross on Wye, where the motor-way became an 'A' road and we pulled in at the first layby. I stayed in my seat, as instructed, while he emptied my rucksack into the rear luggage space. The sack was immediately deemed clear and thrown onto the back seat; understandably, since it had been pur-chased after I had moved into his place, but ten minutes later he slipped back behind the wheel and pre-empted my question with, "Nothing."

My sub conscious must have been mulling things over because twenty minutes later a dreadful truth came to mind, "Shit!"

While I was assembling my thoughts he said, "Go on."

"The first day I called you; I telephoned Libby for your number, because I'd forgotten your surname. All I gave her was your first name and what I did for you, oh and the approximate date. Since then, I thought it was still safe, because she texted me with your number. Nothing was spoken out loud in the house, but she'd have searched the computer for it."

Smudge nodded his head slowly, in acceptance and shortly after nudged me gently, "You couldn't be blamed for that one."

I gazed out of my window, feeling ridiculously grateful for those words.

After shopping for provisions, we drove west out of Hereford and left civilisation at a small settlement named Dorstone, in the lee of the Black Mountains. At some ill-defined point, Smudge took us off the tarmac surface and we bumped and scraped our way along a rock-strewn track that might have been a river in the spring. It felt much longer, but I was assured that it was only half a mile long, ending at a small stone cottage with a view that was worth more than the building.

It smelled damp and when the shutters were opened I noticed that there were mouse droppings along the counter top. The kitchen, come dining room, come sitting room, had a mix of appliances, from a gas cooker and fridge, to an open cooking range which had obviously been used recently. A shelf in the alcove beside the stove contained an eclectic mix of books; their popularity evi-denced by the measure of mould growth. All this I discovered while

Smudge was outside, persuading the generator to fire up. Satisfied that it would do so, he shut it down and came back inside. He explained that the fridge and gas stove were powered by LPG and there were ample *Tilley* lamps for normal lighting purposes. The toilet was a privy in a shelter outside, though there was a 'jerry' under each bed. Furthermore, I was told that the bed would only feel damp for the first ten minutes, after which my body heat will have equalised things. In reality, it meant that the night was spent alternating between damp chills and sweating humidity, but by the second night, a day's airing had solved the problem.

In the meantime Smudge was hungry. I declined lunch, but watched him slice two doorsteps off a loaf and spread them with a thick layer of *Dairylea* cheese spread before laying several brick-sized slices of chopped ham and pork he'd liberated from a can, on top. The smell of cheese and onion crisps finally persuaded me to leave for the bedroom and unpack.

When I came out, fifteen minutes later, he'd finished eating and two mugs of coffee sat on the table, along with my files. He gestured with an open hand; palm up, for me to sit on the wheel back chair opposite, "Right then, today and tomorrow we're going to go through these again; make sure we've missed nothing and then, we'll come up with a plan; yeah?"

"Sure." I said; glad to hear the word plan. I'd already seen enough of his culinary horizons to make a suggestion of my own, "How about I cook dinner tonight?"

He gave me a wry grin, "Sounds good."

"First though, would it be alright if I telephoned Steph, just to keep her mind at rest. I won't tell her anything beyond being OK."

He shrugged, "You can try."

I certainly did, from every side of the cottage, both inside and out. It had started to rain by then, but I still trudged up to the top of a nearby rise, in vain. There wasn't a glimmer of a signal. My whole situation was pretty dreadful, I knew that, but I felt particularly despondent when I returned to the cottage. Smudge already knew of course, but my expression prompted him to offer a solution, of sorts, "Day after tomorrow, we'll go into Hereford for supplies. You'll have a chance there."

Instead of working separately, we decided to go through each file together and by the time we'd finished Smudge's notepad looked reassuringly full.

We were both tired, even though it was only six o'clock, so I offered to start on the meal. He agreed, "Yeah, we've made a good start. Tomorrow, we'll go through the lot again."

I asked, "Any thoughts on plans."

"A few, but they will have to wait until tomorrow."

I checked his box of provisions, which included biscuits, crisps and a variety of canned stuff that would sit between slabs of bread. A quart of milk, pound of cheddar, eggs, onions and tomatoes constituted our range of fresh ingredients. I checked the cupboards and found a variety of herbs, some flour in a *Tupperware* container, a bottle of olive oil and an unopened bag of pasta twists. No problem! After frying the onions I added a can of tomatoes, some chicken stock cubes, mixed herbs and plenty of seasoning. After another sortie into his box of goodies I opened a can of chopped ham and pork, reduced it to cubes and threw those in. In no time, the bubbling red mass was dumped onto cooked pasta and topped off with grated cheese.

It was bloody good; those were his words, not mine.

* * *

They spoke in the mother tongue.

Dominiks had waited in his hotel room until late the following afternoon. The other man hadn't been a friend, but he *had* been a comrade, who would have found some way of making contact before then, if he was alive.

It was only seven in Moscow and the call was answered immediately, though the man on the other end said nothing. Dominiks had rehearsed his report and spoke quickly, "The visit didn't go as planned. Our friends didn't make us welcome, so I came home, alone."

There was a long pause before, "I doubt you will be welcome anywhere. Someone else in the family can take over. In the meantime, come home, you imbecile, I have cars that need washing."

Dominiks gripped the handset so hard it cracked, "I have something to do first."

"I said come home, before you cause any more...," a pause, "Distress."

The call was abruptly ended and Dominiks stared at the receiver, "I intend to cause them plenty of distress before I'm done here, you *zalupa.*"

* * *

Howard Long rose from his desk and stretched. Another two million had just been transferred into his Cyprus account, for services rendered. "Speaking of which." He murmured aloud as he checked his watch, en route to the wine cooler, for the bottle of *Krug Clos du Mesnil* he'd set aside for the occasion.

He double-checked the time before ambling down to the boat, where his second extravagance of the day was due to arrive. He could have entertained her in the apartment, or rather she entertained him, she was costing enough, but it was a pleasant evening and he knew how much she liked to meet on the boat. That much was mirrored in her expanded repertoire.

On Monday, he would face the press and hostility of the shareholders of his next corporate calamity, but that was inevitable. They would squeal even louder when he had the receiver appointed in two weeks time. In the meantime, he would enjoy a bottle of fine champagne and a remarkably versatile call girl.

* * *

It was still raining when we got up the next morning, and the dull gloom was depressing. I found the eggs he'd purchased and we began the day with scrambled eggs on toast. Smudge opted for NATO standard tea; white with two large sugars, while I stayed with industrial strength coffee; black, no sugar.

By lunchtime, we'd gleaned as much as we could from the files, though this time Smudge suggested that we ignore the acts or circumstances and concentrate on the characters. In truth, it didn't tell us any more than we already knew, but we did end up with a list of targets, as Smudge put it. I looked at the name at the top of the list and decided that 'target 1' was a tad ambitious.

The list was short;

Putin

Pavel Ankudinov

'Apeman'

Otto Rilke

Howard Long

We'd included 'apeman', more out of the need to keep him in mind as a threat than a target. I thought that Ankudinov and his sponsor could have been on another planet as far being credible targets was concerned, until Smudge pointed out that they were included as subjects for investigation rather than confrontation.

"So, what about the other three?" I asked.

"If we come up against 'apeman' he'll be my concern, no question. As for the other two, we'll have to see. When we go into town tomorrow, we'll find somewhere that offers WIFI and you can use the *iPad* to see if you can find anymore about them, though I wouldn't spend time looking for 'apeman', he won't be on *Facebook*."

I had a cheese sandwich for lunch, of normal proportions, while Smudge had another doorstep. An empty afternoon lay ahead, so we lingered at the table with fresh coffees. Smudge asked, "Have you ever been married?"

I nodded, "Still am, but I've been expecting the divorce papers to come through for a long time; she's set up home with a solicitor, after all."

He grimaced, "Oops, that's going to sting. Any kids?"

"Two, daughters, both grown up and neither want much to do with me. I don't know why really, I've never beaten or abused them. I suppose if I did anything wrong it was being a workaholic, but they certainly benefited from that."

Smudge looked down at his mug, "Yeah, the absentee parent thing. I was one of those, but I wasn't good news when I was home either. There was a black time. In the end Linda couldn't cope anymore and she went back to her folks in Kent, with Claire. She'll be sixteen/seventeen now."

"Do you see her?"

"Nah, I may do one day, but I still keep making the monthly payments and if anything special crops up her mother gets in touch."

I was suddenly overwhelmed with sorrow. Whatever his problems had been, the man sitting opposite knew loneliness I couldn't imagine. As if recognising the territory he'd ventured into, Smudge abruptly rose and moved to the sink to wash his mug. That done, he asked, "What do you plan to do this afternoon?"

I shrugged and pointed at the books, "I'll try one of those and maybe have a nap."

"OK, I'll leave you to it; I'm going for a run."

* * *

Libby treasured three things in her life; her husband, Trevor, Ann, her daughter and Mack, the golden Labrador who was her shadow, whenever the opportunity arose. While light permitted, the two of them would sally forth to the common each evening, after dinner. There, Mack would leap into his own little world of adventures as soon as the leash was unhooked. It was then a case of tail up and nose down, as he quartered the ground, searching for imaginary prey, unless of course, he came across a friend to play with. They were moments of joy, for both dog and owner.

As always, when it was time to go home, Mack accepted a restraint without hesitation. Unlike the outbound trip, when he would strain at the leash, he was content to trot along at Libby's side for the walk home, which saved her life.

There was always traffic on the road so she paid no head to the car that approached from behind, even when the driver dropped a gear and the engine began to race.

Mack died instantly, a macro second before Libby's knee and femur were broken. Her pelvis, ribs and shoulder were broken when her body slammed into the side of the car and finally, after she had been thrown over the low hedge, into a front garden, she was concussed by an ornamental heron. Had it not been for Mack's presence, the dynamics of the impact would have included a fatal head injury, as her head came into contact with the edge of the car roof.

A pedestrian on the other side of the street saw it happen, another aspect that saved Libby's life, because the paramedic was there within minutes and an ambulance soon after.

The witness provided the police with part of the car's registration number, which proved to be unnecessary anyway, because the stolen vehicle was found on a track near the small town of Ibstock, an hour later, still burning furiously.

* * *

I lay in bed, with an *Ian Rankin* book, having wiped as much of the mould off as I could, though still mindful of the millions of spores still being released every time I turned a page. On the other hand, I reasoned, a chest infection was the least of my worries.

An hour after he left, I heard Smudge call out it was him as he re-entered the cottage. Moments later, I heard the shower being switched on and the boiler in the kitchen fire up, so I decided to get up and make him a cup of tea. There were four decent sized potatoes on the sink, still covered in dirt and therefore, I suspected, recently stolen. Still, it meant that we were having omelette and chips that night.

The following morning, after breakfast, I was left to do the washing up while Smudge went out to check the car over. I soon finished and sat down with his notepad to make a shopping list. I'd been told to buy provisions for up to a week, though just for me, while he ran a few errands. As if to re-enforce that state of affairs, he took me outside and made me practice using the gun; a Glock, I discovered, in better light this time, though still without ammunition. I also learned how to change the magazine; well enough to give me comfort and Smudge some measure of reassurance.

It was mid-morning by the time we set off for Hereford where we found a superstore; I can't even remember the name now. Smudge left me, to have a wander around by himself, while I stocked up with a much more varied range of foods. I also bought some puzzle books and a couple of mould-free novels.

We then headed into town and because it was almost lunchtime, we found a cafe that offered free WIFI, rather than a coffee shop. I welcomed the prospect of an extended break, since Steph would be in the middle of lunches and not home until three.

In the meantime, we agreed to focus on the target list, which reduced the search variables considerably and I began with the name at the top, Ankudinov.

Most of the sites were in Russian, where the Cyrillic letters didn't provide a clue, but I tried 'Russian press agency' and came up with the old faithful, Tass, which also had a site in English. I tried his name in the sub search box and a number of articles appeared, all in English, with the most recent, only two days beforehand. I pulled the full article up, which read;

Pavel Ankudinov, president of ENERGY RUSSIA, the innovative oil and energy company, founded only two years ago, has announced the recent acquisition of the global rights to an exciting new hydro turbine design.

Mr Ankudinov explained that several flaws in the original English design have been rectified by their own development team and licences have been given for over two hundred sites across the country.

This marks yet another Russian advance in sustainable energy.

I tried to find mention of it in the English press and eventually tracked down a small feature in the *Observer's* business section, which read;

Pavel Ankudinov, one of Putin's 'grace and favour' oligarchs is expanding his operations from oil and gas, into Hydro power, using a new turbine design, thought to be the one sold by the receiver of the ill-fated Currentsea Plc.

Let's hope he has more luck than they did.

I showed them to Smudge who took a few notes before propping the *iPad* up on the table between us to check the other TASS articles. They were much of a muchness; 'Lion of Industry' and 'Pride of Russia' sort of thing, but we found four pictures of him shaking hands with Putin, at one function or another, both smiling and at ease.

Having found mention of *Currentsea,* I decided to try the others from the files. *Bio Management Systems* didn't feature but *Bearing Straights Plc* were in the *Financial Times Weekend,* that very day. Rather than pull it up on screen, I ran out to the newsagents a few doors away and bought a copy, in case the digital version had been précised. The article was headed, *BEARING STRAIGHTS SHAREHOLDERS IN UPROAR AT SALE OF FAMILY SILVER.*

It went on to detail the RNS issued by the company late on Friday afternoon, in which they announced the sale of all intellectual rights to their innovative bearing design, to a company in Frankfurt. Howard Long, the chief executive, justified the sale as the only means of survival after the banks had withdrawn their support. He added that they had negotiated the right to continue producing the bearings for the UK market, under licence.

In reality, the company was pretty well worthless now and the shareholders knew it.

We tried the net. I was startled to find that Long was on *Facebook,* until I pulled up his page. There were only two scraps of information and no news feed. It appeared that he went to Colchester Royal Grammar School; class of seventy five and that he lived in London. That was all. There were no pictures and no friends; it was as though he'd decided against the idea very early on and hadn't bothered to delete the tiny amount of detail noted. I expressed disappointment but Smudge thought otherwise, "So, assuming he left school at eighteen, that puts his year of birth at nineteen fifty seven, which makes him forty eight years old and now, I know where to start looking for him." He pointed at the *iPad,* "Keep going."

I looked doubtful, "Bloody hell, Smudge, London's a big place."

In spite of my doubts, a *Google* search came up with a number of entries, mostly by newspapers, chronicling his appearances at AGM's and the like. One feature, from the *Colchester Gazette,* included the best picture we could find of him. He was facing the camera and shaking hands with a gaunt looking chap with a chain of office around his neck. It was a 'local boy done good' affair, marked by an invitation to speak at the local Chamber of Commerce. In contrast to his host, Long was shorter and a good deal heavier. A slightly bulbous nose dominated his face while supporting a weighty pair of horn-rimmed spectacles. He looked as though he was shaking hands with an undertaker, sizing up an imminent heart attack victim.

Smudge used his own smart phone to capture the image. I knew that the pre-paid one he had in his pocket was reserved for our use alone.

The article referred to his success as 'a Captain of Industry' and in the interview, Long sought to re-enforce the measure of his success, by referring to the 'love of his life'; a seagoing motor cruiser named 'Wave Crest'.

There was little else from Google, but Smudge seemed satisfied.

We filled in more time with more coffees, until it was time for me to make my call and Smudge to take a walk.

I knew I had to be upbeat; she'd have been worrying herself sick and would need reassurance. I simply needed to hear her voice.

"Hey Steph."

"Oh Ian, thank God you've called." There was a catch in her voice, "Libby's in hospital; they've got her in the intensive care unit."

My bubble popped, "What? I mean how, what happened?"

"It happened last night, a hit and run. Her dog was killed; the police reckon that's what saved her. They said it was either a drunken driver or a joy rider, or both, because they found it burnt out, not long after. It'd been stolen."

I couldn't find words as I tried to assimilate the news but Steph continued with a plea, "Ian, you don't think this has anything to do with your goings on do you?"

I stumbled, "I don't know. I doubt it. She really had nothing to do with what's happening to me. There'd be no reason to go after her."

"It's a hell of a coincidence."

"That's all it is, I'm certain, but do me a favour can you? As soon as she can have visitors, pop in and give her my best."

"I've already tried, but it's family only."

The spectre of a coma sprang to mind, "Is she conscious?"

"Yes, some of the time, but the list of injuries is dreadful."

Another thought occurred to me, "How did you find out?"

"It was front page news and on the television."

I said, with feeling, "I hope they catch the bastard," not knowing that he was already in Moscow and four replacements were on their way.

All of the casual chatting and endearments I'd been looking forward to had gone out of the window. Instead, I spent another fifteen minutes gnawing at the new nightmare and realised that there was now another difficult call to make. Eventually, I eased the call to a close, but not before I added a final note of caution, "Look love, I still don't think there's a connection, but promise me, if you see anything that causes you concern, call the police immediately. Tell them everything, if you have to."

This time she sounded argumentative, "One minute you say there's nothing to worry about and in the next I'm being told to look out for killers. You're scaring me again Ian."

"Don't be, I'm just being paranoid, but promise me you will."

After an extended pause she said softly, "I will."

"I love you Steph."

"Me you too."

I dialled Libby's home number and Ann, her daughter answered. As soon as I mentioned my name she called out, "Dad, it's Mum's boss."

Trevor came onto the line moments later, "I've got a message for you, from Libby but first, I want you to tell me what's going on."

I owed him some sort of explanation but first, I needed to know how she was. He huffed, as though I had a nerve to ask, "She's stable. With luck, she'll be out of the ICU within a week, but right now she's so drugged she hardly knows us." He went on to detail a list of injuries that made me gasp, adding that he'd had to bury Mack too; a casualty Libby had yet to be told about.

We talked about the wonders of modern trauma care and timescales for her recovery, along with the need to beef up the penalties for car theft. Finally, he said, "Well, are you going to tell me what this is all about?"

I steeled myself for the delivery of more lies, "Firstly, I think it's a terrible, terrible coincidence and nothing to do with what's been happening to me. In confidence, an old friend gave me a bunch of Stock Market tips, some of which caused enough of a stir for someone to have me thumped. They even threatened me with a knife. The police are on to it, but I decided to go away for a while, for safety's sake."

He came straight back at me, "Yours maybe, but not Libby's."

"No Trevor, as I said, the two things can't be connected."

"We'll see, but God help you Ian, if I find out they are."

"You won't, I'm sure, but in the meantime, could you pass a message on to Libby for me please."

"What."

"Give her my best wishes and tell her that as of now, she's a full time employee and on full pay for as long as it takes for her to get back on her feet."

He was ready for that one too, "That sounds like a salve to your conscience."

I spoke more sharply than I should have done, but I had to head him off, for all their sakes, "No! Libby is the only employee I have and I can't afford to lose her. Besides, I'm hoping that news will be a bit of a lift for her. You both could plan a trip for when she comes out; somewhere warm perhaps." There was a long enough pause for me to say, "Hello?"

"I'll tell her, but I have to go now."

I remembered, "You said you had a message for me."

"Huh, yes, she said, good luck. Now, is that all?"

As soon as the call was over, I sagged back against a wall as if the air had been drawn from my lungs and then came despair. No, it wasn't all, I thought. At first I'd taken it to be a message from them, for me to make contact perhaps, but then I realised, it had been a payback; an eye for an eye, or it would have been if not for a beautiful Golden Labrador named Mack.

Smudge's observation was as chilling as I'd expected, "They were out to kill her. She's been lucky."

With an image of 'apeman' in mind I murmured, "Fucking bastard."

Smudge was staring into space, "Stupid one too. He was acting outside of his brief, I'm certain and that marks him as more of a gangster than a professional. There was no strategic value in taking Libby out; it was an undisciplined act of revenge. The mission was to eliminate you, to prevent further damage, and perhaps find out how much you know. Don't forget, the police have a picture of him now, so my bet is that he's been recalled already and a new team is in place. So we've got a fresh set of faces to identify. Meanwhile, I'm satisfied you'll be safe at the cottage; there's nothing to connect me with it. I'll be gone for a few days; can't say how many exactly, but when I get back, we're going after Howard Long. See where that takes us."

He stayed one more night, but when I got up the next morning he'd already left. I hadn't heard anything, but there was a note left on the table, '*Stay here. No walkabouts. Smudge.*'

* * *

At the Royal Infirmary, in Leicester, Libby's whole being was encased in a vacuum of pain and drugs. She'd managed to say a few words to Trevor and Ann, but she still slipped in and out of consciousness. In that darkness, she remained mindful of certain things; of me and the new reality of the threats I faced, along with another sort of pain. Trevor thought the tears were born of pain, but Libby was grieving for her best friend. She knew he was dead.

Chapter 15

Smudge arrived in London at eleven o'clock that morning and checked into a small hotel near Hammersmith. He made a few calls, but it was a Sunday and there was little else he could do until the next day. Even so, he'd been reluctant to spend another day at the cottage. At least now, he was in place and operational.

By noon on Monday, he knew exactly where the boat was moored and where Long lived. An old mate who now worked for the Thames River Police contacted someone at the Thames River Authority who was most helpful. The sketchy plan he started out with began to take on form.

The Nelson at Sunbury on Thames was a riverside gastro pub with a faux half-timbered front. At that time of year, the owners relied on weekend trade and Indian summers to fill the expanse of decking that provided for seventy covers and eight temporary moorings. There was still enough weekday business to cover the overheads, but summer times were essential for profit. They also offered limited accommodation, with eight rooms, which at that time of year; were rarely full.

Smudge checked in for a week's stay, so the landlord was more than willing to give him the room asked for, overlooking the river, just a couple of hundred yards downstream from Howard Long's apartment, which lay on the opposite bank. It was one of four, contained in a square flat-roofed block that might have been built in the thirties, though more recently, larger picture windows had been installed, to take advantage of the view and give the building a slightly more contemporary feel.

A fifty foot band of lawn separated the building from the pontoons and a row of extremely expensive boats. 'Wave Crest' was a sleek fifty three foot motor cruiser, with a flying bridge and expansive after deck. He couldn't see the shore side but he knew what the mooring configuration would be and what he would need to do.

Many of the following seventy two hours were going to be spent in that darkened room; glued to a pair of binoculars, looking for patterns, timings, habits and a head count. Even details of the curtains were noted, which were substantial but not entirely proof against seeing shadowy forms moving inside. They would need to stay away from the riverside windows, for sure. Even so, it wasn't enough. There was so much he didn't know. They would never have sanctioned the op when he was active, not with this level of intel.

His primary objective was to gain access to the premises, find whatever information he could and make a safe exit, without Long knowing anyone had been in there. Secrecy was key; because if the alarm was raised now, all their future plans could be compromised.

He telephoned another old friend, Combo, who agreed to meet up at *The Nelson* for lunch the next day. The nickname meant nothing to anyone who hadn't witnessed his skills.

All that remained for Smudge to do before then, was discover the whereabouts of a couple of specialist outlets and where he might find a traditional butcher's shop. Then he'd settle for a couple of pints and a savagely expensive steak and kidney pie with his accomplice.

Combo turned up on time and accepted Smudge's offer of a pint before they went out to sit on the decking. It had been raining earlier on and low, grey clouds still scudded before a fresh wind, past a backdrop of whiter clouds; a thousand or two feet higher. It was perfect; they were the only ones sitting outside and Combo promptly lit a cigarette, as if to justify their choice of seating.

They both sat facing the river, which enabled Smudge to point out the target and agree plans, though when it was time to eat, the prospect of cold chips forced them inside. After lunch, they took a stroll along the road that skirted around the pub before running along the riverside for a quarter of a mile or so; past Long's place, which gave them an opportunity for a closer inspection, while appearing to admire the boats. Some had already been sheeted up for the winter and many would soon be pulled out of the water completely, until spring.

Access to the river on the other side was much more difficult. Private roads provided exclusive access to very expensive homes, with security systems to match. Too many to check out in the time they had and Smudge didn't want to be seen again on that side, yet.

He'd made one excursion down the approach road and had attracted the attention of one home owner. He had put his hands in the air and smiled as he signalled that he'd taken the wrong turn and did a three point turn. Anything less than a BMW 9 series down there would be logged as a threat. If all went to plan, the next time he ventured down there would be under the cover of darkness and he wouldn't be alone.

Combo shook his head, "Man, this one could go bad, too easily. We'll be going in there blind."

Smudge knew that, but tried to sound upbeat, "Yes, I know, but the downside is limited. If the alarm is set, or there's anyone in there we abort. It'll be a case of non-confrontation, I promise."

There was nothing more to discuss. Mutual trust was a given and arrangements were made for Friday night but in the meantime Smudge would be left to complete the preparations.

That evening, he made one more call, to someone in Reading, in which enough was said for Smudge to know he had recruited his final team member. He never doubted it really, but privately acknowledged he'd taken the arranging to the wire. Last minute planning was never ideal. They arranged to meet for an early evening drink the following day, in the knowledge that they would be operational within twenty four hours; a day before he and Combo would.

The following morning, a slightly perplexed landlord gave him directions to a small and exclusive butcher's shop, which apparently catered to the wealthy locals, without fear of competition from the supermarket chains. Since he was still booked in for another five days, which thus far had included all meals, Smudge decided to provide an explanation, "I fancy some home-cooked ham in a roll, for a picnic lunch."

The landlord made a mental note of having one less cover for lunch, but ventured, "You should have said. We could have prepared a picnic lunch for you."

Smudge nodded his appreciation of the offer, "Perhaps tomorrow."

He'd located a dive shop, just fifteen minutes away, at Kingston upon Thames. Like so many others, the owner had a winter season to confront and all business was welcome, but when the mild-mannered guy declined the range of multi-coloured wet suits, he leapt at the chance to dig out one of the plain black ones they'd had in stock since the eighties. The same went for the fins, snorkel and mask, so that he joked, "You'll be up for some cloak and dagger stuff with this rig."

Smudge grinned, "At my age? I don't think so." He gestured at the racks, "And I'm too old for all that designer stuff too." He then pointed at the price tag on the wet suit; twenty years out of date, "This fits my budget far better."

The shopkeeper realised he'd missed the chance for a spot of re-pricing in the stock room and made ready to deflect any request for a discount, which didn't prove to be necessary in the end. In fact, payment was in cash, which meant that the old stock would never be accounted for.

Back in Sunbury, on the way to the butcher's, Smudge passed a small independent baker's which was selling fresh-baked rolls that were topped with strands of crisped cheese. It was enough for him to do as he'd said and have ham rolls for lunch. The bakery was offering a range of fillings but he settled for butter alone, before heading to the butcher, who carved thick fragrant slices of ham off the bone. He also had tubs of the stuff they would need.

With nothing else to do until that evening, he drove into Kempton Park and found a quiet spot to enjoy one of the finest lunches he could remember.

That evening he sat nursing a glass of tonic water while the man from Reading sank a pint of *Guinness*, observing at one point, "It's the single decent thing I remember from over there." They spoke a little about the old days and the frequent transits over the border, but it wasn't in their nature to dwell on those things. Soon, it was time for business.

Smudge passed a menu across and in due course, the envelope inside was slipped into a pocket. In the meantime he described what was required and shortly after, they took a short drive to recce the location. As expected, there was no call for either an offer, or acceptance and as it turned out, the role would be a minor one, with little or no risk, though timing would be critical. His first task would be no more than a taxi service, the following evening.

* * *

Thursday evenings were often the quietest; a lull before the storm of the weekend, which was why he'd chosen it to effect the first stage of the op, with a stunt they had used in the Yemen.

He left the hotel at eight, so that an observer might think he was going out for an evening meal, perhaps with friends. Instead, he drove up to the M4 and ate a little of the ersatz cod and chips at Heston services, followed by a couple of large *Costa* coffees, during the two hours he allowed to slip by. No one, in the anonymous cavern of the dining area paid him any attention; he was just another faceless entity amongst the hundreds of other travellers.

His thoughts would have startled most of them though. They began with his present circumstances and a growing regret at having got involved. It wasn't just pre-op nerves, he'd had a lifetime of junk food, field rations, bivvying in deserts, crapping in bags; the list went on and on until in the end, he had been ejected into civilian life. Until then, his life had been threatened so many times, in so many ways and places and then there were those he had terminated. Now, in his fifties, he wondered what life would have been like if he'd been a financial adviser. Instead, he was fifty two years old, alone and at odds with the society he had joined. There was nothing else in his life; no alternatives.

At eleven, he drifted out to the car park and checked his gear over for the last time, before drifting with the traffic, back to Sunbury on Thames. All doubts and concerns disappeared; he was operational, again.

He'd already chosen the place to park, at the *Wharf Hotel*; a gastro pub similar to *The Nelson,* but three quarters of a mile upstream from the target. This place only had six rooms available but an extremely popular restaurant which kept long hours. The car park was almost full, which was ideal, for the only spaces left were furthest away from the premises. His car would remain lost amongst the many and the noise of water rushing over the weir would cover any sounds he might make, though with such little gear it hardly mattered. Crouched between two cars, he struggled into his wet suit and hood before gathering his gear and moving down the lawned bank to the river's edge. Without pausing, he slipped silently into the water and took deep breaths as the frigid water found its way into the wet suit, where his body would soon turn it into a layer of warmth. While drifting, he donned the flippers, though they were hardly necessary, for the current ensured that he reached *Wave Crest* within ten minutes. She was pointing upstream and he finned in behind her stern to grasp the edge of her swim platform, where he waited and watched. No one could see him in the shadow of the platform, but he needed time enough to be certain that the whole area was clear. To the north, a large island screened him from the far bank, not that he expected problems from that side; the highest risks at that time of night were private security services and dog walkers.

He could hear the traffic on the other side of the river, but after fifteen minutes all had remained quiet around him. There had been no more than gentle gurgles of eddies, caused by the hull. In that time he had eased into the bank and checked the mooring lines. They were as he'd expected; a bow and stern line with two more ropes, known as springs, criss-crossed alongside. He judged them to be twenty five millimetres, which would be fine. Much less and there wouldn't have been enough of a margin.

Still keeping in shadow, he allowed himself to be taken down to the end of the pontoons where he removed the fins and placed them on the bank before crawling out of the water. The diversion had been necessary, because a climb onto the pontoon might have left enough muddy traces for someone to notice, the next day. After carefully rinsing himself off, he moved slowly for'ard, past four other boats before reaching *Wave Crest's* stern line. There, he reached into the net bag he'd strapped to his waist for one of the butcher's tubs. The click of the plastic lid breaking the seal sounded horribly loud, though he knew it couldn't be heard beyond a few feet and now that he was out of the water, it was not the time or place to dither. He crouched down to each of the lines, using two fingers to apply the beef dripping to an inch or so of the ropes, a few inches away from the bollards and he was back in the water within ten minutes of leaving it. Hidden now, by the end boat, he pulled the hood up over his head and put the fins on while he waited for signs of activity.

Satisfied, he pushed out into the current, using the snorkel this time, so that only black rubber could be seen on the surface. He also needed to fin harder than last time, making sure they didn't break the surface and pointing upstream, at one o'clock to the current, to achieve a 'ferry glide'. In effect, the current was pushing him across as well as down the river. After five minutes he paused to take a quick 'visual' to find that he'd been swept further downstream than he'd thought; past *The Nelson* and he began to fin much harder. His destination, *Rivermead Island* was already coming up and he couldn't afford to miss it. Not only would he have missed the rendezvous, but from then on he'd be amongst houses and traffic.

Rivermead Island was a low, grassy, uninhabited island which was owned by the local authority and designated as a leisure area, which at that time of day and year; would be empty. The only access from the mainland was by a narrow track that passed through a ford.

Another check served to force the pace even further, as the lights from the next island threatened to compromise him. Several times, his fins did break the surface as his kicking became desperate, but he couldn't afford to do less. The fight against the current caused water to burble past his ears and his breathing became louder as a pair of middle aged lungs demanded more air.

Worse, he had no contingency plans. With only one accomplice, none were available. To miss the island could spell disaster, for it would mean exiting the river in a well lit and extremely busy part of the city.

In fact, it was the eddy caused by the very end of the island that finally drew Smudge in and allowed him to land. Five yards further out and he'd have been swept past. Exhausted, he pulled himself on to the muddy bank and collapsed. Minutes slipped by; too many, he knew and his legs trembled when he fought to remove the fins. The effort left him reeling, but he struggled forward on hands and knees, before reaching grass and with an effort of will made it to his feet. He rocked slightly but knew the worst was over, just as he realised new limitations, with a whisper to himself, "I'm getting too fucking old for this sort of caper."

Ten minutes later, he caught a glimpse of reflected light from a parked car, just as a figure appeared at his side and whispered, "All done?"

The man from Reading glimpsed a sight of teeth, contained in a tired grin as Smudge said, "You could say that."

Dry clothes were waiting for him and the filthy wetsuit was dumped in the boot. It was unlikely to be needed again, but he knew it would be clean and dry by the morning, just in case.

Smudge spent most of Friday in his room, 'scoping Long's place out, but that evening he left to collect Combo from Sunbury station. Both were dressed in dark clothing, with soft soled shoes. They also carried black woollen hats that could be pulled down over their faces, to provide cover against CCTV cameras, though Smudge hoped they wouldn't be necessary.

Combo threw a small holdall onto the back seat and clambered in, without a word. The time for questions was over. Now, they needed to focus and deal with shit if it happened. A job like this would have normally been done in the small hours, preferably when the owner was away, but for this plan to work; there had to be people about. During his abortive visit earlier in the week,

Smudge had found a place to leave the car; on a building site, three quarters of a mile to the south of Long's apartment. It prompted another note of concern from Combo. That was a long way back if they were compromised. Normally, there would have been personnel ready to effect a rapid extraction, but they were on their Jack Jones.

The builders had reached the first floor of what promised to be a very large house, fronted by an area that resembled the Somme, but a band of firm ground lay at the side, behind pallets of bricks and con blocks. After slipping rubber overshoes on it took both of them to heave the section of security fencing to one side, but the car was tucked out of sight within a couple of minutes. Only a pedestrian would have noticed it and they were few and far between in that neck of the woods. Ample time had been allowed for getting into position, which meant that a silent wait was necessary, but eventually they got out of the car and waited for a few minutes longer, to ensure that they were alone. Satisfied, Smudge led the way back onto the road. From there on, it was a matter of keeping to shadows and avoiding the occasional camera that guarded a gate.

At last, Combo hunkered down behind a rhododendron bush, fifty yards from the building, while Smudge crept down to the pontoon to check the lines. He was startled to see that one of the springs had already parted, hanging down the side of the boat in a limp surrender. The other three were in perfect disorder though. The rats had halved the thickness of the ropes, leaving a core of around twelve millimetres. He double checked his watch, to make sure they were within the time slot he'd given to the man from Reading. Combo's role would only become time sensitive when things began to kick off.

Smudge removed a multi-tooled knife from his pocket, which was attached to his belt by a lanyard. Anyone who'd been on an op knew that the chance of dropping the thing into the water became a certainty, without such a safeguard. He selected the coarse wood saw blade and rubbed it from side to side, within the rat's dining area, leaving an authentic enough continuation of the fraying they had already caused. The second spring and the bow line soon fell away and *Wave Crest* began to drift back immediately, to collide with the bow of the boat next door. She seemed to settle there, but it was just a matter of time. He had left the stern line untouched, because they needed Long to be able to get on board and sort things out for himself. If she broke free completely he would have to go back indoors and call one of the rescue services.

Meanwhile, the man from Reading had seen enough. He ran in from the decked area and spoke to the landlord who went out onto the decking in time to see *Wave Crest's* bow moving out from the bank, as if pushed by an invisible hand. There were no lights on the vessel and no sign of anyone on board. "That's Howard's boat, I'm sure of it!" They both continued to watch, in case she was actually under control, but then she seemed to straighten up as her stern twisted on the bow of the neighbouring boat and they both heard the crack of breaking glass fibre, even from that distance. The landlord ran inside to call Howard and the man from Reading wandered up the road until he was opposite the target. The necessary number was already keyed into his phone ready to connect with the one on the other side of the river, in Smudge's pocket; set to vibrate only.

Long ran to the lounge window and threw the curtains aside, while holding on to a vaporous hope that someone was pulling a practical joke on him, but the second 'crack' told him otherwise. His beloved *Wave Crest* was impaled on the bow of Mike Startin's boat and held by just one line, which was bar tight. He turned and ran for the door.

Tom from the ground floor apartment was starting to climb the stairs, "You heard it too?"

Instead of acknowledging the man, Long cried, "Shit," to himself; he'd forgotten the keys to his boat. While turning to run back up the stairs, he shouted at his neighbour, "Go and telephone Mike can you please Tom, tell him we've got an emergency."

Each ran in opposite directions, and by the time Long got to the pontoon, a small group of neighbours had gathered on the bank. Two were trying to influence the sixteen ton vessel by pulling on the stern rope and he yelled, "Stand clear of that! If it parts it'll take a leg off." Both men leapt back as though the line had delivered an electric shock.

The swim platform had been forced beneath the water, allowing the bow of the Startin's boat to penetrate the stern cabin, to the right of her centreline, which had temporarily stabilised things, but not for long. With a crackling of fibreglass and screech of tortured metal the wound in *Wave Crest's* stern opened up and allowed the current to bring her all the way around to face downstream and slam into the side of Startin's boat; buckling the chrome safety rails on both. Neither owner had fitted fenders to the outer sides of their boats, so the sounds of destruction continued.

The Startin's boat had been sheeted up for the winter, but Long managed to heave himself over the gunwale and onto the foredeck. He was halfway across when the humming line parted with a crack, followed by the 'whizz' made by the flying rope, as it disappeared out onto the river.

By the time he reached the starboard side, there was already a two foot gap separating the boats, but in pushing the stern out, the current caused the boat to pivot and the bows looked set to enter the gap between the Startin's boat and the next one. He knew that would last only a few seconds and dashed along the gunwale until only a foot separated them. He leapt on board and made a dash for *Wave Crest's* stern. The flying bridge had been sheeted up for winter but the main deck was still open, with a door that provided access to the saloon and wheelhouse. The impact with the next boat was more of a glancing blow but it was enough to knock him off balance, adding vital seconds to his task. By the time he unlocked the door, she was well clear of the bank and picking up speed. Within minutes, she would be matching the five knot current, but he knew his boat well and once inside, he slipped into the seat at the helm and switched the masters on. Moments later, both three hundred horse power Volvo Penta's roared into life and he pushed forward on the stick, but only for a moment.

He engaged neutral and threw himself from the seat with an anguished cry. Almost the whole lengths of the lines were still attached to her and therefore virtually certain to wrap themselves around one or both props if he attempted to move her under power. His chest was beginning to ache with the effort and stress, as he hauled the stern line and two springs in. They had already been swept under the boat, confirming his fears, but remained clear of the props and were soon on board in sodden heaps. He was wheezing with the effort and a glance downstream augured badly. The bow line would have to wait, he'd run out of time.

Sunbury Court Island, on the northern side swept by, leaving scant minutes before the next bend in the river, where he would be driven up against Grand Junction Isle.

He made it, but with only yards to spare. Both engines roared at full astern, he manoeuvred her back into midstream, before bringing the bow around to point upstream and allowing time for him to take stock. The passage back to his mooring would be difficult, but without ropes, tying to would be impossible. She was feeling heavy too, though he had no way of knowing that moving against the current at full astern had shipped water into the aft cabin.

It took two attempts to recover the bow line, due to the speed of the current, but eventually, he had control.

The Startin's had been at the foggy end of a dinner party and none of the twelve participants were capable of maintaining straight lines, let alone managing a crisis. Their house was one of the ones Smudge and Combo had passed earlier and when the raucous group passed by, no one noticed the two figures slip out from behind the bush and into the building. Someone had even propped the main entrance door open, in case the emergency called for outside help and a telephone was needed. It was an incredible stroke of luck.

They heard shouts of encouragement and cries of concern, when the stern line parted but were at Long's door by then, where Combo withdrew a small box from a pocket; similar in size to a spectacle case and set about the lock with the selected pick. As they'd hoped, Long hadn't stayed to engage the deadlock and the door was soon opened, to confirm that he hadn't set the alarm either.

They were both wearing surgical gloves and once inside, with the door closed, they listened for movement, after which, a quick search established that they were alone. Combo went off with his holdall; to search for a safe, while Smudge went to find a desk. He could see the kitchen from where he was and started at the opposite end of the hall where there were two bedrooms. The guest bedroom had an empty chest of drawers and a wardrobe that served as an overflow for suits and coats, while bedding had been stuffed into the top shelf, with nothing hidden beneath or behind. The bedside tables were also empty.

Long's bedroom was a little more interesting, in that the CD's in the bedside table evidenced a taste for the deviant and his toys, a predilection for self-penetration. He ignored the bathroom, knowing that time was running out and he had to find that desk, but suddenly Combo's head appeared out of the doorway beyond the lounge, as he signalled for Smudge to join him.

It was the dining room, with a table, eight chairs and a low credenza, but Combo had removed a picture from the wall above it, to reveal a wall safe. He wore an 'I don't believe it' expression and gave a thumb up sign.

Smudge tapped his watch and drew a question mark in the air, with a forefinger.

Combo grinned and held four fingers up.

Smudge left him to it and moved to the door on the opposite side of the hall; it was the only room left and had to be the study.

It was larger than he expected. Perhaps twenty feet square, yet the mahogany desk dominated the room, largely because it had been placed in the centre, facing towards the window. A quick mental check confirmed that there would be a view across the river.

One drawer held nothing but boating magazines and brochures and another contained computer paraphernalia, such as a couple of mice and various program files. The top one on that side contained a telephone book and a file full of business cards; most of which were those of artisans. The cache of photographs at the back was thoroughly pornographic, featuring a succession of beautiful young women in graphically clear sexual acts. The pictures must have been taken by a third party since Long was in most of them too.

The large drawer on the right was filled with files covering the usual range of household subjects, such as utilities, insurance, cars and the local authority. The one for his bank contained statements which indicated an average balance of around eight thousand, so there had to be others somewhere.

Lastly, the middle drawer was the only one with a lock, but Long's panicked departure hadn't included taking the key. Smudge removed a tiny digital camera from a pocket and began to photograph everything he found in there. There was no time to study the documents or articles; they could be viewed in detail, back at the cottage. With that task completed, he looked at the computer which was still switched on and knew that would be where the real intelligence was. He'd bought a memory stick earlier in the week, but Combo had cautioned against copying anything. Too many programs held records of such activities. It was bloody unfortunate, but not worth the risk.

He was making his way out of the room when a picture caught his eye and after capturing the image on camera he whispered to himself, "Now that's one for the family album."

Combo had emptied the contents of the safe and arranged them in four neat piles. He watched closely as Smudge opened and photographed each item, for they both knew that everything had to be returned to the safe in perfect order. It took over ten minutes to copy everything, during which time Smudge focused on just the photography, but he couldn't help noticing enough to cause a rising sense of excitement. Names, dates, documents and records provided glimpses of a very secret life.

Twenty three minutes after entering the flat, they eased out on to the landing and listened. Smudge had changed into a beige windcheater and Combo wore a pale blue golfing cardigan. Finally, there were just thirteen steps and ten paces to go, before they would be in the clear and able to lose themselves in the crowd.

∗ ∗ ∗

Long was abeam of the pontoons but unable to make himself heard from within the wheelhouse and above the engine noise, so that eventually, he was forced to move upstream a short way and allow her to drift past the crowd, as he left the wheel and called from the open stern.

He was unwilling to use his own ropes until they knew what had caused them to fail, so he called across for fresh ropes. A number of people set off back to their houses for boat keys, because, while most people had *some* spare line, a combined effort would be necessary to replace a full set.

Long took up station midstream and held his position with a mix of main engines and bow thrusters. He'd realised by then, that she had shipped water; probably a lot and knew to keep her headed upstream, hoping that the pumps were making headway.

Tom decided to run back inside for a jacket and was rubbing his arms for warmth when he almost collided with two men walking away from the main door. He gave them a puzzled look and was about to ask who they were when Smudge said, "Hope you don't mind, but we've been sheltering in your doorway. Still, off home now, I think most of the excitement's over."

Tom didn't get a chance to reply, before both men walked away. He did notice the holdall though and hurried indoors to check his apartment. There was no sign of trespass, but he made sure to set the alarm when he came out five minutes later, with a jacket on.

Another hour passed before Long returned to his apartment and it had been a difficult one at several levels. After pumping her out, *Wave Crest* was riding high enough for the damage to be clear of the water, but by then Mike Startin was sober enough to be difficult. They had checked what was left of the lines, leaving Long to rant about 'fucking rats', but Startin's response was meant to be taken in more than one way, "Yes, well, we'll all have to check our lines often enough."

Tom was waiting for him and explained about the two men who had been loitering in the entrance, "I didn't recognise them, though no-one's been in my place, but check yours thoroughly, won't you?" Long was utterly exhausted, "They were probably two of the Startin's guests, but thanks Tom, I'll check the place out." By the time he reached the top of the stairs, the casual dismissal had turned into niggling concern. Surely, it hadn't been a set up.

He hurried inside and began with the dining room. The safe contents were exactly as they always were. Already feeling easier he went into the lounge, reasoning that if they were opportunist thieves, his television would have gone. It was still in place along with the sound system and the microwave cooker remained in the kitchen. Five minutes later, he sank down onto the sofa, with a large scotch and considered the prospect of a huge repair bill. He would also be asking the boatyard for details of the dope they used on the ropes.

An unusually large mouthful of whisky snatched at his breath as he growled, "Fucking rats!"

* * *

Smudge waited until they were three miles away before making a call. On the other side of the river, the man from Reading removed the SIM card from his phone and flicked it into the Thames, before heading home to tell the wife about the week they were about to enjoy in Tenerife.

With that call out of the way Combo observed, "You always did have the luck of the Irish, Foley."

Smudge feigned indignance, "How so?"

"Well, for a start, everything went to plan and we both know that ops don't, usually. Shit happens somewhere along the line. But then, I discover that whilst the alarm system would have been a problem, if armed, the safe was old enough to be the original, from when the place was built. That made things very simple. Like I say, you're a lucky bastard."

Smudge shrugged, "We'll see."

Payment had already been made and little more was said on the journey to Hammersmith tube station, where Combo could get a direct transit to Wood Green on the opposite side of the city. After climbing out of the car Combo leaned back in, "Stay safe mate." Smudge smiled slightly and nodded.

* * *

By the end of the third day I made an oath I haven't broken, to this day. I swore I would never look at a *Sudoku* puzzle again. I'd also finished the two books bought in Hereford and had moved on to the mouldy stock, almost despairing when, after reading a quarter of one, I realised I had read it before. I kept thinking of Steph, as well, and prayed for her safety.

I'd wondered why so many of the contestants in 'Big Brother'; the fly on the wall programme that shut a group of people up in a communal living area; spent so much time in bed but I came to realise that dozing was an effective way of passing the time. In fact, the best way, when there is little else to do. I even practised re-loading the *Glock,* to a point where I might have survived a shoot out, though I doubted it. Some target practice would have been more appropriate. By the fifth day, I had even succumbed to the last tin of Smudge's chopped ham and pork.

Yet the sound of a car coming up the track on the afternoon of sixth day did not cheer me. In fact, it scared the living daylights out of me and I hid in my bedroom, with my gun at the ready. Smudge must have expected as much, since he opened the door very slightly before calling, "It's OK, only me."

He'd bought more provisions, which we packed away and a new laptop, but over coffee, I listened with growing amazement to a summary of what he'd been up to over the last week. He then booted up the laptop and inserted the card from his camera. Rather than use the slideshow facility that would have shown the images in the order taken, he dotted around, beginning with copies of a few pornographic pictures he'd taken out of mischief, before moving on to the contents of the middle desk drawer. A pen and accessory holder took up a third of the drawer and the remainder was filled with miscellaneous documents. None appeared to be particularly important, though Smudge pointed out that the safe would have been used for that sort of stuff. It was too. There were two Building Society passbooks showing balances of seventy and sixty thousand pounds and then we came across an image of some correspondence from a Russian utility company, addressed to Long and with an extremely poor, handwritten translation attached. Smudge observed, "I could have done better than that!"

Soon after, we came across a few photographs of a timber lodge, burdened by a biblical amount of snow. Smudge explained, "That is a Russian *Dacha* and judging by the correspondence, he owns it.

I ventured, "Or was given it."

We moved on to the safe contents, which included four passports; two British and two Russian, all with his photograph, though only one of the British ones bore his correct name.

There were deeds to two properties in the Docklands area, which we guessed were rental properties and then things became really interesting. There were two plastic clip files containing correspondence from two Cyprus banks. The balances totalled over thirty million US dollars, but one of the files began with a letter from an address in Rothenburg, which read;

Dear Howard,

I have enclosed details of the account we have opened for you, with a note of the opening balance.

You must now visit them and establish a unique code.

It was attached to a statement showing an opening credit of four million pounds, but what was equally startling was the signature. The letter had been written by Otto Rilke

Smudge pointed at another two pictures, "Look at these." Incredibly, Long had noted the password codes on the inside cover of both files.

Finally, Smudge backtracked through the images and pulled up a copy of the picture he'd seen on the wall; of three men standing on a frozen lake, around a fishing hole. They were dressed in furs and holding up glasses of what could only have been vodka. All were laughing as they toasted each other. Howard Long and Pavel Ankudinov we knew by now, but once again we had no difficulty in recognising the third man. After all, he was the president of the Russian Federation.

Smudge went to his bedroom and emerged in a T shirt, shorts and trainers, "I'm going for a run."

On reflection, I must have sounded like a petulant housewife, "Oh, hello, welcome back; goodbye. Was it something I said?"

He shrugged, "I need to plan and I do a better job of that on my own."

I sat alone, feeling hard done by, until the realisation of all he'd done for me came through like a slap in the face. With a mix of shame and embarrassment, I had a closer look at the provisions he'd brought and set about preparing the evening meal.

That night, we had sausages, roast potatoes and cauliflower cheese, preceded by a couple of beers and washed down with a fairly decent *Bordeaux*. Afterwards, I ventured to ask, "We know that Long, Ankudinov and Putin are connected. Long has some dodgy money tucked away in a Cypriot bank account, which Otto Rilke facilitated. There are all the other links too, but where does that put us? Where do we go from here?"

Smudge remained silent for a few moments as if he was marshalling thoughts, "I've been thinking the same. You and me, against the Russian Federation doesn't stack up."

"My thoughts, exactly."

He continued as if I hadn't spoken, "So what we have to do is acquire enough intel and then trade. Your silence, in exchange for survival. Obviously, copies of the intel will need to be kept and well hidden, to make sure that our survival continues, but it can be done."

I asked, "Any plans in place, after your run?"

"Some, but they still need the rough edges smoothing out. There are some people I need to speak to tomorrow and then I'll have something I can share with you."

I couldn't stop myself from asking, "How long will you be gone?"

"Most of the day probably, but I'll be back for dinner."

That was something at least and I could use a chunk of the afternoon up by preparing the meal. It was only later, after I had gone to bed that I recalled him saying, 'people I need to speak to', rather than 'make some calls' and even I knew that his old unit was stationed nearby. It wouldn't have mattered if I'd thought to enquire though; he wouldn't have told me anyway. Even so, I would have liked to go into town, if only to telephone Steph.

The following night, we had heavily seasoned chicken breasts, wrapped in streaky bacon, with jacket potatoes and green beans; the last of the fresh vegetables Smudge had brought in. Another bottle of *Bordeaux* was despatched and fruit yoghurts served as a dessert. A *Mars* bar each, accompanied coffee, along with a couple of whiskies. Emboldened by alcohol, I reminded him, "So, you said you were going to share your plans tonight."

I wasn't surprised by the single word response, "Tomorrow."

* * *

The shower being used woke me the next morning. It was only eight thirty and from the state of his trainers, left at the back door, I could tell that he'd been for a run, in spite of the rain. I peered outside to confirm that it was still coming down and saw clouds of fine rain, blurring the view. It was the sort of rainfall that didn't seem so bad, but soaked you within seconds.

Smudge appeared and was keen to get started, packing me off to shower and dress while he made the coffees. By now, he knew that only he would be eating porridge. I refused to eat sloppy catarrh.

He began as soon as I sat down.

"From now on, we'll be poking the hornet's nest, but at least we have an accountant to go after. It's in their nature to keep records, even if they are bent and he clearly is. So our next port of call is Rothenburg. You don't need to know everything now, but you'll be playing a much more active role from now on."

The solitude of that cottage suddenly seemed attractive.

"We'll travel separately, from places far from here; I don't want this place compromised. We may well need it again."

Instead of allowing me to make notes he made me repeat it back to him, though it didn't seem very demanding. The first leg was worriesome though, particularly since it was taking me so close to home, but Smudge convinced me that I would remain untraceable. As an added protection, I was going to be making reservations for journey legs I wouldn't be using and besides, we would be paying cash for everything. The likelihood of our details being picked up was extremely remote and no one would make a move on me without knowing where he was. I knew nothing about his itinerary, beyond an assurance that we would meet up on the other side, but he explained that the easiest way to get me to where I needed to be *and* fit in with our deception plan was to catch the Stansted train from Birmingham; as if to catch the flight I would have a ticket for; to Oslo. Even if they did discover those plans, the destination would suggest that we were interested in the two Swedish engineering companies. I asked where I *would* be travelling to from Stansted and he promised to tell me in good time.

Of course, I took an educated guess, and was wrong.

An hour later, we drove into Hereford and bought my train ticket from the rail station, where the clerk tried to persuade me to take the much quicker option that required two changes. He even listed the stops made by the direct train, adding that the route was so circuitous; it would take me to within eighteen miles of the Wash. I did as instructed and insisted on the direct train and then I headed to a travel agent who sold me a ticket for an early evening SAS flight from Stansted to Oslo. There were no early bird discounts though, for anyone travelling within forty eight hours.

We chose a different cafe for lunch, where I pressed Smudge for more of his plan, but was told to wait. Obviously, I was flying somewhere, but then I thought of the regular shuttle services to the other London airports and realised that I could be flying from any one of four. Whatever his plans were, they had to continue on from Stansted anyway and there were only forty hours left to share them.

The more I thought about the plan I had to hand, the happier I became, even though I'd be passing through Leicester. No-one, outside of the Swedish airline could possibly know my travel plans and that was when another idea sprang to mind.

Smudge showed no surprise when I left him to telephone Steph. It was two o'clock and with luck, she would still be at work. Bill answered the telephone and as soon as I spoke, he broke off and called "Steph, it's your amoureux, my dear."

She sounded breathless, "Ian?"

I was wearing a silly grin, "Hello Steph, how are you?"

She countered immediately, "More importantly, how are you?"

I knew she wouldn't have time to gossip and that I needed to be upbeat, "Great thanks. Still safe and sound, but look, Steph, I'm going away for a short while, until things are sorted out and they will be, I promise, but we just need time."

I heard her cup the mouthpiece with her hand, "Ian, I've been thinking about things too. You *have* to go to the police. If you don't, I will!"

"No!" I glanced around, looking for anyone who had paid attention to my shout before I hissed urgently into the mouthpiece, "Do that and I'm a dead man." As I said the words I wondered if I'd gone too far for her. I waited.

"Ian, I'm so frightened."

"Don't be, I'm being perfectly well looked after *and* I have some good news. I'll be on the direct Birmingham to Stansted train on Wednesday. It leaves Birmingham at ten eighteen so you'll need to check when it stops at Leicester. If you buy a return ticket to Stansted, we'll have a chance to meet up."

"Oh God, Ian, that would be wonderful, wait a minute, let me get a pad." She noted down the details and then asked, "It will be safe though, will it?"

"Yes love, but don't mention it to anyone, OK?"

"I won't. Shit, I'm sorry love, I have to go, we're still busy, but I'll be on it, I promise. Love you loads."

I walked back to the cafe, on air, but later, I gave more thought to what I'd said, about being a dead man. I regretted saying so much, but I couldn't afford to have her call the police. From the moment they became involved, 'apeman' and his friends would know exactly where to find me.

The following morning, Smudge disappeared again, 'for an appointment' apparently.

* * *

He'd known the CO as a Captain, when they were both active. Smudge at the end of his career while the other was just beginning, at least with The Regiment. His welcome was genuine and he was taken to the officer's mess for coffee, but they both knew that a request was about to be made, which could be 'difficult'. But, it was secure too and Smudge detailed all he knew. Whilst civilian money-making schemes didn't count for much, the links with a Russian Oligarch, a *Spetznaz* unit and President Putin was enough for the CO to attend to things. In the meantime, Smudge was handed over to a Sergeant for company, while contact was made with someone in Military Intelligence, who referred it to someone else, who did likewise, which is why most of those in the chain were startled by the prompt clearance to quarantine Smudge's record. Authority for that sort of thing was rarely given for non-serving personnel, but someone at the right level realised that with the Russians involved, this represented a passive opportunity to flush out a leak. Not that they expected one, but the exercise didn't call for resources anyway, so they had nothing to lose.

Whilst the file was sidelined, they would wait and see if anyone ran a search for it.

* * *

That afternoon, after lunch, I told Smudge that I'd start packing. We were leaving at six thirty the following morning, to allow ample time for the drive to Birmingham, New Street Station.

He shook his head, "No need, I've got that covered. In fact, this is as good a time as any to tell you the rest of the travel plans. I sat down as he continued, "You're to get off the train at Cambridge, not Stansted."

My concern showed, but he ploughed on, "Now this is overkill, I'm sure, but just before the train gets into Cambridge, I want you to go to the toilet, but don't engage the lock. Just before the train leaves a station there is always rapid beeping which tells you the door is closing and from the first one, you have about three seconds to get out of the bog and through the door. There are so many stops you'll get the idea. Don't hang about. Go out to the taxi rank and have one take you to the 'Extra' services on the A14; they're about twelve miles away. Have him drop you at the main building and wait until he's gone, then walk over to the lorry park and look for 'Graves International Haulage'; the driver will be expecting you. After that, just do as he says."

I repeated the name, "Graves International Haulage," and then he seemed to read my thoughts, "Don't worry if you fuck up, just get off at the next station, which is Audley End and catch a taxi from there, but don't bother trying the toilet trick again, just get off normally. Like I say, it's overkill, but I'm just being careful."

I couldn't let it go at that, "But you think there's a possibility of trouble though?"

"No, I'm just being careful. Anyway, if they've clocked our travel arrangements, they're more likely to have someone waiting for you at the airport. Just remember, the first beep means the door is moving. Oh, and have a good scrub down tomorrow morning, it could be a couple of days before you get change of clothes."

I went to bed early that night and reviewed my own plans.

* * *

The trip to Birmingham went off without incident and in spite of rush hour 'clots' near Worcester and Redditch, I was dropped off on the forecourt of New Street Station thirty minutes before the train was due to leave.

On board, I found four vacant seats, with a table, halfway along the carriage, that hadn't been reserved and settled into an aisle seat after dumping my rucksack onto the one opposite. If the train was full, I would need to put it in the luggage rack at the end of the carriage, but Smudge had told me to make it as visible as possible. I was going to be leaving it on the train, with its load of three cush-ions and a dozen mouldy books.

I'd decided that Steph mustn't be on the train when I attempted my exit, which meant having her get off earlier, at Ely. Her return to Leicester would still be straightforward.

* * *

Steph dressed as though she was going on a date that was set to end up in bed, which is to say that she wore the sexiest underwear she owned, including stockings and suspenders. Sex in an open train carriage might not be an option, but if there was half a chance, she intended to allow her lover to feel the softness of her 'giggle gap'; the sensual band of flesh that lay beyond the top of the stocking.

She regretted not seeing Libby, now out of the ICU and receiving visitors. Trevor had arranged to take her in that very afternoon, but she had called him during the morning to cry off, "I'm so sorry Trevor, but something's cropped up. I have to go to the station and meet a friend." She asked him to pass on her best wishes, with a promise to visit the next day.

* * *

She looked beautiful, anxious and vulnerable as she entered the carriage and searched the seats for me. I had seen her as the train pulled in, but she didn't see me, because, on the approach to Leicester I'd moved the rucksack into the window seat in case there was someone else I knew, waiting on the platform.

I was as excited as a sixteen year old on his first date, once again; desperate to be close to her but not knowing what to say. I guessed she must have boarded the train a couple of carriages down, because we were several miles out before she reached mine. I stood up and gave a small wave, noting with some relief that our carriage was only a quarter full and most of the travellers, no doubt bound for their own flights, were seated at the ends, where they could keep an eye on their luggage. Just one man sat close by, in a seat on the opposite side of the aisle.

I threw the sack over the table into the opposite seat and shuffled over to the window as she joined me, when I leaned across and kissed her. Small things matter to lovers and I still remember feeling her arm reach around my neck to embrace me. When we parted, she brushed away tears, "Bugger, I knew I shouldn't have put mascara on."

I grinned, "No worries, I love pandas."

She dug me in the ribs and then dropped her head onto my shoulder, "It's so good to see you."

I couldn't tell her where I had been or what had been happening, so I found myself inventing a house near Bromsgrove, overlooked by the Lickey Hills. Beyond that, it was a matter of reassurance, for all of us I realised, when she told me that Libby was out of intensive care. I explained and she understood; the need to keep my next destination secret. What I didn't add, was that it remained a secret for me too, beyond the services at Cambridge.

The man opposite got off at Melton Mowbray and Steph waited until she was sure the seats around us would remain empty before she leaned over and kissed me. This time her lips seemed swollen and her tongue slipped between my lips, but then she broke away and took my hand; kissing it tenderly before taking it beneath the table to rest on her leg, just above the knee and under the hem of her skirt. Any doubts I had were swept away when she reached across and gently caressed the crotch of my trousers. My erection became uncomfortably complete as I ventured upward with my own caress and felt the soft skin of her thigh.

From then on, we gazed out of the window like two perfectly respectable passengers watching the countryside go by, as she unzipped me and teased my aching member through the thin cotton of my underpants. My arm was at full stretch as I reciprocated, feeling her warm moisture soak her panties.

The train stopped at Oakham, then Stamford and still we were left alone, but I was racing towards a climax and made to move her hand. She resisted and whispered, "Shush," as she removed a tissue from her handbag with the other hand, while struggling with my underpants. I eased up in my seat and undid the waist of my trousers, allowing her to reach inside and grasp me. Moments later, my grip on her thigh signalled the imminence of my climax and she quickly reached across to gather it all in the tissue. It was one of the most erotic experiences of my life.

After we had re-arranged our clothing, she gave me a cheeky 'ho ho ho' sort of grin and we kissed again. I whispered, "My mum always warned me about women like you."

She whispered back, "Good job you ignored her then."

Our timing proved to be perfect, because a load of people got on at the next stop, Peterborough. It was time for me to change her plans with more fiction, "Steph, there's someone I have to meet at Stansted, who may be getting on at Cambridge and he won't be expecting to see you. I'm sorry love, but it would be best if you got off at Ely."

She was disappointed, even suggesting that we sat apart at Cambridge, until we were certain whether or not he'd got on board, but I wouldn't have it. In the end, I think the joy of meeting up prevailed. Two stops on, as the train slowed, she leant across and kissed me again, before whispering, "Take care of yourself my love." With that, she moved to the end of the carriage as we entered Ely station. A handful of passengers were waiting to get on, but it looked as though Steph was the only one to alight, blowing me a quick kiss as she made for the exit.

But moments later, another man appeared, obviously from a carriage further down. I didn't give it much thought until he reached my window and looked at me. My breathing shallowed to almost nothing. As the train began to move I desperately tried to deny my fears, explaining it away as a coincidence, but I also remembered Smudge talking to me about surveillance and one of his mantras had been, "There's no such thing as a coincidence."

My heart ached, literally, at the thought of putting Steph into danger, but I had my next move to consider too. We would be at Cambridge within fifteen minutes and I hadn't been paying attention to the closing door warnings.

Everything was being forced into closer focus, because I realised that *if* the man following Steph had been one of them, there had to be at least one other still on the train, watching their main target.

I rested my arm on the table, so that my watch stayed in sight and when I thought we were around four minutes shy of Cambridge, I got up from my seat and asked the man seated on the other side of the aisle if he would keep an eye on the rucksack for me. I had to force myself from looking at the other passengers as I made my way to the toilet and once inside, I rested my head against the door, taking deep breaths and feeling sweat trickling down my neck. A wave of nausea swept over me as the brakes were applied and in no time, it seemed, we were stationary.

When I had a chance to think about things, I realised that it was the whistle that did it. At the time, behind the toilet door, I had no idea that the platform attendant was standing beside my exit, but the piercing squeal startled me into action. I was opening the door before realising it wasn't the signal I should be waiting for and was about to close it when the beeping started. The whistle had given me a second's start, without which I'd have never made it. Every instinct told me to behave in the usual way and back off, except for fear that is.

I went through the closing gap in a sidelong leap and was airborne when the edge of the door struck my trailing foot. As I snatched my leg away, the impact with the closing door rolled me over, so that I landed on my back, at the feet of the attendant. He looked down at me as I struggled to find breath, "What the hell was that? What do you think you were doing?"

As I rolled onto my knees, the train started to move and I caught a glimpse of someone running through the carriage towards the door. I wasn't capable of much original thought then, I just knew that I had to find a taxi and struggled to my feet. The attendant shuffled around so that we were facing each other, "Did you hear me? That was a stupid thing to do."

I tried to smile but it was more of a grimace, "Sorry, I was in the toilet and didn't realise this was my stop."

The man was nodding knowingly, as though he'd seen it all before, then rolled his eyes and shook his head as he walked away, "Gawd's teeth!"

The taxi driver was a chatty sort and once the usual topics of weather, traffic and immigrants had been dealt with he said he'd never taken anyone to the motorway services before. I was testing my bruised ankle for signs of anything more serious and mumbled something about meeting friends for a few days on the east coast. Thus enabled, the driver sought to establish a dialogue, "Blimey, at this time of year?"

I said, "Fishing." Which seemed to satisfy him and provide an opportunity to spend ten minutes telling me about his fishing exploits. My lack of responses finally silenced him, as we passed a sign for the American war cemetery and a few minutes later we pulled into the services. I walked into the main building and pretended to look for my friends, until I saw the taxi exit the car park.

It was a thirty eight ton artic'; with a new, bright red tractor unit. The man at the wheel watched me limp across the lorry park and lowered his window on my approach. I asked, "Are you expecting me."

He was an archetypal lorry driver, thick set, balding, tattooed and looking as though he'd been born behind the wheel, "Depends on whether your name is Ian or not."

I smiled with relief, "It is."

He pointed to the other side of the unit, "Best get in then, we've got a ferry to catch."

We moved off immediately, though he dealt with the basics while negotiating his way out of the services, on to the A14, "My name is Steve. I know yours and all I need to know about your reasons for being here, which is not a lot. For the record, you are my number two; though I don't normally have one on this trip, so if anyone has any questions, let me provide the answers."

I nodded, "Right, thanks."

He kept his eyes on the road and handled the huge rig with consummate ease. Within a few minutes, we left the A14, to head south on the M11, which was when my telephone chirped to tell me I had a text. It read;

U n*ot followed. All gud*

There had only ever been one caller to that telephone, so I recognised the number. Smudge had been tailing me, but for how long? Had he seen the men on the train? Had he seen Steph?

After we had settled into place on the motorway, Steve told me more, "Next stop is Dover and then we'll have a decent meal on the ferry. *Sea France* normally has decent grub. One thing, while I remember, as my number two, you'll be expected to have a class one licence. If you have, fine, but if you haven't, for fuck's sake don't tell anyone. I'll be driving anyway, so no-one will ask to see your licence."

I nodded throughout, even though he didn't look at me. After a short while, he added, "If you have any questions give me a prod, 'cos I love my music while I'm driving." With that, he switched the radio on and inserted a CD.

God, how I've always hated Country and Western music and he was right about the prodding bit, because the cab seemed to vibrate to the monstrous decibel count.

I tried to sleep, with a wholly revised view of the calm at the cottage, but it was useless. In the end, I stared out of the window and felt myself harden slightly, as I re-lived our rendezvous on the train. Gradually though, darker thoughts crept in and I knew that somehow, I had to find a way of contacting her.

Two and a half hours later, we began the long descent into Dover, with those lovely views across the harbour. One ferry was a short way out, bound for France, while another was just coming in past the harbour walls. The sight never failed to thrill me. It was three o'clock and Steve explained that we were early. The original booking had been for the five thirty crossing, though normally, at this time of year they would squeeze him on to an earlier one, "Not this time though," he grumbled, "I've been told to stick with the five thirty one." He asked for my passport which I handed over to see it stuffed into a plastic sleeve that lay on the dashboard. Minutes later, we were weaving around the entrance lanes and into the port.

After clearing the passport control, he drove around to the check-in booths. The clerk obviously knew him and expressed surprise when he saw the ticket, "What, two of you on this one?" I was out of sight, but I saw Steve flick a thumb in my direction, "Yeah, a new bloke. They've sent him over with me to show him the ropes."

I heard the clerk say, "Good enough, at least you'll have someone to share the driving."

We were offered an earlier crossing, which Steve had anticipated and declined, so we were sent to an empty embarkation lane. Steve mumbled something I didn't catch and then said, "Well, at least we'll be first off on the other side."

With two and a half hours to wait, I asked if it would be Ok to visit the loo and buy a coffee at the passenger terminal, which had a variety of shops and food outlets. He held his hand out in that direction, as if to say be my guest, "Go ahead, I'll stay here and listen to some music; mine's white with two sugars."

I soon found a public telephone and called Steph, who sounded as bright as a button, "Hello Bogbrain." I giggled with relief, "You got home safe and sound then?"

"Yeah, no problem." After a short pause she asked, "How long do I have to wait for the real thing?"

"You are incorrigible!"

There was an earthy chuckle, "Ah, but you love me."

I didn't spend long on the line, since I didn't know whether I was doing anything that would upset Smudge, but it had been worth it. If those men *were* bad guys, at least they'd left her alone.

Once on board, I followed Steve to the driver's lounge, where soft drinks and coffee were free and the three course meals from a buffet were only five pounds fifty. Now, much more at ease, I chose meatloaf, peas and chips, of reasonable proportions, while Steve settled for double fish and chips. There were large paper beakers for the soft drinks machine and a little further along, glasses for the two taps that dispensed wine. We had cokes, but I watched a diminutive French lorry driver fill one of the paper beakers with wine; there must have been a whole bottle in there and he'd be back behind the wheel within an hour and a half.

We found a table next to a window, just as we were moving off and before long the place was full. Some had obviously visited the duty free shop before eating. After coffees, Steve left me to, 'point Percy at the porcelain' and stock up on his own duty frees. I declined his offer to accompany him and acknowledged his promise to come back to get me.

Alone, I found it easy to isolate myself from the chatter and clattering around me, as I stared out at the French coast and wondered what lay ahead.

* * *

I had no way of knowing that their mission had been amended; otherwise, I'd have been dead before reaching Leicester. Now though, people in Moscow wanted to know how much I knew and who I had shared that information with. It had been too long since they had listened to everything I said, or seen what had been put on my computer. I had cost them too many millions for the conclusion to be changed though. Once I had provided them with the information I was to be terminated, in a way that would serve as a lesson to others.

Chapter 16

We cleared the Calais docks at eight o'clock, French time and got on to the E15, signed for Reims and Paris. I'd been to France many times and had always been tickled by that. It's an extremely large country, but wherever you are, there will be signs for Paris, even five hundred miles away.

Five minutes later we pulled off into the *Zone Marcel Dorect* and wound our way through the industrial estate, to a large car park, at the entrance to a beer and wine outlet named *Pidou*. He switched the engine off and said, "Do me a favour will you? Pop in there and get me a case of Stella." I suddenly realised that I had no Euros and said so, expecting him to give me some. Instead, he said, "No problem, they take UK currency as well."

Taking this to be my due for services rendered, which seemed very reasonable, I opened the door to get out, but Steve suddenly called out, "Oh, before I forget, let me give you this back." He delved into the plastic folder and handed my passport over. I thanked him and set off on my errand.

When I came out, the lorry had disappeared, but traffic was coming in all the time and I assumed he'd been forced to move out of the way. The car park was huge though and I guessed that he'd have had to search for a space, just as it was my turn to search for him. It took me fifteen minutes of lugging that case of beer around to realise he'd gone and I stood there, muttering, "You bloody bastard," while trying to think of what to do next.

A silver VW Passat eased up beside me, which I realised was a left-hand drive, when the right hand passenger window came down. The light was fading by then and my back was aching; enough to delay me from bending over, so I couldn't see the driver. I recognised the voice though, "Need a lift?" When I opened the back door and put the case on the seat, Smudge said, "Ah, good. You got the beer then."

I got in beside him, "Yeah, along with a fright, thank you very much. Someone could have told me."

Smudge shook his head, "Steve knows all he needed to. He hasn't seen me, or this car."

We drove along the coast to Dunkerque, before heading east, past Bruges, Ghent, Brussels, Aachen, Bonn Koblenz and finally, Frankfurt, where we stopped for a break. We'd been travelling for over five hours and my eyes were feeling gritty, so the coffees and rolls were welcome. It was two in the morning and we were virtually alone; the staff looked as weary as I felt. Back at the car Smudge said, "We may as well get some sleep here, it's too early to make Rothenburg. You take the back seat."

I didn't argue, but two hours later, the cramped space woke me. I raised myself up to look around and check my watch; it was still three hours shy of dawn. Smudge seemed sound asleep in the front, but as soon as I opened the door he woke. I whispered, "Just going to get a coffee."

He said, "Get me one."

I thought about telling him he'd forgotten the magic word, but thought better of it, particularly when he handed a twenty euro note over.

I thought dawn would never come, but at seven o'clock, under a brightening sky, we tottered back into the services. Even Smudge appeared to be stiff. Over breakfast he began to outline his plan, though not before he reminded me to continue using his nickname.

I shrugged, "Of course, but why the reminder?" Perhaps I should have expected as much, but his reply startled me.

Between spoonfuls of yoghurt, he murmured, "I'm travelling under a different name."

I thought of hotels and hire car companies, who asked for passports or driving licences and realised what he meant.

He continued, "OK, we're about an hour and a half from Rothenburg. When we get there, we'll find a hotel then have a look around, just like tourists, but while we're doing that we'll take a peek at Herr Rilke's place. Tell me again, about your telephone conversation with him."

I flapped a hand, "There isn't much to say. I'd barely started before he snapped off a few questions; where I was from, what I wanted and what right I had to ask; that sort of thing. I told him that I was an investor in the Swedish companies and just wanted to know a little more about their crash. He told me he couldn't help me and put the phone down. The whole call couldn't have lasted a minute."

Smudge wanted confirmation of another detail, "You mentioned something in a file about his manner, beyond rude."

I said, "Yes, I remember noting that he sounded frightened, but it might just have been his brand of rudeness. Remember, I was pretty frightened by then, too."

Smudge seemed to be more concerned with scraping the last of his yoghurt out of the tub, but said, "I trust first judgements more than foggy memories." He pointed his spoon at me, "If he is their money man, he will know the lot, pretty well and from what we've seen so far, that includes fraud, conspiracy, money laundering and arms dealing, to name just a few. They're just the ones we know about. Oh, and don't forget two attempted murders.

One thing to bear in mind, is that you being here will compromise him. If Ankudinov gets to hear about it, they'll see him as a weak link and accountants can be replaced easily, We'll have a look, if I'm happy with what I see, you can pay him a visit tomorrow."

"What, on my own?"

"Don't worry, I won't be far away, but if two of us appear on the doorstep he'll clam up. You alone will be another matter. Also, you can talk money matters with him. You two should share that much, at least."

* * *

Bykov, the new man in charge, occupied the same hotel room as his predecessor, Dominiks and looked set to be removed as suddenly. He listened in silence as Ankudinov continued to rant, "Why am I being given clowns instead of professionals. An overpaid clerk lost three of you and has now disappeared. Tell me, is this the best I can expect?"

Bykov had listened to the tirade for long enough, "I believe we underestimated the man he is with."

"So he was on the train too?"

"We can't be sure. I don't have any way of identifying him yet."

"You have a name don't you and some of his background?"

"Only that his is ex-army."

"That is more than enough, what are you people being paid for?" Bykov remained silent, until Ankudinov barked, "Get in touch with Intelligence; they may have something."

* * *

Rothenburg is a beautifully preserved medieval town, contained within the original walls, though modern suburbs lay siege on the northern and eastern flanks. Most of the other half of the town overlooks the Tauber valley.

It is also a significant tourist attraction, which we drove around and through, several times. Smudge decided that we should find a hotel within the old town and behave like tourists ourselves, so we checked into one named *Kloster Stuble* and because it was the low season, there were two rooms available for us that morning.

Soon after, we went for a walk, taking in the sights as we made our way across town and through the arched portal on the eastern side. Rilke's house was in Leydig Strasse, within sight of the wall, in a row of houses that were typically Bavarian, with high, steeply pitched roofs, clad in tiles with half-round lower edges, which gave the properties a 'gingerbread house' look. They all looked well cared for, with a few contemporary timber features that fell well short of the traditional 'cuckoo clock' buildings of that region. Most were large and painted beige, but Rilke's house was half the size and set back, as though it was one of their 'young'. All the gardens were well cared for, with loggias and trellising that still held remnants of summer blooms, except for Rilke's place. The garden was as cared for, in a clinical sense, but there was no ornamentation. It was an anonymous sort of place. We couldn't loiter; there was nothing in the street for tourists, so we turned at the end, as though we'd made a mistake and picked up our pace, back to town.

After lunch, I returned to the hotel for a short rest, leaving Smudge to do as he thought fit, but an intended nap extended to six o'clock. I'd gone out like a light.

An hour after I woke, we strolled up to the Market Square. Because it was light and warm we sat outside one of the cafes and enjoyed a beer. A small group of tourists had gathered on the opposite side of the square for a walking tour, which was signed as 'A walk with the Night watchman'. The guide must have been close to six foot six, because he towered over his audience. He spoke perfect English and was dressed as a medieval night watchman; in a black cape and tricorn hat while carrying a long staff and a lantern, but his delivery was what fascinated me. He had shoulder length grey hair and during his introduction, I heard him say that he'd spent some time in San Francisco. That didn't surprise me, because although he was obviously German, he spoke with the easy manner of a Californian; who'd just enjoyed a joint. We only heard the introduction, but he was extremely funny and in other circumstances, I'd have paid the seven Euros and joined the group, which followed him around the corner like a clutch of ducklings.

Over the evening meal Smudge gave me another pre-paid telephone, for use locally and told me that he'd checked Rilke's place out from a couple of other locations and hadn't seen anything to cause him concern. But he added, "We don't have the options or opportunities we had at Long's place. This is a modern house with what looks like a decent alarm system and you can bet that if he has sensitive stuff in there it will be well cared for. Tomorrow, after breakfast, we'll agree on your approach."

Inevitably, I had a restless night and regretted sleeping for so long that afternoon. Smudge had enforced abstinence after the single beer, which didn't help either. At least he'd brought my iPad, though there were no emails of any consequence and nothing on *Skype*.

We returned to the same street-side cafe in the morning, where I sat and fidgeted, with what Smudge would no doubt have called pre-op nerves. "First," he said, "You must put a foot in the doorway. The notion of putting it there as he slams the door is something you only read about, in detective novels. Speak quietly and reasonably, but you have to say enough in those first few seconds to convince him, at least enough to let you in or take a message. Don't waste time trying to speak in German; we already know he can speak English."

We packed our things, in case we needed to leave town in a hurry and at that time of morning, with breakfasts and check-outs over, the front desk was empty, so we were able to take the rucksacks out to the car, without being seen. Mine was another new one, bought and packed with my things by Smudge, to replace the one I'd left on the train. After a quick check of fuel and maps, we drove out of the walled town; with some difficulty, because the road system limited the number of routes in and out. We exited through an arched portal on the north side and made our way to one of the overflow car parks near the eastern wall and Rilke's house.

Smudge switched off the engine and swivelled in his seat to face me, "You ready? Know what you're going to say?"

I simply nodded and got out of the car. He did too, but walked back into the old town, through the eastern gate, while I made for Rilke's house.

✳ ✳ ✳

I did as directed and put my foot in the doorway as I began to speak, "Herr Rilke, I am a friend and I believe you are in danger."

He glared at me, "What are *you* doing here?" He saw my puzzled look and said, "I recognised your voice. You telephoned me."

My script was fast becoming redundant, "A great deal has happened since then Herr Rilke. Because of what I found out, a close friend has been severely injured and a man has been killed." I omitted to mention that the deceased was one of his lot; sent to kill me.

"Go away; I have nothing to say to you."

"Please Herr Rilke, I need your help and I think you need mine. I,—*we* can help each other see another birthday."

He snorted, "Do you think coming here has helped me? Go, before I call for help."

I noted he didn't say police, "I understand, but please, shake my hand in farewell and I'll leave." I held my hand out, which he considered for a few moments before extending his arm through the narrow gap. The continued resistance to my foot suggested that his other hand was lodged against the inside of the door, but we shook hands and I pulled my foot clear, allowing the door to slam shut.

I walked back to the car with a growing sense of failure and defeat. Short of going to Moscow and confronting Ankudinov, a singularly terminal option, we had no other leads.

* * *

Otto was shaken and now very frightened. He seemed to be faced with threats from both sides and possibly a third, if the Englishman chose to involve the police.

He groaned in anguish as he realised how stupid he'd been when they asked him if an Englishman had contacted him. He'd denied it and now the man had turned up on the doorstep. Which raised the question, should he report this contact?"

He gazed around at the piles of files he'd brought down to the living room and sat in an armchair to read the note I had slipped into his hand.

Dear Otto,

I believe we are two innocents, caught up in things we could never have imagined.

I have help and we can protect you. If you feel able to talk, call me on one of these numbers.

Your friend,

Ian Barber

I'd given him both of the pre-paid telephone numbers, but as I leant against the car, reliving the encounter, my hopes faded completely. I used the spare car key Smudge had given me, to get in and wait.

* * *

Smudge was on the town wall, at an archer's slit in one of the towers. The whole wall was covered with a timber roof so that anyone at ground level could see little in the gloom. Instead of bulky binoculars, he used a rifle 'scope to follow me back to the car, after which, we both settled down to wait in our own ways. He'd known that Rilke wasn't going to invite me in for a coffee and chat. In fact, the accountant did exactly what was expected and sent me packing, but if the man was sensible, he'd get on the 'phone and report the episode. Or would he?

If exposed, Ankudinov would have no use for him in Moscow and besides, he would still be a liability, or worse a blackmail threat. The amount of work required to negate the use of his knowledge would be dreadful, if he was allowed to walk away that is. But then, everyone knew that wasn't an option.

Smudge stayed where he was, intermittently looking at the birds of prey and countryside, just like a tourist. If Rilke made his call to me, they would need to get him and his back-up files out of there quickly, to somewhere safe. On the other hand, if his place was bugged there could be someone on their way there at that moment and for that matter, he may have called his employer anyway, but that seemed doubtful.

The aim was to spook him into flight. If the latest contact failed to produce results, there would be a clumsy attempt at burglary that night; enough to set the alarm off. One way or another, Rilke had to be frightened enough to call for help.

Ten minutes later, things went to hell in a hand basket.

* * *

Smudge caught movement from further down Leydig Strasse and re-focused the scope onto a man walking down the path of a house on the opposite side to Rilke's. The man turned towards the town and a casual observer might think he was going for a beer, or lunch.

But he was military, no question and the bulk of his leather jacket established more. Smudge waited until the man descended the two steps from the street and strode towards Rilke's door before murmuring, "Shit," as he ran for the stairs.

We hadn't expected Rilke to be under surveillance and later, we'd find out that the accountant hadn't known about it either, for their brief had been simple, stay out of sight and watch.

* * *

The doorbell rang continuously, until finally, Rilke gave in and rushed to the door, determined to tell the Englishman to *Ficken Auf*, once and for all. In fact, he'd already shouted half of the expletive before realising that a stranger was standing there. The man wasn't particularly tall, but powerfully built, with a haircut that even Rilke recognised as military. He seemed confident and relaxed as he pushed, first the door and then Rilke's chest, in order to gain access.

Rilke made to protest, but was ignored as the intruder closed the door and indicated toward the living room, "Inside." His sheer presence stunned Rilke into silence and submission, as he led the way into the room. The monosyllabism continued once they were there, with the stranger pointing at an armchair and saying, "Sit."

It all seemed so casual, and unutterably deadly.

Rilke watched as the man checked the back door and scanned the room, before seeming to notice the piles of files on the dining table. He went over and flicked through a number of them before turning to his prey, "You have just had a visitor. Who was he?"

Rilke stuttered slightly, enough to need two attempts at the answer, "Just a man; trying to sell me something."

The Russian accent became clear then, "That was a very silly thing to say Her Rilke. I will begin again."

Rilke sat in his armchair, staring like a rabbit caught in head-lights, at the gun that had suddenly appeared in his visitor's hand. He continued to stare at the weapon during the next ten minutes, even though it was pointing at the floor.

The man had left the threat hanging in one hand while he made a call on a mobile telephone, in Russian and at one point he gestured toward the stacked files. Whilst he hadn't understood what was being said, the body language was eloquent enough for Rilke to realise that his employment was about to be terminated.

The man seemed very relaxed as he pulled a chair out from beneath the dining table, turned it to face Rilke and sat on it. The same casual air applied when he withdrew a silencer from his pocket and screwed it onto the gun.

A sense of surreal calm settled on Rilke, as though the months of fear and anxiety had suddenly cleared. There had been inevitability to it all, from the day he'd agreed to work for them and now, at last, the time of reckoning had come. In a few minutes he would know peace again. He noticed that the gun was pointing at him and that the man was speaking, "So, little chicken, tell me why the Englishman called this morning."

Rilke looked back, as though he hadn't comprehended the question and his questioner shrugged, "Take as long as you like, I have lots of questions and lots of time. You can make this as difficult as you please."

The 'little chicken' spoke dully, "What do you want to know?" He just didn't care anymore.

* * *

Smudge slipped around to the back of the neighbour's house, hoping that the occupants were at work, though he couldn't afford to waste time checking. At the bottom of the garden, shielded by shrubs on both sides of the fence, he slipped over into Rilke's garden and hunkered down in the shade, from where he could see into the lounge/dining area. The man he'd seen crossing the road was seated at the table, with his back to the window and was talking to someone; Rilke no doubt, who was out of sight. There was no way of hearing what was being said, but the man began to nod and suddenly stood to find some paper. He returned to his seat and placed the gun to one side before pulling a pen out of his pocket. He obviously felt comfortable enough to put his weapon down, but rather than use the table, which would have meant turning his back on the other, he picked up a file for something to rest the paper on.

Inside, Rilke was telling all, and much of it was startling and too detailed to try and commit it to memory. The man retraced their steps and began to make notes.

Outside, Smudge considered his options and decided that none were good, but then they were unlikely to improve either. He knew that the windows would be double or triple glazed, so the hollow points in his gun were a waste of time. That much, at least, was remedied by a change of magazine, for the one loaded with seventeen nine millimetre parabellum rounds. This was going to be a shit or bust affair and he had a feeling that all seventeen rounds would be needed.

There was no easier way to do it. If he stayed in the shadow of the fence, Smudge reckoned he could make it to the house without being seen, but once he committed, there would only be time for a couple of rounds, before bullets would be coming back at him and he would be silhouetted like a board target. The man in there was a pro' and would react like one.

Minutes later, Smudge stood with his back pressed against the wall at the corner of the house, now, totally focused. There could be no delay. The target was out of sight and could move at any time. Three, two, one . . .

Rilke was the first to see the figure appear at the window and the loud 'cracks' became louder as pieces of glass burst into the room. The triple glazing served to deflect the first three bullets and by then, the Russian had the gun in his hand and was returning fire.

His first bullet sealed his fate.

Loaded with hollow points, the first round flattened as it hit the glass, punching out a huge hole. Smudge felt shards of glass graze his face, but kept firing, with a new found accuracy that took the

Russian down as he lunged for cover. Two red blooms appearing on the man's chest, as his body was punched out of sight.

The cacophony ended as quickly as it has started and the man at the window shouted, "Otto, open the window, now!"

Rilke stood and stumbled towards the window, sidestepping the body that had fallen at his feet. Doing only as he was told, without conscious thought, he undid the window and pushed it open. Smudge clambered in and quickly checked the Russian for signs of life before kicking his gun away. He grabbed Rilke's arm, "Where's your passport?" The accountant's mouth hung open as he stared at Smudge through dilated pupils. When the question was repeated, he pointed at a leather hand bag, on the bookcase. Smudge snatched it up and checked inside. Satisfied, he took his charge by the arm and hurried to the front door before speaking again, "Listen, we are going to walk out of here and turn left at the street. Do exactly as I tell you and we'll get out of here in one piece. Understood?"

Rilke nodded but as he reached for the latch, Smudge glanced at the hall mirror and saw that his face was covered in blood. He knew the wounds weren't serious, but he couldn't go outside like that. He said, "Wait," and opened the adjacent door. It was a toilet and would have to do. He gathered a roll of toilet paper and dunked it in the bowl before scrubbing his face. After flushing the bloody evidence away, he gathered another handful of paper, to finish off in front of the hall mirror and take with him. Not perfect, he decided, but it would do.

Rilke allowed himself to be ushered out of the door and hurried along the path.

* * *

I'd heard what might have been shots, though I couldn't be sure, but I was startled to see both of them walking quickly towards the car. Smudge was holding Rilke by the arm and hustled him into the back seat, before dodging around the back and climbing into the driver's seat.

Seven minutes later we were on the Autobahn heading south towards Munich on the A7. We'd heard sirens as we drove out of the suburbs, but by then Otto's house was well ablaze.

The Russian's companion had watched as the two men left the house, but realised that a fire fight in the street would be unwise. Besides, there were more pressing concerns. They had been told that whatever happened, the contents of that house must never be seen by the authorities, He grabbed the incendiaries and ran.

Shortly after joining the Autobahn, we turned west, onto the A6 and later, south again on the A81, skirting Stuttgart and Karlsruhe, before crossing the Rhine near Baden Baden. Rilke remained silent for the whole journey and Smudge seemed equally disinclined to tell me anything more than the basics. I did think about trying to strike up a conversation with our passenger, but couldn't think of anything to say. Violent death does little for the art of conversation.

By two thirty that afternoon, we were in France.

I felt a sense of relief and Rilke must have been affected too, because he spoke for the first time, "May we stop please, I have to use the toilet." Smudge didn't say anything, but ten minutes later we pulled into a service area, just north of Strasbourg.

We parked a little way from the building and Smudge said, "Go with him, keep close and make sure he doesn't use a telephone. Oh, and bring me a coffee." I thought, 'you've forgotten the magic word again', but did as I was told, as soon as Otto indicated that he was in a fit state to move. He got out of the car and promptly threw up. I reasoned that if it was a reaction to what had happened, he'd done a herculean job of holding it down. Smudge handed me a bottle of water, which I passed on and was rewarded with a small smile of gratitude.

Finally, he straightened himself up and we made our way into the building. After the toilet, we queued up at the counter. Neither of us wanted food and Smudge hadn't mentioned it either so I ordered three coffees, to go. Otto said, "May we have our coffee in here, please?" After a moment's thought I decided it couldn't hurt, and changed the order to two coffees. We could get a fresh one to take out to his nibs, when we were finished.

We sat in the window; silhouetted and warmed by the late after-noon sun. Nothing more was said for several minutes until Otto broke the silence, "I am not a bad person you know. I had no idea what I was getting into."

I gave him the warmest smile I could muster, "That makes two of us Otto, I had no idea either."

He nodded slowly, "Tell me what happened to you."

"I don't have time to tell you the whole story now and anyway, I'd want Smudge, with me when I do, but I can give you a potted version."

He looked at me quizzically, "Smudge."

I waved a hand, "Oh, you'll find out." Meanwhile, I gave him my potted version.

* * *

In Leicester, Bykov had to concentrate on what was being said on the telephone, over the thumping of the bed head and theatrical panting from next door. The embassy attaché was in any event, soft spoken, but the intelligence was scant and disappointing. Neil Foley had no army records at all. He'd never even been a soldier. They still had no idea who they were up against.

* * *

At Bovington, Shelley Knight, a lance corporal and clerk in the Royal Corps of Transport didn't realise that her army career was over, as such. She'd thought nothing of the favours she'd done for her brother, who worked at an employment agency and sometimes asked her to check someone out; just to make sure they were who they claimed to be. It was no big deal. They had already agreed that sensitive information would be withheld, but if it was just a case of clearing the guy, particularly when it might help him find a job, then she thought, whatever.

It had been low grade stuff therefore, but with time and entrap-ment by default, she and her brother would find themselves ensnared, one day. Then, when the cost of refusal by exposure would exceed that of continuing, greater secrets would have been be shared.

Now though, Intelligence would be watching. In time, she might be of use as a tool, but meanwhile, word was passed back to Hereford and a text sent to Smudge. For the moment, he remained an enigma.

Chapter 17

I took a triple espresso out to Smudge, who acknowledged the necessity with an appreciative nod, but instead of setting off, he downed it in the car before telling us to wait while he visited the toilet himself. It didn't take long and as we made for the exit he explained, "We won't get to where I want to be today; it's close on four already, so we'll pull off and find somewhere to stay the night."

Which we did, fifteen minutes later; in a small *Chambre D'Hote* on the outskirts of Brumath. I shared a twin room with Otto, while Smudge had one to himself, where from the mumblings we heard through the wall, I decided he was making telephone calls. We ate at a small cafe for next to nothing and by ten we were all in bed. Why, I simply don't know, neither of us slept well. We were warm, true, but left alone in the dark, with our thoughts.

At least Smudge looked well rested in the morning and took his time over breakfast. Otto and I looked on, with dulled senses and blank expressions. The coffee helped me recover enough to attack a buttered roll with cold meats and finally, at ten o'clock, we were back on the road.

It took just over four hours to drive across France, past Nancy, Reims and St Quentin to Peronne, a hundred and forty five kilometres north of Paris; for the most part in silence. I wasn't sure whether Otto was sleeping, or just keeping his head down, literally, because he spent most of the journey lying across the back seat. The front seat was less conducive to sleep, feigned or otherwise, but I managed to doze for some of the time, leaving Smudge alone with his thoughts. Somewhere en route, I did ask if he had any plans and the response was a terse, "Working on them." I waited for more, but we continued on in an eloquent silence, which told me to stay quiet and let him get on with it.

My offer to share the driving was dealt with in a similar fashion, because, apparently, I wasn't a nominated driver on the hire agreement, but eventually, we parked on the square, opposite Peronne town hall, where Smudge directed us to a cafe, down towards the river and near a castle-like structure called *The Historial de la Grande Guerre*; a museum of the Great War. He promised to join us there and went off in the opposite direction.

It was warm enough, just, to sit outside for coffee and once again, while we were alone, Otto opened up a little. Perhaps he found it difficult to engage Smudge in conversation, after seeing him kill someone.

He asked, "Who is your friend?"

I shrugged, "Smudge, just call him Smudge."

"No, I meant, what is he? Does he do this sort of thing for a living?"

"Used to, though on the side of the righteous." I thought for a moment and decided to elaborate, in case the translation didn't work, "He is definitely one of the good guys."

"But he is a professional, yes?"

I needed to make one thing very clear, "And he saved your life. He saved mine too, as a matter of fact." Which prompted a question of my own, "Did you know the other man?"

Otto rocked his head from side to side, "I might have met him but I don't,—didn't know his name. I think he was with Sergey Osokin one time, at one of our meetings."

"I've come across that name, somewhere."

Otto explained, "He was the man who appointed me. He works for a man called Ankudinov. You mentioned him yesterday. Both of them are Russian."

I had, in my potted version of things.

After that, we allowed the discussion to move on to more comfortable topics, as though we'd had enough of the bad stuff, at least for the time being. I spoke of my background in Financial Services while he told me some of his, in European accountancy and the mood lightened as we exchanged some anecdotal tales, but his guarded silence returned when Smudge did.

We discovered that he'd been to the tourist information office and found a *Gite* which was available for rent, six kilometres north, in a small village called Moslains. Our cover story was that we were oil rig workers on a month's leave and had decided to sample some of the French way of life. If asked, we were all divorced. He'd also taken my *iPad* with him, which was now fitted with a French data SIM card.

On the way out of town, we stopped at an *Intermarche* superstore for a fairly major shop, which was how I realised we would be staying for a while and why I made sure we included a couple of five litre boxes of wine. On the way out, Smudge had us sit in the photo booth to have our pictures taken and by now, I knew better than to ask why. He would tell us when it suited him.

Moslains was a typically French village, with a cafe bar, an overly large church and a ripe agricultural odour. Our *Gite* was a converted farm building, on the opposite side of the yard from the farmhouse, now redundant as a working concern. The elderly farmer, Monsieur Colbert, had retired from farming and sold the land to a neighbour. As a result, the yard was spotless and the *Gite*, named *Chalet de Lavande*, delightful. It looked more like a cottage than a barn conversion, with one bedroom and a lounge/diner downstairs. A steep spiral staircase led upstairs to a further two bedrooms and shared bathroom. The furnishings were an eclectic mix, from at least five decades and the bed heads were stout wooden affairs that might even have been Napoleonic, but everything was clean and comfortable.

It seemed to be a milestone, marking a boundary, of sorts, from the traumas of the previous day and we sat down to a very late lunch of bread, cheese and pate, washed down with a glass of red wine. It was a feast.

Afterwards, I booted up the *iPad* and connected to the internet immediately. I found a site for the online edition of *Rothenburg*

News, which carried our experience as the main item, though not in the way we'd expected. It detailed how the police had been called to a suspected shooting incident, but discovered a major fire instead, which caused the total destruction of Otto's house. A picture of the charred ruins accompanied the story. The fire department was treating the matter as arson, since a number of incendiary devices had been used, which, it was thought, may have accounted for the explosions first heard.

A spokesman said that the destruction had been so complete and the fire so intense, that they had yet to identify the body discovered in the ruins, adding that the sole occupant had been a single male.

Smudge showed a smidgeon of sympathy, "I'm sorry about the house Otto, but it does mean that the authorities won't be looking for you, at least until they discover that the body isn't yours; if they ever do."

Otto was clearly shaken by the loss of his home which dispelled any comfort there may have been from Smudge's observation, "But Ankudinov will still be searching, I think."

Smudge nodded, "Well, we'll do everything we can to make sure he doesn't find us. For now, if you clear up here, Ian can come and help me empty the car." Outside, he gave me my instructions, "Get as much information as you can from him and write it down, though fuck knows what good it will do us now the evidence has gone up in smoke."

* * *

We took our bags inside and all sat at the table while Smudge began to detail his plans, "You two will stay here for the time being, while I go back to the UK and attend to a few things. It'll be OK to go into town for provisions provided you avoid recording your names anywhere and pay for everything by cash, only. No credit cards; I'll leave you with plenty of cash and the *Gite* has already been paid for." He looked at me, "Don't telephone home. Both Steph's and Libby's 'phones are likely to be bugged, so if you contact either of them, they will become targets. I'll buy three new pre-paid mobiles before I go, but they are only to be used to communicate with each other. Oh, and I'll need your passports. Be grey, don't draw attention to yourselves. Remember, now that Otto has gone AWOL, Ankudinov will be throwing loads more assets at the job."

I asked, "How long will you be gone."

"Don't know; as long as it takes, but I should be back within a week or two. I'll keep you posted."

My spirits fell away as quickly as they'd been lifted. We were going to be left alone, without protection and with a bunch of Russian thugs searching for us.

I was tired though and nothing could have kept me awake that night, so when I woke the next morning, refreshed, logic took precedence. I realised that continued action was better than hiding, until an inevitable end. I said as much to my companions and by eleven that morning we had bought more provisions, three new mobile telephones and were waving Smudge off, who reckoned he would be back in the UK in time for tea.

Monsieur Colbert was in the yard at the time and when he asked if anything was wrong I used the script I'd been given and told him that our friend had been called back on a family matter. He was very charming and when I mentioned our plans to explore the area he asked if we planned on hiring another car. I said no, we would walk or perhaps catch buses, if there were any. All this, in an exchange of my schoolboy French with his limited English, which he'd learned by way of contact with British tourists.

An hour later, he rapped on the door and gestured for us to follow him into a barn, where he had scrubbed down a couple of ancient bicycles. The black, heavy steel frames must have been over fifty years old; the sort that delivery boys might have used, with rods to the brakes rather than cables. The tyres had been inflated and oil still dripped from the chains. He swept his arm out and beamed, "Voila! Pour vous."

We both thanked him profusely and over lunch discussed what to do. First, we needed maps and more tourist information than that found in the dining table draw. However challenging the bicycles might be, Peronne was only six Kilometres away and we knew they had a tourist office.

I saw Otto's smile for the first time that afternoon, when we parked our 'steeds' in one of the cycle racks in the square. The ride into town had been a delight and we agreed to toast our success over a beer, after we had visited the tourist office. There had been plenty of wobbling and once, I veered up onto the grass verge, when I tried looking behind, to make sure he was OK.

We chose the same cafe and poured over a pile of leaflets that promised a multitude of activities, even out of season. There were lots of walks, the River Somme, Canal du Nord and much more. Since we were sitting next to it, *The Historial de la Grande Guerre* seemed to be a good place to start, that very afternoon.

* * *

Smudge switched his UK mobile on, soon after landing at Dover and discovered a number of text messages from the cheap and nasties. Lawyers advising that they were holding four thousand pounds for him, after an accident he hadn't had, or others telling him to claim for insurance mis-selling. But one was from home, or more specifically, the automated unit hidden in his loft, which sent out an SMS if he'd had visitors in his absence.

At the next services he telephoned his neighbour; a key holder, from a call box. "Hi John, it's Neil. I'm still going to be away for awhile, so I thought I'd check to see if everything's OK."

Tom was as relieved to get the call as he was sorry to pass on the news, "Ahh, Neil, I'm so sorry mate, but some buggers have turned you over. They ransacked the place, but there's nothing obvious missing. Your TV and sound system are still there, so the Police didn't seem overly concerned. They made a report, but I doubt that'll do any good. I patched the door up and put a new lock on for you."

Smudge allowed a moment, to ensure that Tom had finished. News that nothing had been taken should have been welcome, but Smudge knew better and was cursing himself for it, "Thanks Tom, I'll square up with you as soon as I get back, but in the meantime, would you do me a favour please? Pop back in and check on something; I'll call back in half an hour."

The next call confirmed his fears, when Tom said, "No chum, there's no picture there now. Was it valuable?"

"No, just sentimental value." Smudge hadn't told him what the picture was, just its location. Now the Russians knew that he was ex-army. More particularly, they now had a picture of him and the uniform would speak for itself.

* * *

That evening we toasted our success over a glass of wine, while I prepared dinner. With the prospect of so much time to kill, I'd decided to spend more time cooking and that evening we enjoyed pork chops in a creamy red peppercorn sauce, with buttered baby potatoes and green beans. We then did as the French do and followed the main course with a cheeseboard, before a sweet finale of T*arte Tatin,* topped off with calvados-laced whipped cream.

Over Cognac and coffee Otto thanked me and asked, "I am a very bad cook, will you teach me some, please?" I was delighted and said so.

The following morning, we went for a walk through a local wooded area, called *Bois Saint-Pierre Vaast* and didn't see a soul. The calming influence of the trees silenced us to begin with, but in time, we began to compare notes. This time, I went into much more detail, having failed to find an opportunity to share it in Smudge's presence and Otto seemed both shocked and reassured by the story of my would-be assassin. Gradually, we moved onto the Russians and there, Otto was able to confirm all the links with my experiences. He knew it all, though I was fascinated to hear about each conspiracy from the opposite perspective.

After lunch, when Otto discovered a chess game and challenged me to a match, I had to admit that I'd never learned the rules. He seemed delighted, "Then I shall teach you, in exchange for being taught how to cook!"

That evening, I taught Otto how to make a sauce, or more specifically, for that meal, a red wine sauce, to which we added, sliced mushrooms, sautéed in butter. We were both delighted with the result and the elevation it gave to the Toulouse sausages. There was enough *Tarte Tatin* left over from the previous day to provide another two desserts, but over coffees and cognacs, we agreed on menus for the next two days, before preparing a shopping list. Incredibly, the badly perished bicycle tyres had stayed up, but we added replacements to the list, along with a puncture repair kit.

* * *

Smudge stayed with Combo for the first night, but left early the next morning to visit an address in the East End, where he was startled by the increased costs. Terrorism, it seemed, had caused the risks and penalties to rise exponentially. Many of the lads had one or two passports of their own, that no-one knew about and Smudge had kept his. Thankfully, the forger recognised him, so credentials didn't need to be established. As expected, the documents would take more than week to prepare, particularly now that he had been forced to add two more, for himself. Since his photographs wouldn't be ready for ten days, a further day would be needed to complete the job, so he returned to the cottage and worried. For the first time in this op, there was a void. They could hide away there for some time, but the threat would remain, unless they could find a way to eliminate it. Ultimately, the key to their problem now lay with Otto.

* * *

Ankudinov saw things differently, not least of all because the relationship he'd enjoyed with his sponsor had deteriorated so badly. Removal of political threats was a way of life in the new Federation and no matter what the Western press made of things, their system would continue to protect the powerful. But this was different. It was personal and well outside of Russia's jurisdiction. Rilke was a boil that needed lancing, before he was tempted to share his knowledge, but there was one positive at least. The accountant now lacked any evidence and nothing would be gleaned from the ashes of his house.

Bykov's team in Leicester had been doubled and another was on standby, in Moscow. Sooner or later, all three targets would be found and dealt with, under the new orders, issued at the express wish of the sponsor, to 'Liquidate on sight'.

* * *

Our journey back from Peronne that afternoon was a hazardous affair, with tyres and inner tubes slung over our shoulders and a shopping bag each which made chattering incursions into the wheel spokes.

We'd had omelettes for lunch, at what was now our regular cafe, during which Otto spoke of his home and town. When I explained that we'd only had a day of sightseeing in Rothenburg he said, "So, you did not see any of the Riemenschneider carvings?" When I said no he was shocked, "Oh dear, then you must go back. Tilman Riemenschneider re-defined wood carving in the fifteenth century. His work is truly remarkable." He went on to do a fine job of describing the work and I regretted not seeing any of it. After lunch; we took a walk along the banks of the Somme. With so few people about, the wildlife in the mosaic of pools and cut offs was a delight. Conversation drifted around to boats as Otto described the type of yacht he had always wanted. I didn't agree and described the sort of floating gin palace I had in mind, though I was prompted to say, "If we get out of this lot, why don't you and I rent a boat on the Norfolk Broads and cruise for a week?"

He smiled, "That would be a fine idea. What are the Norfolk Broads?"

Another half an hour slipped by, as I told him.

That evening, we had calves liver in a honey and sherry vinegar sauce.

* * *

Libby had a wonderful meal that night too; at home. Everyone remarked on her speedy recovery, even though she was still on painkillers and barely coping with her crutches, but she didn't bother to differ; at least she was home and alive.

She often thought of her boss and prayed for him, in a fashion, given that as a relaxed agnostic, she didn't know who she was addressing her prayers to.

But she did know who her boss was up against and deep down, she felt certain she would never see me again. Those moments of cognition were terribly saddening and couldn't be shared with anyone, particularly Steph, who was now a regular visitor. Whilst they shared the same knowledge, she thought Steph was too vulnerable to contemplate the worst.

Libby was right about that, though not in the way she thought. Steph could be as tough as anyone, normally, but not when she was three months pregnant.

Steph had started to miss the odd period before she met me and took that to be the beginnings of her menopause, so she didn't give a second thought to the recent absences; until her breasts became tender and more tellingly her days began with morning sickness. A primeval instinct told her to keep it secret, for as long as she could. She couldn't see or hear them, but the threat was out there and real. She prayed every day, to a God she believed in, for both the child and its father.

* * *

After the first week, Otto had become a creditable chef, while I made little progress at chess. He summed up my approach to the game with, "You are too aggressive. You play like a bull elephant, with no finesse or tactics."

More notably, we had become firm friends. I told him about Steph and how much she meant to me, while he admitted to being a bit of a loner; by accident rather than choice. I knew only too well, that working from home isn't the way to meet women, though he added that at least I saw clients, whereas he only had the Russians for company. We knew that as one of Putin's cronies,

Ankudinov was ex-KGB so I joked about the days of the Cold War, where women were used to trap foreigners into spying, "So don't you think they'd still have a few knocking around, if you'll pardon the pun?"

Otto pulled a face, "Perhaps, but remember, the Cold War ended twenty years ago. They will all have moustaches by now."

That called for faux sympathy, "True and don't forget the extra few pounds they'd have put on with all that sausage. Still, some prefer their ladies to be built for comfort rather than speed." That jest took a further five minutes to explain.

On the twelfth morning, after breakfast, I suggested another bike ride, but Otto shook his head, "Ian, I have decided to tell you all I know. Who knows, you may be able to use some of it to help you out of this predicament." He held up a hand, "But, there will be a small favour I shall ask in return."

I asked, "What is that?"

"I shall tell you, soon, but for now, I have a lot of other things to tell you."

It was an enormous step for him to take, but all I could think to say was, "Thank you."

He placed a pen and notebook on the table, in front of me, "You will need lots of notes I think."

Lunch marked a welcome break, in a day I shall never forget. The stream of information beggared belief. I learned of fraud and embezzlement at every level, along with trades in everything, from arms to atomic material, drugs, currencies and extortion. The list went on and on. Even countries were being looted, including Russia itself. Almost all the proceeds were screened by Trust companies, using Cypriot banks.

Towards the end of the afternoon I flicked through my notes, "This is astonishing, is that the lot."

Otto sighed, "Even now, there are some things that you would be better off not knowing, but that is almost all."

I scanned the notes and tried to do some mental arithmetic, "Hell, there must be millions in those accounts."

He chuckled, "You are joking I think."

I certainly wasn't, "What then, tens of millions, hundreds?"

Otto held my gaze as he spoke, "The last time I checked, there were nineteen billion US dollars."

I sat back and shook my head, "We are minnows Otto, in a lake full of sharks. What hope do we have?"

He thought for a moment, before, "Perhaps we must carry on as we are doing, by surviving each day; until the sharks lose interest and move to another pond."

"Is that likely?"

"Who knows? Perhaps a change of leadership would blur things enough. All we do know for certain is that we have already survived for another day and you have a good friend in Smudge."

I countered, "He's a friend to both of us."

Otto smiled, "Perhaps."

I didn't sleep well that night. The enormity of Otto's disclosures were so boggling, I needed time to think about them and perhaps how to use the information. The next morning I decided to do just that, alone. I asked Otto, "Would you mind if I went for a walk on my own this morning? I want to think things though."

He patted me on the shoulder, "Of course not my friend and while you're gone I shall think of something to do for dinner tonight."

* * *

The emptiness of the *Gite* was the first thing that struck me. I whirled around, pulse racing as I scanned the farmyard for attackers. None were evident, but I locked the door and ran for the stairs and my gun, which is when I saw the note, propped up against the kettle. I sat down at the table and unfolded it;

Dear Ian,

I wish we could have met in happier circumstances. These last few days will stay with me forever.

Perhaps one day, we will be able to continue our friendship and you can introduce me to Steph, but for now, I think it is time for us all to hide.

I am the one they most want and therefore it is best that I leave you. Tell Smudge that I already had another passport and there is somewhere I can go.

Therefore, do not worry for me, but take great care of yourselves.

Your friend,

Otto

PS. This is my mother's address in Wurzburg. Would you keep it safely please.

I read the note again and realised the significance of the address. If he didn't survive and I did, he wanted me to visit her.

I had never felt more alone, not even when Dee walked out on me. The silence and serenity of my surroundings suddenly felt suffocating.

That evening, as if on cue, a text message came up on my mobile. It was from Smudge, 'Bak 2moro late pm'.

When Smudge arrived the following evening I was mildly pissed and close to a drunkard's tears. Moreover, if my gun had been to hand, I'd have probably used it on him, in the circumstances. Anyone who strode through the doorway, looking like a stranger, deserved to be shot. Of course, given time, his voice would have saved him. It was the only thing I recognised.

His hair was dark, along with the new beard and moustache. He'd changed his features further with a lightly tinted pair of gold rimmed spectacles.

I didn't waste time with greetings, "Otto's gone."

Smudge's jaw dropped, "Gone where?"

I shrugged, "I haven't a clue; he just left this."

He took the note and read it before glancing back at the door, as he murmured, "Shit." A period of time passed as he considered the change in circumstances and then sat down opposite me, "Talk to me."

I described what we'd done in his absence, until I reached the part about Otto's disclosures and then I passed over my sheaf of notes.

During the silence that followed, I was tempted to re-fill my glass, but thought better of it. I did get him a beer though.

Occasionally, he would break off to ask me about a financial instrument or transaction, but for the most part, he read in silence. Finally, he read my last note; the one I had underlined three times and said, "Sweet Jesus, nineteen billion?"

I nodded, "That was the last time he looked. I shudder to think what the daily interest amounts to."

He gathered the sheaf up and tamped the pages into order, "Well, even without the evidence, this intel would be useful to someone, but it's no use to us. In fact, if Ankudinov suspects we have it, we'll become as much of a priority as their accountant."

I felt a mild resentment at that, "Otto, you mean." He didn't bother answering.

Instead, he said, "I've been thinking about our next step. We're fast running out of options, but how close do you think you could get to sounding like a Canadian?"

I thought about it, "It'd be English with a bit of a bur I should think."

"I thought so too, but we'll work on it over the next few days. We'll listen to some Canadian news channels on your *iPad,* though it doesn't have to be great, you won't be speaking to any Canadians. After that, I need you to fly over to the Caymans and open an offshore account." He handed me my Canadian passport.

I asked the obvious, "What with?"

"You'll tell them to expect a transfer of three million within the month, with more to follow." I waited and he obliged, "Mr Long is going to lose them out of his Cyprus account. Not enough to have him squealing to the Russians, who will see it as gross negligence on his part, but it should be enough to make him meet with us."

"And what then?"

"One way or another, we have to make him talk; to us first and then the authorities. Right now, it's the only thing I can think of; to make it all so public they have to call the dogs off."

I was sceptical, "But the Russians hold grudges don't they. You know; dodgy umbrellas and the like."

Smudge shook his head, "Those people were political enemies and don't forget, Ankudinov and Co will still have their pots of gold in Cyprus. No, the only fall guy will be Long and even he will have enough of a stash over there to justify three or four years in the nick. Eventually, people like him want out, but the people behind them won't allow it. What I'm hoping is that he's at that point, or close enough, to see this as an opportunity to get out alive. Don't forget, what we're doing will be telling him his cover's been blown."

The following day, we drove into Peronne and kitted me out with casual, but expensive clothes, suitable for the Caribbean. Since I was only going to be away for four days, we bought a leather holdall that would fall within the 'carry-on' limits.

Back at the *Gite* we both made arrangements, on the basis of 'each to his own', though periodically Smudge would listen to my attempts at sounding like a Canadian.

Three days later, we made our farewells to Monsieur Colbert, who sought to refund the unused rent and was quite startled when we declined. He ran inside and returned with two jars of Rhubarb conserve, the recipe for which had apparently been handed down through countless generations of his family.

Although I had a longer wait at *Pidou's* beer and wine outlet, I returned to the UK in exactly the same way as I had left it, with Steve, who sadly, hadn't lost his taste for Country and Western music. This time though, I alighted at Maidstone Services, where Smudge was waiting for me, in a UK registered hire car. We stayed at a nearby *Travelodge* and the next day, I boarded a British Airways flight out of Heathrow, for Grand Cayman, as a Canadian national named Andrew Links.

I discovered that flying First Class is an extremely civilised experience, at every stage, from check-in onwards. Smudge explained that the people at the other end would expect nothing less. There would be someone to meet and greet me at the airport, before whisking me off to a meeting with Lee Bodden, of AJC Trust Management Services. From then on, I knew my brief. Some years earlier, I had helped a client set up a similar arrangement in the Isle of Man, so I had a good idea of what to expect.

Though I didn't realise it at the time, the first class option also saved my life. Check-in took less than two minutes, after which I took the 'fast track' route through security. Smudge was somewhere in the background I knew, because we'd discussed the possibility of watchers, but what I didn't know was that they could only spare one man at each of the London terminals, which included Luton, Gatwick and Stansted. Terminal five has a huge length, which couldn't be monitored from a single position and therefore the man they posted there had to stay on the move, monitoring the check-in queues. Later, Smudge told me that he had identified the Russian almost immediately, though well away from my check-in desk for the short time I was there.

After a brief stop at Nassau, in the Bahamas, we landed at Owen Roberts International airport, Grand Cayman, just before five in the afternoon.

A chauffeur, dressed in dark trousers, a white short sleeved shirt and tie held up a placard with my new name on it as I entered the arrivals hall. After introducing himself as Owen, he took my bag and asked if I would care to follow him. The Caribbean heat washed over me as I left the building, so much so, that I took my jacket off and did a mental review of the clothes we had bought for the trip.

The *Cadillac* had been left in a VIP waiting area, with an attendant standing beside it. I realised why when the rear door was opened and a wash of cool air gambolled out to greet me. Obviously, the engine had been left running.

Fifteen minutes later, I was delivered to the *Ritz Carlton Hotel* on seven mile beach, during which time Owen advised that he would collect me at ten, the following morning, for my meeting with Mr Bodden. As I exited the car he expressed a hope that I enjoyed my stay, passed my bag to a bell boy and made his leave.

We'd paid for my stay in advance, at the French travel agency and a pre-paid travel card, laden with US dollars passed muster at the check-in, to cover all other expenses. The hotel was delightful and the beach, everything a tourist could hope for. I took a walk along it before dinner, instead of crashing out; the way I usually did after a trans-Atlantic flight, but twelve hour flights are nothing, when they include silver service meals and a lie-flat seat.

* * *

I could have walked in the time it took to drive the short distance to into George Town. The offices of AJC Trust Management were contained in a terrace of timber-framed buildings that had been painted in a variety of colours. My hosts had chosen pale blue.

Lee Bodden was a Caymanian who spoke with an Oxford accent. He already knew, from our earlier telephone conversations, that I was there at the recommendation of a colleague. Not surprisingly, when I chose not to elaborate, he hadn't asked for a name. He beamed and extended a hand, "Welcome to Grand Cayman Mr Links, is this your first visit?"

"No," I said truthfully, "But this is my first time on business."

We took a little time to exchange small talk, but he soon got around to business, "I understand that your first transfer will be in the region of three million US dollars."

I nodded, "That's correct."

"OK, well, as you know, discretion is a byword here and one of the ways we can ensure as much; is to form a trust company. Rather than have you appear as a director, I and one of my colleagues will act as nominees, obviously constrained to do only as you instruct."

I explained that I had made similar arrangements for others, though only as an intermediary.

"Excellent, then my work this morning has become somewhat easier. I have arranged to meet up with your future banker for lunch; a Mr Harvey Tibbetts of the Eastern Caribbean Bank and Trust, though I should be able to answer any of your questions in the meantime."

One thing had been troubling me, "I wouldn't want the transferor to have the details of my account."

Lee opened both hands, palm up, "Of course, that is no problem. The funds can be directed to the bank's client account and you may then use the appropriate codes to have them transferred into your own account."

After explaining the mechanics of international transfers, along with their day to day obligations and service, he moved on to costs, which seemed considerable compared to my income levels, but he did ask what my total transfers might amount to. I was about to pull a figure out of thin air, when I remembered Otto's revelations and thought, what the hell, this is pure fiction anyway. I maintained a dead pan expression as I said, "I can't be certain yet, but it is likely to be in excess of three billion."

He scanned my features for any sign of levity, but found none, "In that case Mr Links, you may be sure that our fees will be eased appropriately. When that time comes, we will also use more than just one bank."

I said, "Speaking of which, are there any issues I shouldn't raise over lunch?"

"No, absolutely not, you may ask whatever you like."

Harvey Tibbetts was an extremely cheerful Caymanian who obviously worked closely with AJC Trust Management and lunch was a very pleasant affair, though little time was spent discussing business. Obviously, matters of due diligence had been taken care of. In fact, they spent more time telling me about their islands and places I should visit. Lee offered to give me a tour of Grand Cayman, the next day, but I cried off, saying that I'd prefer to drift at my own pace.

We all returned to Lee's office and by four that afternoon, the paperwork was complete. I had an account number and my password had been established via a secure link.

Max took me back to the hotel where we agreed a collection time for my return to the airport, the next evening, which left me a day to be a tourist.

I hadn't realised how stressful the day had been until I got back to my room and after digging a scotch out of the mini bar, I crashed. In fact, I woke two hours later, propped up against the headboard, next to a damp patch left by the half glass of scotch I had spilled.

The following morning I joined a half day tour of the island which pulled in visits to a distillery, sculpture park, turtle farm and an area of black limestone called 'Hell'. Two cruise ships had deposited five thousand people into the system, so by lunchtime, I was happy to be back at the hotel, where I bought a pair of bathers and a book for an afternoon on the beach.

My flight home landed at Heathrow, at noon the following day, where Smudge waited to greet me. He had spent two hours in the arrivals hall and declared it to be clear. With four airports and nine terminals to watch, manpower had to be an issue.

Three million pounds disappeared from Howard Long's account, twenty six hours later.

Chapter 18

It took Howard Long three attempts to log on to his computer; with hands that were shaking so much.

His banking file, with the passwords and codes, lay on the desk beside him and minutes later he was staring at a nightmare. The transaction lay at the bottom of his online statement, like a malignant growth, just as the caller had said.

He thought about calling Ankudinov, to ask what the hell was going on, but dismissed the idea as quickly as it had formed. It would unwise in the extreme. The caller had known so much; enough to compromise both him and the Russian. Worse still, the man told him how they had come by the knowledge, which made him responsible. He was still staring at the screen when the next call came in, five minutes later, as promised.

He didn't give me a chance to speak, "What do you want?"

We'd rehearsed this thoroughly, "A meeting, that's all. You can keep the rest of your money." That much was a given, since we all knew that the password and codes would be changed within minutes of the call ending, if they hadn't been already.

"A meeting? What about?"

"Oh come on Howard, don't ask silly questions."

Long squirmed in his seat, "I'll put it another way then; why? What do you want, if it isn't money?"

"To discuss how we may help each other stay alive."

"I don't have time for riddles."

I sighed, "You won't have much time left for anything, unless you talk with us. We can talk with you or Ankudinov; your choice."

It was enough. He snapped back at me, "When?"

"Tomorrow evening, at seven."

"Where?"

I made it sound obvious, "At your place, alone." We had no intention of doing so, but he would be ready and a telephone call would soon have him on the move, to a place of our choosing.

That was it. The call ended as abruptly as it had started. We stepped out of the call box and strolled back to the car park. I glanced at Smudge, "Do you think he'll play?"

My guardian's mouth turned down at the corners, "Don't know, but right now, he should be feeling as threatened as we do."

We drove back to Combo's for another night in his spare bedroom, in which it was my turn for the air mattress, on the floor and Smudge's for the single bed.

Howard Long finally managed to overcome the nauseous panic and think logically. He was in trouble, that much was certain and plans had to be made.

In essence, he had to either deal with the threat or run. The former would entail speaking with Ankudinov and he had no taste for that. First though, he would need to discover the measure of the threat, which meant going through with the meeting, but before then, he could plan for the worst.

He began by purchasing a ticket for first available flight to Moscow, following the meeting, which was at eight fifteen, the morning after.

Next, he went down to the boat, now back at its berth, just days after the boatyard had completed the repairs. He stripped the winter covers off, checked the fuel and started the engines, while continuing to try and think of other solutions. With an air ticket and his boat, he knew that getting out of the country would be straightforward, but there was still the question of the Russians, who had already warned him about me and given instructions of who to call if I, or my accomplice, made contact.

That last recollection provided him with his solution. It was an epiphany. He didn't need to mention the money, or the weight of information we had. So far as the Russians were concerned, we were dead men walking anyway. It would be enough for him to say that I had linked him with the ruined companies and was attempting blackmail. With a credible motive for the meeting, all he had to do was make a call and there would be a welcoming committee in place.

* * *

I'd come to realise that when Smudge was operational, his silences signalled planning rather than isolation. He did mention once that the core plan was the easy bit. Planning for shit was much more difficult; which explained why the following day was a quiet one.

We drove past *The Nelson* at five the following evening, at a conveniently slow pace thanks to the rush hour traffic. I was lying across the floor behind the front seats, as instructed, or I might have questioned why we were leaving so much space between us and the cars in front. A number of impatient drivers had accelerated past, noisily and cut in. But then I knew nothing about evasive tactics and one eighty degree turns. I *did* know that it was a 'recce', because he'd told me that much, but when I heard him murmur, "Shit", I said, "What?" and began to rise. He snapped back, "Stay down."

We drove for another twenty minutes in silence; until he was satisfied we weren't being tailed and then pulled into a hotel car park, where I was given permission to sit up. He was staring out of the windscreen, thinking, before finally looking at me in the mirror, "I counted three, which means they have at least six and that's on this side of the river. They probably have twice that number around Long's place."

My heart sank, once again. There seemed to be inevitability to it all. I couldn't even bring myself to ask the question, but Smudge provided the answer anyway, "We need to find out what's happened to Long." He pulled out his mobile and keyed the pre-entered number.

It was still ninety minutes shy of our appointment, or the call wouldn't have been answered, but it was, almost immediately, by someone with a distinct accent, who was probably expecting a call from someone else, "This is Howard Long."

Smudge spoke in perfect Russian, "Let me speak to him."

The man at the other end spoke in his mother tongue too, but in a suspicious tone, "Who is this?"

Smudge snapped, "Don't ask stupid questions on an open line."

"Sorry."

Smudge continued, "So, your first job is done?"

"Yes."

"And you've tidied up?"

"Of course."

Smudge cut the connection and swivelled in his seat to face me, "He's dead."

This time I did ask the question, "What now?"

We were already moving when he answered, "Back to the cottage, to pray for a miracle."

Dominiks put the telephone down and mentally re-played the conversation. Something wasn't as it should be and he couldn't afford to fuck up again. It was only because they needed so many assets in place that he'd been given a second chance. He turned to his colleague, "I think we've been blown. I'm going to call in."

* * *

Ankudinov seemed ambivalent about the news, though in reality, he was relieved. Just an hour earlier, his benefactor had insisted on a change of plans, arguing that our attempt at blackmail suggested we knew more than they imagined. It was vital they found out how much more.

Long couldn't, or wouldn't provide any more details, though it was enough that he'd been compromised. That, at least, had been remedied.

The operational orders were changed once more, to 'Terminate, after interrogation'.

We didn't stop for a break or provisions on the way back to the cottage; I even had to pee into a pop bottle and on arrival, all we had was tea, coffee and a couple of pizzas in the freezer. They were enough though, for neither of us felt particularly hungry.

Smudge drove into Hereford for supplies the next morning and also bought a data SIM card for my *iPad.* Towards the end of our last visit, we discovered that a weak signal was available, two thirds of the way down the track and that was to be my boundary for the duration. Smudge did all the shopping while I stayed out of sight.

I spent hours in the car, its windows misted up; deepening the autumn gloom even further, while the rain pattered down on the roof. It was a miserable experience, re-tracing the steps Libby and I had taken and searching for any fresh developments. It was a for-lorn project too, but seemingly, all we had left. I even tried to *Skype* Terry again. The only nugget of news I did find, three days in, was the discovery of Long's body.

They found it in the Thames, two days after Dominiks had chucked it in and judging by the damage, it had been drawn through the propellers of at least one vessel.

The police went to Long's apartment and could find nothing out of the ordinary, apart from an apparent failure to set the alarm.

On board *Wave Crest* though, they found an open, but almost empty bottle of scotch on the flying bridge. Immediately below, they found a smashed glass on the main deck along with traces of blood and hair on the gunwale, which would be matched with Long's, just as the fingerprints on the bottle were.

If by some chance Long had made it to heaven, he'd have found a soul mate in Noddy, from Sharpness docks.

* * *

After two weeks, things became difficult. For the first time, Smudge became morose; no longer the thoughtful silences in which I could sense his concentration, but a bleak air, littered with irritable criticisms, often of himself. In response, I became petulant and snappy.

Still, my research had failed to produce anything of consequence and I realised that Smudge had run out of options. It was as though we were waiting for an inevitable confrontation.

I began to take my mobile down the track, on my research forays and if challenged, I'd have told Smudge that I was keeping it to hand in case he needed to contact me. In truth, I was determined to speak to Steph, if only for that last time; as soon as I plucked up enough courage, or became desperate enough to do so.

I received Otto's text two mornings later.

Somehow, they had found him.

* * *

Anna had been a close friend at university. She was studying languages and he, accountancy, but they shared a common interest in astronomy, at the small club formed for the purpose.

At one point, they might have become lovers, but while trying to find a way of taking the initiative, he watched on, as other suitors gained precedence. His pragmatic acceptance of the status quo ensured that their friendship remained intact, though as the years passed by, their communications had dwindled down to an annual exchange of Christmas cards. But she always remembered to invite him for a visit.

When he left the *Gite*, she was a translator, based in Barcelona.

She was delighted to see him too. He explained his sudden appearance as the need for a quiet period of reflection, after being dismissed from a high pressure post. She insisted he stay with her and her husband, in the second bedroom of their apartment, which was only a hundred metres or so from *Las Ramblas;* the bustling, tree-lined pedestrian way connecting Placa de Catalunya in the centre with Port Vell. It was major tourist attraction and the crowds gave him some comfort.

But it wasn't enough. He still felt isolated, in spite of his host's welcome. A week after arrival, he and Anna were having lunch alone, at the apartment, when he murmured, "Actually, I wasn't dismissed. I ran away." After that, he was unable to hold back. Two hours later, she held him when he began to weep.

It took them another three weeks to find him and then they sought to flush him out, in a typically Russian fashion. Since he had shared his story, his friends never let him out alone. Someone accompanied him everywhere and isolated spots or passageways were avoided, yet the two thugs stood out in the crowd. They made no attempt to contact him, but ensured that he saw them. It suited their purpose to merely spook him into flight.

Back at the apartment, they discussed alternatives, but eventually, Otto insisted that there was only one, which needed a degree of subterfuge to begin with.

The following morning, he and Anna stepped out to buy bread, from a bakers shop nearby. Unusually, Otto wore a large felt hat, which might have been taken as a forlorn attempt at disguise, but while the watchers were watching him another man entered the apartment building. He was the same height and build as Otto, with similar features, though his hair was black.

Half an hour later, a taxi pulled up at the same door and Anna, her husband and someone dressed in Otto's clothes ran out of the building and clambered into the vehicle. There was no attempt at subtlety; they were making a run for it. The Russians called for their car and followed.

Another of Anna's friends, named Carlos, dropped Otto off at Barcelona Sants station at nine fifteen that morning, in time to catch the nine forty seven train to Paris Nord, a journey that would take six and a half hours.

Otto marched away from the ticket booth towards his platform, always staring ahead; too fearful of what he might see if he looked back. Since the journey commenced from there, the train was already in place and the platform was empty, which gave him some comfort. He even managed a brief glance back as he boarded, to see that only a young woman with a child had followed him.

The carriage was only a quarter full and he slid into a forward facing seat, so that his back would be toward anyone joining the train. His luggage was just a small rucksack, which he clutched firmly to his chest, as though it was a talisman, as each minute taunted him with its tardiness, until finally, the doors closed and the platform began to roll by. He was completely drained.

He was also frightened and singularly unable to deal with the threats that now confronted him. Yet an instinct for survival still prevailed. There were just two people left in the World he could turn to.

The journey dragged by in a dichotomic stasis, in which fear prohibited thoughts about his situation, yet wouldn't allow him the latitude to think of other, less troubling things. An observer might have thought he was in a trance.

He arrived at Paris Nord at four thirty in the afternoon and had to run in order to catch the four forty to Calais. As a result, he had no time to look behind and was simply pleased to have made the connection. Even so, as his pulse settled, he felt less than cheered at the prospect of another two hours of claustrophobic containment.

Only one of the three Russians on the platform bothered to board the train. They knew where he was going now and two more men would be waiting for him at Calais Frethun station, by which time, the end play would have been decided.

* * *

The irony of it wasn't lost on Otto, who, as a German, was finding comfort in the sight of the white cliffs of Dover, still visible in the darkness. He and a number of other passengers had gone out on deck to enjoy the last three miles of the crossing.

He glanced back towards France; glad to be off the continent and saw them, thirty yards away and walking quickly. There was no attempt at discretion; they held his gaze as they came for him.

With his heart fluttering like moth's wings, he fled inside and managed to gain some distance by dodging around a column of school children being marched to an assembly point for disembarkation. He dashed out onto the other side of the ship and ran towards the stern, but on reaching the rail he stopped. The sound of water, rushing through the vortexes of propeller wash marked the end. He had nowhere else to run.

Otto Rilke's last act in this life was to recall the draft message he had stored on his mobile and press the send button. When he looked up, one of his assassins was just ten yards away and approaching quickly.

Otto flipped his telephone over the side and smiled at his killer. He didn't see the fist sweep up to deliver him into unconsciousness, or the hands that lifted him over the side, into oblivion.

A member of the crew found his rucksack much later and after recording the time and date of discovery, consigned it to the mass of lost property

Just like Long, the body wasn't found until two days later.

Chapter 19

I was in the car, vainly looking for something on the internet when a signal finally found its way into my mobile.

I read the message several times, in disbelief;

Ian, it is over for me. Please honour your promise and visit my parents as soon as possible. Give my love to them. Both of them.

I walked back into the cottage and spoke softly, "They found him."

Smudge was seated at the table and whirled around, "What?"

"Otto; they found him." I pulled up the message on the screen and placed it in front of him, watching for his response. When it came I was surprised by the strength of feeling.

He rested both arms on the table and clasped his hands together, "Poor bastard. He had no-one." Suddenly he stood up and said, "I'm going for a run," and left without another word, leaving me to sink into a trough of despair.

He came back an hour later, soaking wet and splattered in mud, but this time he didn't even kick his trainers off at the door. I was in my bedroom when he yelled, "Ian, get your arse in here!"

I was confronted with a complete transformation when I stepped into the kitchen. His eyes were alive again and his whole body gave off a aura of nervous energy. He sat down and pointed at my chair, "Sit." I did.

Satisfied that he had my full attention, he began, "We need to get over to Germany, now. Otto knew that he'd be sending you back into the lion's den, yet he specifically told you to do so as soon as possible. There's something over there he wants you to have."

He hadn't sold it to me. In fact, I looked at him, aghast, "You do realise that they live in Wurzburg? That's just an hour away from Otto's home. Don't you think they'll be under surveillance too?"

Smudge's eyebrows popped up, in a dismissive acknowledgement, "They would've been, I'll grant you, but now he's dead, there's no need."

"But surely, if *you* think there's something there for me, someone on the other side will be thinking the same."

Smudge considered that for a few moments, then shook his head, "In that case, they'd have been in there already and ransacked the place. If we find that has happened, we'll probably turn around and come home."

"But in that case, whether or not they found something, they'll realise that at some point we'd try to do the same. Wouldn't that be enough reason to keep the place under surveillance?"

"That's a risk, but a small one. My guess is that they have most, if not all their people over here. The last time we popped up was when we tried to arrange the meeting with Long and they'll have guessed that Otto was trying to meet up with us." He put up a hand to stall me, "What else are we going to do? Sit here and wait for them to find us, because they will, eventually."

I still didn't *want* to buy it, but I had no answer to that one, either.

Smudge hadn't just reached a conclusion on his run, he'd been planning too. "We'll go into town tomorrow and buy tickets to Frankfurt, from different travel agencies. On the same flight mind, but we'll travel separately. At Frankfurt, you will catch a taxi to the rest area on the autobahn, while I rent a car and meet you there.

A thought occurred to me, somewhat belatedly, given the number of hire cars we'd used, "I take it you'll be using one of your dodgy passports?" He nodded.

"Then don't you need a driving licence and credit card to go with it?"

He nodded again, "Of course."

Silly question.

I was troubled by his insistence on buying single tickets rather than returns, which would have given me some reassurance, but he explained, "We don't know what we'll find there, how long it will take to recover it or where we might need to go for it. For all we know, this could simply be the first step in a long trail and even if it is there waiting for us, we don't know what form it will be in. We can book tickets for a return flight, just as easily as the outbound one."

The lady at the travel agency was most helpful and didn't seem perturbed by my faux Canadian accent. The *Lufthansa* flight out of Birmingham, was at seven the next morning, so she was able to print my boarding pass off as well.

However foolhardy it may have been, I welcomed Smudge's suggestion that we have lunch in town. It was the most normal thing I'd done in a long time.

Back at the cottage, Smudge tinkered around with dye and scissors, until he was satisfied with what he saw in the mirror and passport. I went for a doze, again.

* * *

Once again, the drive up to Birmingham was straightforward and the flight was only half full. We pushed back from the jetway on time too. In recent years, I'd always used the low cost airlines for short flights, in which the coffees cost almost as much as the ticket, so I was pleasantly surprised to receive a *pain au chocolat*, orange juice and coffee without charge.

I was equally pleased to have finished them by the time we landed, because the captain decided to turn off the runway as early as possible, by applying full reverse thrust and stamping on the brakes. The sound of luggage being flung forward in the overhead bins could be heard over the sound of screaming engines and the inertia forced most of us into the brace position. It didn't end there.

Twenty minutes later, after taxiing halfway around Northern Bavaria, we drew up to an 'off piste' stand, well away from the extendable boarding bridges that would have afforded direct access to the terminal. That startled me too. Frankfurt is not tropical; in fact the weather can be dreadful for chunks of the year, yet we were expected to exit the aircraft and dash across the tarmac to a flexi-bus, which was overcrowded and lacked enough handholds. Almost everyone was embarrassed by the bodily contacts occasioned by sweeps around tight corners and braking, though I supposed that professional gropers must have had a field day.

Eventually, the bus pulled up at an entrance to the terminal. I'm still certain it was an act of considered mischief, for the trek from there to passport control would have traversed an English county. Worse, a flight from the Far East had just beaten us to it.

That I should choose the wrong queue in these circumstances was a given and something I've always been noted for. I watched others overtake me in the adjacent queues, while two separate travellers at the front of mine underwent lengthy questioning and were eventually taken away by officials. A third failed just as spectacularly, but by then, they had run out of officials, so the officer behind the desk pulled his shutter down before exiting his booth, to take the poor wretch away himself. As they passed the queue, he waved an arm and issued an edict, "Go,—other queues."

Eventually, exhausted, I made it out to the taxi rank and with the aid of the driver's road atlas, managed to establish where I wanted to go. Smudge was already there, waiting for me, with two new pre-paid telephones.

* * *

The parent's house was smaller than Otto's, but the garden had received much more attention. Even at that time of year it was evident that someone spent a great deal of time working in it. We drove by twice and then Smudge dropped me off in town, having arranged to pick me up at the same spot later that day, after texting me.

Which left me with a dilemma. It was only eleven o'clock; I wasn't hungry and there were only so many coffees I could consume, but the thought of wandering around in the open, terrified me.

In the end, I decided to spend a little while in the cathedral.

Like so much over there, it had been rebuilt after the war and my first impressions were ambivalent.

It is a huge Romanesque building, with an entrance, rose window and clock that sit between two square bell towers, such as those found in Venice. Most of the exterior consists of rendered pale panels contained within reddish stone surrounds, lending the place an almost prefabricated air. Inside, there seemed to be a discordant mix of ancient and contemporary, yet the longer I spent there the more I realised how mistaken my first impressions had been.

Whilst I'm not particularly religious, the huge windows and the radiances they gave to the place are breathtaking. In addition, every corner reveals an equally beautiful feature or artefact. The domed approach to the altar is adorned with gold decoration and a large cross is suspended over the aisle. But it was the startlingly white, wedding-cake walls that most impressed me, when they joined with the stained glass and gilding in a celebration of light.

After my tour, I bought a guide and sat near the front of the nave where, incredibly, a sense of peace washed over me; so much so that I became reluctant to leave. In fact, I spent over two hours in there and by then, I felt hungry enough to wander into one of the adjacent cafes for a hot chocolate and cake.

Smudge's text came through before I'd finished them.

I clambered into the car and sat in silence; allowing Smudge time to finish whatever he was planning. We drove back to the suburbs and parked in a non-descript street of modern boxes. He switched the engine off and swivelled to face me, "I didn't see anything to cause us concern." Though he added a caveat, "In the time I had, which wasn't much, but we can't afford to hang around here for long. In fact, I want to be out of here today."

I was delighted to hear that, but not so thrilled by his next idea, "I think it would be best if you paid them a visit alone. We don't want to intimidate them and I'll be nearby, watching closely."

I'd become a professional devil's advocate, "What if there's someone in there with them; one of Ankudinov's men?"

Smudge shook his head, "I don't think that's likely. An arrangement like that couldn't continue for more than a day or so. His parents would be held prisoner, effectively and sooner or later, it would be noticed by people trying to visit, the postman, or neighbours. Besides, they wouldn't do anything to you there; it'd be too messy and would entail killing all three of you. They would take you somewhere quieter and I'd be right behind them." He saw my expression, "Trust me Ian, I wouldn't be sending you in there if I thought there was any real prospect of contact."

I sat quietly, while he dived into the boot of the car, to make his own preparations, which included two tasers he'd purchased at the autobahn rest area. Later, when I discovered them, he told me that they could be obtained legally in Germany.

* * *

While sitting there, I wondered what someone like Dick Turpin would have made of modern travel. We had left Birmingham at seven and travelled to the German city of Wurzburg, via Frankfurt, in the time it would have taken him to get from London to St Albans. The take off at Birmingham would probably have triggered the need for a laundry bill.

So it was, that by mid-afternoon I made my way down the path to Otto's parent's front door, which was a heavy-looking wooden affair, with a small panel of glass at head height. I rang the door bell and waited; for long enough for me to consider flight, but eventually, the door was opened by a tall, slim lady of some presence. I recalled Otto telling me that she spoke English very well, so I didn't inflict my schoolboy German on her, "Good afternoon, my name is Ian Barber. I was a friend of your son's, Otto." I realised that I'd used the past tense and mentally kicked myself.

She wore a cream blouse, which buttoned up to the neck and a dark pair of trousers, with creases that could have been used as weapons. Her grey hair was done up in a tight bun.

It was a matter of mutual scrutiny, which seemed to last for a long time, but eventually, she inclined her head slowly and opened the door further, "Please, come in."

I followed her down a hallway, into a sitting room, where a man was rising from an easy chair. She introduced him, "This is my husband, Albert." She then turned to him, "Albert, this is Otto's friend." She smiled slightly, "Otto wrote to me about you. He described you well. My name is Elsa." We all shook hands. Hers were slight and smooth while his were like hams. He was dressed in a check woollen shirt and denim jeans that were held up by a stout pair of red braces. He might have been a fit, barrel-chested sort of chap once, but a Bavarian diet had converted his whole torso into that shape. An extremely thick-set sort of chap, in other words, with a thick mop of dark hair.

Elsa said, "Would you care for a cup of tea Herr Barber?"

I smiled, "Ian, please and thank you, that would be welcome." She directed me to sit on the sofa but as she left the room Albert returned to his seat and picked up the newspaper he'd been read-ing, leaving me with a side on view of him. Evidently, he didn't wish to engage in conversation. It became extremely awkward as the minutes rolled by, but at last, Elsa appeared with the drinks and sat beside me. She didn't waste time, "I think perhaps, that you have some bad news for us."

I was taken aback. The thought of having to tell them their son was dead hadn't occurred to me and I didn't know how to begin. Elsa recognised my dilemma and sought to help, "Otto also told me in that letter, that he feared for his life; also, that you had saved him on one occasion."

I looked at her squarely, "Otto and I became close friends. We were both running from the same people."

She clasped her hands on her lap and focused on them, "He told me a little about the people he was working for and seemed frightened of them. Two men came here a few weeks ago, shortly after Otto's house was destroyed and were,—unpleasant. They even searched the house."

I asked, "And they haven't been back since?"

"Why should they? Nothing was found here, but please, what news *do* you have?"

I recognised so much of Otto in her and realised that half-truths and platitudes would be inappropriate, "The last message I received from Otto, was that they had found him. He asked me to give both of you his love." Albert shifted slightly in his seat, which made me realise that he hadn't participated at all.

Elsa's eyes moistened, but she straightened her back and looked at me, "I thought as much. Thank you for being a friend to him and thank you for coming."

She wanted to hear about our stay in France and in return, she told me a little about her son's childhood, though soon, things became stilted and it was obviously time for me to go. But I still had an agenda of my own, "Forgive me Elsa, but did Otto leave anything to pass on to me, or perhaps he posted it to you?"

"No, we only received one letter; the one in which he mentioned you."

"Perhaps a message then; or something passed on by another friend?"

"No Ian, I am sorry."

My heart sank. I knew I should leave, but I needed longer. There had to be something and I was missing it. When someone is overstaying their welcome, it is often a sound tactic to offer them another drink, which usually prompts the response, 'Oh no thanks, it's time I was off.'

Instead, I accepted her offer immediately and was left in Albert's company once again. He was still reading his newspaper, which troubled me. He hadn't shown any reaction to the news of his son's death, apart from shifting his backside slightly. I decided to address him, "Albert, I'd like you to know that it was a privilege to meet Otto and beco.."

He didn't even look up, "That is good! I am pleased for you."

I wasn't going to let the fat bastard get away with that, so somewhat disingenuously, I said, "I am so sorry Albert, I shouldn't measure my loss against yours, as his father."

This time he set the paper down on his lap and stared at me, clearly irritated, "I will support my wife, just as I always have done, but, you must understand, Otto and I had little in common. He was what you English call, a mummy's boy." He shrugged, "But that is how things were, I could not change them."

All sorts of things sprang to mind. Was it a result of a particularly toxic teenage period, or was Otto gay and his father homophobic? I certainly hadn't seen any evidence of such inclinations, but it might have explained why Otto had been such a loner. I felt an unspeakable sorrow for my friend.

Elsa retuned and the following fifteen minutes were taken up with small talk, though I was able to include a few anecdotal tales of Otto's cooking, but there were no other clues for me. Elsa stood when I did and said, "I will show you to the door."

I almost said goodbye to Albert, who had returned to his paper, but his ignorance had been too extreme. I left him in what I hoped would be a very troubled peace. As I led the way down the hall I thought, 'How could any father treat the news of his son's death that way?'

And then it came to me, as Elsa was opening the door. I was at the point of leaving and didn't have time for subtlety, "Elsa, forgive me, but Albert is not Otto's natural father, is he?"

A shadow passed over her face and she glanced over her shoulder, before ushering me outside, where she joined me, pulling the door to, "What makes you say that?"

"I read the signals. It must have been very difficult for you, bringing Otto up."

She would have none of that, "He's a good man and has always provided for us both!"

"Please Elsa, tell me who his real father is, I have to find him. Don't do it for my sake, this is for Otto, so we can hurt the people who killed him." She stared at me for a full minute, in an agonising silence, before hurrying inside. The door was left ajar, thankfully, so I knew she was going to return and she did, a few minutes later, with a piece of paper. She thrust it into my hand and said, "Good luck Herr Barber, I will pray for you." As I turned to leave another thought occurred to me, "Elsa, did you or Albert tell the other men about this."

"No," she said quietly, "It is never spoken of."

I walked out of the gate and turned right, as Smudge had instructed, but before I'd reached the end of the street, he pulled up alongside. As soon as my door closed, we moved off, though in silence. I put my head back, against the rest and closed my eyes; utterly spent. Smudge kept quiet for a few minutes, until finally, he said, "Put your belt on mate, this beeping is doing my head in." The simple act of putting a seat belt on brought me back; there were still things we had to do.

Any doubts I had were dispelled when I dug my UK mobile out of the sack and retrieved Otto's message;

Give my love to my parents. Both of them.

It was obvious, or should have been. If he'd have wanted me to give fat Albert his love, the message would have simply read, '*Give my love to my parents*'. I switched the phone off and stared out of the screen, "Whatever he wanted us to have is with his real father." I passed the slip of paper over, "That's his address."

The name must have driven Albert nuts.

Otto Shenke lived in a block of flats near the town centre. It was close to five when we got there, with the rush hour traffic heading in the opposite direction. At least the exodus out of town made parking easy. Smudge did a quick reconnaissance while I waited in the car, but we both thought it unlikely that Ankudinov's men had made the connection. Moreover, we wanted to get it over with. He was back within half an hour, "OK, I didn't see anything, let's go for it."

He made me dial his number, so that I only had to press the green button twice for the call to go through. His instruction was simple, "Don't bother speaking. If this phone rings I'll be on my way."

Otto Shenke was an old man; at least ten years older than Elsa, but he recognised me immediately and without a word, turned and walked away, down the passageway, leaving me to follow. I stepped inside and closed the door. The flat smelt musty and the decor looked tired, but the thing I noticed most was the silence. I followed him into a sitting room that changed my perspective, completely. It was a scene of organised chaos. Bookcases that lined two walls had been filled long ago, with an overspill that covered every available surface, including much of the floor. He was almost completely bald and very thin; with the opaque skin of old age. The stoop was accentuated by the clothes that hung on his small frame; clean, so far as I could see, but without an ironed crease in sight.

He stepped around a large oak desk that was stacked high with books and took a largish envelope from the middle drawer, before grasping the spectacles that were hung around his neck with the other hand and wriggling them into place. Then he withdrew a photograph from the envelope; looked at it and then at me. Finally, he spoke, for the first time, "Guten abend Herr Barber, so my poor Otto is dead."

I said, "I'm sorry, Herr Shenke, for the short time we knew each other, he was a good friend to me."

"And you were to him." He put the photograph back into the envelope and withdrew two sheets of folded paper, "Otto told me everything in this letter." He walked stiffly across the room and held out the envelope, "He also told me to give you this and not to keep you. I understand why, of course, but will you promise me one thing please?"

"What is that?"

"Find a way of telling me, if you succeed in avenging my son

I didn't hesitate, "You have my word."

He placed the envelope in my hand, "Then go and good luck."

We drove back to the autobahn and stopped at the first rest area we came to. On the way, I had pulled the photograph out of the envelope and saw that it was one of me, taken on the banks of the Somme, during one of our walks. I remembered him taking it with his mobile. There was another envelope inside the first which was addressed to me. It was too dark to read the letter it contained in the car, but there was a small key and ticket of some sort in there as well.

Inside the services Smudge told me to find a quiet corner while he brought the drinks and once seated, I saw that the letter to Herr Shenke had been posted from Barcelona. Someone had probably posted it for Otto. I opened the envelope addressed to me and began to read,

Dear Ian,

If you are reading this I am probably dead. In which case, you may stop worrying about me.

I am sure I read a motto somewhere, that was something like, 'Don't get mad, get even'.

The enclosed ticket is for something I deposited in the Left Luggage facility at Frankfurt airport, some months ago. I hope it will help you do that.

Your friend,

Otto

* * *

We parked in the multi-story car park at eight that evening and strolled into terminal one of Frankfurt's airport. Smudge accompanied me, with both hands hanging loosely at his sides, though I took comfort from knowing that he had both tasers in his jacket pockets.

As luck would have it, the Left Luggage facility was on the ground floor, near the exits; well away from the check in areas upstairs and the arrivals hall. The watchers, if there were any, would be concentrated in those two areas.

The two windows to the facility were encased in a wall of stainless steel, with a conveyor belt on one side which protruded a metre or so from a cavity in the wall. Luggage would have to come through the screen of heavy plastic strips, leaving little time for owners to grab their bags; I guessed that most would have been dumped on the floor. Both windows were occupied by young men who had better things to do than serve customers, or so it seemed. We waited patiently for a few minutes, until the topic of their conversation had been exhausted and then, they obviously identified us as Brits, for they both spoke in unison, "Yes?"

Smudge handed the ticket over and three minutes later, I caught a dark blue, leather holdall at the point of ejection.

Five minutes after that, I sat in the back seat of the car and used the key to open the padlock Otto had used to secure the holdall. Whatever we found in there could determine what we did next, though contrary to Smudge's belief, we couldn't buy a flight ticket home whenever we wanted. The eleven o'clock flight was full. We'd established that much by telephone, earlier.

The bag was beautifully made, with two broad straps over a zipped opening. The first thing I saw was a light grey piece of clothing that proved to be a track suit top, which was followed by the other half, some shirts, socks, underpants and a sweater. Then finally, I came across the first of three files, all neatly secured, along two CD's, in plastic cases and an old fashioned cash box. I cast an eye over a couple of the documents and suddenly found it difficult to breathe. I looked up at Smudge with an expression that contained a mix of shock, delight and horror, for if nothing else, the information I had in my hands had irrevocably affirmed our death sentences, "It's all here, at least as far as I can tell. Records of transactions, bank accounts and their statements and God knows what else is stored on the CD's, or in that box."

The tension in that car became almost tangible, until Smudge broke the silence, "We need to get out of here, sharpish. Pack that lot back up while I go and pay the ticket."

Since a flight was out of the question, I asked, "Where are we going."

He was already halfway out of the car, "To the cottage, where do you think?"

We stopped just once, to refuel and stock up on cans of *Red Bull*, reaching Calais at two the next morning, where we bought two foot passenger tickets for the two forty P&O crossing. Most of the vehicles were HGV's at that time of day and there were only a handful of cars. With the commercial drivers up in the driver's lounge, the main body of the ship would be almost empty. Even so, we hurried to the stern rail and watched the remaining vehicles being loaded, not that I'd have recognised one of the Russians if I'd seen one. While we were there, Smudge telephoned the hire car company, who thankfully, were pan European, but they still applied a charge for the vehicle's recovery. He told them where he'd parked it and settled the account.

I will never understand how Smudge did it, but we only stopped twice more. Once, at Birmingham, to hand in the car we had hired at Calais and secondly, to refuel our main car, halfway back to the cottage. That garage included a convenience store, where we bought a few pasties, milk, bread, eggs and a few packets of biscuits, one of which we devoured immediately.

We arrived at the cottage at nine thirty in the morning, twenty five and a half hours after leaving it to catch the Frankfurt flight. Dick Turpin would have been catatonic.

$$* * *$$

Perhaps, because we were *so* tired and slept very deeply, we, were both up by four that afternoon. Smudge had beaten me by half an hour, but wouldn't venture into Otto's holdall until I was present. He did, however, place it at the centre of the kitchen table, stalling any other plans I might have had.

We folded and piled the clothes carefully, as though Otto was watching, but soon, the table was laden with the important stuff, in separate piles.

There were three bound files with black plastic covers; filled with photocopies and therefore on A4 paper, though the original documents had obviously been of different sizes. The one I thought would be the most interesting, from a first glance, was put to one side, on the basis of saving the best until last, but they all held surprises.

The first contained a collection of notes, in chronological order; some no more than a scribbled record of instructions taken on the telephone while others were minutes of actual meetings, using codenames for those attending, except for Otto. There was correspondence too. We even found a copy of the letter Smudge had photographed in Long's apartment.

The second file held copies of the correspondence Otto had received. None bore names or addresses, but many were signed. We identified Ankudinov's signature, but the rest were indecipherable. Others would identify them though, I felt certain.

As suspected, the third file held the real treasure. There were copies of bank statements, spanning a period of three years, for a number of accounts; all in Cyprus. The balances looked like telephone numbers.

Eventually, we loaded the CD's onto the laptop, which thankfully, weren't password protected. The first one only had digital copies of the document files we'd already seen and the second one, when we loaded it, indicated a file size of only two kilobytes, but as they say, all good things come in small packages. We sat staring at the passwords and codes for each bank account.

I looked up at Smudge, "This is incredible! I need time to go through this lot."

He asked, "How long?"

"A day, at least."

We were both wearing stupid grins and Smudge said, "Fair enough, I'll cook dinner tonight, while you get started."

I pointed at the cash box, before you do; let's see what's in there.

We were both startled to find a collection of bolts, ball bearings and small socket spanners, until I pulled a black metal tube out, which had some sort of toggles at one end, "What's this?"

He had already recognised it and was digging around in the box, "Very clever, that is a gun barrel." Suddenly he retrieved a stubby, black handgrip and moments later he'd assembled the weapon. It was tiny; perhaps half an inch wide and less than six inches long. He passed it to me while he dived back into the box. I hefted it in the palm of my hand and guessed the weight to be less than a pound. Meanwhile Smudge was lining the bullets up in a row as he found them. There were four in all. He was pretty dismissive about it though, "It's not something I'd choose to use. You'd have to be very close to your target and anything less than a head or heart shot would still leave the other bloke in a fit state to return fire; not forgetting that whoever we come up against is going to be packing something a lot deadlier."

I said, "Otto might not have known that, but then, from the look of it *and* where the holdall had been left, he was hoping to get through airport security."

Smudge acknowledged that much, "He may well have got away with it too, particularly if it went through as checked baggage."

* * *

The pasties were an undemanding menu and a welcome break from pizzas, though he did find some chips we had left in the freezer, which bulked things up nicely. We were famished. At one point, I asked if he'd still eat pizzas, with ten billion in the bank. He grinned, "Only ones from my own restaurants."

In spite of the excitement, or maybe because of it, we were still exhausted and by nine that evening; I'd had enough.

I was up before Smudge the next morning and got back to work immediately. He came through shortly after and made himself a coffee, but in the continuing silence; it soon became clear that there was nothing for him to do and he went for a run.

When he got back, an hour and a half later, I had stacked everything to one side and looked as miserable as I felt. The file review hadn't been completed, but I'd seen enough to reach a dreadful conclusion, "We're stuffed!"

He leant against the sink and folded his arms, "What do you mean?"

I explained, "We could sell this information to the highest bidder, or strip the funds out ourselves, like we did with Long. Either way, we'd be dead men walking."

Smudge grinned, "Nineteen billion buys a lot of security."

I shook my head, "It's a poisoned chalice. There isn't a person on this planet that couldn't be bought with the sort of money the Russians would throw at it. It would simply be a question of time. We'd spend the short time we had left on the run."

Smudge wasn't having any of my argument, "So why don't we do what we did with Long and take a percentage?"

"We'd still know too much; still be in exactly the same situation we are now."

"OK, so we negotiate our way out of this. Let's take all the money and offer most of it back to them, in exchange for a pardon."

I shook my head, "Would you trust the Russians? We'd still know too much for their comfort."

"Fuck it Ian, are you saying we can't do *anything* with this?"

I exhaled, audibly, "That's the way I see it."

"Surely, if we know too much, we're still going to be running from them anyway, so why not hurt the bastards?"

"No, that isn't the case." I waved a hand at the pile of files, "They don't know that this lot even exists; or that we've seen it. If you don't count it, the information we do have is limited. In two or three months time it'll be old news and they'll move onto other things. The cost and risks of having gunmen running around the UK will outweigh any embarrassment we might cause them and that is all it will be, embarrassment. Big deal, I haven't seen Putin apologise for much yet, have you?"

We argued about it for hours and sometimes Smudge would come up with an idea that needed a closer look, but eventually, I would reach the same conclusion. By nine that night, we were tired and embittered. I went to my room for a troubled night's sleep.

* * *

Smudge pushed my bedroom door open and called, "Get up, we've had a visitor."

I left my bed like a frightened jack rabbit and struggled into my clothes, noting as I did that Smudge had put the kettle on, so there couldn't be an imminent assault, could there? A cup of tea in a crisis was simply too much of a cliché.

When I entered the kitchen, he was bending down to put the milk back into the fridge and nodded at the piece of paper, lying on the table, "That was pushed under the door."

It was addressed to me;

Ian,
Find a WIFI connection at ten this morning. Somewhere private.
Your best friend.

I looked up at Smudge, "That has to be Terry."

He nodded, "I think so too, or whoever has been pretending to be him. It certainly wasn't the Russians. This place is ideal for their purposes; no witnesses and out of earshot. They wouldn't have let this opportunity for a full assault slip by."

He seemed to address the next question to himself, "But who delivered that and how the fuck did they find us? In any event, this place has been compromised, which means we get out of here, today. If one lot found us the others will." After a moment's pause, he concluded, "We've been careless, somewhere along the line."

I felt his tension, "So what now."

He looked at me as though I hadn't been listening, "Pack of course, then we need to get down the track to find you a signal."

* * *

The *Skype* melody came on at ten prompt and I 'fat fingered' the accept button twice before establishing a connection.

I was expecting an IM message as usual, but instead of text the screen shivered and suddenly, there he was, looking older than I remembered, but tanned. He was also wearing a Jewish kipa on his head.

He spoke softly, as if apologising,

"Hello mate, how are you?"

Wrong question.

"Well, funny you should ask that question; I don't know where to begin. How does 'alive' sound, for a start. That much should surprise you, as much as it does me."

"Ian, I'm so sorry this has happened. I never thought things would go this badly for you."

I had already switched the camera on at my end, so he saw me wave a hand,

"Hold it. Let's go back a step. Who did they bury, or is it a box of bricks?"

I was taken aback by his candour,

"He was one of the homeless, living on the streets, in London. Had no family, but at least he had a decent burial. Please don't do anything rash about that. The only people you would hurt are Mum and Dad."

That sparked another thought, about why loving sons should do that to parents but this time he held his hand up;

"Please, Ian, this call is unauthorised. We don't have much time."

I still wanted answers;

"So what about all those other calls, were they unauthorised."

He was obviously discomforted,

"They weren't me. They used the information I gave them, to implement an agenda my people had in mind."

I spoke quietly but with feeling,

"You bastard."

"Perhaps, but we have been keeping eye on you, for some of the time. Your friend Smudge, certainly made things difficult for us. Peronne looked very pleasant though."

I was too shocked to say anything for a moment and then the *Kipa* triggered a memory.

"So you're in Israel then, with family."

He continued as though I hadn't spoken;

"You have some goods that seem too heavy at the moment. As you say; a poisoned chalice, but a return to sender is not an option. The sender will charge you in full, no matter what you do. His staff may come and go, but you are both permanent members of an incentive scheme."

I heard him typing on his keyboard as he spoke;

"This is your only option, I swear. It's an attempt to put right a wrong and a measure of my shame. I have to go now Ian, we won't communicate again; shalom"

I shouted at the screen,

"Wait, Terry!"

But the connection had gone. At the bottom of the screen was a single line of text;

US Wit. Prot.Spk to Amy Johnson US Embassy.

He had tacked a London telephone number on to the end of his written massage and we both stared at it for some time. Eventually, I broke the silence, "What do you make of that?"

Evidently, Smudge was trying to reach his own conclusions and spoke slowly, "Well, I figure 'Wit Pro' stands for Witness Protection Programme, but if you were right about him being in Israel and the headgear supports that, it might mean he's with Mossad."

I interrupted, "Well we thought as much didn't we? At least about the secret service stuff, though I thought he was mixed up with our lot."

He looked up from the screen, "Yeah, but he said that 'they' used the intel he gave them to implement the agenda 'his people' had in mind. That's two separate entities, so MI6 might have been in the frame. It certainly wasn't the Russians."

I countered, "So why is he telling us to contact the US Embassy?"

"They may have been involved as well."

I shook my head, "That doesn't feel right. All the information they fed me was focused on the UK Stock Market and I remember Terry telling me that some of his information came from our own authorities."

Smudge raised a finger, "But, the consequences were international."

I corrected him, "With a specifically Russian bias."

"And who are the Russian's main opposition?"

I wasn't convinced and continued to shake my head slowly, "It just doesn't feel right. By now, we have become aware of the different players; even Terry's Israeli connection, though the Mossad link is a new one, I'll grant you. But there hasn't been a hint of US involvement."

He added quickly, "Don't forget, MI6 have already dumped you. The two spooks that visited you and the 'Dear John' Skype message made that clear." Then he asked, "So, back to your question, how come we're being directed to the Americans?"

I wrestled with my thoughts for a few moments and spoke as a wider conspiracy came to mind, "I don't know, but the Israeli's have always been closer to the US, so maybe this whole mess has been thanks to an alliance between them and Terry's put a word in for us."

Smudge looked vexed, "Yet something doesn't fit. Terry said his call was unauthorised, so any arrangements he has made have been under the counter, with contacts of his own. That doesn't suggest an alliance and we're going around in circles."

We sat quietly but eventually, in the absence of anything new, I asked, "So, do you have any conclusions?"

Smudge stared out of the windscreen, "Just one. If Terry is with Mossad and they reckon that we're in the shit, then we are; big style." I began to speak but he continued, "Which means that we're running out of options. He said as much when he told us we were 'permanent members of an incentive scheme'. In other words, the contracts out on us will stay in place, no matter what. Being shoved into a witness protection programme usually means there are no alternatives."

I had reached the same conclusion, but asked anyway, "OK, so what now?"

He picked his telephone up and looked at the iPad screen for the number, "We make a telephone call."

The telephone number turned out to be one of the more private lines into the US Embassy and when Smudge asked to speak with Amy Johnson, the spoken words were identified and triggered a warning light, which signalled a need to put the call straight through to Andrew Kellman, who knew the identity of the caller, from the use of that name.

* * *

We sat in the car and tried to think things through; to make sense out of them and evaluate what they entailed. The appointment wasn't until nine in the morning; two days hence. Smudge had opted for the extra day, arguing that we needed time to plan for contingencies and prepare our scripts. There would be no second chances and failure would mean certain death; in the very near future. We agreed that Ankidinov and his sponsor would throw every resource they could get their hands on to find us; way more than they were using at that moment. Smudge added, rather gratuitously, I thought, that it would be a nasty end too, for they would want to extract an awful lot of information first, even if our opening lines were the truth. It wasn't the Russian way, to take that sort of thing at face value. Though he added, "One thing at a time; we need to focus on our meeting with the Americans first."

We sat in the car for a few moments, while Smudge planned and I thought about Steph. Since everything had already been packed in the car, I asked, after a while, "Where shall we stay tonight?"

Smudge realised that the cottage had been under *benign* surveillance, but his professional pride had been hurt. Worse, Terry's people had been at Peronne too and that was just one place he had mentioned. At worst, we could have been shadowed from day one; in which case, someone else knew about the Russian we'd dumped into Thornton Reservoir. There was no doubt in Smudge's mind that the watchers should have been detected. He sighed, "It'll have to be Combo's. I'll have the air mattress."

Thankfully, it was only for the one night. On the drive there we began to formulate a plan and I set about drafting a presentation, of sorts, along with a schedule.

As we made our way around the M25 I read the schedule back to Smudge for the third time, having had him tweak the previous ones, but in repeating it, I realised that we were, finally, at the end of the road. Once I carried out the first task on our list, we'd have thrown the dice. Terry might have played for such high stakes, but I certainly hadn't. Or had I?

Whilst only a pawn in the scheme of things, I suddenly realised that my stake had been on the table for a long time; since the day I started to take Terry's messages seriously; I just hadn't known it at the time. I'd spent most of my working life telling clients that if it sounds too good to be true, it probably is and then I'd gone ahead and ignored myself. Talk about cobbler, sole thy shoe!

Neither of us slept well that night, albeit for different reasons. I couldn't shake a sense of foreboding for Steph. She had to be at risk now, or she certainly would be the next day. They would either use her to flush me out, or simply harm her out of malice. Smudge's slumber started off well, but his air bed sprang a leak and he spent half the night in an armchair downstairs.

We looked a sorry pair the next morning and Combo said as much. The need to be well rested and to guarantee getting to the embassy on time, prompted Smudge to suggest finding a hotel in the City. After a few *Google* searches, he chose a *Radissson*, near Hyde Park Corner. Comfortable, anonymous and within a few minute's walk from our rendezvous. This time, we would be sharing a room, because he was determined to keep me within sight. At nearly three hundred pounds for the night, I couldn't disagree.

We checked in at five that afternoon and hunkered down, even to the extent of having our meals brought up to the room. It was fairly standard fare, but tasty and a welcome diversion, which when added to a couple of game shows helped us through to nine o'clock, when we turned in. I didn't think to ask Smudge, the next day, but I slept surprisingly well.

At eight o' clock the next morning I changed the passwords on the Cyprus accounts.

I turned to Smudge and whispered, "That's it; the clock's ticking. There's no going back now."

Having come around to my view of our situation and the short term nature of our status as account controllers he said, "Yep, if we don't get a result this morning, you'd be better off using that *Glock* on yourself". I huffed, "What about you?" He gave me a small grin, "My exit will come with a price."

We set off out of Portman Square and along Oxford Street in a dismally grey drizzle, though nothing much registered with me; I had simply numbed out after we left the room. Until we turned south onto North Audley Street, where I couldn't help noticing the people who were preparing to begin their own days.

One young man, at a coffee shop, was setting tables and chairs out on the street, in spite of the weather. I remember thinking that smokers needed to be a hardy lot nowadays. A small lorry, with half its wheels on the pavement, was attracting the attention of a traffic warden while the driver carted boxes into an Italian restaurant and elsewhere, in shops and eateries, others were preparing to open up.

No one was smiling. It was just another gloomy, damp and depressingly routine day.

Lucky sods.

Neither of us spoke, though no doubt Smudge was planning still. For the time being, my mind wouldn't allow me to go there.

* * *

Eleven agents were scattered around Grosvenor Square watching us as we arrived at the embassy, ten minutes before time and approach the lady at the lectern, who seemed to be dealing with all enquiries, before directing people to whichever security point was appropriate. A 'suit' was standing next to her; around six feet tall, with a crisply trimmed head of greying dark hair, but I most remember being aware of his scrutiny. As soon as I mentioned that we had an appointment with Amy Johnson, he stepped forward, "Mr Barber, my name is Andrew Kellman, AKA Amy Johnson; would you come with me please?" As he turned away I noticed that he was speaking to someone or something, though too softly for me to hear anything, but the tiny cable that fed from his ear and disappeared beneath his jacket collar suggested that he was carrying a complete communications package. We bypassed the security station and were shown through a small private entrance before following him into the depths of the building. The deeper we went the quieter it became, though not before Smudge had an opportunity to whisper, "Never thought we'd make it into the US Embassy with a couple of *Glocks*." I felt a ridiculous urge to giggle.

The meeting room was cosy, with pastel coloured walls and plush carpeting. There was a round table in the centre, surrounded by eight chairs and to one side, against the wall, another table laden with cups, saucers and a coffee percolator, with a full flask of fragrant coffee. We all helped ourselves and sat down.

Kellman began, "Thank you for coming in. I understand you have something you wish to share with us."

Smudge cut in before I had chance to speak, "No, we have something we wish to trade with."

The agent smiled, "Then perhaps we should *begin* with that aspect. What is your price?"

I said, "That's a little back to front isn't it?"

He shrugged, "It's often the quickest way of establishing the value of something, though that is often a little subjective."

Smudge spoke, "An entry into your witness protection programme."

"OK, well that was concise. What do you have to offer in exchange?"

"Well, nineteen billion dollars, for a start."

Kellman hid his surprise well, "That is a considerable sum of money. May I ask how you came by it?"

I said, "We haven't, yet, but we can show *you* how to."

"Perhaps you'd better start at the beginning."

We did. Smudge asked me to tell the story and towards the end, I passed over my handwritten copies of the previous three years bank statements from Cyprus. We sat in silence as he read them closely, until finally, he asked, "May I borrow these for a few minutes? Not to copy; I just need to make a call.

Smudge shrugged, "Sure."

Kellman made his way to another office and made the call, to his section head, in Langley. After covering the basics he said, "Get this, one of the transfers in was made by *The Butterfly Trading Company,* for six million." There was a pause, before, "Christ, that information alone is worth putting him into the witness protection programme."

America's closest ally was unaware that the US intelligence knew about the company and that it was used as a conduit for the illicit transfer of funds. The leverage those statements would give them, when called for, would be immense.

But there was so much more, as the section head pointed out, "Do you realise what this means? With the supporting documentation this guy claims he has, we'll be able to identify and date hundreds of deals we've only suspected until now."

Kellman asked, "So you'll request clearance to put him in the programme sir?"

It was a foregone conclusion, "Consider that authorised, as of now. Go ahead, do whatever it takes and do it quickly."

* * *

I accepted their terms with equal haste, though subject to a crucial caveat, the importance of which was acknowledged and their offer amended. They would have the documents and CD's but the passwords would only be passed over when I knew Steph was safe.

Smudge surprised both Kellman and me, by declining the offer of relocation, "With you out of the frame, they're not going to waste resources on me and I kind've like this country. Sorry chum, but I'm staying."

I knew better than to try and persuade him to do otherwise.

* * *

Three SUV's left the embassy car park at the same time. The one we were in took us back to the hotel where two agents remained with the car and the other two waited in the lobby while we went up to the room. The other two SUV's drove north.

We hurried in to grab the bags off our beds, mindful only of the wonderful result we'd just achieved. In less than a couple of hours, the Russian threat would be lifted from our lives. It was so remarkable; I needed more time to fully appreciate it. In the meantime, I would ride the wave of deliverance.

Neither Smudge, nor I was aware of the figure that slipped out of the bathroom behind us.

I was the first into the room and therefore furthest away from the gunman when he opened fire, but I was already glancing back when a 'phutt' sound accompanied the explosion of bone, gristle and blood that blew out from Smudge's knee. Smudge howled as he collapsed to the floor and clutched at his leg, just above the knee

I looked up from the horror, to see 'apeman' step into the room, pat Smudge down and remove his *Glock*. He then stepped over him and walked towards me. It became a case of déjà vu when he punched me in the face, though this time he didn't break anything.

I bled though, like a stuck pig, while he span me around for a pat down and took the *Glock* out of my jacket pocket. He turned me back to face him, held my gun up and sneered, "I bet you don't even know how to use this." He removed the clips from both guns before throwing them onto the bed. "Down, little man, there, against the wall."

Terrified, I sank down the wall and pulled my knees up beneath my chin, with my hands clasped around my ankles, rocking to and fro.

He spat at me and turned to Smudge, who was propped up against a chair, "Now, Mr Army man, you have some information for me."

Considering the pain he must have been in, I was surprised at how calm Smudge sounded, "Fuck off, there's a good chap."

Dominiks kicked the injured leg, just below the knee, causing Smudge to give out a grunt as he flattened back to the floor. It took a minute or two for him to gather his wits, by shaking his head clear of the shock and pain, but Dominiks didn't appear to be in a hurry. Even now, I am certain he was having fun.

"I have been told to find out what you know. Convince me and I'll end things easily. Otherwise, we shall continue to play games. He glanced back and said, "You," to let me know that he was addressing me, but turned back to watch Smudge, who was the clearest threat. "You have ten seconds to start talking, or your friend's other knee will be destroyed."

I didn't say a word.

Instead, I shot him, with Otto's toy gun, which had been stuffed inside my sock. I aimed for the middle of his torso and destroyed his right lung instead, or at least, enough of it to drown him in his own blood, given time, which was something I didn't have. Dominiks rocked slightly but remained standing and turned to look at me in surprise. He hadn't made a sound and now he was raising the gun. My mind went blank, but my eyes caught a blur of movement and my ears heard the 'snick' just before the flick knife Smudge had strapped to his calf, was buried into the Russian's groin. He screamed and dropped the gun, which Smudge caught on the drop, to put two taps into the thug's chest

'Apeman' collapsed to the floor like a leaden sack, but Smudge was already lunging for the *Glocks* and telling me to find the clips. While putting them in, he nodded at the bedside table, "Give me the phone; quickly, he'll have at least one friend nearby."

I stretched the cable as far as it would go, but he still had to shuffle around the corner of the bed. He didn't groan but the pain was evident, from the sweat that poured from him. I gave him the receiver and dialled the desk, as instructed. A moment later, he spoke to the receptionist, with the same urgency. Putting a call out for two US Secret Servicemen in the lobby would have been unwise and too slow. Instead he said, "Go out to the black SUV at the front door, immediately please. Tell the men in it 'Room four four eight, immediate'."

He passed me a *Glock,* "You remember how to use this?" I nodded and as soon as I'd taken it from him, he manoeuvred his way round to face the door. This time he grunted with pain and rested for a few seconds before being able to speak. He'd begun to lose a lot of blood and I ran to the bathroom for a couple of bath towels, which we wrapped around the knee. The waistband off one of the hotel's dressing gowns served as a tourniquet, but by the time we had finished he was showing signs of shock. Once again, he shook his head, before telling me to stand just inside the toilet and what to say when the next visitor knocked the door. He added, "Stay back, because if I don't hear the right response I'm going to open fire."

* * *

Both agents leapt out of the car and one told the doorman to keep an eye on it, as they ran inside. Both were wearing heavy overcoats and were joined by Kellman as they reached the lifts. The other agent made for the stairs.

I heard the light tap on the door and steeled myself for mayhem, "Who's there?"

"It's me, Kellman."

I stuck to the script, "Who was our appointment with?"

There was no hesitation, "Amy Johnson." I looked at Smudge, who seemed to deflate, but he nodded, "Let them in."

I opened the door just as the door opposite began to move. From where I was standing, I could see the figure appear but I didn't see his gun. One of the overcoats was already covering that door and yelled what might have been "Down!" I couldn't be sure because of the noise. The machine pistol he had brought with him, beneath his overcoat, sounded like a shipbuilders rivet gun, though by then I was already being thrown to the floor. The two agents outside cleared the opposite room and I was allowed back to my feet. Kellman had run over to Smudge and was inspecting the wound. He shook his head, "I'm sorry sir, we won't be able to take you."

I decided that wasn't going to happen and said so, but Smudge pointed his finger at me, "Fuck off, sharpish. Catch that plane and stick to the plan!"

I almost wept, "What are you going to do?"

"Go to fucking hospital, what did you think I was going to do?"

Kellman had already instructed one of his men to make the call, "That you are. An ambulance is on the way; I'll leave one of my men with you." He turned to me, "We have to go, now!" He grabbed a handful of toilet paper from the bathroom and passed it to me, "Be discreet using this, don't walk through the lobby looking like we're kidnapping you." He pointed at my blood splattered shirt, "Do your jacket up and cover that."

It seemed like an hour, but it had taken less than four minutes, from when Kellman knocked the door, to my hustled passage along a corridor filled with the pungent smell of spent ammunition. The experience continued in the same vein, all the way to the car in a blur of professionalism. We were on the move when I glanced at my rucksack and Smudge's words came back to me, "Stick to the plan."

Kellman was seated in front of me and I tapped him on the shoulder, "The files, they're not here." He swivelled around to look at me as I explained, "They're somewhere else; safe."

* * *

No one would know how they had traced us, though by then they had over thirty men in the City, looking for us. One theory was that they may have networked with the thousands of Eastern Europeans working in London at the time, particularly in the hotel industry. One of them could easily have recognised us, or more probably, me.

By the time we had returned there, with Dominiks waiting in the bathroom, our room had been searched carefully, without any sign of intrusion, but nothing had been found.

* * *

It took an hour to claw our way to Wood Green and Kellman became tenser with each minute. I could tell he was angry too. After half an hour he spread a map out onto his lap and telephoned someone. I listened to him discussing an aircraft and eventually, mention Luton. He seemed to relax a little then, to the extent of sharing his news with me, over his shoulder, "The aircraft was at Farnborough, but it's re-positioning to Luton, so we won't have to drive back across the city."

As Combo handed me Otto's holdall, he asked after Smudge and I was tempted to tell a white lie, in the interest of expediency, but thought better of it, "He's been shot, but he'll be OK."

Combo snapped, "Which hospital."

I said, "I'm sorry, I don't know. The ambulance was on its way when we left."

Kellman, who was at my side; cut in, "The Warwick, in Kensington." He glanced at me, "It's the one we use." He nodded at Combo, "I'm sorry, we have to keep moving."

Combo extended his hand to me, "By the sound of it, you do. Good luck Ian, I'll look in on his lordship."

In that split second I felt my eyes begin to fill and hurried away as I fought to regain control. A kind thought or gesture can be a wickedly powerful thing at times.

It only took forty minutes to reach Luton, during which time I asked why we didn't just continue north for ninety minutes and pick Steph up. Kellman explained, "Our people have only just got there. They'll need to scope the place out a little before collecting her. In the meantime, the sooner we get you off UK soil the better. Every minute counts.

I had no idea that they were as anxious about MI6 as they were the Russians.

The formalities at Luton were soon dealt with and the shiny *Gulfstream* jet was already on the apron, refuelled; with the flight plan already filed with Air Traffic Control. The first engine was being started before I had even sat down and the pilot must have secured clearance to taxi immediately, for the second engine had barely come up to speed when we began to roll. I watched the main terminal slide into view, looking drab and miserable in the persistent rain, but before I knew it, England disappeared beneath a cloud base of only eight hundred feet. I would never see it again.

I glanced at my watch; it was only one forty five, just four and three quarter hours since our appointment at the embassy. A whole life erased in less than half a day.

Kellman had passed the holdall to a man who had been waiting on the aircraft and I saw him walk aft, to a desk and work station. The stuff would be loaded onto the computer in no time, except for the disk labelled passwords and codes. That one was protected with a password of my choosing, which I would share as soon as Steph was airborne.

* * *

The American was a late arrival, at one thirty, but at least he only wanted a sandwich and a coffee. He wasn't planning on staying long either, because he asked for the bill only fifteen minutes later. He didn't need to ask her name, her badge provided that much information, but he did smile and palm a fold of paper over to her when she came back. It was common enough for clients to be discreet about their tipping, as though it was an illicit act, which so far as the Inland Revenue were concerned, it often was, since tips were rarely declared. But when cash was handed over in that way, protocol called for the money to be kept out of sight until she reached the kitchen. Americans were usually good tippers, so she was keen to see what colour the bank note was.

It was a note of a very different kind and one that needed reading twice, before she ran to the telephone and began dialling the number it contained. Any doubts had disappeared the moment she recognised my writing.

"Steph?" Bill didn't exactly ban incoming calls, but he did discourage them. On the other hand, making calls out during working hours was an absolute no no; unless the person concerned looked at him, with the feverishly, frantic expression he saw then. He raised both hands, palms outwards and walked away.

We were still climbing through cloud when her call came through. Kellman passed me his telephone, "For you."

"Hello?"

"Ian! Is that you?"

"It is love. Are you OK?"

"Yes, but what about you; where are you?"

"I don't have time love. Listen to me, this is important. The man who gave you that note is on our side and will bring you to me. Trust him and do exactly as he says."

"Ian, I'm at work."

"Steph, your life is now in danger. Every minute counts. Please, trust me."

"You're frightening me."

"Good. You need to be, now go to him." I cut the connection; we couldn't afford to waste time.

Steph returned to the American's table, with her coat on, "Ian says I have to do as you say."

The man nodded and spoke into a throat mic she hadn't noticed before. He waited for a few moments, until the response came through and stood up, before taking her arm and escorting her out of the door. When they stepped outside, a black SUV swept up to the steps and a man leapt out of the side door, as Steph's escort hurried her across the patio. Normally, she'd have been bundled inside, but in the circumstances, he was unusually gentle.

It was still slick though, and seconds later they swept out onto the lane, past another SUV and headed for the motorway.

They had spotted the watcher almost immediately. Since parking in the restaurant car park would have attracted attention, he'd been forced to park fifty yards away, on the verge. But Dadlington is a small village, dissected with narrow lanes, which made such waiting obvious and mildly hazardous. The second SUV had moved in first; sweeping into the kerb, in front of the parked Ford Fiesta and reversing up to within inches of the front bumper. The Russian inside couldn't see the occupants of the SUV, but he did see the two gun barrels pointed at him and decided to remain still; very still. He watched the other SUV leave and fifteen long minutes later, the SUV on his front bumper drove off at speed, leaving him to begin breathing normally again and make his report. There was no need to check inside the restaurant; he knew his subject had been lifted.

At that moment, she was at the northern end of the East Coventry By pass. The crew of the *Gulfstream* at Coventry Airport, ten minutes away, were already running through their pre-flight checks.

As things turned out, she was airborne just forty five minutes after me. They were still climbing out of Coventry's airspace when the call was put through and Kellman passed his telephone over, again.

Her panic and anxiety was immediately evident, "Ian, what's going on? They won't tell me anything. All I do bloody well know, is that I'm on a private jet that's just taken off from Coventry airport!"

Time was running out and I knew that explanations would have to wait; our future and possibly lives could depend on the next few minutes, "Oh my love, please, please trust me, I haven't got time to explain now, but I'm on a plane as well; to the same place you're headed for. The main thing is that you're safe. I'll tell you everything when I see you, but there's something I have to do now. I just needed to know you were safe first. I'm sorry love, I have to go now. I love you." I cut the connection before she could respond and handed the telephone back to Kellman, who was obviously ready to launch himself out of his seat. Even so, I couldn't resist telling him, "She knew the password all along, when spelt the right way around."

I dictated it, letter by letter, NIARBGOB and watched him run to the rear of the cabin.

Twenty minutes later, at exactly three o'clock UK time, the US of A was twenty two point three billion dollars better off.

Half an hour later, Kellman sat across the aisle from me and leaned over, "You did the right thing."

I looked at him, "Pardon me?"

"When you told me the stuff was elsewhere I was taken aback and then we lost an hour getting it, when minutes counted. I was *anxious* shall we say."

I grinned, "Mad as hell, I thought."

He smiled, "Whatever, but like I said, you did the right thing. If the stuff had been left in your room, we'd have lost it."

I felt a twinge of anxiety, "That was Smudge. He's been the tactician throughout and I owe my life to him. He's ex SAS you know."

I realised that I'd just answered an unspoken question as Kellman nodded, "It figures."

* * *

Moscow time is two hours ahead of ours, which meant that when we were being led into the US embassy, Ankudinov was in his limousine, en route to the Kremlin and one of the most important meetings of his life. He was expected there at eleven thirty in good time to join his benefactor in welcoming the Chinese delegation for a Presidential lunch, which would be followed by an afternoon of negotiations. The bulk of their pact had already been agreed and the agenda for that day was aimed at finalising a few details and signing everything off. It was to be a joint venture in Africa; that would extend the plundering of that country's mineral wealth to a level that would shock the World. Ankudinov's inclusion would show returns that would dwarf his current, yet considerable wealth.

He had left instructions that under no circumstances should he be interrupted and that would remain the case until late evening.

By then, it was too late.

Nevertheless, the meeting went well; splendidly so. Ankudinov signed the agreements on behalf of his conglomerate and his sponsor, who was present throughout the proceedings, though tellingly absent from the documents. With the agreements in place, others would attend to their implementation over the following eighteen months, but in the meantime the two Russians in charge, looked certain to become global rankers.

Gifts were exchanged prior to the delegation's departure and after, Ankudinov accompanied Putin back to his office for a few more vodkas, even though the President hadn't taken any alcohol that day, as usual. But an occasion such as this called for boldness in one and indulgence in the other.

When he tumbled into his limousine, numbed by vodka, there were a number of messages waiting for him. He called the London and Leicester teams first; who both made reports that signalled the introduction of a US interest, along with a major deployment of assets. As a result, they had lost two men.

The targets had been spirited away; even the woman too, which meant they were being re-settled, at least for the time being. That could only signal one thing; the two Englishman knew far more than had been suspected. A worm of doubt began to uncoil inside his stomach and he snapped at the driver to make haste.

He had sobered by the time they reached his house and within minutes, he knew the worst. The passwords to every single Cyprus account had been changed and therefore undoubtedly, they would have been emptied. With a howl of rage, he swept the keyboard and monitor from the desk.

He was finished, financially and almost certainly, literally.

* * *

When I first saw the private jet, visions of executive travel, with endless drinks, caviar and an attentive cabin crew came to mind.

The decor and fittings were certainly upmarket, but this flight was courtesy of the US taxpayer. Refreshments were limited to sodas or coffee and the food, if it could be called that, came out of packets; all self service, which made me take a more objective view of the cabin. It had been filled with seats, albeit rather pleasant leather ones, but the only table was a desk at the rear; populated with a computer and communications equipment. As a result, I decided that it was a rather cramped experience, without the sense of space afforded by wide-bodied jets. At least, I only had to share the space with four fellow passengers, instead of the three hundred or so I was used to.

Once again, I tried to consume the hours by way of sleep, as I had done at the cottage, but this time the strategy failed, terribly. In the twilight zone between consciousness and sleep, I was left alone with unwelcome thoughts. My mind recalled the experiences of the last ten months. The fears, frights, violence and the dead came back in dreadful detail. How could so much have happened in less than a year?

In the end, I leant against the window and gazed out at the endless ocean, thirty five thousand feet below and tried to focus on finer things.

Ultimately, there was only one. My previous life was lost now, save for Steph.

* * *

We stopped briefly, at a US Air Force base near the east coast to refuel, though I wasn't allowed off the aircraft and the window blinds around me were closed. From there we flew over a myriad of landscapes, from snow laden mountains to deserts, but eventually, we were descending over a huge urban area in the middle of a desert. Kellman told me it was Phoenix, in Arizona and that we were about to land at Luke Air Force base.

As we descended past an altitude at which I could make out details, the wide straight roads, huge trucks, malls and bright cream industrial buildings impacted on me to a far greater extent than ever before; predictably I suppose, but it was another reminder of how much my life was set to change. I continued to gaze out of the window, but without focus, as the list and images of things I would miss, continued to grow. Our way of life, of communicating, working, spending, saving; the street markets and sole traders; my clients and Libby, trains every hour and of course, warm, malty beer. I realised, with a pang of guilt, that I should have included family in that list, but dismissed the thought as quickly as it had emerged. In spite of the hundreds of clients and a number of friends, there was still that one person in the World I could say was a soul mate, and she was about to join me.

I stepped off the aircraft and welcomed the change of climate, at any rate. We'd exchanged a dull wet November day for a dazzlingly bright twenty five degrees, though not for long. Moments later, I was shown into an air-conditioned hospitality room, where I was offered more sodas, coffee and snacks. It was typically military, in much the same way as UK bases were. I was certain that the same decor and functional furnishings would be replicated in most other bases. Only Kellman stayed with me and he settled into one of the easy chairs, with a coffee and magazine, but after more than ten hours in the air, I only wanted to pace around the room, with an arctic soda in my hand.

Naturally, it had nothing to do with the fact that the woman I would propose to later that day, had yet to arrive.

We waited until the aircraft carrying her had taxied to a halt, before being allowed out on to the apron and as I approached, the cabin door opened and a set of steps materialised. An agent appeared at the doorway, but turned to extend a hand back into the cabin and then she appeared, holding on the agent with one hand and reaching for the rail with the other. Both of them were more concerned about negotiating the steps safely, than to notice me as I stumbled to a standstill and looked on, in absolute delight and shock.

She was dressed exactly as she was on the day I met her; even the name badge remained in place, but there was more, much more. I waited until they were safely on the ground before yelling, "Steph!"

It would have been nice to say that we ran into each other's arms, but she had just been on a ten and a half hour flight and I walked, intent on setting the pace. I didn't want her running. Eventually though, we did fall into each other's arms and wept; both of us.

I don't know how long we stayed like that, but everyone kept a discreet distance. Eventually though, we eased apart and I place both hands on her swollen belly. I gazed at it and could barely speak, "I had no idea."

She caught and contained a sob, with a great gulp, "I thought I was going to have to bring him up on my own."

I looked up at her smudged and beautiful face, "He?"

She nodded, "I've had a scan." Then she choked slightly, "I was going to call him Bogbrain."

Epilogue

We are different people now, with new identities and lives, in a friendly community, with a number of new friends. Although we are British, the reasons for being here are entirely credible and have been accepted, though I'm unable to share them with you.

We also have a three year old son, named;—well you'll have to guess.

Both of us are employed, in jobs that are enjoyable and fulfilling, though Steph's is only part-time, at least until his nibs reaches school age. We rarely speak about the old days anymore, for bad things are often better served by being locked away, but sometimes I think of Smudge and Libby, who I would have dearly liked to have kept in touch with.

Even now though, I can barely credit the speed at which things came to a close. After all those months of fear and pursuit, the end play was chaotic and quick. But then, it had to be. From the moment I changed the passwords, Smudge and I were dead men walking. Our only hope lay in discrediting Ankudinov and furnishing the CIA with so much intelligence that a continued pursuit by the Russians became unwise.

Ankudinov was arrested for embezzlement of state funds and a few other lesser charges. The trial ran its course, but the result was a foregone conclusion, to the extent that the judge was required to read what was supposed to be his summing up and sentencing.

It was reported that he had obviously never seen the document before, let alone written it.

As well as the forfeiture of his title to the energy conglomerate, Ankudinov was sentenced to twenty years imprisonment. No one, including him, expected his survival beyond the first twelve months.

I transferred two hundred and fifty thousand out of Long's money into Libby's account; without any explanation, though I'm certain she would have known who'd sent it.

Herr Shenke received a note, posted from London which contained a simple assurance;

Otto can rest in peace.

As for Smudge? Well that became a little contentious. In the end, I had to become belligerent until finally, they agreed to let me go ahead with my plans.

I sent him a Christmas card; unsigned and also posted from London. It contained the message;

Will be having a quiet Christmas Eve morning, thanks to you. See you in hell."

* * *

On Christmas Eve, they flew me over to Grand Cayman in a smaller *Gulfstream.* I was accompanyied by a monosyllabic agent named Grant something or other and we were met by two more agents at Owen Roberts airport, who bundled me into a ubiquitous black SUV.

I'm not sure how long it took to get to Hell; probably close to an hour, but I stared out of the windows and savoured the views. Everything there, the colours, people, beaches and turquoise hews of the ocean were so uniquely Caribbean. Hell post office is a gaudily painted gift shop, as well as a post office with an amusing postage stamp, but the attraction that draws visitors to it lies at the rear.

I found Smudge on the viewing platform, overlooking an area of black limestone that looked more like a solidified lava field. He and his crutches were leaning against the rail.

Being Christmas Eve, there were very few tourists there and I'm sure the black SUV and agents prompted the American contingent into cutting their visit short.

He'd lost weight,—and half a leg. The dressings were still evident and I guessed he was still in pain.

We didn't hug, or even shake hands; it didn't seem necessary somehow, but I did point at his leg, "Sorry mate."

He shrugged, "Occupational hazard, though this bit of convalescence is welcome. Thanks for the first class ticket, it was an enlightening experience." He added, "I kept the rest of your money though."

I grinned, "Not enough." Then passed a large envelope over, "Merry Christmas Neil, I owe you; always will."

He took it and smiled slightly, "Smudge, please."

I left then; it seemed the right thing to do; to leave him a moment alone, before he opened the envelope and found a million dollars, in bearer bonds.

Other Books by Jeff Hawksworth

Graham's Chronicles

A Heart Warming Trilogy

A Child's Eye View

Graham's Gang

Help Out House

* * *

The Tack Chest

* * *

The Carpenter's Gift

(May be downloaded free of charge from
http://www.jeffhawksworth.com)

A Child's Eye View

Graham's Chronicles I

Graham Parsons is a *man ordinaire* whose well-ordered life is changed beyond measure when he witnesses the manslaughter of a 7 year old boy, Christopher. Whilst holding the dying child he experiences a profound out of body experience and minutes later suffers a life threatening attack, leaving him with permanent disabilities.

His recovery brings with it a telepathic connection with children who need help. An affinity which threatens his sanity, marriage and eventually his life.

This tale of discovery begins with a fearful and confused denial which takes him to the edge of reason until eventually, he accepts and employs his remarkable gift with a charming pragmatism that disarms doubters and helps to salvage blighted young lives. His simple, candid honesty wins the support of four friends from very different backgrounds; Christopher's mother, a GP, a Child Protection Officer and a Detective Sergeant.

This story chronicles the shocking, moving and yet sometimes heart-warming episodes in his new life.

Graham's Gang

Graham's Chronicles II

Graham has come to terms with his special gift. A telepathic connection with children who need help, but his efforts to help them are often accompanied by calamity.

The tiny group who know his secret decide he needs their protection, but just how effective can Nancy, his partner, a GP, a social worker and an overweight detective sergeant be?

They are joined by Harvey Calder, a wealthy business man. He and his wife Audrey are indebted to Graham for saving their granddaughter's life, which prompts them to give Graham, Nancy and their foster child, Jimmy, a holiday of a lifetime. But *'life'* takes on a whole new meaning when Graham confronts an American, set to become a Senator, who will do anything to discredit and remove a threat.

Graham's false imprisonment does just that and the situation seems back under control, but no-one has told the Senator about the Hell's Angel, 'Big Bob'.

Help Out House

Graham's Chronicles III

Graham Parsons is back in England, a fugitive from US law, but his freedom is still threatened by a vengeful US Senator and extradition.

His life goes on hold, in a stasis of anxiety while in America, Chrissy Haddon and her mother confront their own demons of abuse and alcoholism. Is it time for Senator Haddon to answer for his deeds and make amends?

The *'Gang'* rally to Graham's side once more, with support and practical help on both sides of the Atlantic that become quite extraordinary. But like Graham, with his telepathic connection with children needing help, they all know others would think their experiences were no more than fiction.

As things begin to fall apart help comes from an unexpected source and the US State Department are persuaded to join in.

Meanwhile, in Leicester, Lori is a frightened fifteen-year old, trapped in a world of drugs and prostitution. Yet in the darkness shines a tiny glimmer of defiance. Only she knows her real name is Marya, until she sees Graham's advertisements and 'puts her message in a bottle', triggering a dreadful reaction which causes Graham to suffer one of his worst nightmares.

The Tack Chest

. . ."but there's something else as well. Grandma had a box at the foot of her bed, which she used as a linen chest. It's a bit tatty; she covered it with a rug, but it looks a bit like the one in your picture.

You're welcome to it if you want it; only it had blankets in it, not tack." I had nothing to lose, "Yes please Audrey, if you could hold on to it, I'll pick it up at the weekend."

There were more than just blankets in there, much more and so began an odyssey of discovery I couldn't have imagined if I'd tried. Dad had passed away a few years earlier, another victim in a lineage littered with heart attacks, so the hoard I discovered was as mysterious as it was startling.

Weapons, loves, scandals and crime. Just how well did I know my father? Fact or fiction? This book became both. Stranger still, this is a book that leaves the reader knowing more than the author.

The Carpenter's Gift

Arnie Osborne is a sixty eight year old florist, and alone, save for the beautiful companions in his shop. The business is barely viable, thanks to the superstores and would have disappeared long ago if it hadn't been so close to the hospital.

He knows he has cause to feel bitter, but then there are the children. The ones who don't realise they're about to be orphaned, knowing only that they want to take a gift in with them. It is enough to keep him going, to justify dragging his creaky old bones out of bed each morning.

Until he has the nightmare.

About the Author

Jeff Hawksworth

After thirty years in the insurance industry, latterly as a pensions consultant, Jeff decided to take a gap decade.

His life has been filled with formative influences, such as those imparted by his woodwork teacher, 50 years ago, who gave him a lifelong love of wood and taught him how to work it. You might say Mr Dunkerley was Jeff's *Mr Chips.* (No pun intended).

Not forgetting Pam, his wife of 41 years, his son James and daughter Kim.

More recently, a master carver named Mike Painter taught Jeff how to carve and so wood carving has filled a significant part of the 'Gap', along with a new found love of France; it's culture, food and of course, wine.

Felling trees, cooking and a short but very enjoyable spell as an examinations officer at a local college also helped to fill time but the real surprise was fiction. Writing it that is.

What started as a vivid dream that stayed with him, became a four year journey of discovery that resulted in the publication of Graham's chronicles, *A Child's Eye View, Graham's Gang* and *Help Out House.*

Oh, nearly forgot, Jeff is 9 years into his gap decade. Watch this space.

www.ingramcontent.com/pod-product-compliance
Lightning Source LLC
Chambersburg PA
CBHW051239210726
48287CB00002B/311